INFERNO

KAT TURNER

CITY OWL
PRESS

INFERNO
Coven Daughters, Book 5

CITY OWL PRESS
www.cityowlpress.com

Cover Design by MiblArt. All stock photos licensed appropriately.

Edited by Tee Tate.

For information on subsidiary rights, please contact the publisher at info@cityowlpress.com.

Print Edition ISBN: 978-1-64898-410-5

Digital Edition ISBN: 978-1-64898-409-9

Printed in the United States of America

PRAISE FOR KAT TURNER

"A fledgling witch finds love with a mature rock star in the midst of occult danger in Turner's magic-heavy debut and series launch. Turner sets up a promising world that readers will be pleased to return to in subsequent installments. Paranormal fans should check this out." – *Publisher's Weekly*

"*Hex, Love, and Rock & Roll* is clever, witty, and captivating from chapter one. Helen and Brian pull you into their world and refuse to let you go. It is utterly a bewitching love story that has it all: chemistry, mystery, *love*, but most of all– rock and roll." – *Jaqueline Snowe, author of the Shut Up and Kiss Me series*

"In *Blood Sugar*, readers can expect Turner's trademark snark mixed with magical and metaphysical mysteries, a well-paced plot full of unexpected twists, and two layered and complex characters winning their happily ever after." – *Janet Walden-West, author of Salt + Stilettos*

"I adore Cynthia and Raven! The chemistry between them is off the charts and they are both such badasses. *Fallen Angel* is pure paranormal joy. From the scintillating opening scene to the satisfying ending, it grabbed me and didn't let me go. Kat Turner has not only provided readers with a fascinating new addition to her series, she's given them a story and characters that feel distinct and fresh. I loved every moment of it." – *Rosanna Leo, author of Darke Passion*

"*Song of Virgo* is an intense and perfect combination of magic, mystery, and love!" – *Jaqueline Snowe, author of the Shut Up and Kiss Me series*

"Absolute magic. *Hex, Love, and Rock & Roll* delivers thrilling suspense, steamy chemistry, and a sexy British front man. Anyone who's ever had a crush on a rock musician or wished on a star will fall in love with this debut." – *Mary Ann Marlowe, author of Some Kind of Magic*

ALSO BY KAT TURNER

COVEN DAUGHTERS

Hex, Love, and Rock and Roll

Blood Sugar

Song of Virgo

Fallen Angel

Inferno

COVEN DAUGHTERS ORIGINS

Embers

For My Readers.

ONE

MEGAN O'NEIL SCOOTED TO THE EDGE OF HER BED, CREEPING SLOWLY as not to disturb Logan. He lay facedown, his shaggy blond hair obscuring his features. A tangle of white covers stopped at the small of his back to showcase his impressive, tanned slopes of muscle.

She felt nothing except mild guilt for using the Instagram influencer as a temporary fix to fill the hole in her heart. Only one man had come close to bridging the ever-present gap, and that man was not the Internet lifestyle sensation whom she'd slept with. As the months without the one she wanted dragged on, her void had only grown larger and more unfillable.

She threw on her favorite robe, padded to her bathroom, and gargled mouthwash. The antiseptic sting burned away the alcohol-fueled taste of the previous night. After scrubbing her teeth and tongue, she attacked her face with a makeup wipe and inhaled the calming cucumber scent. Mascara remnants left dark smudges under her eyes. When combined with her mess of red hair, the effect made her look like a clown. Fitting. Thirty-six was too old to still be doing this shit.

"Hey, gorgeous," the deep, raspy, male voice spoke from behind her. Logan's jacked arms circled her waist. She hadn't noticed him slinking in after her. She hadn't really seen or noticed her latest lover at all, in a sense. "We look good together." He caressed her belly, his big hands parting her robe before skating over the jungle-and-flowers tattoo that splashed color all over her chest. He cupped her large, painted breasts. "You're fucking hot. Hot body." He tugged the piercings that speared her nipples, his touch making her squirm in discomfort even though his moves were skilled and sensual. "Beautiful face too, with those green eyes and fat lips. Hot redhead. Fucking hot. You're, like, the hottest chick ever."

Megan cringed, the former English professor in her recoiling at his limited vocabulary and stilted syntax. She hadn't hooked up with Logan for his intellect, that was for sure. He was right though—they looked good together and fit on paper. "I had a great time last night." She maneuvered out of his hold, the sight of his waxed, bare chest and six-pack abs failing to stimulate her interest in another round of sex.

"Me too, baby, me too." He licked his shapely lips and reached for her again, his dark blue eyes lighting up with desire. "How about we both have a good morning. You know what I mean?"

She pulled her hair into a ponytail and tightened the tie on her robe, hoping to send a message. "I actually have a pretty busy day ahead, with getting ready for the *Bump in the Night* shoot. The trip to that haunted hotel is coming up."

"You're, like, the hottest ghost hunter on the planet, you know that?" An impressive erection speared the material of his boxer briefs. He pulled at her waistband. "You ever fuck in one of those haunted locations? That'd be hot."

Now there was a dumb idea that would surely release a ton of bad mojo and piss off some angry spirits. Megan was seasoned enough in her trade to recognize the no-nos. Her expertise had helped her land the paranormal reality show that was on its way to becoming *the* Internet television hit. "Hard pass." She left the bathroom before he could get his hands on her again. "What are you doing today?" Leaving would be a good start.

He stood in the doorway wearing a sad puppy look. "I was hoping we could hang out. Grab breakfast, on me of course. Maybe talk about our game plan while we walk around the zoo or something fun like that. We're still gonna collaborate on that podcast, yeah?"

Megan sucked her teeth. Had she agreed to do a project with Logan when she'd been tipsy and flirtatious at the party where they'd met? "I'm not sure what my schedule is going to look like for the next few months. I'll call you."

His golden boy face crumpled in defeat. "Oh shit. You're ditching me. I screwed up, didn't I? Did you not come last night? I misread the signals sometimes." Logan flashed his naughtiest grin before loping back to her bed and throwing himself on it, propping his arms behind his head. "Don't you worry, sexy lady. Want me to go down on you again? Or get out your vibrator? I'll make it up to you, I promise. Just tell me what to do and I'll do it."

The inkling of guilt unspooled into a cloud of shame. Logan had been an excellent lover, tending to her needs and ensuring that she got off, and multiple times. His sex skills weren't the problem. Neither was he. She was the asshole in this situation. "No, you were great. I swear. I had an amazing time. It's just that I'm not ready to start seeing anybody right now as more than a one-time thing."

Not Logan, at least. Because Logan, like all the guys she'd been with recently, failed to wipe her memory of the man she really wanted, the one whose stubbled jaw, laugh lines, and thick cock had filled her mind while Logan was working her to climax. The man she really wanted was twice Logan's age and a thousand times sexier.

"Shit." He scowled and stood up, grabbing his t-shirt off the floor. He hopped into his jeans one leg at a time. "This is your deal, huh? You use guys and throw them away like trash?"

Yes, unfortunately, and she wasn't proud of it. She'd burned through plenty of women too, but that was beside the point. "You aren't trash, Logan. You're talented and funny and a great lay. You're a twenty-five-year-old millionaire. I mean shit, you're awesome. It's just that I'm in a weird place emotionally—"

"Whatever." He yanked his shirt over his head before jamming his hand in his pocket and snatching his phone. "Your loss. Do you even know how famous I am? Like, for real?"

She rolled her eyes while he was busy putting on his shoes. Sure, Logan had millions of views on TikTok and had won an endorsement with a popular line of men's grooming products. His online fame was what had landed him in her tiny town, where he'd booked a gig at nearby Stillwater College. He was a rising star, but she could pull men more famous than him without even trying.

A certain mega-famous rock star, for example, whose talent with the bass guitar burned as hot as his smoldering English accent. The one and only Thom James, whom she'd walked away from long ago but had never been able to forget, was the only man in ages who'd meant more to her than a night or three of no-strings fun. "Totally." She tapped her foot and checked the time on her phone. At least Logan was moving things along. "You can find someone better than me."

"Damn right." His keys jingled when he swiped them from her dresser. "Your ghost show is dumb. And fake. Everyone knows you use rigged tables and lighting tricks and shit."

She'd never faked any of the scares or encounters in her show. Paranormal authenticity ran through her blood like the fire magic she was learning to wield. Arguing with Logan, though, would accomplish nothing except prolonging their time together. "Okay."

He glowered at her before theatrically pushing a button on his phone and bringing the receiver to his ear. "What's up, Trina?" Logan addressed the person on the other end while aiming a surly stare at Megan. "Nah, I'm not doing anything important right now, just killing time. What are you up to? Wanna hang out?"

Trina must've agreed, because Logan flashed Megan a triumphant, bratty smile before storming out of her apartment while making plans with Trina.

Once the door slammed, Megan shed her robe and put on sweatpants and a tank top. She ran her hands down the full-sleeve arm tattoos she'd gotten in an ill-fated attempt to forget about Thom. She should have joined him on his tour like he'd invited her to do before they'd tearfully parted ways. What was even the point of being his groupie if she rejected his attempts to turn the relationship into a more serious arrangement? Wasn't that the Holy Grail of groupiedom, having the rock star ask you to be his girlfriend? The women she'd met and hung out with while chasing rockers around sure had that outlook.

She'd wanted to be with Thom too, so much that it hurt. Yet she'd shied away, making excuses while putting up her wall.

She really needed to work on her commitment issues. And all her other issues while she was at it. She scrolled through her phone and pulled up the number of a therapist she'd sorta connected with a while back. Megan's heart fluttered while she scrolled a bit farther down in her list. The last messages that she'd exchanged with Thom stared her in the face like relics from a time capsule.

There wasn't any harm in reaching out, right? They'd left on amiable, albeit supernaturally charged, terms. Before she could change her mind, she pulled the trigger on a text.

Hey. How's the tour going?

Thom might not respond. He was busy, with Chariotz of Fyre in the middle of a massive tour. Yes, she'd stalked their schedule online and toyed with the idea of showing up randomly to one of his shows when the tour was close-ish to her Iowa town.

She watched the dead zone of her phone's screen for signs of life. Business aside, he might have forgotten all about her. The man was a legendary player who'd dated famous actresses and pop queens, filling the gaps with top-shelf porn stars and an endless string of groupies like herself. Who knew what music's most legendary bad boy had seen in her that cut through the feminine clutter?

Still no response. She switched from the chat app to her photos. Megan would afford herself ten minutes, no more, no less, to think about Thom. Then she'd delete every trace of him and move the fuck on. *Yeah, right.*

She pulled up her favorite photo of them, a random pic taken by the mailman from when Thom had stayed with her. Her eyes were open and bright, her face angled upward toward his. Thom stood behind her, his arm laid over her breastbone in a protective pose. His brown hair hung loose and free at his shoulders, and his smile was tender, extending to deepen the crow's feet near his eyes. He'd worn his leather jacket on that cold night and looked like a pirate with a heart of gold. She'd glowed with the telltale aura of a woman in love.

Pain radiated through Megan's chest. Had she been in love? Was that why she'd gotten scared?

Her phone dinged. She gasped like an idiot and checked. Just her spin studio offering her a promotion for more classes. She was about to hide her phone from herself when another message came in.

Megan O'Neil. Hey, stranger. It's been good, but I'm ready for it to be over. Tired. I'm at some promotional party. It's boring. Missed you. What's going on?

Her stomach fluttered. Had he really missed her, or was he just being nice? One way to find out. *I missed you too. Been thinking about you a lot. Wish that I'd come and hung out on the tour.*

Same. How's your show?

Going well. Views are growing. I don't think I'll have to teach anymore if I don't want to. After being fired from her last job, she really didn't. The show and studying her spell book were plenty.

Congratulations. You have any breaks coming up?

Good sign, good sign. He wasn't blowing her off yet.

We're wrapping next week. She had stuff to do beforehand, but work could wait. She chewed her lip and watched three white dots bounce.

Ever been to Chicago?

Yeah. I love it.

We'll be there for a bit. I'd like to see you. Ticket's on me.

With any other guy, she would have worried about looking too eager, about presenting herself as desperate. Thom was different though. With him, she could be herself, authentically and always. *That'd be great.*

Say the word and I'll buy it.

An inkling of worry wormed into her. Despite the potency of her connection to Thom, they'd never even begun to figure out a plan to make a consistent, stable relationship work. He wasn't slowing down, and she was busier than ever. Taking a vacation the week before finishing her show's second season wasn't the most responsible move. And that was just the mundane stuff, to say nothing of the weirdness that orbited the perimeter of their courtship.

Not that responsibility was Megan's strongest suit.

Yes.

When he texted her his hotel room number followed by a plane ticket confirmation, all she felt was the girlish thrill of anticipation mixed with a twinge of fear.

She was about to walk back into the life of the one who got away, the one who made no sense as a permanent person, to see if second chances were possible.

A rush of chemicals flew through Megan's system. She pushed the button to buy a ticket for an earlier flight.

Screw waiting around. She was going to surprise Thom by bringing her best game. She slithered into a black leather miniskirt that barely covered her crotch. No underwear, no problem.

Her core was on fire just from getting ready. She rounded out the outfit with a leopard print halter top that bared her fit, inked arms before donning lace-up high heels that a dominatrix would envy. The time spent leaving her apartment and calling a car both dragged and whizzed by in a blur, every moment stirred into a cocktail of impatience.

Her wheeled bag trailing behind her, Megan turned every head in the airport. She felt like a star while deplaning and sashaying to the transportation area.

A balmy breeze danced through the dark night air as she waited for the next car. Her heart beat to the drum of her desire. The rideshare driver kept sneaking peeks of her in his mirror, and she crossed her leg high on the thigh. Let him look. Let everyone look at her, wild and in her element. She rolled down the window and stuck her arm outside as if to collect a trace of the night magic, the skyline whizzing by in its sensual, decadent light show.

The driver's lusty look changed to one of confusion as he pulled up to the curb alongside the arena, the band name splayed in spiky red font on the glowing jumbo screen. "You don't want to stop at your hotel to drop off your suitcase first?"

"Nah, I'm good." Someone would stash her luggage in a safe place. People here would know her. Instinctively, she tapped the clutch looped around her wrist to feel the hard circle of her demon-trapping watch. Her sacred heirloom had been dormant for a while, its gears frozen in stasis, but she kept it close for comfort whenever possible. When her prized possession started working again, she'd be by its side. "Have a good night."

Megan walked to the ticket window, her heels clacking on concrete.

A young man working the booth looked up from his phone and shook his head. "Sold out."

Not for her. "Megan O'Neil. Thom James is expecting me."

Her phone dinged. She'd deal with it later.

He raised his eyebrows. "He's seriously expecting you?"

"Serious as a heart attack." She'd fuck Thom until the muscle in his ribcage pounded for mercy, that was for sure.

The employee shrugged, turned away, and said a few words into an intercom. After putting it down, he slid her a jet-black pass with the band name printed across the front. "Checks out. He's in Room 110 on the lower level. Are you somebody, or what?"

In this space she was. Megan accepted the pass and slung it around her neck. Inside, fans milled about and ordered drinks, killing the last thirty minutes before showtime. She recognized people from past shows, but they didn't halt her forward momentum. She wasn't there to visit with anyone except one man.

A ride down an escalator took her to the mouth of a wide hallway staffed by two security guards whom she breezed right past. More staffers hustled around, speaking into headsets as they completed pre-show prep.

Thom's door was the third on the right. Blood rushed in her ears. The anticipation was deadly. She knocked twice.

He answered immediately, the first sight of him stealing her breath. He wore a faded blue t-shirt and a cowboy hat and gazed at her like she was the only person in the world. His brown eyes smoldered with desire, his dark hair crashing onto his broad shoulders in messy waves.

Thom looked every one of his fifty-one years in the best way possible, the lines on his face telling a story of hard living and rejected inhibitions. The soft golden glow of his vanity lights wrapped him in the aura of fame. "I never stopped thinking about you." The smoky timbre of his English accent called her home. "I was afraid I was doomed to lose you and never forget you."

She stuck her bag off to the side and launched herself into his arms, running her hands up his back to make a study of firm muscle. His body felt the same, deliciously stocky, like a bear in human form. He'd put on his sandalwood aftershave, and she craved a taste of him with the same ferocity that possessed her the first time she'd gotten near him. "Make me remember you."

Thom lifted Megan by the waist in a single, confident motion, pulling her feet off the ground. She wrapped her legs around his waist, her heels digging into the small of his back, their bodies moving fluidly together in a dance of desire.

"Megan," he whispered, his eyes half-closed, his lips millimeters from hers.

Her heart was full to bursting. Arousal flooded her center in damp, humid pumps. "I can't wait anymore."

He crushed his mouth onto hers, tasting of mint and tobacco, his tongue plunging in to claim her in one hot strike. He shoved the door until it shut with a click. Her clit throbbed. This was going in one clear direction now. No doubt remained.

She kissed him in hungry gnashes, sucking and moaning, grinding her bare pussy against the front of his belt until her motions warmed the leather. She wanted Thom to devour her. Probe her mouth so deeply that she felt completely and utterly fucked by his tongue alone.

He walked them backward to the chair by the vanity and sat down. Megan hovered her hips a few inches above his and barreled her stare into his. She reached down and tore into his belt, button, zipper.

"You're a goddess," he groaned, unknotting the strap of her halter and sliding the fabric down to expose her breasts.

"I was dying without you." Breathless from the kiss, she had to gasp out the words.

She reached into his open fly and freed his erection, his dick as hard as a bat and thicker than any cock she'd seen. Frantic and fumbling, she managed to remember the condom she'd brought. Her stupid phone pinged again, but she had more important matters to attend to. Megan ripped open the foil with her teeth. A bitter burst of latex brushed her taste buds. She rolled the sheath over Thom's length while he watched. He jerked his stare up to her eyes once she was done suiting him up.

He buried his hands in her hair. Through silent eye contact alone, he spoke a litany of profound words.

She lunged forward and took him in one more kiss to end all kisses. Using the rocking motions of her pelvis, she slid down on him until he filled her up with sweet, tingling pressure. "You feel like heaven," she cried out, grinding forward and back to enjoy the penetration to the fullest. The buildup had already begun deep inside of her. This would not take long.

"I thought of you every single night," he grunted into the side of her neck, holding her tight, his hips bouncing like he couldn't get enough. "And after I fell asleep, I dreamed of you. My heart broke every morning when you slipped away."

"Touch me." She squeezed his shoulders, bit his earlobe. "Touch me everywhere, all at once."

He stroked her breasts, rubbing each pebbled nipple between the pads of his fingers, and dragged clawing fingertips down her neck and arms. Every nerve ending in her body sparkled. He slid two fingers between her legs and rubbed her clit in steady motions.

The thread was about to snap. She was taut and tense, hurling to the edge, shoving forward and back against him, wet enough that barely any friction hindered his slide. Megan cracked, flooded by that delicious release, coming apart in shocks and waves that left her trembling.

Thom threw back his head and cried out, stiffening all over. Twitching, he squeezed her breasts, locked in the freeze of his own long climax.

They caught their breath together, slackening even as their embrace spun them up tighter, a sticky mess of body heat and sweat.

Thom released a satisfied exhale, cupped her face in both of his big, callused hands, and stared at her with a crooked smile and hazy eyes. "Welcome back, baby." He put his cowboy hat on her head, the whimsy of the gesture making her giggle. "You haven't changed a bit."

Her phone dinged again, then rang. Thom's statement wasn't quite accurate. She'd been through quite a few changes since they'd seen each other last, and now she had to figure out how the hell to make it all add up now that she'd stirred Thom James back into the chaotic mix of her life.

TWO

To say that Megan O'Neil was back was an understatement, and Thom hadn't much taken to the English knack for understatement. He moved through life as big and bold as the bass lines he played, his impact warbling deep in the world's bones.

Megan had once again thundered into Thom's life like only Megan was capable of doing, crashing against him in a tornado of red hair, hot pussy, and hungry lips. Megan O'Neil made Thom want to die fucking. Megan O'Neil was to be mainlined, not sipped. Megan O'Neil was original sin. Megan O'Neil was the reason the word *sex* was invented.

She was all of that and more. He gazed into her jungle-green eyes, lost in the wilderness of her seduction as he recovered from the euphoria of orgasm, his heartbeat and blood chemicals stabilizing. He'd never let her slip away again. It was a declaration of fact. The universe would have it no other way.

"You got new tattoos. They're pretty." He kissed an indigo-and-ebony butterfly that wrapped around her throat, brushing his lips against pink lettering that curled from her jugular to her ear in a cryptic, foreign language that trailed off like a lost myth. He liked her new designs. There was a beautiful frenzy to the mishmash of text and image, a labyrinth of ink that made up a pattern known only to its owner. "Where's my name in here?"

She smirked and dismounted him, tugging her skirt down to hide the red hair between her legs. "I wanted to feel something." Gracefully, she lifted the strap of her top and tied it around the back of her neck. Her trim, shapely biceps flexed as she covered a portion of the color splashes that now painted her chest, arms, and neck, sparing only her face and the bottom of her chin.

Megan had been working out. She'd been busy without him, going on with her life. This made him sad and happy at the same time and even more determined to win her for good.

He peeled off the condom and threw it in a wastebasket, taking care to cover up the other condoms with a few tissues. Thom didn't feel bad. He'd bet all his multi-millions that Megan hadn't stayed celibate for him either, and he didn't care. They were together now. "Did you feel something just now?"

She pulled a cigarette from her purse and lit up. "Do you really have to ask?"

He'd felt her contractions and the rush of fluid when her body locked up against his and she breathed in a series of shallow pants. Her moans were unmistakably true, and he'd heard fake cries of ecstasy burst from lesser mouths. But he never squandered the opportunity to drop a good line. "No." He gestured to the gray wisps drifting up to frame her face in a dark mockery of a halo. "I thought you were quitting."

"I am. I only smoke after sex now." She lifted her head like a baby bird and blew smoke rings. Even the women he'd known who'd made being bad girls their entire identities hadn't mastered that trick. None of them had been as confident as Megan either, nor as raw.

He laughed. "I tried that rule. I was still smoking too much."

Megan cast a knowing glance at the wastebasket. "Shocker."

A twinge of pain pinged in his chest. He couldn't quite tell if she was bothered, if she'd seen the evidence of his un-chastity and her feelings were hurt. In addition to being sexy, smart, and talented, Megan was a master of sarcasm and deadpan. Thom stood up and fixed his pants, looking her in the eye once he was decent. "I should have had a clear conversation with you about what our expectations were. I'm sorry if I let you down."

"You didn't let me down. You lived your life." She closed her eyes briefly, touched her temple with two spiky, black fingernails, and stubbed out her cigarette in a makeshift ashtray made out of a coaster. "Actually, it's me who should be apologizing, leaving us in limbo like I did." For a second, she looked stunned. "It's been over two years."

He simultaneously felt every month, day, and minute of those two years and had compressed the timeline into a matter of hours. They'd picked up where they'd left off, not missing a beat, their instruments perfectly tuned and playing in harmony. The only other people he shared such rhythms with were his bandmates. Megan was inner-circle caliber. "How did we let that kind of time get away from us?"

She shook her head. "I think I was scared. Correction. I know I was scared. The whole incident in the haunted site, well, I didn't know how to process it. My watch was going crazy. I was worried if I kept hanging around you, you'd get hurt."

A heavy load of memories hardened throughout his body. His relationship with Megan hadn't been all skipping through fields of flowers or some such sentimental bollocks. She'd talked about demons and childhood curses and bad energy lurking around his band. He hadn't cared. He'd wanted her too badly to care about a little kookiness. But then kookiness had turned to terror.

He'd slept in a decrepit asylum that smelled of mold and death, where he'd woken up paralyzed and staring into the vacant face of a living shadow who wanted to kill him. Then there were the things that Megan hadn't told him, her darker secrets that seemed to seethe in a hole at the center of her very self. But that was the past.

He gathered up both of her hands. Her skin was like silk. "It hurt more being without you." A lump formed in his throat. Megan was so beautiful that it pained him to look directly at her. "Don't abandon me again, okay?" He kissed the tip of her nose.

This was all nuts. Thom was the one who ate the hearts of willing women who welcomed the privilege. He was a man for whom lovers were as temporary as the cities he played. Yet here he stood, puny in the thrall of this person who held his emotions on a short leash, her heel piercing the base of his neck.

Four knocks struck the door in a brusque, speedy pattern. Thom's stomach did an embarrassing turnover that hit down low. If this was a woman coming by to tend to him before the show, the resulting encounter between the three of them would sure be awkward. Megan supposedly didn't care about what or who he'd done over the last couple of years, but deep down she did. He saw the truth behind her eyes and sympathized, because he didn't want to think about who she'd been with either. He stepped away from her and opened the door to face his fate.

Just a lanyard-wearing staffer, thank God, a curvy brunette in artistically ripped jeans and a political shirt that looked handmade. Thom didn't screw the staff. He had enough decency and ethics to draw clear lines in the right places. The worker acknowledged Megan's existence with a curt greeting before saying to Thom, "Brian wants to see you."

That was odd. The band did a customary pre-show huddle, but they had another thirtyish minutes before it was time to convene. "Why?"

"He didn't say." The young woman fiddled with an earpiece and walked away talking about unrelated matters.

Megan asked, "Everything okay?"

Suddenly, Thom felt strange, creepy-crawly, and out of body, and Megan appeared to him as a character in a movie might. He shook off the weird haze before it got the better of him. "I'm not sure. It's out of the ordinary. I guess I'm about to find out." He grabbed his phone and stuffed it in his back pocket. An off-kilter sensation still had its hooks in him. If he was being honest with himself, he wasn't entirely sure how to process the reemergence of Megan after a two-year hiatus. And now Brian wanted to delve into an important-sounding topic at an inconvenient time. The control freak Fyre front man never disrupted his cherished routine, yet here they were. "Can I ask you a question?"

"I have a feeling you're about to."

He found a hair tie on the vanity and pulled his hair back into a ponytail. At least there weren't loose ends right in his face. "I don't mean for this to come off as insensitive or ungrateful, but why now, after so long? Is something the matter, or do you need to break some news to me?" He didn't allow himself to speculate on what the phantom fantasy "announcement" might be. He supposed that he was searching for a puzzle piece to restore a sense of order.

She chewed on the side of her lip. "I'd better go and let you deal with Brian. I'm sorry I barged in like this. I shouldn't have. My impulsive act caused a major disruption, like always."

He heard another voice in her mouth, a parent or teacher who'd been scared of her power and set out to crush her spirit. Thom mentally kicked himself for being an arse. "No. Don't go. That's the last thing I want. Stay, please. We'll have time to catch up after the show. You're welcome to stick around while I talk to Brian. I can't imagine he has anything confidential to say. Otherwise, feel free to do your own thing. I don't mind."

Megan was a familiar face in the rock and roll circuit and had been a staple of Fyre's touring party scene a few years ago. She was one of those people who had quickly transcended the rank of mere groupie to carve out her own unique status, exalted yet undefined. She was simply Megan O'Neil, someone who was around if the night was an interesting one, a harbinger of a lit-up time. She might have plans at the arena that didn't involve him. In any event, she wouldn't be bored.

"I'll stay," she said, her voice softer and free of its usual husky edge.

"Perfect." He meant it. She belonged by his side. "Do you need anything?" He took her hand and interlaced their fingers, careful not to act too territorial while also making it known through touch how much he valued her. A part of Megan was vulnerable. This piece of her didn't like to stay buried and required a practiced nurturance that Thom was honored to provide.

Holding hands, they strolled down a hallway as wide as a Wal-Mart aisle. Recorded Fyre music came from somewhere, and people with and without headsets called his name in ignored attempts to get his attention. The energy was picking up, and his status was hitting the right notes, but he didn't have the bandwidth to play his fame-doused, arrogant-but-lovable character at the moment. Not when he had Megan. "Is it fun to be back?"

Several of the ambient background people greeted her, and she afforded them smiles and waves. "Yeah, I'm having fun. Want to go out later, for old time's sake?" Her smile was vixen incarnate. She was definitely back, and his cock was half-hard again.

The second Thom had spotted Megan at that promotional party two years ago, his attention had zeroed in on her with the focus of a laser. Her signals had been nakedly sexual, with her bright red corset top and false eyelashes as thick as two spiders. Fishnet tights even, for heaven's sake. Megan's look was commonplace among the women he met on nights like those. They led with their bodies, and he followed.

Make no mistake, Megan was no good girl who complemented his dirtiness with her innocence. She was a clear and present fuck for the taking, leveraging the usual stock-in-trade. Even then, buzzed and horny, he'd seen through the superficialities. Megan was tall and proud and charmed every person in the room. She talked, she listened, and she told tales with her hands while others watched, rapt. The woman moved like a troubadour, a bard, stitching vagabond tribes together with the power of her words.

Then there was the matter of music. If her looks were the hook and her personality was the reel, her taste closed the deal. Led Zeppelin's "Immigrant Song" had been playing, and Megan had mouthed every word perfectly.

Lip-synching would have been lame if it had been a Fyre song; lots of groupies advertised their bona fides as true fans. No, Megan was a real rocker bird. She'd swayed her hips to Muse and flashed the hand horns when Sabbath came on. She knew obscure Iron Maiden and iconic Radiohead.

Everyone had wanted to be near her. She was almost famous, a magnet, the female element of an electric outlet. She'd created the scene that night, not the other way around.

Thom could get a piece of tail with a snap of his fingers, but until then he had trouble admitting that he wanted more—a woman who completed him. Megan was all woman, pure woman, a breathing celebration of female sexuality with crimson blood spurting through her veins.

She'd caught him staring and approached, head high and shoulders square, Crüe's "Dr. Feelgood" her soundtrack. Was he the doctor or was he her patient? Ah! His knees had gone weak, and he'd ceased to be a big man with an axe. He was as dumb as Wayne and Garth in an instant, an unworthy wanker bowing beneath the divine she-gaze.

Next, she'd led him into a bathroom, sat on a toilet, and swallowed his prick whole. He'd thought he was having an aneurysm when he shot his load. That was the moment when she became a superstar.

"You still have your tongue rings?" He studied the apple curve of her ass. They turned a corner, and he accepted a thumb drive from a short-haired girl in a yellow blazer.

Megan ran her tongue across her top lip, flashing a triptych of silver studs laid in a perfect vertical line.

"You got a third one." His head swum in hormones. His balls tightened. Brian's issue might have to wait.

"What's on the USB?"

"Huh?" He texted an assistant and asked him to buy ten pieces of the hottest, most expensive lingerie available, all in Megan's size. "Oh, the thumb drive. A demo, probably. I try to listen to a few per week in case there's a diamond in the rough. Give the up-and-comers a fair shot." He stole a look down Megan's generous cleavage, disinterested in the kid's music for now. He'd listen to the aspiring young musician's work later.

She laughed her fullest, roundest, most beautiful laugh. "You're old. How is your dick still running your life like this? Viagra?"

"Is that your new nickname?" Thom's horniness cooled as they approached Brian's room. He hoped Brian was okay. The man could be annoying, but Thom loved him like a brother. Thirty-plus years of band life inspired either lifetime loyalty or blood hatred. Fyre had lucked into the former. "Because you certainly have that effect on a man."

"How about The Notorious M.E.G.?" she offered in a jesting tone. "We just have to figure out what the letters stand for."

My Electric Girl? They'd work on it.

A small group of women in club clothes and body glitter caught up to Megan, chattering excitedly. She paused outside the dressing room to talk with them.

Thom kissed her cheek and bumped his fist on Brian's door. He was comforted that Megan had friends. She held her own, and he didn't have to worry about her not fitting in or getting pushed around.

"It's open," Brian called from behind the door, his posh voice more clipped than usual. The auspices of the meeting were dubious. "Close it behind you."

Thom entered to see Brian hunched over the vanity and shuffling loose sheets of paper. His jaw was hard enough to take a punch, and his short hair had amassed more brushstrokes of gray. He wore a track suit instead of his usual pre-show attire of fitted jeans and a button-up dress shirt. The singer's typical stage costume winked to when the band had played in school uniform attire.

Emulating the AC/DC aesthetic for commercial cache had been the label's idea, of course, and the sellout style had sucked up loads of teenage cash. Brian never completely dumped the getup, not even after the cheeseball execs had stopped insisting through their porcelain veneers.

Whatever. Once upon a tacky time, dancing near the line of boy band fandom had made Fyre nearly as rich as the Stones. "How can I help?" Thom asked with sincerity.

Brian huffed and sorted, unusually disheveled. This was all maximum weird. The only thing more organized than the man's methodical approach to singing and lead guitar was his rigid preparatory protocol of funky virgin drinks and vocal cord voodoo. "Jonnie and I are leaving tonight for a couple of days. Can you handle my meetings while we're gone? Andrea has contracts that need a look, and there's a shedload of legalese surrounding Pepsi and Rockstock 2024. I need you to look through those contracts *very* closely and keep your cool. There are parts buried in there that are only for you to see. I'm in a position of having to slide things by the higher-ups, and buried layers is the way to do it. Stay focused and trust in the process."

Thom popped his head out the door to check on Megan, who was lost in conversation, before closing himself in the room with Brian. He had no desire to play a trashed-out campsite propped up by mass-produced goods, but the music festival was beside the point. "What do you mean, leaving tonight? Where are you going? We have more shows after tonight."

"I'm aware, and I'll be present for them." Brian finished with a sharp smile. "My schedule doesn't concern you. Can I count on you to take the lead on these matters?"

Somewhere along the way, Brian had morphed from a charismatic rock star with a clean-cut chin, male model bone structure, and preternatural talent into a grinding business executive with a head full of numbers. Brian Shepherd was too uptight to have ever been a real rebel, but now he was a right and proper data-driven professional.

Brian's efforts to start his own record label had gone tits-up for reasons that were never quite clear to Thom, and Brian had been overcompensating ever since. The lawyers and managers loved him. His presence occasionally made Thom's teeth ache from sympathy clenching.

However, the request to meet with those capitalists presented an opportunity for Thom to involve himself more in band matters, and if he played his cards right, the added responsibility could be to his benefit in shaping the direction of Fyre's next phase into one with less soda pop and more bourbon on the rocks. "Yeah, I'll talk the turkey talk with your favorite suits, sure. What are you and Jonnie conspiring about now?"

Those two had an irritating habit of cliquing up that they'd formed a couple of years ago, right around the time when Fyre's then-manager died suddenly and things started getting strange. That was also when the woman who became Brian's wife entered the picture with her crystals and woo and totally Yokoed out on everyone in the studio that one day (Yes, he knew Yoko Ono was a legitimate artist in her own right before she met Lennon. Grant him the bit, okay?) Thom would get to the bottom of all that goofy shite eventually.

"It's a personal thing." Brian looked to the side. Dark circles ringed his blue eyes, and his wrinkles popped into stark relief in the overhead fluorescent light. "Andrea needs a meeting tomorrow at nine sharp. Get sober sleep and try to have the groupies gone by then. You ought to be thinking straight. Major money's on the line." Brian slapped Thom on the shoulder and stuck his mystery documents into an actual briefcase that he locked with a tiny key. Oh, dear. "Major Money" was in top form. "I'm going to change and go through my warm-ups. Thanks for being a team player. See you in twenty."

"Teamwork makes the dream work," Thom said sarcastically before leaving Brian to get in his zone. At least the man still had a passion for the music and left his heart on the stage. He could rock a crowd's face off despite all the corporate crap.

After reconnecting with Megan and making a bit of small talk with her friends, Thom gave her a tour of the backstage layout and pointed out the food, bathrooms, and pop-up bar. His mind was still locked on Brian and Jonnie's clandestine date. Megan must've noticed, because after eating a bacon-wrapped appetizer that she snagged from a passing catering cart, she asked, "What was that about? You seem distracted."

He didn't want to talk about it. He was probably jealous that he'd been left out of the guitarist bonding reunion like any other lowly bassist. He had better things, and people, to focus on besides whatever the toxic twins were concocting. "Just business. What are we doing later?"

Her face lit up, which lit him up. "People seem into the idea of going out. There's a new place a block away called Mixed. It's hip but intimate. Dance floor, good deejay. Some of the girls know a promoter who can reserve it for us on this super-short notice."

Perfect. A night out with Megan provided plenty of incentive for him to bust through the concert at his best and give these people what they'd bloody well paid for and much more.

IT ENDED UP BEING A BANG-UP SHOW, WITH A LOUD CROWD THAT filled the bucket seats from floor to balcony. Light on geriatrics, children, and the hipsters who enjoyed Fyre ironically. Hot chicks aplenty and sky-high energy.

The band was on the right wavelength, Jonnie and Brian attacking those guitars and strutting their stuff down the runway that bifurcated the pit.

Brian delivered the hits with an intensity that brought Thom back to their schoolboy days, when the four of them were a bunch of outcasts, uncool nobodies hungry to break big. He had his head thrown back, and his fingers were moving over that fretboard at warp speed. Thom's respect for Fyre's leader was immense. That man could *play*.

Brian had never cared about pussy or parties. He was better than Thom in that respect. His goal from age fourteen onward had been singular. Chariotz of Fyre: Legendary.

Not fame—fame was cheap plastic that eventually ended up in a landfill. Legends inspired myths, like the ones that shaped Fyre's epic albums: *Prometheus, Avenged* and *Crystal Mountain Reins*.

His obsession was scary until it came true.

Sweat poured down Thom's back and stung his eyes, all the pomp and spectacle giving him spine-tingling chills. The crescendo of "Deep Dark Woods," their version of "Stairway to Heaven," threaded through the center of his essence. The explosions boomed, reverberating through the nominal barrier of his earplugs.

Pyrotechnics baked the backs of his legs and singed his nose hairs with a chemical burn smell. Thom looked skyward and grinned at the undersides of the two psycho horses that he'd nicknamed Pony and Tony because making fun of Fyre's signature set piece pissed Brian off.

Thom had to cope somehow. He'd grown sick of the ridiculous prop that hung over the stage, a mythological black chariot pulled in two directions by a white Pegasus and a nightmarish steed with a coat of flames dusted by painted-on singe. Those fuckers shot fireworks out of their eye sockets. No shit. He wasn't having you on. The worst of KISS and GWAR stuffed into one stage piece, he'd been known to bitch. On his worst days, he hated the band name too, derivative of Def Leppard when you considered the context. Brian loved it, naturally.

Tonight, though, Thom had no potshots to hurl. Tonight, he loved every bit of what they'd built. His life's work. His legacy.

He jammed in accord with Jonas to crank out the rhythm section magic. Jonas thrashed those skins and cymbals, his dark arms built like bricks, his dreadlocks a whipping whirlpool. Thom stuck every lick, his bass beats as rich and deep as a swamp creature that crawled out of the Muscle Shoals mud.

Scratch the surface of rock or metal and you get the blues, and Thom aimed every goddamn time to flay that surface as raw as the pads of his fingers when they lost the battle to his fat brass strings.

He was heaving at the end, drunk on shouts and applause, blood and adrenaline drowning every cell. He cried tears of joy when the band bowed at the end to a thunderous applause. The show had gone off like a tight machine, each gear lubed and precise to turn at full function. They weren't all like that.

His heart was a war hammer of the gods. His cock was steel. He was phallic, unstoppable, possessed. Time for his favorite fix.

Megan stood backstage, hanging in the vibrating field of his vision like a juicy, teasing talisman. He stomped offstage the second the curtain dropped, shoved his instrument into the hands of a tech, and grabbed her. The contrast of stage lighting and darkness was severe enough to shadow an entire side of her unspeakably stunning face. She looked like a devil, a witch—biblical. He dragged her into a storage closet, bent her over an amp, and shoved her skirt over her pale bottom.

"Yes," she moaned, spreading her legs into a wide V to give him a nice view of her openings from behind, both holes swollen and ready for the plunder. Thom was honest enough to admit that he'd stuck with the musician's life for the express purpose of moments like these. "Yes, yes. Now. Please."

"I appreciate the clear consent, but my name isn't *yes*." He whipped out his dick and rolled on a condom, a vein on the side of his shaft throbbing. Her arousal smelled like the sea and made his heart pound into his ribcage. He felt his nostrils flare. His eyes watered. He wanted to eat Megan O'Neil alive.

"Fuck me, Thom, fuck me now." She arched her back and stuck her luscious cheeks in the air, her sculpted legs elevated high by those stilettos she wore. "Wherever you want, however you want."

Maybe they'd take the back road eventually, but for now he craved a hit of straightforward pussy. He shoved in and stroked, finding her sweet-slick and softened to perfection. "There is not one thing I'd rather do." He grabbed her hips and thrust, the pressure building fast. Out of his mind, he slammed in and out, the obscene sounds of wet skin slapping making music to his ears.

The tips of her long nails tickled his driving cock. She was playing with herself. He loved that, and he kept pushing. His member was a shining staff of pride that disappeared into her before emerging victorious to fuck again and again, in and out.

She cried out, shaking, her walls clenching around him. She clawed the amp she was hunched over with five black talons. Her back hole opened and closed like a greedy little mouth. A blanket of red hair hid her face. Megan's climax pushed Thom to the brink as every nerve inside of him wound to a pinpoint of tension. "On your knees," he gritted out. It was time for a glorious reunion, a throwback to their first date.

Megan obeyed as soon as she finished coming, whipping around in a sea of flame before she dropped down to kneel. She gazed up at him, her glossy lips parted. He ditched the rubber, held the sides of her head, and pushed himself in all the way to the back of her throat. She gagged, and her eyes stretched wide, but she took control and wrangled her reflexes before getting down to it.

She sucked him, those metal balls on her tongue working the most sensitive areas of his cock's underside, her head bobbing fast. Megan stroked the base of his shaft and squeezed his balls, her green eyes fixed on his while her candy apple lips wrapped and slurped.

He couldn't take it anymore. Two more pumps and a flick of her tongue tip at the base of his crown, and he pulled out and shot white all over her face, like he'd done in that bathroom two years ago.

A clap like thunder went off in Thom's ears, angry and round and terror-loud. Pressure squeezed his skull from all sides. He staggered back, his spent prick still out, and pressed his hands over his ears to stop the noise. He tried to ask what was happening, but he didn't hear any words come out. Was this a stroke? The explanation sounded plausible until two orange wings sprouted from the top of Megan's back, flapping and unfolding in an arson of sun-colored feathers. Their movements roasted his face, the glare forcing him to squint in the wake of her twenty-foot wingspan.

THREE

"I THINK I NEED AN AMBULANCE." THOM SUNK TO THE FLOOR OF THE storage closet where he'd rocked Megan's world a moment ago. His pants stayed unbuttoned. He slumped forward.

Both proud of her work and buzzed from her orgasm, she found a roll of paper towels behind an amp and used a handful to wipe off her face. "Relax, you're fine. I give great head. We both know that."

She treated herself to a cigarette and enjoyed a drag of the bitter, smoky flavor. Thom was still crumpled in on himself. She crept forward on her knees. "You okay, babe?" She shook his thigh, concern setting in as a dull bite above her navel. Was it really a thing, a man having a sex-triggered heart attack? She'd long since written that off as a joke or an urban legend. Thom wasn't even that old. "Do you really need help?" Megan crushed the cig and took her phone out in case he was being serious.

He snapped out of his daze enough to sit upright and button his jeans, easing her worry. Thom pressed two fingers to the side of his neck to take his own pulse. "I'm okay." He watched her for a long time. "Did you experience anything...out of the ordinary just now?"

What was he talking about? Was he messing with her? Thom could be a jester at times. She mirrored the humor tack. "Is this the part where

I say I've never come that hard in my life and only you can do that to me?" She'd be telling the truth, but it really didn't look like he was fishing for an ego stroke.

He responded with a watery smile. His complexion had washed out to an ashy pallor. "I'm sure that's all it was. You're a powerhouse, girl. You're gonna kill me."

She wasn't ready to be cute. Thom didn't look good. "Do you have a heart condition or need medication?"

He shook his head and adjusted his hat. "I got a bit worked up is all. Between the show and you, well, I might not be able to rock like I used to without paying the price." He laughed, but there was a touch of nerves in the tone, like he hadn't convinced himself of his explanation.

She let it go. If there was more to the story, it wasn't going to come out now. "You still wanna go to Mixed? They serve food. I'm starving."

"Definitely." She fretted when he stood up quickly, but his balance was solid, and he seemed to have recovered fully from the post-coital episode when he offered her his hand.

Megan rose with the assistance of Thom's firm hold and met his eyes once she was on her feet. She searched for a clue behind his pupils. Her intuition hummed with a disturbing undercurrent. He hadn't been acting melodramatic. An unusual occurrence had unfolded. Maybe he'd tell her after a couple of drinks. She pulled up a rideshare app and called them a car to the after-party.

MEGAN'S ACCURSED PHONE MADE ANOTHER DING THAT POPPED THE trancelike bubble of the house music bumping through Mixed. If Gary called or texted again, she'd tell him to cool it and wait until she got home to talk production logistics. He was wound tight like a spring for reasons uncertain, but it didn't matter. There would be no *Bump in the Night* without her, and Gary wasn't her boss. It was the other way around, which his male ego needed to accept.

Then there was that meathead mosquito Logan Pax, stink bombing her with shitty text threats. That asshole wasn't getting any reaction other than an ice-cold ghosting. His jilted ass had no power to fuck up her show, despite his bluster.

Nestled beside Thom in a circular booth and flanked by friends, Megan stole another look at her phone before vowing to put it away. Four new messages, the number as red as a siren. An anxiety ball bounced off the walls of her stomach.

Gary: *Seriously, where are you? Shooting starts in two days. Need to test equipment. CALL ME.*

She whipped off a reply that had better suffice to placate him: *Personal thing. Back tomorrow or next. Chill.*

Against her better judgment, she read Logan's latest micro-tantrum: *Bump in the Night could use a rebranding without the tits and the tats. Hmmm. Thinking!*

What a childish pain. Why was he being like this? He had Trina, money, and plenty of his own projects. Had the guy never been rejected in his life?

Megan pulled the bottle of champagne from the ice bucket in the middle of the table and refilled her glass. She drank, washing away the bitter taste in her mouth that Logan had brought up.

Though the bulk of Thom's attention was taken up by a talkative Asian man in a football jersey, he had rested one of his hands on the inside of her bare thigh and was caressing her in lazy strokes. His touch was grounding, a relief, and she laid her hand over his. Their appetizers wouldn't arrive for another ten minutes. She needed to get out of her head and away from her phone. Megan leaned in to Thom and raised her voice over the music, "Wanna dance?"

Thom stood up and clutched her hand, and they moved to a dance floor where bodies were packed front to back, undulating in sexual, serpentine motions that matched the music and atmosphere. A leggy blonde with fine bone structure passed out bioluminescent shots from a clear tray. Megan threw one down her throat and threw herself into Thom, rolling her hips, grinding her butt against his crotch, and busting out a range of typical dance club choreography.

He matched her, spun her, held her, his motions fluid testimonies to the allure of good rhythm. He was a natural when it came to all things musical. The gel-filtered lighting turned him uncanny, rendering the man into a surreal version of himself. The way he stared down at her with a look that was somehow both dominant and enthralled sparked her like a match.

Bass beats forever trembled in her core, transforming the bouncing club into one big sex ritual. She half expected Dionysus himself to twirl into the middle of the floor, clomping his cloven hooves while women shrieked. Her heart beat to the rhythm of the drum. Thom was the drum, a bang in perpetuity. She draped her arms over his shoulders and got lost in his eyes, his smell, his solidness. Why the fuck was she fretting about what that turd Logan was up to when she had a man like this? She needed to calm down.

They danced until last call and then ate, even though their food was long since cold. She chugged warm champagne from a half-spent bottle bobbing in melted ice. He kissed her while her mouth was still full of alcohol. Confetti covered the table. The snuffed remnant of a sparkler jutted up from the little lake in the champagne bucket. The final song was a triumphant female anthem. She was free.

Thom called his own driver this time, summoning a white Lexus that shimmered steedlike on the curb and reminded her of that Pegasus suspended from the stage. Her brain floated in booze bubbles. He was famous and massive and he freaking liked *her*, a rando from Iowa. She held tight to him, a warm breeze blowing meaty scents of street food in her direction, trying not to think about Logan and the show and whatever had happened in the storage closet that made Thom go to pieces.

She rested her head on his shoulder during the car ride, and he stroked her hair and allowed silence to transpire.

He didn't vocalize his concern until they were at the door. "Part of me wants to ask you if you're okay and mention that you seemed stressed when we got to the club, but I suppose I'm the one who made this night intense and heavy in the first place." He waved a key card over the digital pad and turned the handle once he got a green light.

There was a lightness in his speech that cut into the tension. "It's just my work. I need to get back to the show." Thinking about *Bump in the Night* made her think about the spell book, which made her wonder how much she should tell Thom, in light of his episode. It stood to reason that her dabbling in magic was connected to his unexplained event. But how to gauge the timing on introducing a subject like that? "Between that stuff and what happened to you before we went out, my head just feels a little full."

Thom turned on lights and brought to life a suite laid out like an apartment. She'd never stayed in a hotel room fancy enough that the bed had its own dedicated space behind a closed door. Her bag rested against a navy accent wall that gave way to the kitchen. Beside it sat a sleek, cream-colored sack with a mahogany ribbon for a satiny handle. The name of the boutique, Lovely, was written across the front in elegant cursive.

"That's for you, but I confess I'm too exhausted to enjoy you again properly. Why don't we get rest and regroup in the morning?" He dropped a lazy kiss on her lips before yawning into his fist.

She wanted to see what was in the bag but was just as tired as Thom. Her feet ached from walking and dancing in heels. They'd had sex twice. She'd drank most of a bottle of champagne and two shots. He had to be more wiped from his show than he was letting on. The performance had taken it out of her, and all she did was watch. "Not gonna lie, I'm ready to swan dive into that bed back there."

Thom had showered at the arena, and Megan got her own, scrubbing off everything from the flight to the club sweat. Fancy hotel products delighted her senses with scents of lemongrass and lavender. The bottles weren't even bolted to the wall. Apparently the hospitality chains weren't worried about rich people stealing.

She brushed her teeth and all the rest before climbing into bed with Thom and tucking her clutch under her pillow. Before it petered out, the watch would have diagnosed the energy of the closet incident, had it been malignant. Maybe someday she'd figure out how to revive it, but that time was not now.

Once swaddled in cool, fresh sheets, her eyes started to close. She snuggled into his warmth and ran one of her hands through the thick hair on his chest. He put his arm around her and kissed her goodnight before nodding off. She could get used to this but probably shouldn't. Fairytale dreams had never been written for girls like her.

✳

MEGAN WALKED TO THE EDGE OF A CLIFF, HER BARE HEELS KICKING UP bursts of fire. Fyre's classic mythological anthem, "Deep Dark Woods," played in the open air. How apropos.

Beyond the cliff was a canyon. Would she fly if she jumped, coasting on flaming wings that carried her to the land where Prometheus was avenged? Would she land at the bottom of the crystal mountain?

"Jump," Folly, the coven sister of chaos and governess of the magic system, whispered in her ear. "Jump into my arms."

Megan jerked back to consciousness. She stirred awake on a mattress, her mouth dry and her head aching.

"Deep Dark Woods" wasn't pouring through the clouds from some mystical heavenward speaker. The song was coming from Thom's phone, his ringtone, the device shaking on his nightstand. She pushed the pillow into her ears as the dream left and shame and queasiness swelled to the forefront of her mind. She was too old to drink as much as she had.

Thom grunted, his deep voice thick with sleep. He looked at the phone and groaned, "Oh no."

"What?"

"They're here." He vaulted out of bed, ran to the closet, and grabbed a dress shirt so hard that the hanger clattered to the ground. Thom was gargling when Megan heard the knocking. "I have to do a stupid meeting on Brian's behalf," he said through what sounded like a toothbrush. "I overslept. Thought I set the alarm, but I guess I forgot."

"I've been there." Megan didn't count punctuality among her virtues and didn't judge Thom for his lapse. She rubbed her eye with the heel of her hand. "You want me to leave?" She could call one of her old scene friends and go out for coffee. She needed caffeine.

"Whatever you want, baby. I don't want to run you off. I want you here." He kissed her on the lips. "Good morning. You're beautiful. I'll try to get rid of them quickly, but it's your call if you'd rather get air."

Thom was charming even when flustered and thrown for a loop. A breeze in the face of stressors and disruptions, one who wasn't prone to emotional reactivity and could keep the stress chemicals at bay. The casual coolness looked good on him, endearing and true to form.

She stood up, the motion bolting nausea to her center. "I'll slip out and try to find a decent cup of coffee." She wasn't quite up for socializing, but hanging around while Thom did business didn't sound great either.

"Come on, man," a woman called from behind the door. "Up, up. The morning is wearing on."

Megan shucked her sleepwear and was halfway into jeans and a t-shirt when two company types powered through the main door. The man had blond hair, frat boy energy, and carried a leather-bound folder. The woman was short and severe, a nondescript plain Jane with a pinched countenance and a brisk stride.

The man tossed a quick sideways glance into the bedroom. "Brian says no more hookers. Fyre is shows before hos. This has gotta stop."

"That's not the putdown you think it is," Megan clapped back while wrapping her clutch around her wrist and jamming a deodorant stick up into her armpit. Hookers were shrewd hustlers and no joke. She probably could have made a lot of side cash had she charged for her time over the years. "Sex work is honest work." She bet that jackass with the folder had hired a prostitute or two during a cliché Vegas bachelor party.

"You have quite the nerve speaking to my guest that way. I ought to fire you both and send you on your way. Brian's not my boss, I might add. His vision for my life is a suggestion at best."

An ensuing pause tumbled into the abyss before the dudebro finally cleared his throat with all the awkwardness of bad news message delivery. "Band leadership structure is actually one of the matters we're here to discuss."

Yikes, the meeting was getting serious and had veered sharply into "none of her business" territory. Megan popped on her go-anywhere sport sandals and exited to the living room. Thom looked miserable in the presence of the two middle managers in their suits. Three neat stacks of paper rested in the center of the coffee table, a smattering of sections marked with neon sticky flags. The execs appraised Megan with a combination of disinterest and contempt that bounced off the shield of her skin.

Thom came over to her, shaking his head. "Don't let them get in your mind. I apologize for their rudeness. For all of this."

She didn't want to stick around for whatever was going down, but she didn't blame Thom. She'd kept him out late and distracted him from his obligation. "No worries. I need breakfast. Want me to pick you up anything?"

"If it's convenient. Don't worry about me. I'll make this fast."

She kissed him goodbye and saw herself into the hotel hallway, a generically tasteful space accented with mass-produced paintings and the scent of powder and class. Megan was halfway to the elevator when voices behind a door snagged her attention, in particular the cadence of a man talking in an English accent. She made herself a fly on the wall.

"If the spell is in the music," said a British man in all seriousness, "do we have control of its effects? Do we shape the course or guide it, or is it acting in accord with its own will?" In her estimation, this man was not thrilled to be engaging on the subject at hand but had no choice. He said, "I did my best to block off the two main songs. We'll see if my plan works."

She held her breath. Spells and magic tracked her down one way or another, even when her book wasn't present. She fingered her watch through the material of the clutch. Who was this man?

A woman responded, "We aren't sure about the control factor. That's why we need to get to Peru, and immediately, to run those tests. Last night would have been the best time, but the second-best time is now. Cynthia and Taylor are there already, and they have this woman Rachel with them who seems promising. That makes five of us. Five beats two."

There had to be a second woman under consideration for this Peru quintet who wasn't already down south. Megan's exhale puttered out in choppy jumps. An anxiety monkey unleashed bedlam in her belly. Her book had six sections, each marked by a distinct element. Her speculation ran amok. Did she...fit? She'd longed to be a part of something larger than herself, but not like this.

A different English man spoke, "I'm not sure if Thom and Jonas can hold it down for a couple of days. I lack confidence your proposal will be taken in stride. Frankly, I think you mishandled the setup."

The drama behind the door came home to roost. In a flash, Megan saw herself and someone she cared about as small, targeted, and pinned in the crosshairs.

The original man: "They'll have to cope. This can't wait, right, dear?"

"Right." Based on the clipped intonation of the woman's voice, whatever was being planned mattered gravely and could not, in fact, wait. "It's not ideal to have only five out of the six, but we need to assemble before the next ritual and work through this song magic theory."

Ritual? Megan's backbone turned to an icicle.

"The last thing I want is to be enacting mind control programming unintentionally," the second man put in, sounding pressed.

What the hell? Footsteps approached from inside the plotting room. Megan beat feet to the vending machines and pretended to buy a snack. She caught the reflections of four people in the plexiglass. The women, she wasn't able to place. The men were Brian Shepherd and Jonnie Tollens.

Thom had hit the target. Those two were definitely up to something. She hated her inkling that it concerned her. Or maybe she was spinning stories, remiss to trudge back to Iowa and face her own dramas. Either way, this was his circus. She had her own, and there wasn't much she could do except grab her suitcase, peel herself off Thom James, and get her ass back to work.

With a chime, the elevator carried away the conspirators. She stayed put in the vending area until the dude-bro and Plain Jane walked by yammering jargon before they made themselves scarce.

After halfheartedly purchasing pop and prepackaged sugar junk, Megan dragged herself back to the room. Should she tell him what she'd heard? Probably. But how to frame the rundown? She let herself in with the spare key and found Thom sitting sunken into on the living room couch, staring at the ceiling. The carcasses of those contracts lay fallen at his feet in a mess of shredded scraps and crumpled wads. Uh-oh.

She sat beside him. "Meeting didn't go great?"

"I think I'm going to be sick."

She handed him a Coke Zero and opened one for herself. "Wanna talk about it?"

Thom glared at his bottle of pop. "Fuck soda. Fuck all this shite. Fuck these companies and their parasitic thirst for artists' souls."

She was desperate for a sweet, cold, fizzy drink but felt super weird about reaching for her Coke now. "We don't have to talk about it, on second thought."

"I'm sorry. Thank you for the drink. I just can't reconcile what was put in front of me. Not by you. By them." He propped his elbows on his knees and crushed a hunk of fallen paper underfoot. One of the small, gummy flags stuck to his bare big toe.

She rubbed his back. She cared about Thom but wanted to go home now. Even dealing with Gary's misplaced bossiness and Logan's jilted lover juvenilia sounded better than all the craziness swirling around Chicago and this Hilton Hotel. Whether Brian Shepherd was into mind control rituals or Thom James suddenly hated pop didn't have to impact her. Bottom line was that Chariotz of Fyre shit wasn't her shit.

She had her own shit, which was stinking up the nether parts of her unconscious where she'd tried to shove the rapidly growing heap. "I'm here if you want to talk."

Thom tore a sheet of paper into neat strips that he stacked on the table. "Brian wants to buy me out. He offered six million dollars on the condition that I surrender my share of the rights to all Chariotz of Fyre songs. No more royalties, writing contributions, or leeway to play those songs on my own. I'd be a hired gun and paid a salary. He'd have the final say over how long I stay with the band. He'd be my boss in reality, not just in his mind."

There had to be more to the story, a "more" that involved Peru and song spells and whatever else was being broken down in that room across the hall. "Why would he do that? What's his motive? There's no Fyre without you. It's self-sabotage to break your bond like this."

"Money." Thom kicked a ragged chunk of paper. "He's a capitalist pig now I suppose, just like them." Thom extended a middle finger at the closed door. "I've suspected as much for a while but let myself deny the truth."

She gingerly opened her bottle, avoiding a carbonation explosion. A cold drink of chemicals and caffeine got her brain parts working better. "Do you think there might be another angle of this that isn't visible from our immediate vantage point?" Bringing up what she'd witnessed might accomplish nothing but upsetting him even more. With any luck, he'd work through the conundrum on his own. Thom had his own, independent suspicions about Brian and Jonnie. He had to have seen or heard a clue.

"Sure, a gross brand management scheme." Thom sagged into the cushions and stretched his arms over the top. The pose would've looked sexy, except he was stewing in bitterness and defeat. "It's all connected. Pepsi and Rockstock 2024 and Brian and Jonnie running around like conjoined twins. They're definitely up to something, and I think that thing is taking us in a disgustingly commercial direction. They want our image to be even more high concept than it already is. I'm talking real Dungeons and Dragons bullshite. I loved the Tolkien angle, but they're itching to cross the final Rubicon. I've felt it. I need to call Jonas and debrief." Thom stared blackly into the middle distance. "And then there's Helen."

Now there was a warm lead. "Who is Helen?"

"I shouldn't have even brought her up. I don't want to be the jerkoff band prick who blames my grievances on women."

Hmm. "Well, just because she's a woman doesn't mean she's blameless. Women are people and therefore capable of being just as awful as men."

His half-smile was resigned but kind. It was nice to see Thom's easy charm and playful personality return, though he had grounds for being mad. He was clearly going through an upsetting situation, and she didn't hold his anger against him. "True."

"Who is she and what did she do?"

"That's the thing, I'm not altogether sure. Maybe nothing. Brian started dating her during a strange time. They're married now. She was visiting Brian the day our manager died under unexplained conditions. Suicide, murder, I never figured it out. That whole weekend was bizarre and cocked up. As soon as she shows up in L.A., the world tilts on its axis. Brian went missing for a short time. She lied about getting called to audition at a fitness studio and then snuck back into his house. Who does that? We played a show that went sideways—the prop came crashing down and everyone had to be evacuated. She runs a yoga place in the Midwest and claims to offer services like energy healing and crystal readings." He pinched the inner corners of his eyes. "Could she be organizing cult stuff and pulling them in? Is cult recruiting what this is?"

Megan drowned in overwhelm. That was a lot to process. Was Helen a murderess? A kidnapper? She didn't have the capacity to grapple with whether some ruthless rock star's wife was those things and/or a cult leader, or simply *in* a cult, and what any of those scenarios meant. Maybe the woman did nothing but lie about being scouted by a Los Angeles fitness studio to appear cooler to a bunch of famous men, making her phony but not dangerous. "Does Peru mean anything special to you?"

He drew his brows into a confounded crunch. "No. Why?"

A whole bunch of different thoughts crashed down on her at once, combined with feelings that she struggled to process. "What happened in the storage closet after we had sex?"

She could practically see his head spin. "I don't know. I hallucinated. Maybe someone put LSD in my drink."

He hadn't hallucinated or been drugged. This was witchcraft, and she'd lost control of hers. Everyone had lost control.

When it came to witchcraft, everyone lost control eventually.

Her book said as much.

The fabric of life was fraying as entropy gained momentum. "I have to leave." Her physical presence was not an asset to bringing the situation back down to earth. The least she could do was clear the field of her overcharged chaos particles.

"Megan, wait." He jumped to his feet and held out his hands. "Did I frighten you? Confuse you?"

"No." She was shaken. Squirreled out. Free-falling. She'd been able to stay cool as long as supernatural stuff was off the radar, but the reprieve had ended. Her own life was quietly imploding in the background, and that wasn't even taking into account Peru and Helen and Dungeons and Dragons bullshit and cult leaders and dead managers and the missing pieces of the Brian/Jonnie saga. She'd hit a tilt. "I need to get home and take care of stuff. I'll call you."

FOUR

"MEGAN, PLEASE." THOM CHASED HER INTO THE BEDROOM, WHERE SHE stuffed her pajamas into her bag and gathered up her odds and ends. "Not now. Not like this." The bottom fell out from beneath him. He desperately tried to hang on to Megan without crossing the line into domineering psycho possessiveness. He simply couldn't bear to lose her. He'd shatter. "Let's talk about this. Please, sit. I shouldn't have dumped my band nonsense on you like I did. Give me a chance to reset the rest of the weekend. We'll have dinner and relax."

She shook her head, her eyes bloodshot and pinned. "I can't. I need time and space to think. This was my fault, crashing back into your world unannounced. I stirred the pot. You have real, tangible things you need to focus on. I do too." She pulled the handle on her bag, and with the click of the extension he knew that he'd lost.

A red kick thundered in to replace his sadness with fury. This was Brian's fault. If Brian hadn't gotten all craven and greedy and pulled his strings at the worst possible moment, Thom and Megan would be lounging in bed at this very moment, laughing and talking and making love. Brian and his obsession with personal power had ruined Thom's life.

He tried to stand in front of Megan, but she was too fast.

Out the door, down the hallway, she blazed her trail. She'd made up her mind. He kept up with her, jogging barefoot, issuing his pleas. "I can't be without you for another two years. Promise me you aren't leaving for good. Tell me that you're just going home for a minute to regroup. Don't do this to me, Megan. I'm sorry I lost my skull over those papers."

Once they were in the elevator, she threw up her hands. "I can't breathe right now. My show is in trouble, and someone is harassing me. I have to figure out what happened in that storage closet and how I'm implicated. The more I hear about this Brian and Jonnie situation, the less I understand and the less I want to understand. It's not you. You mean a lot to me, Thom, you really do. More than you know. But our lives aren't meshing right now on this very practical level."

He scrubbed a hand over his face, scrabbling for words. His stomach lurched in twisted jerks. He was about to puke or cry, or both. His heart was chopped-up stew meat. He was unwashed, unmoored, and facing losses unprecedented. He had to reach down and find the right words to say that would make her stay. "You complete me, Megan. I've never felt this way before. Without you, I'm nothing. A hollow shell of a man." He got down on his knees. "Do you have any idea how special you are?"

The elevator doors opened to a lobby frosted in cut glass artwork and jammed overfull with people. Many stopped to gawk. Phones came out with zombie automation and filmed. A teenage girl in combat boots said "Aw." Two boomers wearing matching family reunion sweatshirts winced, grasping the root of the situation. A line wound around the breakfast bar, and a coiffed Black woman played a baby grand piano.

Thom ignored the cluster and bluster and followed Megan, fuzzy, blue carpeting tickling his bare feet while he begged.

And then he spotted the motherfucker himself. The big cheese. The self-crowned king. One arrogant, unfeeling rock star extraordinaire staked his claim near the coat check as if he owned the damn hotel.

The architect of Thom's professional, emotional, and spiritual demise wore his stupid sunglasses indoors. A complete and utter caricature.

Brian Eugene Shepherd stood by the revolving entrance doors, flanked by his two-faced wife in her ridiculous athleisure attire, that traitor Jonnie Tollens plus the mortician he'd married, and a few entourage pawns. Brian claimed center circle like the self-absorbed sod he was. He spoke into a cellphone by holding the device away from his face, the speaker pointed at his mouth.

The way Brian held that phone made Thom angrier than he'd been all day, and that was saying a lot. Brian was so faux-slick that he kept everyone at arm's length. Everyone including Thom, his supposed band brother, whom he'd demoted to hired help.

"How dare you!" Thom shouted. Gawkers gasped. The music stopped. Phone camera flashes reflected in Brian's lenses. "How dare you spring that on me like you did, and under the guise of legalese about a music festival? Do you have any idea the betrayal you've caused? The humiliation? The hurt? What has possibly possessed you to tear us apart like this?"

Brian pressed his lips into a line. He handed his phone to a guy who was built like a pile of mashed potatoes and wore a low-slung fanny pack.

The slight movement revealed the worst part of the situation yet. Brian was wearing a Chariotz of Fyre shirt. Merch from the 2004 tour, when they'd debuted the album *Crystal Mountain Reins*. *Crystal Mountain Reins* built out the mythology of *Prometheus, Avenged*, adding a plethora of new characters and layers. Each song was both a fully contained episode and a part of a larger arc that spanned Fyre's entire oeuvre.

There was the blind troll prophet and the sorceress who pushed the disc of destiny. The initiates who lived inside the crystal mountain below the ocean had to choose a new door every day from an infinite selection. *Reins* introduced the four-headed steed, which ruled over luck and inspiration, with each head representing, well...

The liner notes even came with a detailed map of the world. *Crystal Mountain Reins* was a masterpiece, and even the normally unimpressed reviewers who made their careers from hating Fyre agreed on the scope and breadth of the album's genius.

Thom would have rather been decapitated by Brian directly than have to endure the sight of him in that shirt.

Crystal Mountain Reins solidified Fyre as a band built in story. *Crystal Mountain Reins* was a reunion, a revival, and a breakthrough. "Have you no self-awareness?" Thom grabbed Brian's collar and shook. "You have no right to wear this. You don't deserve to. It's a punch to the face of everything we've bled and cried for all these years." Seams ripped as Thom tore the fabric, set to rip the goddamn travesty right off Brian's back, right there in the lobby while everyone and their dog rubbernecked.

"Let go of me and get ahold of yourself," Brian hissed, using his forearms to shove Thom back and dislodge his grip. "If you would have listened to me and actually read those documents carefully like I asked, we'd be on the same page. I crafted those materials meticulously with a precise intent for your eyes only. You didn't read, did you? Let me guess, you climbed off some woman just in time to stumble into the living room and skim those pages, seeing only what your petty, jealous, resentful ego wanted to see."

Thom got close enough to Brian to smell his overpriced, cool-water-and-stockbroker-spunk cologne. He yanked the sunglasses off the front man's face and threw them to the ground. "Don't you dare gaslight me. That buyout was as clear as day. Look into my eyes like a man and tell me the goddamn truth."

Jonnie chimed in, "It's not like that, Thom. You're not thinking straight."

"Shut up." Thom jabbed his finger in the dark-haired guitarist's direction. Lanky old Jonnie thought he was cooler than cool in his studded belt, leather pants, and role as right-hand knob polisher to the big man. Little Jon was in for a rude awakening. Brian would screw him over too. That's how these things worked. "Condescend to me again, Jon. Go for it and see what happens. What, you think you're Jagger and Richards now? Tyler and Perry?" He scoffed at the both of them, two has-beens flying high on a flight of fancy with their enablers and flunkies blowing smoke up their arses. "Page and a half-dead houseplant?" Brian looked wrecked. At least deception didn't suit his appearance.

"Step outside," Brian spoke through vise-grip teeth, his shirt now marred by a three-inch tear down the center.

"No. We do this here. I won't be *handled* by you like I'm a crazed fan or discarded staffer."

"It's not about me handling you." His whisper could have punctured skin. "It's about the fact that there are hundreds of phones aimed at us. Outside. Now." He pointed at each of his three hangers-on, the fanny

pack man and two stoic creeps who may have been Mormon twins.
Thom noticed two other extras in the mix, frowning shadows with
workout bodies. One wore a holstered gun. Bodyguards, probably. Thom
had never felt the need to hide behind armed men. Brian barked at his
help, "Clean this mess up. Call security and get this crowd dispatched."

Thom shoved his way outside before Brian finished directing his
crew. He needed air. That part set him straight. He glanced back and saw
Megan. She looked leveled with shock but was still there. He counted
that as a partial win.

Sunday mornings in these big cities were comparatively quiet, lolling
in hangover mode, but there was still enough activity to create decent
cover and deflect any starstruck interlopers who happened to stumble
into the fray. Taxis idled out front, other cars honking as they cruised
down the street facing the hotel. A green-haired homeless man stood in
front of a department store window, ranting about how he was selling
bus tickets to Jupiter. Disaffected millennials shuffled by, disposable
coffee cups in their hands and wireless headphones in their ears. A gaggle
of goth kids smoked outside of a shoe store.

Brian showed up.

Thom used his eyes to send every ounce of his pain right into Brian's
soul.

"I'm sorry," Brian said hoarsely. "I know this is a lot to digest, and it
doesn't make sense."

"It's not that it doesn't make sense, it's that it's senseless. You tried to
buy me out and sneak that bit of backstabbing into all that crap with
Rockstock 2024 and Pepsi. You buried the lede. It was cowardly. How
was I supposed to take it?"

"Again, you didn't listen initially. But you know what? That's my fault.
I was rushed, and I rushed the process. I should have sat down with you
when we had hours to discuss and unpacked the entire predicament."

"What process? What predicament?"

"I need you to not play Fyre songs until certain things blow over.
Don't even think about Fyre songs or hum them in your head. Take that
ringtone off your phone. The energy is too heightened for the next
twenty-four hours. Fyre songs are extremely porous right now, and

borders have to be closed. Locked behind one of those doors in the crystal mountain. A few select songs in particular need to be hemmed in." Brian made the shape of a box with his hands, his wedding ring catching a wink of sunlight. "Controlled. Prevented from leaking out of a certain set of limit lines that I'm about to spend the next day establishing. Once I return, I'll know more. Until then, Fyre content needs to be hermetically sealed. It's for protection. All our safety." Brian spoke at a normal pitch, pace, and register, but his words were all wrong. They were schizophrenic.

Thom wasn't sure how to feel. He gaped at Brian. The stench and yowl of the city assaulted his senses. Concrete scraped the bottoms of his feet, and the feeling of invisible bugs all over him made his skin crawl. Everything was falling apart. Revulsion and panic tore at his fabric, splitting him into a human gash. "You sound unhinged, mate. What's happening? Are you in trouble?"

"Yes," Brian said with earthquake gravitas. "We all are. More than anyone can comprehend." His eyes watered. He let loose a small gasp.

Thom stepped back. He'd never seen Brian break down from emotion. He had nowhere to turn. "I need context."

Brian moved in on Thom and grabbed his arms. "There are forces in this world that are dormant until unlocked. Many don't have our best interests at heart. We've opened a portal, Thom, somewhere along the line. 'Deep Dark Woods' did it, or *Prometheus, Avenged* or some combination of vocals and music. We dug too deep into mythology, or tarot, or the *Bhagavad Gita*, and we struck an energetic tap. We chanted an incantation or painted a summoning sigil with our compositions. Our songs lifted a ladder into the middle of the mountain. The chariot of the gods is spinning its flaming wheels now, faster than it ever has. The ship landed, and we steered it. But the chariot landed in the wrong place. The steeds failed in their tasks. We let the Titans loose. The archons are coming. The hologram trap has sprung in a honeycomb all around the universe. We'll soon be stuck and harvested unless we act fast. It's been prophesized."

Thom bent over and retched in a gutter. Vertigo turned him inside out. "Tell me you're pranking me. Taking the piss. Tell me this is an elaborate put-on."

"I'll write for the witches. They say they can help. I'll see if the book takes to me."

"You've lost it." Thom jutted his thumb at the hotel lobby. "This began with Helen, didn't it? She got in your head and fucked you up. The weekend that Joe Clyde died. That's what started the downward spiral into this hell."

Brian folded his hands in prayer over his lips. "Not her fault."

"Bollocks. Name an alternative inciting incident."

"Us, Thom, us. Chariotz of Fyre started it all. We turned the wheel and lit it aflame. That burning wheel tore the firmament with its incantations and let in archons, Titans, and various hitchhikers. We released the books of the coven daughters from their dormant states."

"That's your ego talking. In no way is one gimmicky British pop-metal band responsible for the downfall of existence as we know it."

"There's codes in our music that weren't put there by us."

Satanic panic derivation; get Brian a mental health evaluation. At least he hadn't been of sound mind when he wrote up that awful buyout contract. There was peace to be found in the funhouse of madness. "I can't listen to any more of this. What's next, a warning not to play the records backward lest we open a hell mouth? Or how about we stir different rock and roll conspiracies into the mix?" Thom lifted his bare foot and pointed at it. "Am I barefoot because Paul McCartney is dead, just like the Beatles tried to tell us with *Abbey Road*? Am I sending you secret messages with my every move?"

Miraculously, chillingly, the next words that Brian spoke were perfectly ordered and coherent representations of his true self. "I have business to attend to in Peru. It's a long story, and I know that you feel left out, but please don't. I wish you'd read the contract how I intended, but that's in the past. I'll be back before the Indianapolis show. Can you give me until then to prove to you I'm not a backstabber?"

Thom croaked out bewildered words of agreement because he'd rather agree and move on than risk getting plunged back into the black hole of delusion that had sucked up both of them minutes ago.

Brian yanked Thom into a hard hug and slapped his back. "Brothers in arms. Always. I swear, mate. Don't turn away from me. You're my man." His plea came as warm breath against the shell of Thom's ear and was ripe with vulnerability. He heard the shake that previewed tears. All he could do was hug Brian in return and hope to end all hope that normalcy returned after the weird Peru excursion.

"Brothers, mate." It was Thom's turn to fight a crying jag. He nearly wept from exhaustion, frustration, fear, and the all-around roller coaster of it all. But Brian was back, and the circumstances didn't seem as awful as Thom initially assumed. Awful in a different way that he'd have to assess later. "It's Fyre till the end. Us. Always."

A red van pulled up alongside the scene, and a man with a thick Middle Eastern accent hung out the window to yell Brian's name. Brian said goodbye to Thom with a final slap to the arm and gestured to the hotel lobby. Odd that they'd hired this random driver and not called one of Fyre's personal chauffeurs, but the break with transportation tradition was way down the list of inexplicable happenings that day.

Helen, Jonnie, Jonnie's wife Eve, and the entourage filler trekked outside. The bodyguards and Mormons hauled the bags. Thom tracked Helen with his stare. He'd never really liked her. She was busy and sketchy and could never just *be*. She was around every time that things weren't right.

He caught her alone while the others were distracted loading bags and dealing with the driver. Wishing to throw her off-balance, he dredged up some darkness from their shared past. "Did you kill Joe Clyde?"

Her light brown eyes betrayed not one iota of remorse. "No. Joe Clyde sealed his own fate." She walked away from him, her brown ponytail shining him off as it swished.

Brian was in the car now. Thom didn't have to worry about setting him off by confronting Helen. Besides, Helen deserved to be confronted and held accountable. He followed her to the curb. "Why did you lie about that audition? What happened when Brian went missing? You're into witchcraft, right? What the hell do you do with that anyway? Get inside people's minds and drive them barking mad?" He'd stood beside Brian at the wedding, supporting his mate like a good usher when he really ought to have listened to his instincts and objected. Now it was too late. The wheels were off. "Or how about we talk about cults. Let's do that. Do you run one, with your yoga and crystals and droned-out bagboys? Or are you still working your way up the ranks, reeling in big kills for your pyramid scheme like my mates in that van?"

Everyone from the Peru crew was in the van now except Helen, who had paused with her fingers curled around the door handle. "I made mistakes in the past, yeah. Big ones. I'm not sure if what's happening now is because of those mistakes, but I'm trying to fix the problem with my input. I love Brian. I swear. I'd never do anything to hurt him. And he cares about you to an extent that's truly moving. Try to trust the process, and don't fixate on me too much. I'm a cog. Excuse me. I need to work now." She got in, sending a parting whiff of fruity air freshener his way when the van door opened. Helen closed herself in with a slam, and the red van disappeared into traffic.

That red van might as well have hit him head on for as wrecked as he felt. There was nothing left for him on this street corner. In a day, the world around him would make more sense. He'd trust the process, because he had no other viable options. Thom turned around and walked back inside. To his surprise and relief, Megan was waiting for him.

FIVE

THERE WAS NO RUNNING BACK TO IOWA LIKE A WHINY BABY NOW.
This was too hardcore. A Rubicon had been crossed, like Thom had said.

Megan embraced him in the middle of the hotel lobby and felt his pain. People brushed by her with their bags and curious glances, the presence of others no more significant than the easy listening background noise. She and Thom were a united front. Gary and Logan could abide her timetable and await her response. Their whims didn't rule her.

"What are you going to do?" She held Thom. He'd hugged Brian at the end too, kindling hope that the mess had blown over. She didn't want to leave him. Not at all, and certainly not like this.

"Wait and see what he says after Peru, I suppose." The circle of his arms managed to comfort her, even though he was the one who clearly needed support. Tinkling piano tunes from the music lady added romantic, cinematic ambiance to the drama. Megan was in the middle of a big disruption. "Can we go upstairs and talk?"

Downtime had a head-clearing effect that'd be good for both of them. They could plan their next moves from a place of calm. One item that belonged on the discussion table was her witchcraft book. That problem wasn't going away.

The ride up the elevator cooled her jets and gentled down her fried-out nerves. There was no crisis, urgency, or angst in their midst. Chaos had fallen dormant. "You're okay-ish though?" The scene with Brian wasn't pretty, but at least it had resolved into a semblance of closure, opening a space for reflection.

"I'll be fine." He chanced her a sheepish glance, rubbing the back of his neck. "I kind of flipped back there, huh?"

Eh, she'd seen worse. Conflict between loved ones wasn't always tidy and civilized. "From what I heard, Brian had it coming."

"I'm not sure he's to blame, that's the thing. You should have heard him talking, Megan. He wasn't himself. It was as if a different voice was coming through him." Thom fidgeted with the elevator buttons. He traced his toe through the swirly carpet pattern. "Like he'd snapped. Or was possessed."

Fretful gibberish junked up her thoughts, like it had when she'd grabbed her bag and jetted because she hadn't figured out what else to do. She was worried about her book again, what consequences she'd caused by reading it. She'd known since she'd dug that book out of the orphanage floor that it had been infused with a forbidden force. Of course she'd looked anyway, puppeted by the voices in her head and her own cat-killing curiosity.

Spirits had danced close to the veil, and demons had been pushing against that thin membrane. None of the calls she'd made that day were measured. She was a paranormal hunter though. What was she supposed to do, hide under the bed when clear signals of supernatural activity were blaring in her face, coaxing her to go further? That shit had been *gold*. "You remember that old book I showed you the day we slept in the orphanage two years ago, right?"

"I remember the book. And how you put the watch over a page and the gears moved."

They got off on his floor. "I heard voices that day. Voices from beyond, telling me to do things."

He looked at her in a tortured way. "I thought that Brian was having a psychotic break."

Her mouth went gummy. This stuff would always find her. There was no fleeing. "That's what happened outside?" Brian's antics, based on

Thom's description, struck her as cruel but not insane. She hadn't been able to hear the conversation on the street. She thought about mind control, the implications, and who the controller(s) might be. Brian and Jonnie had brought up those topics in the hotel room. They were looped in.

"He went on about how our songs unsealed otherworldly portals. How there was magic in them. He told me to take 'Deep Dark Woods' off my phone. It was bizarre."

At least the stuff about song magic was consistent with what she'd overheard while eavesdropping by the vending machines. If the stories stayed straight, that was better than the alternative of lies or deliberate misdirection. "Has he been into esoteric stuff in the past?"

By the time they ended up on Thom's rented doorstep once again, Megan was thankful for the absence of industry execs, Helen, and the Brian/Jonnie operation. At least there was peace. She and Thom finally had a decompression opportunity, even if their conversation had circled back to this perennial backdrop of woo-woo witchery. "Only insofar as mystical topics inspired our music and identity. Not in a serious belief way. Not since Helen." He got out his key card. "It all sounded like something she might say. Maybe it was her voice in his mouth."

"I actually don't think she's patient zero." Megan watched him let them back into the room. Visions of her book haunted her imagination, those ugly, occulted pages flying every which way like a haphazard pack of bats. She should have known better than to dig a buried artifact out of a floor. "I think it all started with me. My watch, and how it acted around you."

Thom went to the bedroom and sat on the end of the bed, his dress shirt wrinkled and his face bearing the burden of the last thirty minutes. "Brian said that it started with us. The band."

She racked her brain for other significant paranormal investigations or moments that had transpired in her career. There was that trip to the theme park with the hidden chambers and tunnels underneath. All she'd found was a room full of costumes and what was probably a sub-basement and definitely not a torture dungeon. "We can't keep spinning our wheels like this. It isn't healthy." She propped her bag against the wall. Thom's "hallucination" was another hanging thread. "I'm gonna shower." Hot water had a way of clearing out gunk of both the literal and metaphoric varieties.

He took her in with a long stare that was reverently wicked. She got a wonderful chill. Thom could speak many emotions with his eyes alone. "May I join you?"

Her thoughts turned a corner into more appealing images, because continuing to think about scary stuff exhausted her, and because Thom was Thom. Even disheveled to the point of shabbiness, he was sexy. Even more, really, with the unintended irony of the button-up shirt. Thom didn't make a very good businessman, which was kind of awesome. He was a mirror opposite of Brian the sellout.

They could escape together, if only for a few minutes. They had their chemistry to hold onto in the midst of reality dissolving into an acid puddle of dark magic mayhem. She undressed before his gaze. "Get in there."

Megan turned on the water, hot steam and pounding spray battering her with spa-worthy luxury. Her mind went blissfully blank. Thom joined, the waterfall saturating his hair until it was a sheet slicked to the back of his neck. Droplets beaded on his skin, and she licked a trail up his pectoral. Problems circled the drain. They were starting over. She used a handful of that frou-frou body wash to soap his chest, massaging his shoulders on the way up. He moaned in pleasure, and she let go on another level.

He nuzzled her neck and slipped two fingers between her legs, her lubrication oily against his wet, firm hand. She responded by lathering suds on his cock until he was nice and hard, curved with alertness under the jets. Megan was about to turn around and offer herself up when Thom said, "Let's move to the bed."

His proposition was a ballad. They hadn't had each other in a bed during this trip. After a bout of mutual soaping stimulated her imagination—all that white foam streaking down skin—they left in a cloud of heat, air conditioning wrapping around her midsection when he opened the door that connected the bathroom to the bedroom.

Megan laid herself down while Thom put a condom wrapper on the nightstand. The lingerie in the bag crossed her mind, but mostly she wanted to skip foreplay and get right to his body. He settled on top of her and kissed a path down her neck and stomach before diving between her legs. His skin was warm, and softer than normal from the water.

He used his tongue and went to work with an unbeatable, even-paced method, lapping her up and down until she was taut and tingling, her fists full of bedsheet.

She twisted her hips to get more. Thom picked up the pace, strands of his wet hair licking the insides of her thighs, and the onset of climactic conclusion hit with a winning resonance. Right before she went off, he targeted her clit head on with the tip of his tongue. The technique was sharp—brutal almost—and decadently effective. She screamed, molten and ruined, clamping his head in place with her palms because he'd better not stop.

He didn't cease until she was all the way done, when he rose up and knelt between her legs, ripped open the packet, and suited up. His weight lowered down on her, heavy and protective, pushing out all her headaches as he slid in.

She threw her legs in the air, taking him easily to the hilt. She was perfectly juicy. They didn't talk, just watched each other's faces. She touched the side of his cheek while he bounced up and down. It felt good, right, and she arched her back and gave as much depth as he'd take. A few more pumps at a practiced angle took her apart again, bringing deeper reverberations and a whole-body release.

Right at the end, he pulled out to a shallow depth, stroking only his crown with short plunges. The corded muscle in his forearms clung tight to the bone. He pushed the mattress away to hold himself up. A curse, a grimace, and a squeeze of her breast finished him off.

He crashed to his back. She rolled to her side and traced small, meaningless patterns below the dip of his collarbone, her body still buzzing, her mind mellow for a change. Right now, it was safe to be spontaneous. "Come to Iowa with me."

His chest rose and fell as he caught his breath. He scooted closer, making a study of her with lidded eyes. "I won't be in the way?"

"No. I want you there." If Gary and/or Logan decided to go haywire, the presence of a more powerful man might drain the gas from their tanks. Not the most feminist of reasoning, but everyone needed help at times. Besides, in that scenario, she and Thom would be together, and she hated to think about him marooned in Chicago, all alone in the hotel room except for the desecrated remains of his loathsome contract. "Just until your next show. We'll have some time to catch up, and after this production wraps, I should be able to get away again."

"I'd love to." He walked his fingers down her arm. "I miss your place. Your room was inviting and dainty. The sunlight streamed in and illuminated all those perfume bottles on your dresser. There was snow outside, heaps of it, and frost on your windows. You had pale yellow sheets with blue flowers on them. I'd never felt more content."

What a charitable memory he had of her shitty, low-rent apartment. All she noticed lately was a building where a stoner screamed at his video game before work every morning and a different neighbor's free-range pet rats had escaped and started their own feral colony in the wall behind the laundry room, where they mated angrily with their sewer-spawned brethren.

The weekend that he visited, Thom told her he was in love with her. It had been cold outside but warm in bed, warm in her heart.

She held him tight. Was he still in love with her? It would be weird to ask, right? Clingy and weak? "Do you have a guitar with you here?"

"Yeah, why?"

"Will you play a song for me?"

"I'd be honored. This seems like a good time to reconnect with my solo experiments."

"Silver linings." A Fyre song would be cool, but not if it loosed a plague of evil or made everyone insane or whatever else was possible in this hellscape.

He got up and put on boxer briefs from the dresser, tossing her a crooked smile. "My nerves are wracked. These pieces haven't gotten much airtime. Be gentle with your criticism."

Thom's solo work was understated, short on airplay, and hadn't achieved anywhere near the commercial success of Fyre, but his skill with vocals and a six-string was hauntingly, devastatingly beautiful. His voice mixed Jeff Buckley and Robert Plant. His acoustic melodies spun together a sense of past, future, fantasy, and nostalgia with such prescience that listening was déjà vu in a bottle, making her churn and yearn and ache for somewhere she'd never been in a time that had never existed. He tapped an ephemeral well of universal humanity.

She'd binged all his stuff on YouTube even before she'd developed a crush on him. Come to think of it, it might have been his work that did her in. Those songs felt like secrets that she'd discovered. A treasure chest with a gilded M on the lid, buried underneath the sprawling castle that Fyre had built for the world.

"Are you taking requests?" She crawled under the covers, where somehow being tucked in struck her as more vulnerable than lounging around naked.

"Of course," he said through a sharp exhale, smiling big even as he patted his chest in a clear display of jitters. He walked to the closet humming a tune. "What do you want to hear?"

"'Candle on the Freeway.'" The first time she'd heard that ballad while commuting to her old job at Stillwater College, she'd wept for a lost, precious moment that she didn't remember but had never forgotten.

"Who is this?" she'd said out loud through the salty taste of tears, astonished that this song had been written just for her and she'd never heard it before. For those four minutes and forty-seven seconds, the pieces of her entire being clicked into place. She'd been *seen* by someone out of touch, out of reach, and corporeally undefined. An idol. All she'd had was his song, and it was enough. At first.

"Okay." He held a guitar pick between his teeth when he returned, carrying an acoustic guitar made of dark wood. The polished lacquer shone with a gleam. The guitar pick blunted his speech and pulled his lips into the contrivance of a slight sneer. Both effects enhanced his appearance in a fittingly erotic way. "That's a deep cut, my lady. I don't think I've heard another person mention that song in five years."

She pulled her knees into her chest. "That's too bad. It's a masterpiece."

He hugged her with one arm before situating, crossing his legs at the ankle. Thom took a deep breath. "Pressure's on." He did what seemed like a vocal warm-up exercise that vibrated in his throat. "Hello, performance anxiety, my old friend."

Thom's vulnerability was sweet, even more so because he was letting his guard down around her. That arrogant swagger was nowhere to be found. "Nobody's listening. Just me."

He warmed up on the guitar, his fingers and hands moving with a sinuous ease as he pulled notes from the strings. "Don't minimize yourself. It breaks my heart." The gentle yet stern way he spoke made her listen. Megan did put herself down a lot, come to think of it. "Your opinion matters to me more than anyone's." His hands were both beaten and graceful, flexible and smooth moves wrapped in lived-in skin. A pale pink scar in the shape of a sickle dragged a groove from the webbing of his index finger to his thumb.

"How did you get that?" She laid a quick tap on the raised track of tissue.

"2012." His dark hair draped his face while he watched his own fingers move up and down the fretboard and pluck the strings, practiced skill flowing out in the range of notes he struck. "We did a six-show blowout in the month of December to celebrate the curtain call of the world. That was the year that the Mayan calendar ended, and lots of conspiracy theorists were saying that it was about to be lights out on civilization. Prime Fyre time for spectacle and mythological melodrama, you know? Thus, the Dark Your Calendars mini-tour was born. Long story short, this Christmas Eve Seattle crowd short-circuited. Fights broke out. I ran out back and into an alley to save myself from the melee combat. I got bored and challenged a bum to a game of dice. The wager was our clothes. I won, and he wasn't happy." Thom flashed his scarred hand. "Forget escaping melee combat. But the good news was I got a tie, a porkpie hat, and a faire isle cardigan despite the scrap."

She'd heard about the Dark Your Calendars West Coast tour but not about a concert in Seattle going majorly sideways. Talk about rock star shenanigans. "Really?"

He winked, then repeated with the opposite eye, increasing the pace of his back-and-forth eyelid trick.

"You got me, you jerk." She punched his arm and couldn't help but giggle. "Seriously. How did you get it?"

"Omaha. Sometime in the late nineties. I can't remember exactly how the exotic animal breeder ended up backstage—"

Laughter and the scary, trespassing rush of falling in love shot from

Megan's throat in a bubbly avalanche. She grabbed a pillow and smacked Thom over the head with it. "Quit messing with me."

"You asked for a story," he growled, putting the guitar beside his leg and pulling her in tight before ticking her side and making her squeal. "I told you a story." He flipped her until her back was on his lap, and he looked down at her with a fake, comically exaggerated scowl. "Are you saying that you don't believe my tales of rambling nomadic adventures?"

"No, because you're full of shit." Her sides hurt as she laughed out her words, nestling deeper into him. She shot off a flurry of tickle bullets under his arm, jumping back with a victory screech when he squirmed and released her. "I win."

"Get over here." He grabbed her ankle and yanked her across the bed, prowled up her body, and French kissed her.

They had sex again, rotating through every position known to man. Fifty minutes and three orgasms later, Megan was dripping with sweat and bouncing on top of Thom like a piston, singularly focused on her goal of getting him off even though her hope had begun to wane. "Come on," she gasped, banging her hips in hard, wet shoves, chunks of damp hair blocking her view of his face. She was getting angry. Sex was stupid if the other person didn't come. "I know you have another one in you. You've got this."

"I might need a few more hours and a protein shake." He gripped her midsection right below the waist, his expression dazed and amazed but not orgasmic. "You're remarkably athletic. What have you been doing in the gym?"

"Focus. Think about your dick. Look at my tits."

"Who said romance is dead?" He obeyed, pinning his stare on her bouncing breasts, and she played with her nipple rings. Her inner thighs burned. There would definitely be a chafing situation in the morning.

Finally, finally, he cried out, thrusting his pelvis into an arch. She shouted along with him, throwing her hair around, vicariously sucking up this climax that she'd coaxed from him with a marathon runner's tunnel vision determination.

His eyes rolled back in his head, and he dropped his grip on her and went limp.

Two hard pokes jabbed at each of her shoulder blades from the inside, pressed taut against her skin. They retracted. She froze. The odd, disturbing sensation passed as quickly as it had arrived. Playing it cool despite *what the fuck*, she gingerly slung one leg over Thom, dismounted, and laid beside him.

Thom patted her bottom. "What was that? It didn't feel like you came again."

"Just a cramp." Had to be. Except it felt like her bones shifting or merging. "I worked hard up there."

"You sure did. I'm impressed." He got rid of the condom.

"Can I still hear the song?" Otherwise known as the perfect distraction from her organs and bones apparently spontaneously deciding to spring a getaway attempt from her flesh.

"No rest for the wicked." He pushed his hair out of his eyes before maneuvering the guitar back into his lap. "And yes, of course. My pleasure."

After turning the knobs and running through a few notes with the pick, he launched into her favorite song. It was uncanny at first, listening to him sing one-on-one. Now that she had a person to pair with this tune she adored, a clearer picture of why the song mattered to her came into focus. Thom's voice was uncut and gruff, scraped of pretense. His voice was shoeless walks through rough-hewn rocks laden with warm, sticky mud. He was better than Brian, and Brian was good. The ballad rolled on and washed away her worries in a rainstorm of hazy dreams and lonely hearts.

A candle will burn, on the freeway
Its passion drives by as I wait for you
Miles high, in the nighttime, red lights
The secret will die
While you wait for me
The pain it won't stop
Can't stop
In the details
A candle will rise on the freeway
I cradle you down, down deep in the nighttime
Red eyes, the lights, they wait for me
Can you see now, the signs?

Can you see now, the signs?
I wrote you in my sleep, can you hear me?
With the help of the angels, can you feel me?
Turn the dial, hold the glass, and see me
My love, while you wait for me
A candle will rise, on the freeway

MEGAN REACHED THROUGH SHEETS OF FLAME TO OPEN THE BEATEN, amethyst door with the crystal knob, and that's when she knew there was no turning back.

SIX

THOM SLUNG HIS FABRIC GUITAR CASE OVER HIS SHOULDER AND PATTED his pockets to double-check for his wallet and phone. He'd changed the "Deep Dark Woods" ringtone to a generic jingle. He couldn't wait to walk away from the monochromatic void that was the Chicago hotel room. The space was beginning to feel as heavy and tainted as the muggy street corner outside the building.

Megan had the right idea. Quality time and a change of pace was incoming. "What's the latest with your show?"

She'd been texting up a storm at the club in a way that looked work-related, and not in a good way. An expert in fielding professional stress, Thom recognized the signs. Perhaps it would help to have him around. If not, he'd give her whatever space she needed. He'd head to Indy early if he had to and sightsee while he waited on Brian and Jonnie to wrap up their side trip. Jonas might hang out. The drummer was a fun sightseeing companion.

Megan piled her thick hair on top of her head and tied it in a bun without using a hair elastic. She was full of those types of subtle aesthetic graces. "I think Gary's mad at me. I guess I'm about to find out."

"He ought to be thanking you for coming back." Thom detoured into the living room, brushed the contract scraps into a pile, and stuck them in his suitcase. He supposed that he ought to put the pieces of his relationship with Brian back together, literally and figuratively. If Brian was having big problems, he'd need support and understanding. "What's the show without your charisma and sense of humor? A bunch of blokes stumbling around a condemned flophouse with all the lights shut off? Sounds like a drag to me."

"I appreciate it, but I'm just the eye candy."

He went to her and held her chin with two of his fingers. "What did I say about putting yourself down?"

Half of her mouth ticked up, but there was a sorrowful layer quivering behind her pretty eyes. He moved his hand to the back of her neck and massaged her while she spoke. "I'm trying. I'm worried, though, that he wants to take the show in a different direction. More seriousness and less sex appeal. You'd have to have your head in the sand to pretend like my presence plus the name *Bump in the Night* isn't selling fantasy and innuendo. The hot spooky chick. Happy Halloween to boners everywhere, no slutty witch costume required. Blah, blah, blah."

This Gary git was an utter fool if he didn't see the value that Megan added to the production. Yes, she was a beautiful, sexy woman, but she also knew her stuff inside and out. Why break what didn't need fixing? "Could be anxiety talking. After I'm away from my obligations for a bit, I start to fixate on worst-case scenarios. My brain goes round and round like a hamster on a wheel. I don't know if that problem strikes you as relatable."

"Yeah." Sadness left her face, yet her forehead remained drawn in a frown. "That's a sensible perspective."

"You don't seem convinced." He checked the wall outlets for forgotten chargers or cords. If only he could help Megan feel better about her show in a way that wasn't meddlesome or reliant on platitudes. "You want to talk through it more?"

"I'll be okay. I'm not a big fan of conflict, I guess. I just have to be ready to stand up for myself and prove my worth. Sing for my supper and all that."

That comment surprised him. Megan struck him as confident and self-assured, although he mostly knew the side of her that let her hair down once she was off the clock. He didn't want to go all bossy and tell her how to run her working life. He looked instead for a way to build her up. "For what it's worth, I adore your show. You breathe life into the entire operation. We should watch it together when we're back home. I'd love to have an exclusive look at the second season. Hot off post-production."

She raised an eyebrow, a big smile betraying her feelings. "You watched my show?"

Well, of course. Why wouldn't he have when it was his only access to Megan? Besides, *Bump in the Night* was a genuinely good show, modern and cheeky in its tone with plenty of jump scares. Megan was hands-down the star. Thom had seen enough television efforts in his years in show business to recognize who had camera presence and who didn't. Megan had that X factor, her allure augmented by a sharp yet humble wit that she leveraged to make good entertainment. "I binged the first season in two sittings. I wasn't about to go gushing about it. I was afraid that might come off like something a stalker would do."

"No, not at all, I'm completely flattered that you saw value in my little YouTube videos when you probably know movie stars and people whose content is top-tier in production value."

There was the self-undermining again. "Megan."

"It's just overwhelming. In a good way." A pale pink blush tinted her cheeks and nose. "Thank you for watching."

"I mean, if you're looking to expand and move to a network or streaming platform, I could ask around my contacts." She was right, he'd seen a lot of movies and television, and lots of it was garbage. Unfortunately, heaps of hack garbage got pushed to the top of the pile for various reasons. Life wasn't fair, and the entertainment business was worse, but Megan was talented and deserved a fair shot.

"I'd love that." She stepped closer, looking up at him with an expression so lovely that he nearly got out his phone and took a picture. She could be a model if she wanted. Do ads for makeup or hair dye. How had this woman not been discovered and hit the big time? "Thank you."

Megan deserved the world and to feel like a queen. Thom couldn't give her all that she deserved, but if she wanted his support, he'd sure lend it when he was able. "Let's get to your studio. I'm in *Bump in the*

Night withdrawal. I have two days before Indianapolis and not a moment to waste."

She knocked into his side. "Why are you this nice to me?"

He'd fallen madly in love with her two years ago and in no way fallen out. After he'd chased her through the hotel following the contract fiasco, she had to know how he felt, or she should know. He wasn't about to press the issue now and grab on too tightly. He best bide a bit of time and put space between himself and his meltdown, lest he trigger another retreat. "Because I care about you."

"Same." She pushed on one of her long nails. "I'm glad that this is more than sex."

Another fact that ought to be self-evident by now, but it was true that their relationship was very sexual. He'd show her more romance and thoughtful moments and ease her worry. "If our relationship was only about sex, there's no way I would have poured out my soul to you with that forgotten song I hadn't played in years." They left, the door shutting behind him with a nice click of closure. Already his breaths came in fuller and deeper.

"I can't wait to hear more off your album. 'Blue Letter.' 'September's Last Blossom.' 'Wave Once out the Window.'"

He covered his mouth, his face heating, embarrassed yet delighted. His solo work had never been paid much mind beyond college radio stations and dusty midsized venues where his appearance dates got squeezed between local stand-up comedians and niche podcasters. He rather enjoyed that semi-anonymity, as it gave him a chance to truly dive into the well of inhabiting another persona, but it felt damn good to hear that Megan found value in his projects. "Anytime. I'll play for you in Indianapolis. It'll be a palate cleanser before going on Fyre autopilot." He cleared his throat, having gotten too eager and made an assumption. "If you'd like to come along to Indianapolis, that is."

"I'd like that. Despite your mixed metaphor."

He held her hand and simply looked into her eyes. The stare lingered, but she was looking back with a tender expression on her features, and he let it play out. It was nice to enjoy a long, delicate interlude with someone when most of his interactions with other people over the years had been a blend of rushed, surface, and transactional.

Thom stopped outside Jonas's door. The courteous thing to do was check in with one of his mates about his whereabouts, and right about now he was more than ready for the contagious influence of Jonas's mellow demeanor. Besides, the rhythm section of a band had to stick together, doubly so when the guitarists and singer started acting out.

Jonas answered Thom's knock and greeted him with a hug. The drummer wore workout clothes and had his dreadlocks bundled into a ponytail. His portable treadmill and free weights were set up against the window overlooking the city, and he'd placed a picture of his wife and three kids on the kitchen table. "You want to come in or are you headed out?"

"Headed out. Jonas, this is Megan O'Neil. Have you met?"

Jonas extended his hand. "Jonas Kilmead. Pleasure to meet you." Megan's reputation preceded her, meaning Jonas knew who she was, but the courtesy he displayed was classy. Jonas was one of the best men Thom knew. He was made up of equal parts dedication, kindness, virtue, and talent, a golden mean of ratios striking sublime balance. "Are you having a good time? Is my mate here taking good care of you? Watch out for this one. He's trouble, but I'm sure you already know that."

Following the pretend ribbing and a good-humored exchange of pleasantries, Megan said, "It was awesome to finally meet you, Jonas. You steal the show up there, and your writing is brilliant." She hooked her pinky onto Thom's. "I'm gonna to grab food before we ride to the airport. Want to meet in the café downstairs?"

Thom had nothing in his stomach and wasn't about to save himself for airline cookies, but he sorely needed this check-in with Jonas, both for friendship and confirmation that he wasn't losing his marbles. He kissed the top of Megan's hand. "I'll be right there."

Once Megan had left, Jonas turned to Thom and said with one glance that it was time to get down to the bottom line—a certain elephant-sized bandmate in the living room. "What's up with Brian? We were supposed to meet today to go over foreign rights details, but he cancelled at the last minute and sounded rather fried. Not himself at all."

The existence of the meeting didn't startle Thom, as Jonas was one of Fyre's main songwriters and would certainly be at the table for a discussion about song rights. The important part was that Jonas had picked up on the flaky behavior. Brian was all over everyone's radar. If Jonas had insight into what was going on, Thom would take it along with the cold comfort of assurance that he wasn't nuts. "Did he say anything specific?"

"No, but you seem troubled about it as well."

"The implication being that you were also troubled."

"Somewhat." Jonas rotated one of the beaded bracelets on his wrist. "I wasn't sure if he cancelled the entire meeting or just my attendance. I hate to think he's cutting me out of business that he's doing. The other part of me is worried for him on a personal level. That there's an issue with Helen or Tilly. Or his parents."

Brian's daughter was away at college and could certainly be struggling. Tilly didn't attend a school in South America though. "Does Peru mean anything to you?"

"No."

Thom sliced glances up and down the empty hallway before keying Jonas in on the other major development that took place in Chicago. "Has Brian ever tried to buy you out? Or suggested that he might, or even brought up the idea in an almost performative way? Like, to manipulate you or psych you out by making you think he's about to buy you out, but really, he's coding other intent into the effort?"

Jonas looked bewildered. "Never. That would be a strange move, and counterproductive if you ask me. Career suicide. Remember how Brian's solo career never quite took off like he'd hoped? Destroying Fyre would not be in his best interests, and alienating you and me would destroy Fyre from the inside. I don't see why he'd pretend to sever ties. Unless there's something else he isn't telling us. A card in his back pocket." Following a heavy-eyed contemplation of the middle distance, Jonas added, "It makes me ill to think I can't trust Brian. He's never even scratched me off his Christmas card list. Where's this coming from?"

"I think that there's definitely something he isn't telling us, and I think that it's happening down in Peru." Thom chewed on his finger, his thoughts drifting to fuzzy and half-formed images of unseemly secrets unfolding in the darkness of a hidden jungle. He wasn't quite ready to show Jonas the torn-up papers or offer up the explanation that Brian had delivered. That'd stay close to the chest for a minute while he cobbled together a more complete picture. He'd square this maddening circle one way or another. "Do you remember that day a couple of years ago when Helen came to Brian's house while we were practicing in his studio? When she asked us all to leave so she could tend to an important matter that couldn't wait?"

Jonas's chest swelled under his sweatshirt. He drew in a long inhalation. "Absolutely. I took Tilly for the rest of the day so Helen could have the house to herself. She was insistent, and they'd been dating for what, a few weeks? Nobody knew where Brian was at the time."

"Joe Clyde died that night. Or the next day." Thom's stomach contracted. They were getting somewhere. That one day was meaningful. "I think something bad happened around that time. Something not right that changed the course of all our trajectories."

"Tilly certainly seemed to think that."

Thom perked up. "How?"

"She said that Helen came to the door earlier, wearing an evening gown and babbling incoherently. It struck me as a made-up story at first, but then I got to considering that her account was way too specific to be fabricated. She got rattled when she talked about it and would have no motive to hurl such an off-the-wall lie at me."

"I never gave it much notice before, how Helen advertised that she was into energies and crystals and all the rest of the new age pursuits. But now I'm beginning to think that whatever she does, or did, transcends harmless dabbling or spiritual practice and goes into graver territory."

"You mean what, like black magic?"

Thom nodded. "Celebrities attract freaks, and malevolent ones." He tried not to think too much about how Megan owned an occult book and artifact watch that sensed ghosts. She might have an offbeat side, sure, but she wasn't sneaking around, disappearing people, or speaking in tongues.

Frightening occurrences didn't follow her. Well, except for the night terror shadow person and the bout of sleepwalking. And when she'd told him that she sensed dark energies orbiting around his band. That was different, though, and not uncommon. Lots of people dealt with unexplained phenomena on a personal level and became over-invested in those narratives. That didn't mean they let a supernatural bent run their lives or other people's. The comparison wasn't apples to apples.

Megan had a haunted house show and a fascination with the paranormal. That was it.

"That one day sure was dark," Jonas conceded. "But come on, mate. Helen's nice. She invited us all to that yoga retreat by the beach. That was a lot of fun. And she can hold her liquor, I'll give her that. She's funny and laid-back. Well-read. Laura loved her."

"I'm glad that you and your wife have fond memories, but please don't get sentimental. We need to take a bird's-eye view and shore up our objectivity. The darkness didn't end with that day. It kept rolling. Remember when Pony and Tony fell down and nearly killed Brian? That was the same week. Then after the stage disaster, he and Helen abruptly move to Minneapolis and Brian sells his L.A. house. He pulled Tilly out of school. That felt really sudden, yeah?"

"All at once. Yes." Jonas leaned against the door and tapped his foot. Thom was grateful for the advancement of Jonas's allyship, however reluctant his conversion. "The circumstances sure seemed skewed."

"Like he was hiding a detail from us. Information having to do with Helen. When we reconvene in Indy, I'll try to get more information out of him and figure out what happened in Peru. He wasn't lucid before he left. It was scary. I thought you should know."

Jonas's brown eyes bugged out. "What do you mean not lucid? Like he was using? He's never abused drugs."

"No, not like that. Like a mental health episode. He was speaking in word salad. It's hard to describe."

"Oh, man." Jonas rubbed his temple. The faint wrinkles creasing his dark brown skin seemed to cut clearer paths from his nostrils to his lips.

"Exactly. I'm afraid between that weird sham buyout and the display out front, he may not be in his right mind."

"I feel awful for him, in that case. And the situation you describe isn't sustainable for any of us."

"We haven't even scratched the surface. Do you remember when Jonnie collapsed onstage *that same year* and then broke out of the hospital? He went AWOL for a time too, and I swear to fucking God he said that he went to Peru. What was that all about? He's never been willing to talk about it."

Jonas's Adam's apple bobbed.

"All I'm saying is that we need to be mounting a more robust fact-finding mission here. We've stood idly by while really whacked shite has been happening because, if I'm being brutally honest, we tuned out because the stuff didn't affect us. Except now it is. Fyre's in jeopardy, and God knows what plot those two are hatching down in Peru. I can't say for certain that they're sane anymore."

Jonas massaged the sides of his face, looking burned out and weary. Thom felt bad for interfering with the man's workout, but this conversation needed to happen. "How can I help?"

"That's the thing, I'm not sure. I'm going to spend a day with Megan and try to clear my head. I'm praying that once we're all back in Indianapolis, we'll be able to sit down as a group and urge them to come clean. They owe us an explanation."

"I mean this as your friend. Please don't take this the wrong way, but do you think you could be overreacting? What if Brian and Jonnie just decided to go visit the rainforest for a day? Maybe that's on both of their bucket lists. Is there a sense you're focusing on this because you feel hurt and left out?"

Yes, there was a streak of envy mixed into the jumble of Thom's emotional reactions to the whole matter. The contract that Brian had served up before running off with Jonnie certainly didn't help Thom feel like he belonged. Still. This mess was bigger than Thom sulking because he hadn't gotten an invite to the cool kids' party. "They aren't camping for fun. Can you imagine Brian roughing it in a tent, with the bugs and the elements and the hard ground?"

Jonas snorted. "No way. Not even cabin camping. But what if they went to visit one of the cities? We can't assume the forest was the destination."

"Fair enough. They took Helen and Eve. Let's look at that angle. Why not invite you and Laura and the kids, if the reasoning is that I'm being ignored is because the trip is a family gathering type of deal?"

Jonas shook his head. "I've got nothing there to counter your point."

"Because it's rooted in weird, that's why. That's the tie that binds all four of them."

"All I ever wanted to do was play music," Jonas sighed.

"Me too, man, me too. But we can't run away from this any longer. I'm concerned about Brian's next move. What if he's truly out of his mind and goes and fucks with our livelihoods in a way that causes real damage? You should have heard what he was saying about our music. He was talking about the songs being cursed and how they ought to be sealed off. Stuff like that."

"I see how you're drawing your conclusions, yes. Let me sleep on this. I'm staying the night here. I'm going to call Laura, get some rest, and then ship off to Indianapolis. Maybe we can meet up before we have to be at the Sprint Center. Megan is more than welcome to join."

"Great plan." Thom patted Jonas's shoulder. He felt the relief whoosh out of him in gusts. It felt good to talk. Get it out of his system. "Take care, mate. I'm sorry for having to dump on you like this. Thank you for your patience."

"Hey." Jonas grabbed Thom's arm before he walked off. "Thanks for filling me in. I needed to hear it, even if I didn't want to."

Thom snagged the drummer in a big bear hug before shifting his focus to Megan and her world. He'd have more clues on the debacle with his band sooner than he'd like.

SEVEN

MEGAN MANEUVERED THE STEERING WHEEL, ANGLING HER TOYOTA Camry into a spot near the front of the nearly vacant parking lot. She spotted Gary's Ford, Lindsay's scooter, Chris's hatchback, and a couple of stray vehicles that she didn't recognize.

A fluttery, unsettled sensation skittered through her belly. Gary hadn't answered her last text, the one confirming that she'd show up at the studio at the specified day and time. His reticence annoyed her. It felt like a power play.

She had to keep reminding herself that Thom was right. She was an important member of the *Bump in the Night* team, not a slacker employee on thin ice.

"Thank you for coming with me." A relaxing dinner after the flight would have been preferable, but Gary was right that they had work to do. Who cared if it was random to bring Thom along? Having an ally in her corner would help her focus, and he had good ideas. Gary had met him. It wasn't uncommon for the rest of the crew to invite guests to the studio. The atmosphere was informal in that way. Or it had been.

"I'm happy to be a fly on the wall or pitch in, whatever's appropriate. After that talk with Jonas, I'm just relieved to have a break from band intrigue."

"Yeah, what happened with that?" He hadn't said anything until now, and she hadn't asked, committed to honoring a boundary between his life and hers.

She turned off the ignition and slipped an assessing stare his way. He'd changed into a button-up shirt and darker jeans, a respectful move though one that wasn't necessary. Thom could've rolled into the studio in sleepwear for all she cared. His presence was good enough.

"We're going to check in once we get to Indianapolis. Have a band meeting, if you will. I think that's the best approach. An honest conversation about what's happening."

"Smart." Maybe she'd misheard Brian and Jonnie in the hotel, being all jacked up over the run-in with the corporate types. This might all be a big misunderstanding. Such an explanation didn't suffice to put her mind at ease. She was still too spun, her nerves tweaked, all the pieces of her life flying around her in a circle. She hesitated to get out of the car and stalled by playing with her keys. "Okay, ready?"

He cupped her leg above the knee. "It'll be fine. You're in control. Don't overthink. You aren't in trouble. Your colleagues don't have the authority to put you in trouble."

"I'm in control," she breathed, pushing herself out of the car before she wimped out. Thom was right. Her mind wasn't always her friend, and narrating stories in her head didn't accomplish anything except making her feel bad about disasters that hadn't happened yet. Which led to perpetual misery in suffering the consequences of hypothetical disasters. "I'm in control."

The *Bump in the Night* production studio made its home in a strip mall one town over in an office space sandwiched between a miraculously resilient Radio Shack and an unemployment office that was always closed. Rent was six hundred dollars per month, and the electronics store sold equipment in case they needed a cord or surge protector in a pinch. Pull-down curtains on the door and windows hid the gear inside.

The remaining storefronts were mostly empty, save for a makeshift church with dirt-brown carpet and the corner lot, a true rathole called Ai Hong Kong that ostensibly served Chinese food. The faux-restaurant hosted the only other people who ever came around, a revolving door of scoundrels who looked to be involved in shady dealings. Megan was thankful their hustle was lucrative enough that they'd never bothered to break into the studio and steal equipment.

The sun beat down hard and bright, summer making an early debut. Megan didn't reach for Thom's hand because her palm was already sweaty. The welcome chimes trilled when she pulled the door.

Lindsay sat at a desk scored from dumpster scouting, hunched over one of the computers they'd all pooled their money to buy. She took a break from fiddling with editing software to offer Megan and Thom a friendly-enough wave before resuming her work. For a woman who lived in cargo pants and banged-up souvenir tees, Linds was uncharacteristically business casual in a skirt and blazer getup. She'd even flat-ironed her otherwise frizzy hair. Especially odd that she'd dressed up, considering that she preferred to work behind the camera as opposed to hamming it up in front of a lens.

Megan spotted Gary near the back wall by the filing cabinets, his posture military straight even though he sat on the shitty Craigslist couch that smelled like wet dog. Glassy-eyed and hypnotized by whatever he was watching on a laptop, he wore headphones and his mouth hung open slightly. He, too, looked crisper than normal despite his zombie expression. He'd shaved for once, and his fancy new sneakers belonged on someone ten years younger. Megan groped for eye contact like an idiot. He ignored her completely.

Chris, their fourth musketeer, was crouched goblin-like in a corner, his dark hair tumbling in tangles all the way down to his plumber's butt. Chris talked to himself while tending to a charging station, juicing up three cameras and a digital energy rod. He acknowledged Megan's existence with a grunt and plugged in a fourth, smaller camera. "This one gets the money shots," Chris said to nobody.

Bile crept up Megan's throat. The studio energy was all wrong, and not in a haunted way.

She circled back to Lindsay, who'd at least had the decency to eke out two seconds of cursory politeness. "Hey, Linds. You remember Thom, right? He stayed over at the asylum that one winter."

"Nice to see you again." Thom angled around Lindsay's side but failed to stir a reaction.

"Yep. Hi." Lindsay didn't budge this time, a jarring show of rudeness that Megan excused on the grounds that she was sunk deeply into Final Cut Pro. Lindsay wasn't all that savvy with computer software, and she hovered near the flat tail of learning curves that involved pushing buttons. Her strongest suit involved operating cameras and onsite equipment.

"What's the occasion? You guys all seem both distracted and super-focused." Megan surveyed the studio for clues of unusual activity of the non-paranormal sort.

A bounty of the ghost hunting equipment that they used for onsite excursions dominated the surface of an Ikea table in a black box legion. MEL meters, infrared cameras, portable motion detectors, voice-activated recorders for EVP, and gadgetry that even Megan didn't recognize trespassed into her field of vision, all smug and self-satisfied. The crew had been busy in her absence. They should not have been working with field equipment. "Why is our gear out?" She pawed through an unzipped polyester equipment bag and removed a sand-colored egg. "And what's this?"

"You guys are high-tech, I'm impressed." Thom walked through the space, dodging the one-shelf research library and the repurposed end table where a dozen cords were curled like sleeping snakes into figure eights. "What does all this stuff do, in layman's terms? Give me the abridged rundown, if you don't mind."

"Clearly, you've never seen a ghost-hunting show," Chris muttered, condescending when he finally bothered to converse.

"I have, actually," Thom said. "I've watched yours."

"Then you should know what all of *this stuff* does." Chris used an irritating, whiny singsong that he probably envisioned as a self-righteous "gotcha" but that actually just made him come off like a little bitch.

Megan's heart went into freefall. Why were her people behaving like this? Not only did she look like a friendless loser in front of the man she wanted to bring into the fold of her life, but the rejection of being out-grouped socked her square in the chest. "I don't know what's going on."

Gary mumbled a rejoinder under his breath that sounded snotty despite being indecipherable.

"I can leave." Thom put up his hands.

"No, stay." Megan grabbed one of the tan eggs and marched over to Lindsay. "What are these? They look new."

"EMF readers." Lindsay slid her cursor to the cutting tool at the bottom of her screen, trimming off a few seconds of video footage. Megan lacked any context for the still video image frames on the monitor. Some were black-and-white, other night-vison green, still others full color. "I stuck in flash drives to timestamp any spiking, which will help track changes over the course of a shoot. Electronics companies made them back when people were worried about cell phones giving them brain cancer. They check to see if electrical fields are floating through the air. The health nut demographic eventually fizzled, but now ghost hunters use them because ghosts cause electromagnetic energy. Cool, huh?" Lindsay enlarged a frame. Onscreen, Gary waved a wand. A phosphorescent ribbon thinner than a pencil slithered from left to right.

Thom put his arm around Megan's waist. "What am I looking at here?"

"Ribbon energy," Lindsay mumbled. "We also caught an orb, a swimmer, and maybe even two funnel ghosts. Gary may have even spotted a glimmer of a full-body apparition by the payphone station. Payphones! There was a whole row of them by the bathrooms in that old restaurant where the gentry dined. Hardwood everywhere. Like a time capsule. Overlook Hotel vibes. The entire space filmed beautifully. That night was a cash machine." The next frame was crushing in what it revealed. A ballroom, once grand but now derelict, rotted in defeat. Gilded plaques hung cockeyed on torn wallpaper, and cobwebs draped sagging chandeliers in gauzy sheets. There were even a couple of overturned round tables and the abandoned remnants of a splendid meal, left to decay. "Look at these readings," Lindsay breathed. "Milligauss city. These meters are unmatched in their ability to detect magnetic fields. When one of them shows a reading, there's usually a ton of excitement on screen."

The Mayfield Ballroom was *perfect*, a ghost junkie's paradise, and Megan had missed out.

Correction—she'd been left out.

"I know what a milligauss meter does, Linds," Megan gritted out. "Don't talk down to me like I'm stupid."

"She might have been talking to me," Thom said, his voice tight because he obviously knew he was giving Lindsay too much credit. "If that's the case, please, Lindsay, enlighten me on the technical details of a milligauss meter."

"It just means that the Pytheum Hotel was a ghostie hotspot. Think of it as a really strong Wi-Fi signal," Lindsay said. "The milligauss meter is the phone searching for the network."

Megan's ribcage squeezed in a tight contraction. Her vision wobbled at the edges and refused to focus. She sniffed the first humiliating taste of tears. The worst-case scenario was confirmed. "You shot footage at the haunted hotel without me?"

"Chill," Lindsay said. "We tried to call and text. You weren't around."

"You never said you were going ahead with the shoot."

"You snooze, you lose."

"I wasn't snoozing. You went behind my back."

Finally, Linds spun in her office chair to face Megan, a pinched look of exasperation screwing up her pretty face. She'd applied wings with liquid eyeliner, a choice that didn't flatter her features at all. "Like I said, we reached out. If you want to run off to Chicago and party instead of sticking around for the shoots, that's cool, but don't expect us to wait on you."

She hadn't been partying. Well, maybe a little. Enough that she didn't have as much of a claim to indignation as she'd like. "There wasn't a rush. You could have waited. That hotel isn't going anywhere, and our sponsors don't need to see the new season for another two weeks."

"Talk to Gary." Lindsay circled back to her work.

"Fine. I'd love to."

"I can talk to Gary," Thom said.

"No. I need to fight my own battles." She marched over to the smelly couch and kicked Gary's dumb, trendy shoe. "Hey. Take off your headphones." He did, at least, regarding her with a dull look. "Why is everyone acting aloof? I'm sorry I didn't answer your calls and texts right away, but I was busy. I do have a personal life. You remember Thom James."

Thom offered a tense raise of one hand. With each passing minute, he looked like he wanted to be in the studio less and less. She didn't blame him.

"What's up, man?" Gary tossed out before addressing Megan. "We had a really cool opportunity drop in our lap, and I wanted you to be a part of it. This connection we've made could really blow us up big, get us on Bravo or even Discovery. But you weren't here, and we pushed on without you. We didn't want the chance to slip through our fingers. Time sensitivity and all. I frankly don't see what's outrageous about looking out for the show's best interests. Yeah, everyone was a little frustrated, but it's better now."

Hardly better. Gary had a point though. Putting the show first was smart. In his defense, he had tried to get in touch. "You never told me exactly what was going on." He was still in the wrong, at least partially. "Had you gotten specific and explained the particulars of this new opportunity, I might have felt more motivated to act. What was up with that?"

Gary winced. There were six fresh, white ball caps on the cushion next to him, bills unbent and emblazoned with a lime green lighting bolt logo. "It's a bit sensitive." He craned his neck, checking his phone before warily eyeing the door. "Given, um, your history. I didn't want to get into it on the phone. This was an in-person conversation."

"No, that's a poor excuse," Thom said. "You owed her honesty and straightforward communication."

"Please butt out," Gary said.

"What is going on?" Megan snatched one of the hats and threw it in Gary's lap. "Who brought these?"

"Our fairy god-dude." Chris snickered at his lame joke.

"What are you talking about?" Megan asked a ripe pink pimple on the tech's ass. "Pull up your pants."

The door chimes tinkled again, and the door swung open, followed closely by an extended leg that wore a shoe identical to Gary's. "Whazzup, ghost bros. I come bearing sustenance."

Megan would have rather seen a rat waddle into her workspace. Strutting onto the scene, carrying a cardboard drink tray loaded with

Technicolor frozen confections, was Logan Pax, a cheesy smile on his face and one of those branded ball caps on his head.

Logan walked to Lindsay and handed her one of the Starbucks treats. She proceeded to gawk at the bubble-gum-colored goo, oohing and ahhing.

"That's a 'Stink in the Pink,'" Logan explained, beaming. "Venti frap with mocha chips, the strawberry crème base, a splash of oat milk, one-point-five pumps of caramel, and a squirt of sugar-free syrup for complexity. Finished with whipped cream and a dash of holiday sprinkles." Logan sauntered over to the couch. "They totally keep the holiday stuff in storage. Don't let them tell you it's unavailable."

"Logan knows all the best Starbucks menu hacks." Chris stood, pulled up his pants, and accepted a beverage the color of toilet bowl cleaner.

"Awesome." Megan crossed her arms over her chest. "Now we're blacklisted by every barista in town. What are you doing here, Logan?" He'd made good on his threat to interlope in her life, and in a big way. This was very bad.

"Hey, Megan. No frowns. Sorry I didn't get you one. Didn't know you'd be crashing." He popped his own drink out of the carrier and sucked on the straw before handing a purple monstrosity to Gary.

"I'm not crashing, this is my studio. What are *you* doing here?"

Logan slurped up glop the color of cat vomit, sucking his straw until his cheeks hollowed. He stared at Thom with squinted eyes. "Are you on television?"

"Now and again. I'm Thom James, bassist for Chariotz of Fyre. You are?"

Logan giggled. "I love how this guy talks. What a trip." He nursed his sugar bomb. "Aren't you guys doing Rockstock 2024?"

"Apparently," Thom said.

"Apparently," Logan parroted in a terrible, fake British accent, chuckling all the way. Megan wanted to die. Or kill Logan. Or die killing Logan. What the hell was this douche all about and why was he intent on torpedoing her life? He'd used her just as much as she'd used him. "That's cool, bro. That shit's gonna be *lit*. Three days. Four stages.

Thirty-plus bands. Bungee jumping, two bars, an open-air cannabis court, and *X-treme* entertainment."

Thom checked his phone. "I think you just about covered it."

"I'll be there too, promoting my rad new kicks. Maybe we can grab a quick lunch if my schedule opens up. I'm totally down with rock music and would be interested in exploring a collaboration if the fit's there." He lifted one leg in the air. "Cool, right?"

"Sure."

"This guy's kind of serious." Logan scrunched up his face and turned to Megan. "Don't tell me you dumped me for him?"

"I didn't dump you because we were never together. What are you doing here?"

"Taking your shit to the next level." Logan threw his body on the couch and mock-wrestled Gary while calling him "Spooky Dude."

Chis put on a ball cap. "Logan has big time on-camera sparkle. He cracked us all up on the hotel shoot." Patting his hat, Chris added, "These bad boys looked great in the footage."

"Ghost bros!" Logan bellowed, throwing his arm around Gary and making his free hand into horns that he shook in the air. He stuck a hat on Gary's head. "Try one on, Megan. Pull your ponytail through the opening. It'll look cute. Chicks can be ghost bros too."

A bad taste flooded her mouth. The cringe fest in the studio was deteriorating rapidly. "Gary, why does he keep saying ghost bros?"

Gary took on a hangdog look, grimaced, and pulled his hat bill down enough to hide his eyes. "We just think the title would pop more and do a better job of catching the right kind of attention at networks and whatnot."

"No, that title's awful," Thom said. "It's juvenile, crude, and an obvious cheap attempt to capture a lowbrow demographic."

"Whoa, we got the king of England over here, regulating on our shit," Logan said before getting lost in his phone. "*Ghost Bros!*"

"I'm not wearing that hat or going along with that title." Megan slashed her hand across her throat. "This is a bad idea, Gary. We don't need Logan's brand to go places. Logan's brand doesn't fit our image at all."

"Nah, you guys embody the *Ghost Bros* ethos." Logan stuck his tongue out at Megan. "Except maybe you."

"Megan, simmer down." Wearing his stupid hat and shoes, Gary jumped up. "This is huge for us."

"You can do better, I promise," Thom said.

"I can't take you seriously in that getup," Megan said to Gary. "Take the hat off."

Logan threw a different hat across the room, maybe aiming for Megan, but the cap missed her by a good two feet and landed by the charging station.

Chris picked it up and layered it on top of the hat he was already wearing.

Megan burst into a peal of cynical laughter.

"I know this is new and seems like a curveball." Gary tried to rest his hand on Megan's shoulder, but she shirked him before he could patronize her through touch. "But give Logan a chance, okay? He's passionate, energetic, and has a great vision. He has connections. We could get off YouTube, like for real."

Thom had better connections than Logan and his social media C-listers. Thom could get *Bump in the Night* off YouTube. But if she brought that up, she'd look like a social climber who was using sex to advance her career or an unserious flake who'd showed up to parade around her sugar daddy. She had no tenable strategy. She felt small and frozen. "No title changes. Please."

"Megan, don't let him intimidate you." Frustration lanced through Thom's voice. "Stand up for yourself, like you said you would."

"Why are *you* here?" Gary tacked his hands on his hips. "Our show isn't any of your concern."

"No, but Megan is, and none of you are treating her very well at the moment."

"That's because she needs to be here to focus on her work instead of chasing your washed-up band around." Gary pointed at Megan. "You're better than this."

Water wobbled in her vision. Selective muteness stole her tongue. She didn't feel better than anyone or anything, even a lump of dog shit.

"Says the man who's simpering to an Instagram model while wearing

his clothes. What a paragon of dignity and self-respect you are, Gary."
Thom rolled his eyes.

"That wasn't very nice. I'm an *influencer*." Logan sulked.

Lindsay rushed over and fussed at Megan's side. "Hey, hon, do you
need to step outside and relax? I know this is a lot."

"Oh, it's my fault I'm not in lockstep with your little plan to ruin our
show? I should just shut up and take it, right?"

"Everybody, stop." Gary got in the middle of the circle and threw his
arms up in a peacemaking pose. "Megan, we're going on a shoot
tomorrow. You should come and get a feel for things. Actually, your
influence would be perfect. This is that old reform school that became a
brothel in the nineteenth century. We can't have the on-camera presence
at a shoot like that be a sausage fest, and you know how Linds gets
performance anxiety." He chanced a glance at Logan, who now had
earbuds in, before saying to Megan in a low voice, "I'm not totally sold
either. Come tomorrow. We'll talk, okay? Sort everything out and reach a
mutually agreeable conclusion. But if you want to be a part of that final
verdict, you absolutely have to be present."

Her ears buzzed. Numbness blotted out her emotions. She didn't
want to only be needed because the shoot was in an old brothel and she
looked like sex. Plus, tomorrow was supposed to be Indianapolis with
Thom. They'd barely spent any quality time together. But she couldn't
miss the haunted brothel. That would spell the end of her stint on *Bump
in the Night*—oh, wait, *Ghost Bros*. She had to go. Had to do this shoot
with Logan there, tormenting her and messing up the entire vibe.
"Okay," she said lamely. "I'll be there."

"Good deal." Gary went back to Logan.

Thom pulled Megan aside, and they stood over by the Ikea table,
away from the fray where everyone else orbited Logan Pax like a mass of
light-drunk moths. Thom rubbed her arms. "It's okay, baby, it's okay.
Don't cry. Let me help you."

Fuck. Was she that obvious? She sniffed and blinked until the wet,
stinging sensation passed, though her eyes were still raw. "I'm good."

"You don't need them. I can help your show. I promise. We'll get you
new people. Better people. And a better space to produce in. This joint
smells like goats and pancake batter."

A laugh squeaked out of her. "Yeah, it stinks in here. And I appreciate the offer, but I need to set this right. I can't turn my back on these guys. They're my friends, even if they acted crappy today. I won't feel right if I rely on you for something as big as my career. I need to be independent. For my confidence."

"I completely understand." He hugged her warmly and for a long time, then pressed a lingering kiss to her forehead. "I admire your conviction. I wish that you were coming with me to Indy, but we'll link back up when your shoot is over."

The tears threatened again. He was about to slip away. Who knew what would change once he was back in his element, siphoned up in a carnival of glitz and money and an endless supply of women like her? On top of all that, Thom had to wrangle his missing-in-action bandmates and solve his own paranormal debacle. She was losing him. But keeping him meant losing her identity. "I hate this." She covered her face.

"Me too." He pursed his lips. "I'm going to level with you and tell you that I don't think I'm serving you by staying here at this time."

Her heart crashed to her shoes. "But we had tonight."

He ran a hand through his hair. His eyes looked tortured. "I know. It's just that I'm afraid I'm throwing off your process, and more than anything I want you to succeed in this show. I can tell that you want more than anything to succeed in your show."

A wall of rock closed in on her throat. "This is goodbye."

"It's not goodbye, it's just for a couple of days. I swear on my life. Stay strong for me, okay, Megan? We'll be back together before you know it."

Megan was numb and skeptical, but she honored Thom's wishes. On one level, not even that far below her surface, she knew that he was correct. Through no fault of his own, and despite all his attempts to build her up and put a tiara on her head, she shrank in the shadow of his largesse. It was a knee-jerk automatic or subconscious thing that she had to figure out. The first step of mapping the route to her power while trying to be with someone high above her was to get a handle on the *Bump in the Night* issue. Thom was spot on, but the pain still killed her.

She drove him to the airport, where they sat in her car while she wailed in his arms, choking out ugly, wracked sobs. He assured her this was temporary. She believed him but not enough to stop the crushing pain. She was broken and pathetic, addicted to a powerful man and unable to stand on her own.

Once Thom's brown leather jacket and shoulder-slung guitar case disappeared into the small crowd of the Cedar Rapids airport, Megan bawled until she had no tears left.

EIGHT

Sightseeing in Indianapolis had fallen by the wayside. Thom's interest in museums or historical attractions had cratered in the absence of Megan. An hour early to the arena, he navigated the usual network of wide corridors, dodging the typical array of people. A sadness monster ate away at the center of him.

Megan's tears had crushed his spirit, but he hadn't known what else to do besides step away. His presence at her studio was a detriment, not a benefit. He hadn't lent the support that she needed, or hadn't done it in the right ways, a failure that left her scattered and insecure. She shrunk in his wake, which was the last thing he wanted, but he didn't know how to do a better job of showing her how wonderful she was. His efforts all seemed to backfire.

The best choice had been to let her sort out her situation on her own, but he still felt like the heel who had abandoned the person he loved. Damned either way.

He said hi to a Black man in a suit and an androgynous person with a buzzcut and feathery earrings, both of whom acted like they knew him, even though he could not place them. That was commonplace. He met heaps of people, meetings that imprinted on their memories but not his. He wasn't being arrogant—it was actually embarrassing and kind of a headache. Thom wasn't all that great with names or faces, and an endless procession of individuals moved in and out of his life with carefree ease. That really was a depressing way to live, when he thought it over.

He reached his dressing room and took the sheet of paper with his name on it off the door. He couldn't be bothered with attention and craved anonymity. These spaces varied a lot in what they offered, but this one was decent, with a green loveseat and a small wardrobe rack stocked with a few changes of clothes. The crew had set up a snack table with sliders and water and brought his Fender into the room.

The creature comforts centered him. He sat on the green couch and called Brian, shaking a restless leg as the phone rang. The only silver lining of Megan not being around was time and mental space to focus on his other problems.

"I'm here," Brian said. "Just got in." Not much to go on, but the words he did say came off as measured and stable. Small wins.

"We need to talk. Can you come to my dressing room? I took down the sign for privacy, but my room is right around the corner from the locker rooms the basketball teams use. You'll know you're in the right place because the crowd gets thicker."

Jonas and Jonnie needed to be part of this conversation eventually, but not right away. Brian was the eye of the storm. If he felt ambushed, he might close up.

"Of course. I'll be over in twenty." Brian hung up.

With not much to do and no interest in his usual preshow distractions, Thom opened his wallet and took out the USB that the young woman had given him in Chicago. He twiddled it in his fingers and cased the room for a compatible device. After coming up empty, he stuck his head out the door and said, "Can I get staff help, please?"

A Latino man who looked all of seventeen scooted over to the threshold with pep in his step. He wore a headset, a pressed uniform shirt from a temp company, and a laminated pass. His haircut was impeccable. "Whatcha need, sir?"

"Call me Thom, please." After tanking with Megan in a spectacular show of ineffectuality, he wasn't really feeling his status. He'd rather just be a man for the rest of the evening. A musician, a friend, and a music fan. "Can you get me a laptop with a USB port? I need to screen a demo."

The guy's already huge brown eyes stretched to saucers. "You listen to people's albums?"

He probably shouldn't have admitted that. Word would get around and he'd find himself devoting hours every day to checking out albums, graphic novels, artwork, blogs, books, podcasts, and more. Oh well. There were tons of creatives out there, and most didn't get a fair shake, through no fault of their own. Thom figured that he'd better give back, and his method had a more direct impact than donating to faceless charities. "When I have a moment. I beg of you, don't spread that to everyone you know."

"You got it. One laptop, coming right up." The guy returned five minutes later carrying a silver computer and a cord. Piled on top of the machine was a spiral-bound manuscript as fat as a doorstop, three folders in various colors, and a black plastic bag. The staffer sucked his teeth. "I said the word 'album' and got dogpiled."

"Don't worry about it. It's flattering, really." He gave the young man a generous cash tip. "What's your name?"

"Leo."

"I'll see you around, Leo."

The manuscript looked to be a screenplay for a horror movie, and inside the folders were charcoal sketches of anime characters. A jumble of USB drives, business cards, stickers, and even a pearlescent ashtray in the shape of a unicorn head filled the bag. He set the rest of the loot aside and plugged in the Chicago girl's demo.

Her band was good. The base layer was punk, thrashing and relentless, more Sex Pistols than Green Day. Underneath were notes of heavy metal. The tracks told a story of damnation and redemption that involved fighting skeleton adversaries in a hell dimension. Gothic and high-concept. He could see why she thought that a member of Fyre would be the right person to hear her work.

Three songs later, Thom was lost in a tale of a Valkyrie sword fighting a hydra for a chance to escape the underworld when Brian walked in.

"This isn't half-bad," Brian said. He wore his show costume and looked decently rested and put together.

A muscle deep inside Thom's middle unclenched. He exhaled and turned down the volume. "I love that aspiring musicians think of us when they think of narrative and mythological songwriting." Not that he wanted to go down the road of a discussion on branding or image, but those topics were good ways to break the ice with Brian.

Brian stayed standing. He put his hands in his pockets. "Look, I want to apologize for everything that happened in Chicago. From the contract to the scene outside. All of it. I wasn't myself."

He could say that again. "I appreciate it. I apologize for losing my skull. What happened?"

The man looked steamrolled with knowledge that he didn't want. "I'm not sure you'll believe me. I don't even know where to start."

"How about with Peru?"

"I don't think that's the best starting point."

"Okay. Let's do the contract. That's the part that has me the most out of sorts."

Brian walked to the couch and sat. He stayed there in silence for a rolling lapse of seconds, watching his hands, sighing and articulating syllables in false starts, and shaking his head.

A monstrous bird unfurled its wings in Thom's chest. His despair was bigger than the universe. This encounter was right on the verge, about to flop sideways and shatter into pieces. Sometimes intuition doesn't lie.

"What if I told you..." Brian cleared his throat. "...that there is much more to this world than we can see? That there are invisible forces everywhere, and many don't have our best interests at heart. These forces can manipulate the perceptions that we take in through our senses. They can get inside our minds and toy with them. They can make us into someone we aren't."

Here we go. How to proceed with this? He had to humor Brian in order to most effectively figure out what they were dealing with. "Who or what are these forces and where do they come from?" He felt dumb, like when he was a child asking his mum about God.

"From what I can tell, it's a sentient, pre-biblical deity. The main one, at least, is the engineer of where magic comes from. That's who has compromised our songs and co-opted them to advance the hologram prophecy."

Thom wanted to cry. What had happened to his dear friend? "Do you think that maybe you need rest, mate? You're clearly exhausted. Let's call off the rest of the tour. We don't need the money. The fans will understand."

"I know what you're thinking." Brian ran his finger through the crease of his perfectly neat, rolled-up sleeve. He didn't sound insane, except for the actual words. He was shaved and showered, positioned normally on the sofa, and didn't smell of alcohol or any other intoxicant. "This was a lot to accept for me too. At first I didn't believe any of it. I rejected the whole lot: magic, spells, nonhuman entities, other dimensions. That was before I saw the proof with my own eyes."

"What's this got to do with the contracts?"

"It was a test. To see if she's able to rewrite text outside of the spell books. One of her powers is altering records and erasing words from documents. I wanted to see if the ability extended to different types of materials. Two of the contracts were pure. One we think she reached. Now we know that she's able to manipulate us from within."

"What was I supposed to see?"

"A business plan for branding. That's all. But as we know now, she has the ability to alter the record and warp any mention of our songs into an emotional and psychic weapon to be turned against us."

"Who exactly?"

"Her name must not be spoken. That's how she amasses power."

Thom hit a breaking point. He was able to swallow this type of content only in bite-sized chunks, and now he was full. "Is Helen running a cult? Or part of a cult? Is that what's happening down in Peru? Is that what you're swept up in?"

Brian sliced a scalpel look Thom's way. A high-voltage current ran beneath the surface of his blue eyes. "Don't accuse Helen of being a bad actor. She's innocent. On our side. She's trying to help. That's what she's doing right this minute. Working hard to put a stop to this prophecy."

"Is this performance art? Are you having me on?" Fyre had made a deep dive into Mayan calendar mythos and spirituality during the Dark Your Calendars mini-tour. The stated purpose had been to bolster their knowledge for the purpose of infusing the shows with authenticity.

Maybe Brian was reconnecting with the spirit of the method actor he'd channeled during that tour, play-acting as a conspiracy nut for the purpose of packing more power into Fyre's set. Back then, his half-nutty, eccentric rock legend act had earned them heaps of press and publicity, prime real estate in gossip rags. But why now? This was just any other tour, not a special or themed cluster of shows.

"I wish I was taking the piss," Brian said. "You ought to open your mind, though, before it's too late."

Arguing with Brian had proven to be a dead end. Thom experimented with other approaches. "You know what? You're right. Whatever this is is meaningful to you, and for that reason I'll give it a listen. What can I do to support you, to support us?"

"At some point, you'll need to come down to Peru and be a part of the work we do there."

Yes, he would. He needed to witness the madness firsthand. "When's the next time you're headed there?"

"I think that we're set until after the tour. At least on my end. Helen I'm sure will have her own obligations before then. But I'm here for us now and fully present." Brian patted Thom's upper arm in three friendly, reassuring taps.

Helen and her "obligations" directly impacted Thom and his best mates. Naturally, the eye of that storm swirled to the surface of his mind. "She's still there?"

"No, she came back with me. We're wrapped up for the time being."

Good to know. She had to be somewhere in the vicinity, and it wasn't doing any good to continually grill Brian about his wife. By default, Brian would protect his spouse and disclose as little as possible. Thom would have to track her down and get the story directly from her lips. "I'm glad that you have a break from running around."

Brian sat up straighter. A gleam illuminated his eyes. "I'm actually quite glad that I have one-on-one time with you. I do have good news to share."

Thom proceeded with cautious optimism. "Do tell."

"I have it on good authority that we've secured an opportunity to play 'What's Your Sign?' at the Super Bowl halftime show next year. That's not one of the impacted songs, meaning there's no additional concerns."

Thom groaned, though he was glad to have his usual rapport with Brian back. He'd rather bicker about the artistic direction of their band than listen to the front man talk about curses and evil entities and his wacky reconnaissance missions to South America. "No additional concerns my arse. I have additional concerns. Namely, do we have to sell out *that* hard? I don't care to pander to the lowest common denominator. 'What's Your Sign?' sucks."

Brian looked wounded. Even though one of Fyre's old managers and the production company had been largely responsible for unleashing "What's Your Sign?" on the world, the poppy, three-minute piece of power-chord candy was one of Brian's sentimental favorites. When Brian played that song, he caught residual bursts of Fyre's first taste of mega-fame. He'd chase that high until he drew his last breath. "'What's Your Sign?' is our 'Pour Some Sugar on Me.' 'What's Your Sign?' is the definitive pop-metal anthem of a generation. 'What's Your Sign?' is the thread that stitched a few hits together into a never-ending party."

"In other words, it sucks."

Brian summoned his glass-melting glare. "You're a curmudgeon."

"You're commercial."

"You hold yourself back and fear success."

"You need to lay off the pop-psychology leadership slogans."

"You're the most stubborn person I know."

"You're addicted to fame."

"Get over here." Brian grabbed Thom and squeezed him tight in both arms. "Let's stick to fighting about band business, okay? I don't want to fall out with you."

Thom hugged Brian in return. It was good to see the man being himself. Thom would rather talk about the Super Bowl and Rockstock 2024 and all the rest than witchcraft and scary occult forces. "I'm sorry I ripped your shirt."

"That's okay. You had grounds for being angry. I like the aesthetic of the tear. Makes me look edgy."

"Prudes can't be edgy. That's an inherent contradiction in terms."

"I'm principled, thank you very much."

"That you are." Thom could only hope that Brian's principles kept him safe when he was down in Peru, swept up in whatever mysteries eluded the far reaches of Thom's imagination. Brian did have a good head on his shoulders. That much at least instilled Thom with confidence.

They broke the hug at the same time. "We good?" Brian smoothed his own hair.

"We're good." Which didn't mean that Thom's curiosity was put to rest. He had another lead to pursue.

"Alright, well, I'm off to do my routine. See you at the huddle." Brian stood, brushing a nonexistent wrinkle off his ironed jeans.

"You bet. I'm going to finish up this demo. The band's called Forgotten Words. I plan to contact the person who handed me this demo and see if we can find an opportunity for their act."

"Good plan. A few shows with an opening act would enhance our brand ahead of Rockstock 2024. Infuse us with that down-to-earth, relatable image we wear so well. Say hi to Megan for me."

An ache spread through Thom. He needed to call her after he took care of other business. Was she still sad? That wouldn't do. "Yeah. I will."

As soon as Brian left, Thom took out his phone and brought up Helen's number in his contacts. The front-man's pre-show routine would keep him occupied long enough for Thom to try to get a real answer or two before reconnecting with Megan.

He sent Helen a text: *I need fifteen minutes of your time. You around?*

A reply dinged. *Why, so you can accuse me of murder again?*

Thom figured he had that one coming. *I apologize for losing my cool. That wasn't fair to you. But we do need to talk.*

Fine. Sure. There's a coffeehouse around the block from the venue. Meet there in a few?

You got it.

Thom gathered himself up and hopped to it. He wasn't quite sure what to expect, but the time to have a real conversation with Helen about the past and present was urgent. Sprinting to a discreet back exit, he spotted his new friend Leo. Leo and a few other staffers had taken over a storage room, where they were awash in Fyre merch, packing peanuts, and cardboard boxes.

"Forgotten Words," Thom called over his shoulder while Leo stuffed Fyre-branded tote bags with black candles and other swag. "They're good. If you know anyone in that band, tell them Thom James will be in touch."

Leo dropped a folded Fyre t-shirt onto a card table, where it joined a towering pile of others identical to it. "I sure will. They'll be thrilled."

Leo's shirt-folding companion, a graying woman with dyed hair and faded tattoos, parted her lips. "You and Thom James talk? How'd you manage that?"

Thom didn't stick around for more interaction. He slipped out into a drab day, muggy air smelling of city curling around his skin. The usual cacophony of car horns, music from bars, and the occasional shout provided a nice backdrop to get lost in.

He found Helen's coffeehouse straight away and went inside, finding himself in a hippie hole-in-the wall where fliers covered the walls and obscure, alternative rock played over the audio system. There were only four tables, and Helen sat at one of them.

Though the aroma of coffee was certainly enticing, Thom's mind was already plenty stimulated. He bought a bottle of water from the barista, a white woman with rainbow dreadlocks, and took his place across from Helen.

His chair creaked. They watched each other in silence for a moment. She drank from whatever was in her mug. Helen wore light makeup and a wrinkled shirt with a witty Internet saying on the front. She looked like she wanted to be somewhere else. Of course she wanted to be somewhere else. He'd never made the prospect of his company appealing to her.

Thom thought about the version of her that Jonas had described and felt ashamed and guilty. Maybe he'd never given Brian's wife a fair chance. "I'm sorry for what I said in Chicago." He toyed with the cap on his water bottle before opening it. "For what it's worth, I suppose I've never gotten past all that happened the year you and Brian got together. And now it seems like it's starting up again."

Helen pursed her full lips. She was a beautiful woman in a natural, approachable way, but Thom mostly saw the tension in her face. "It is. Starting up again. It is starting up again. More accurately, it never stopped. It's accelerating." Her eyes moistened. "Maybe it is my fault that Joe died. I could have done more to reach him about the dangers of dark magic. Even though he hated me, maybe there's a way I could have framed the topic or an action I could have taken that would have brought him around."

The only other customer at one of the coffeehouse tables, a buff man in a wheelchair, lowered a book below his eyes to observe the conversation.

Thom gave the eavesdropper a look that returned him to his reading. "Don't beat yourself up." He dropped his voice to reassure Helen. "I should not have cast blame on you. I just want to know, Helen. What happened back then? What's happening now?"

"The short answer is black magic. Lots of it, and it's powerful." She stared into her beverage. "I never tried to harm anyone. I didn't even know what I was doing. All I asked for was money, not knowing how volatile of a current currency was." She brought her gaze to meet his again, the mistiness in her eyes having hardened into resolve. "How much do you want to know?"

His mouth had dried. A drink of lukewarm water barely helped. "As much as you're able to share." Not knowing was torture. He'd learn for himself if knowing was worse.

"I'm a witch. I've been aware of this since you met me. I tried to step away from it all after everything that went wrong that year because I wanted to lead a normal life. But magic found me again. It always finds us, along with these books. There are six of us total—witches. Four in Peru. That's why I go there, to work with them. Brian and the rest of you are implicated in this prophecy through your songs. I need his help. We aren't sure how the forces at play got ahold of your songs or what caused that, but we think we closed the loop for now. There are big problems to worry about, namely a prophecy that will do real damage. Six witches have to be assembled in person to have a shot at halting it. I have one more witch to find before our coven is complete. Once I have her, I'll be able to connect these final dots. She's proving to be the most elusive."

Thom couldn't believe what he was hearing, but he was starting to take this line of thinking seriously, or at least humor it. Even if he didn't necessarily believe in witchcraft or the occult, everyone else certainly seemed to. Meaning there was something of merit to examine. "Why is she the most elusive?"

"Her element is fire. What we've deduced through our research is that fire is the hardest element to wield, if it can even be wielded at all. It's almost symbiotic with the other elements. Free-floating. Depending on her level of practice and experience, she might not even know when she's casting spells. And that's not a good place to operate from. I've been there, and it was bad." Helen raked her hand through her loose, windswept hair. "I did a divination spell in Peru and got the sense that this fire witch is putting her magic into other people. Or another person. Giving them visions, precognition, access to her powers. Involving them in her process. I don't think she's cognizant of it. Part of my work down there last time, after you confronted me about Joe, was to get a clearer picture of what this fire witch is doing and to whom. I hoped that if I keyed in on the current of her practice, I could locate her. But no such luck."

A dark iciness spread over Thom's skin. He'd had a fiery vision after being with Megan in that closet. She had a book too, and her unusual watch. Could it be that Megan was the missing piece that Helen was searching for? Was Megan putting magic into him? Did he believe in magic now?

"You got quiet," Helen said.

"It's a lot to take in." He wasn't about to say anything to Helen about this witch business until he consulted with Megan. To do otherwise would amount to a betrayal of trust, like giving her up. "Thank you for your honesty."

"It's all I have to offer at this point." She rubbed the underside of one of her eyes. "I wish that we would've started out on better terms."

Whether his future with Helen was as a friend or a foe, he had nothing to gain by pushing her away. "I don't know what to say except let me know if there's anything I can do."

She watched him for what felt like an unsettlingly long time, like she was trying to read his mind. Or maybe all of this talk of spells and witchery and dark prophecies had succeeded in freaking him out. Either way, he had a show to prepare for and Megan to check in on. "Thanks again, Helen. I hope that next time we meet, it'll be as friends. I appreciate your time."

"Of course." Her smile was casual and kind, though her expression retained a certain intensity that destabilized his equilibrium. She'd gotten in his head, which wasn't automatically her fault. "Text me any time. Maybe we can catch a movie. I'd like to get to know Megan better too."

"I'd like that," he said, though he didn't wholly mean it. He wasn't ready to offer up Megan, not without running this latest twist past her.

Thom left the coffee shop and didn't look back, though he felt Helen's eyes on him until he reached the arena.

NINE

MEGAN SLID HER NIGHT VISION GOGGLES TO HER FOREHEAD, RUBBING her cheeks when the release of pressure made her face throb. She squinted, fuzzy splotches blurring her vision. Squeezing her eyelids shut and opening them, she readjusted to darkness. There was a physicality to haunted shoots that she never completely got used to.

Gary called, "Lights in three, two, one."

The musty room flooded with painful light, making her wince. After a round of blinking, her surroundings swam into relief. The small bedroom where they'd gotten their final clips was minimally furnished with an antique dresser, a queen-sized bed stripped of its sheets, and a stand-up mirror mounted in dark wood. A layer of dust coated every object along with the floor, revealing several sets of messily stamped footprints. Megan buried her nose in the crook of her elbow and sneezed.

"Bless you," Gary said, the nicety reaching her like an olive branch in the aftermath of the less-than-stellar reunion with Thom.

Scouring for any final bits of good content, she opened the closet door and peered in, but all the clothes had been removed. "You get anything good?" she asked Gary. There was no point in giving him the silent treatment.

He sat on the bed and fiddled with his wand. "Yeah, glimmers and swimmers. A few whispers in my EVP. Stuff that'll shore up well in postproduction. You?"

Megan hadn't picked up any lights or noises, certainly nothing jump scare worthy to rack up those likes and subscriptions, just feelings and impressions. The women who'd lived and even died in the old brothel were trying to communicate with her on a subtle level. "We'll see once we sit down with the footage. I did get a sense that spirits were trying to reach me, but in less obvious ways. I felt the presence of a few women though. Some were happy and content, like they enjoyed their time here with their clients and each other. Others were miserable and trapped. A mixed bag of highs and lows, but this place is full of emotions."

Gary smiled. At least he wasn't wearing Logan's hat anymore or acting like his yes man. It amused Megan that he'd quietly defected from Logan Pax once the cameras started rolling, as if douchebag was contagious and he didn't want to catch a bad case.

Maybe her colleague was more on her side than she'd initially assumed. He'd been rude to Thom, and she was still mad at him, but she wasn't willing to throw away their working relationship.

"It's good to have you back, Megan," Gary said. "What you just said right there will lend thoughtfulness to the show that only you can offer. That's what we need to fill the gaps when we can't deliver straightforward scares, which you know. Maybe you can give a longer interview segment where you talk about the connection you formed with the women. Take creative license in fleshing out their backstories. Name them. We'll see if we can dig up information on the Internet on real inhabitants of this place, or we'll take our best guesses." He poked his head out the door and looked both ways down the hall before ducking back into the room. "Logan's vision for the show strips away all that depth. It's basically just yelling and shaky cam shit. A total disaster."

Megan leaned against a wall and crossed her arms. "You think I didn't notice? Shooting with him was a pain in the ass, with him shouting the entire time and doing all of that 'I dare you to show yourself and face me' crap. That didn't fit the atmosphere here at all. He's not sensitive to the paranormal. He just wants a new toy to play with and toss around social media, and *Bump in the Night* is that toy."

"We need the money. All we have to do is keep him happy for a little while, and he'll continue to front the cash we need. It's a fine line, but if we can walk it long enough to get on television, we're set."

"We're surrendering any pretense of artistic integrity. Got it."

Gary scoffed. "Don't get all self-righteous and try to pretend like you weren't thinking the exact same thing when you hooked up with him."

She hadn't been thinking enough, actually, and certainly not about consequences. "Wrong. I just wanted to get laid, and he was there. He's only inserting himself into the show to upset me because I didn't want to date him. I can't believe you don't see through the act."

"I don't care about your after-hours activities. I'm looking out for the future of our show. That's it."

"You don't care, huh? Is that why you were rude to Thom when I brought him by the other day?"

Gary set down his meter and threw his hands in the air. "I was just frustrated. You'd vanished, left us high and dry, and I didn't want to hear an arrogant rock star's opinions on how to run my production."

"*Our* production. And he's not arrogant. He's caring. He wanted to help. He would still help if we asked."

Logan interrupted the back-and-forth by strutting into the room, tossing a camera into the air, and catching it. He was decked out in the branded attire that he'd debuted in the studio plus a matching t-shirt. "What up, ghost bros. That shoot was kind of a bust, huh?"

"It wasn't a bust, I got great inspiration for a breakaway segment," Megan said. Working with Logan was exhausting, and they'd only done one shoot together. Circumstances would have to change. "And stop saying ghost bros."

"Ghost bros, ghost bros, ghost bros." Logan turned the camera on himself. "What up, ghost bros. Turns out the haunted whorehouse was a great big bust. Get it? I guess the hookers were too busy giving happy endings in the afterlife to stop by and give us any of that sweet lovin'. Peace out!" He aimed a megawatt grin at Gary. "Good outtake, yeah?"

"The camera wasn't on. You need to push a button and wait for the red light," Gary said with a dry condescension that no doubt went over Logan's head. "Was it like that for the entire shoot?"

"Oh shit." Logan fumbled with the camera, flipping it upside down in a failed effort to find the switch. His technological ineptitude was a relief. He probably thought he'd gotten two hours of footage that they now didn't have to deal with, making room for serious content. "Where is the on switch and why isn't it all huge and obvious?"

"Think about what I said," Megan told Gary before leaving the room. "Are we ready to wrap?"

"What'd she say?" Logan finally got the camera on.

"Just strategy, don't worry about it," Gary said.

"Where's Thom?" Logan asked like the question was a gotcha. "Took his fat stacks of cash to another chick's show or what?"

Megan ignored the childish remark, though Logan's comment had her wondering what Thom was doing at the moment. He would have been fun to have on the shoot, if only as moral support and a buffer against Logan's nonsense. She stayed ten feet ahead of her ex-bedmate as they gathered up Chris and Lindsay and piled in the minivan to drop off the equipment and screen footage.

Megan was watching the parts she'd recorded for ideas on her narration when an unusual image blipped on the screen, a flash of connected black lines no larger than a handprint. She paused the footage and slid the digital tracker backward.

"You get good stuff, Megs?" Lindsay called from the Craigslist couch, where she'd cozied up with her laptop. "I heard you kind of gasp over there."

"I'm not sure yet." Megan leaned in closer to the screen, starting and freezing the frame. The shape only hovered in the visual field for a split second.

"Ghost hos getting dirty?" This from Logan, of course, who was halfheartedly unpacking while playing with his camera. "Dudes, that's the name of our episode. Ghost bros and ghost hos."

Chris, returning equipment to its proper storage places, muttered a phrase that might've been *Please shut up*.

Megan certainly hoped that she'd heard Chris correctly and that everyone was getting tired of Logan's antics. After a couple more attempts to nail down the right frame, she smacked the pause button in the right spot. A simple black triangle appeared to be painted on one of walls, where it stayed for an eye blink before vanishing into the ether.

She hadn't even noticed Gary watching over her shoulder until he said, "What was that?" making her jump as a shot of adrenaline zapped her extremities.

The symbol could in theory mean many things, though it held one feasible explanation to her. "The symbol for fire."

Gary hummed a groove. "Cool. Any thoughts on how we spin the significance?"

She scooped up her purse. Her book was calling her, or the spirits were calling her to her book, just like they had when she'd dug it out of that old floor years ago. She'd have more ideas to share with the crew once she flipped through pages and reconnected with the witchy words. It'd been too long since she'd studied. That was the message. Bonus points if she was able to blend cool witchcraft concepts into the *Bump in the Night* storyline. What a way to halt Logan in his encroaching tracks. "Maybe. I have to go home and read up."

"What's the hurry?" Gary looked on with interest while she fished her keys out of her bag.

The last thing she wanted to do was bring up her special book in front of Logan and accidentally give him ideas on how to screw with it. "Don't want to lose my inspiration. Great shoot tonight. Talk soon."

"Don't be a stranger," Gary said, more worrisome than warning.

"You can count on me. Promise."

"Hey, since the king of England isn't staying with you tonight, can I come over?" Logan wagged his eyebrows.

"No!"

"Logan, dude," Lindsay said in a stern tone. "You're being kind of sexual harass-y right now."

"Fine. I'm going clubbing. Who wants to come along and siphon off the leftovers and extras of that sweet, sweet tail that Logan Pax reels in?"

Megan rolled her eyes and bolted to her car before anyone answered, choosing to believe that nobody took Logan up on his offer. If she got quality writing done while her brain was still running hot, she'd have the leverage she needed to wow the entire crew and convince them to dump Logan. His designs on the show were not a fit with hers, but once she made moves to get him ousted, she'd better have a lot of impressive material to bring to the table.

✳

MEGAN DIDN'T REALIZE HOW STIFF SHE'D GOTTEN UNTIL SHE FINALLY stood up from her office chair and took a break. Her foot was asleep, reducing her to hobbling around on one leg and shaking off the pins and needles. Her elbow ached, and her hand was cramped into a claw.

Around and around her thoughts went, full of incantations, cryptic pronouncements, and various and sundry witchy words.

The session was productive though. Her notebook lay cleaved on her desk, the pages filled with blue ink. The spell book sat beside her notes, a study in contrast with its warped paper and deckled edges.

She'd read a good fifty pages of the witch's tome before her brain melted and she found herself rereading the same script, or reading new material when she thought that she was rereading, totally lost. The witch book, otherwise known as a grimoire, was evasive like that. Its contents muddled and confounded, as if it didn't always want to be perceived and understood.

Still entranced by the grimoire, Megan closed the volume before reopening it to study the inside of the cover. She stared at the sigil of the coven daughters until the hexagon with the handprint in the middle danced through her imagination like a diabolical elf. Why had the symbol for fire appeared in the video of the brothel? Why did knowing more of this magic paradoxically lead to knowing less? How would she solve the mysteries?

Before the hypnosis sucked her in even deeper, Megan jumped out of her office chair and went to the living room. Even though she was supposed to be quitting, she shoved open a window, hung out into the warm night air, and lit a cigarette. The bitter flavor calmed her down, and she watched gray clouds dissolve into darkness that was cut only by the lone orange glow of the streetlight that marked the boundary between her parking lot and the street.

Not many cars kept her sad sedan company. It was Saturday night, which the residents of her building spent bar hopping in Cedar Rapids, or Ames if they felt like road tripping for the sake of getting hammered.

New Denmark was a lonely town, propped up by nearby Stillwater College, the Catholic church, and a rubber factory that hobbled along on its dying legs. She felt the ache of aloneness too, especially since she'd lost her college colleagues.

Oh well. Megan had her show, and she was grateful that she'd pulled *Bump in the Night* back from the brink. She stubbed out her smoke on the windowsill, the nicotine having cleaned the fuzz out of her head. She shifted back into the right frame of mind to work.

When she turned around, the sight of a chilling trespass smacked her still.

Her witch book sat on the sofa, closed and perfectly centered in the middle of a couch cushion like it had been observing her. Her chest was an airless place, pierced by icy-hot spears. A tremor raced up the back of her neck. Invisible bug legs scurried over her limbs. Her rational mind scrabbled for purchase. She must've zoned out and carried the book into the living room.

No. She'd left it on her desk. For sure. Unless she was going crazy. Megan fought through a visceral wall of revulsion and snatched up the book. She felt stupid for feeling freaked out. If the book was trying to send her a message, wasn't that a good thing?

She stomped back to her office, chanced a tweaked, furtive glance over her shoulder, and plunked the book down where she'd left it. She didn't realize that she'd been holding her breath until the book obediently sat still for many seconds. If the grimoire had a standard repertoire of antics that it deployed to scare her or even just talk to her, that'd be one thing. The problem was she lacked any frame of reference to make sense of its behavior.

Her pulse thready and her breath sputtering out in choppy puffs, she fumbled for her phone and took a snapshot of the tome. At least if it moved again or didn't show up in the picture or did some other freaky thing, she'd have proof that she wasn't mentally unravelling.

She had a text notification. From Thom: *Thinking of you. How was the shoot?*

The distraction was nearly as blessed as the reminder that he was thinking about her.

Productive. I captured footage that I'll be able to use. I'm back on good terms with the crew. What are you up to?

Pinches of anxiety and jealousy put her on edge. Thom was

surrounded by eager women constantly, wasn't known for his restraint, and hadn't had a personality transplant since they'd started hanging out. She refused to get her hopes up or set herself up for crushing heartbreak.

Just relaxing in my hotel room. Got dinner with Jonas and Laura, then J and I played a bit of music. Mellow night. Brian seems to have calmed down. Jonnie's normal too.

A knot inside her loosened. Megan was typing out her reply when an anomaly snagged in her peripheral vision before dread crashed down like an avalanche.

Her book was on the floor, sitting there eerily as a creepy, mute witness on her butterfly-print area rug. She backed against the wall, her stare pinned to the worn cover with its mysterious engravings. She poked her photos app and checked. Sure enough. The picture showed the book on the desk. It had moved without a peep, and independently. The hefty volume had not fallen or been bumped by her.

What was wrong with her? The book was sending messages, so what? The circumstances felt all wrong though. Bad and twisted, deep down in her gut.

Clinging to her lifeline of contact with another human being, Megan wrote back to Thom. *Living alone sucks sometimes.*

Why do you say that? Are you okay?

She gulped, squeezing the phone to steady her shaking hand. She didn't want to scare him, but she didn't want to lie. *I'm not sure. I don't know how to explain it.*

Megan, what's wrong? Is someone there who shouldn't be? Is somebody bothering you?

No. It's not like that. I probably just spooked myself at the haunted shoot.

I'm coming to you. I'm worried about you.

The muscles in her chest tensed. This wasn't a good look. She was coming off as a clingy, fragile damsel in distress, terrified of her own shadow and whining for a man to come save her. Worse, she was passive-aggressively pulling him away from his own life to drop everything and tend to her. At least it might appear that way. Not that she was being silly on purpose. The damn book was moving on its own. She had incontestable visual proof.

Don't feel like you have to run to me. I'm probably overreacting.

Megan chewed her cheek, grimacing at the book. Of course she wanted Thom to come see her. She ached for his touch, for him to hold her all night long and reassure her that there was nothing to be scared of. So what if she was being dumb? Every cell inside of her body craved the comfort of his presence.

I don't care if you're overreacting. I can find a chartered flight and get there in an hour and a half if I'm lucky. Leaving now.

The book had moved ninety degrees on the butterfly rug. She could tell by the angle of the sigils on the front. What was it doing? Casting a spell of its own accord? She was made of shivers.

Thank you. I miss you.

She set her phone down. Rubbed her face. Circled the book and debated picking it up before deciding to leave it alone. The damn thing was too overstimulated. She'd better let it cool down. That made sense, right? She chided herself for not having wrangled a better grasp on the rules of magic by now.

She'd studied a lot but only fallen deeper into an occulted labyrinth of un-meaning.

A heavy, sour feeling curdled in the pit of her belly before floating to the surface.

That was it. That was the curse of this magic system. Knowledge didn't beget knowledge, knowledge begot confusion, chaos, and madness. The thought made a light go off. She'd cracked the code and dug up the key tenet of the magic of the Coven Daughters Prophecy. The underlying principle of this dark work was dense, awful, and a truth as pure as snow.

She returned to her desk and scribbled down her observation in her notebook. She'd barely finished her thought when an eight-foot shadow slithered through her open window, its spindly arms and jagged mouth spanning the surface of an entire wall. Her neck hairs stood. Goosebumps flared on her arms. *Just a tree.* There were no trees outside her window.

In a flash of dark motion, the shadow retreated through the route that it'd come in, and her book rotated another ninety degrees.

Megan swiped her laptop and scurried backward onto her bed. With one eye pinned to the smug, observant book, she curled into a ball, stuffed herself into a corner for a false sense of security, and halfheartedly watched a feel-good movie on her computer.

The ring of the doorbell cut through the charged silence like a knife, startling a jerk out of her that set off a spray of scuzzy, nerve-wracking chemicals through her bloodstream. She laid her palm over her hammering heart and only stood once she felt confident that she wouldn't act like a nervous wreck.

Remiss to turn her back on the book but not interested in touching it, she left her looming companion alone and walked to the front door, counting down from ten to smooth her breath. A glimpse in the peephole confirmed that it was indeed Thom who had arrived.

Megan whipped open the door, pulled him inside by the sleeve of his jacket, and buried herself in his hug. He smelled like outdoor air and aftershave, and with every second they hugged, she stitched herself deeper into his grounding energy. "I'm glad you're here," she spoke into his shoulder, not caring how vulnerable she sounded. She sure didn't feel like a tough badass right now. She was massively in over her head without an idea for how to dig herself out.

Thom stroked her hair, tugging the strands in gentle pulls. "I'm glad I'm here too. I'm relived you're alright." He broke away and held the sides of her arms while gazing at her, the tenderness in his brown eyes penetrating right down to her essence. "Tell me what's been going on. Tell me what you need from me."

Stress rushed out of her system in a flood. Contentment filled the void. "Right now? I just need you." Megan stood on her tiptoes and pressed her lips into Thom's, the warm pressure of their kiss erasing the angst that had piled up over the course of the night.

Settling into him, into her peace, she slid her tongue into the hot, sweet welcome of his mouth. Their kiss was slower than the others they'd shared since they'd reconnected, more languid and sensual, but no less hungry.

She urged him with a pull on his wrist to follow her into the bedroom. What she needed from him was to escape. To him and with him. To remember, and to forget.

TEN

BACKING TOWARD HER BED, MEGAN HELD THOM'S FOREARM IN A territorial grip. If he was with her, then she wasn't alone. The closer she got to him, the easier it was to push away the darkness. Thom pulled a suitcase behind him, a good sign that he wasn't planning a quick exit. She guided his free hand past her yoga pants and into her underwear, moaning when his fingers brushed her swollen wetness. "Do you feel how ready for you I am?"

He nibbled her neck and trailed a line of kisses to the corner of her mouth. The two of them moved as one down the short expanse of her hallway and to her bedroom. "I sure do. And you know exactly how to erase my mind." With a heavy sigh, he pulled his hand out of her crotch and let go of his bag to touch her face. "Are you sure that you want to do this right now? Do you want to talk first about what was bothering you?"

As soon as the threshold was crossed, she kicked the book under the bed while he was distracted by playing with the spaghetti strap of her tank top. "No. I don't want to talk about it. I want you. Now." After stepping out of her bottoms, Megan pulled her top over her head and threw it to the floor, leaving her in her bra and underwear.

His eyelids fell to half-mast. "If you say so. Because I definitely want you more."

"Oh yeah?" She laid herself down on the mattress and parted her knees. "Prove it."

He shed his jacket and shirt and dropped them on the rug. "I'm always up for a challenge." The outline of his erection bulged against the material of his jeans, straining in stark relief.

The sight of his excitement made her pulse slam. A heat wave consumed her whole. Though their absence had been brief, she'd missed him with abject ferocity.

"I can see that." Megan stroked herself over her panties, arching her back when her fingertips connected with the swell of her clit, giving Thom a show.

He unbuttoned, unzipped, and prowled on top of her until their bodies were perfectly aligned. Rubbing his hardness over her mound, he asked in a gravelly voice, "You feel me?"

Tingles rose from the pressure point to the depths of her core. Despite the cloth between them, the feel of his cock drove her mad. "I want to taste you."

"Me first." In one skilled motion, he unclasped her bra and threw it aside.

Her nipples pebbled against the cool air of her bedroom.

Thom leaned down to suck on one swollen tip, pulling her stud piercing between his teeth until a sharp pinch made her cry out. He responded by flicking his tongue over the rock-hard point of her flesh. He pushed her breasts together and repeated the irresistible pleasure-pain tease on the other side until she was writhing and groaning and her clit was throbbing. She was certain that it would explode.

"What if I want to slide my cock right in here?" he grunted into her cleavage. "Spray all over your perfect tits?"

"Anything." She wrapped her legs around his lower back and bounced her hips for more grinding leverage where she needed it. An animal thirst drove her feral. She distilled down to pure lust. "Do anything you want to me."

"Let me think about that. I know I want to get off on these." He cupped both breasts. "I also want to try this." He traced her waist and hips with his palms before gripping the sides of her ass and pressing her deeper into the delicious temptation of his bumping hips. "Though

I'd love for you to suck me off as well. We'll have to go more than once."

She could not argue. "I want to go all night. Again and again and again and never stop fucking."

"Have I told you lately that you're perfect?" Thom lifted his face from her chest and pinned her in a moment of deep eye contact.

She smiled at him before reaching down to stroke the length of his stiff member, lingering on the head until his eyes rolled back in his head. "No sentimental stuff right now."

"Fine." His tender smile shifted to a randy smirk. "Give me what I want then." He dove down fast, taking hold of her knees before dividing her legs into a deeper spread. The jolt of fabric ripping shocked her senses. That was it for her underwear.

Thom started in right away, the lack of build-up erotic in the filthiest, most desirable way. His tongue pinpointed her bulging clit with laser precision, darting over the spot relentlessly in a speedy, lapping motion.

The tension catapulted in an instant. She wasn't going to last. He'd broken out a power move designed to take a woman down in seconds, and she was halfway to succumbing. Megan blanked her mind, tried to meditate, and even thought of baseball, but those tactics only got her through three licks. He must've sensed her efforts to hold out too, because he pulled her clit into his mouth and sucked hard.

That was that. Megan let go, pulling his hair, coming into his mouth in violent spurts of sweet release. She'd barely reclaimed her bearings when Thom was back on top of her, his hair shaggy in his face and his expression dark-eyed and wicked. He shoved his pants and underwear below his ass. His hard cock popped out.

"Where do you want this?" He gripped himself at the base until his crown flushed a plum color.

"I thought you were picking." She pushed her breasts up to her chin, her nipples peeking between her fingers, and wiggled her butt, presenting herself as a symbol of pure temptation.

"We're picking together." He winked. "What turns you on the most right now?"

Megan angled her body upward and kissed Thom's freshly shaved cheek. Consent really was sexy. "I want you inside me. My pussy."

"You do have unbeatable pussy." He reached for his back pocket, pulled out a condom, and ripped the wrapper open with his teeth.

"I'm still on the pill. And I'm STI-free. If you're more comfortable using condoms, that's fine though."

He threw the packet across the room, the spontaneity making her laugh. "Works for me. I had an STI test right before we started seeing each other again. I passed with flying colors."

Megan laid back and welcomed the added degree of intimacy. While having sex without condoms wasn't representative of an earth-shattering change in relationship status, there was a degree of mutual trust inherent in the agreement that elevated their encounter to the rank of milestone.

Thom hooked one of Megan's legs in the crook of his elbow and slid into her in a single, effortless push. They fit together. She circled her arms around his broad shoulders, the hair on his chest tickling her breasts, and moved with him.

After they'd found a groove and she was nice and warmed up, he slipped his hand between their bodies and rubbed her clit. His pumps sped up. His touch worked her with precision, and as he struck her internal spot over and over at the perfect tempo, she climaxed again, this one wracking her insides with high-impact reverberations.

"I'm gonna come inside of you." Thom thrust faster, his speech both clipped and awestruck, like he didn't quite believe what was about to happen. He lost his rhythm and plunged at a desperate clip.

She encouraged him with her moans of affirmation, dragging her nails down his back like he enjoyed.

He grunted three times and slackened on top of her, the tension in his body having been spent.

She snuggled into his warmth and caught her breath. Relief and afterglow trickled away as the book howled a silent scream from its exile beneath the bed. Megan knew of one way to banish unpleasant thoughts of the occult sort. She nuzzled Thom's earlobe and rubbed his stomach. "How much longer until you're ready for me to give you a killer blowjob?"

Instead of answering, he turned to his side and held her hand. "I'm starting to worry that you're hiding something from me."

She was. Literally. And from herself. She was hiding from a relentless onslaught of terror and overwhelm that was barreling toward her like a juggernaut. "It's more that I don't want our time together to be tainted by negativity."

He lifted a lock of her hair and coiled the strand around his finger. "Right, but ignoring that negativity doesn't make it disappear."

Unfortunately, he was correct. Megan considered her words with dutiful care. "I think I've gotten in over my head."

"How?" His voice dropped in register, softened by a slight tremor.

The last thing she wanted was for Thom to interpret her statement as being about their relationship. She'd better tell the truth or risk confusing him. "That spell book that I showed you last time is unpredictable. I've been reading and studying it, trying to figure out how best to use it in service of my show. It started doing weird things."

His Adam's apple bobbed.

A nervous laugh popped out of her throat. "Great, now you think I'm crazy like Brian."

"I don't think that you're crazy. Or that Brian is either, for that matter."

"If I tell you something really off-the-wall that happened to me today, you won't judge?"

"I won't judge. I promise."

"The book started moving on its own. Following me around the house. Then a shadow came out of the window, and that's when the book started rotating on the floor in this deliberate, clock-type pattern."

Thom's features pulled into a grimace. He looked over his shoulder. "Where is the book now?"

"Under the bed. I didn't know what else to do with it. I don't know what's worse, seeing it or not seeing it."

He smiled wryly. "Seeing it. Good call on out of sight, out of mind."

A sobering realization settled in the depths of Megan's chest. "I should have told you before you came here. I'm not actually sure that it's safe for you to be here."

"I'm not afraid, Megan." He spoke the words with a conviction that rocked her. She'd never felt more cherished with few words. "I'm here for you. I want to be with you. It'll take more than low-level paranormal scares to stop me."

She traced aimless shapes over his torso, running a finger across his skin while making a study of his birthmarks and freckles. In her opinion, the scares weren't low-level, but Thom's confidence reassured her that the sky wasn't about to fall. "What happened in that closet?"

He watched the ceiling for a few long seconds before laying his hand on top of hers. He knew what she was talking about. "I had a vision. Loud noises and sensations accompanied it."

"What was the vision?" If he saw the symbol for the fire element, his experience would at least line up with what'd been happening recently. While not exactly reassuring, consistency at least offered a paltry bulwark against total chaos.

"You had these fiery wings sprouting out of your back." He scoffed. "It sounds absolutely absurd to say this out loud."

Not absurd, but not immediately meaningful either. She pictured the book under her bed, and a chill danced through her. "I think that I read things that I shouldn't have. Got too close to mysteries that I didn't understand and let in forces that don't make sense to me."

"Brian said something to that effect." He pulled her closer until they held each other. "But about the four of us. Fyre. I thought that he'd gone mad. Now I'm not sure."

"Did he say anything else about the songs?"

"Yes. He said that he sealed them for now. I'm not quite sure what to make of that, but I suppose I'll take it."

Her thoughts tapped along in problem-solving mode. "I wonder if there's a way for me to seal off any openings I've created."

Thom studied her in a long, curious look. "Beats me."

Megan certainly wasn't helping the cause, whatever that was, by hiding her book away and letting herself get spooked like a child terrified of demons in the closet. She jumped up and put her clothes back on. Being naked while doing witchcraft seemed overcharged and dangerous, though she didn't have a logical explanation for the hunch. Not that logic was steering this supernatural train. "I might have seen a spell or incantation for blocking energies. In the fire section. A firewall."

"Are you sure that this is a good idea?" He sat up in bed.

"No, but doing nothing doesn't seem to help." Megan tugged the book out from its hiding place and laid that hunk of horrors down on her desk once more.

While Thom looked on, she opened the text to the fire section and read a part about using fire to block unwanted influences, calling upon the principle behind a wall of fire and its power to stop the momentum of anyone who would pass beyond the flaming barrier.

Intermediate to advanced practitioners of the craft may summon their element to halt the intentions or progress of others, seen or unseen. This action may be taken literally, to erect a guard against intruders, or in an energetic sense.

"Now we're getting somewhere," Megan said, Thom watching from the periphery of her vision.

A fire witch may pair an emotion in her heart with her element, set an intention, and build a mighty wall around whatever needs protection.

Megan tried to read on, but her vision blurred and her head swum. She reread the same sentence three times, stuck from moving on to the next paragraph.

"Follow the stairs down, down, down the crystal mountain," Thom murmured in a soporific timbre of pure hypnosis. He sounded like a blend of himself and Folly. "Once you arrive on the lowest level, turn the sixth knob on the sixth door."

"What?" Megan was drowsy. She fought against the fall of her eyelids. Her thoughts grew muzzier by the second. Each word floated out of reach before she could finish thinking it. Far, far away. "What did you say?"

"I asked if you'd found any promising leads." His regular voice sliced through the haze, measured but thick with worry. She wrestled to reclaim her composure. "Are you okay, Megan?"

"Fine. Fine." She wasn't about to wimp out on her sacred duty. The magic content was intense, sure, but she had to master it. If not, it was going to take her out and win this sick game. "And yes, this section that I'm on looks useful."

Though her perceptions remained cloudy and surreal, she forged ahead, squeezing her eyes shut and reopening them until her drifting gaze stayed focused and the words registered with full, crisp clarity.

Fire witches with a penchant for sex magic may involve a partner for optimal results. Enlist a companion on the wavelength, and at an opportune moment, mentally repeat the following incantation six times.

Sister Fire, build for me, secure my borders, certainly. None shall pass, friend or foe. All who breach must surely go.

She pictured herself walking down a spiral staircase whose clear steps glimmered with the brilliance of cut diamonds. Six white doors waited for her at the base, a row of crystalline slabs ringing an iceberg floor. Six knobs adorned each door in two symmetrical rows. Five of those knobs were the elemental symbols. The sixth was a twisted coil.

Her perception sucked outward and inward in two heavy pulls. She fell too far away, then too close, before resettling in her office chair, where she stared down at her book. A piece was missing from her, and at the same time she was overfilled. Too much and not enough. Winged flutters took flight in her bones. She shuddered.

Thom kneaded her shoulders in a firm, delectable massage that had her melting from the sweet ache. She'd been out of it and she hadn't noticed him walking up beside her. "What if we put this aside for the night and do something else to clear our minds. Watch a movie. Go out. We can have a late dinner."

She swiveled in her chair until she looked up at him. He'd put on his boxers but stayed shirtless. "I can stop this right now. Well, we can. The instructions are right here." She tapped the page that laid out the incantation. "No more visions or symbols appearing out of nowhere. If we get lucky, the firewall might even block whatever force is manipulating your songs."

He craned his neck in the direction of the pages. "I'm interested. How do we do that?"

Excitement curled around her midsection. As far as spells went, they were getting a pretty good deal on this one. Stop the onslaught of questionable magic and have a good time in the process? She'd take the win. "Go sit on the edge of the bed. I'll show you."

"Is this about what I think it is?"

"You're perceptive. Yes. You okay with trying out a little sex magic?"

He scratched the back of his neck and sucked his bottom lip into his mouth. "Absolutely. You're the expert."

"Damn right. Close your eyes too."

Thom did as directed, his cooperation kindling the first stirring of renewed horniness. He was a rebel and a bad boy at heart, down for a little experimentation even if the practice wasn't strictly vanilla or even safe. The daredevil ethos suited Megan. Exciting things happened at the edge of danger, and at least this one would bring productive results.

Megan went to where Thom had dropped his luggage and picked up the lingerie bag. What a perfect opportunity to enjoy her presents. She pulled out a bodysuit the color of charcoal that was sewn in the most delicate of lace. Merely touching the fine, silken, stretchy fabric made her feel wet and scandalous. She changed right there in the hallway, shimmying into a sheath that caressed her sensitive parts while leaving her back and shoulders bare. The neckline plunged for easy access to her breasts, and a quick-release snap held the crotch together.

Dirty, dirty Thom, identifying this whore's costume as a perfect choice for her.

He'd chosen perfectly.

She strutted back into the bedroom, walking as tall as a goddess in her new piece. He was already hard underneath his boxers, as if he could smell her arousal and hear lust in her breathing. "Don't open your eyes yet." She settled on her knees before him and cupped the stiff bar of his excitement.

"I want to look at you," he breathed, grunting when she gently pinched his tip.

"Not yet." She grabbed his waistband, sending a cue for him to sit up enough for her to pull the shorts to his ankles.

Megan licked her lips at the sight of Thom's thick, curved cock, all proud and ready for her. "You like when I get down on my knees and suck your cock, don't you?"

"More than I like life itself." He fisted wads of the unmade comforter. Fabric bunched at both sides of his hips.

She fluttered her pierced tongue against the underside of his dick in feathery, teasing laps. "You can look now," she whispered before dragging her tongue up the length of his shaft, gazing into his blissed-out face. His eyes popped open and were instantly drowned in a pool of lust.

"Fuck, I about blew my load just there from that visual. All over your face." His breath came out choppy. He cupped her cheek and watched her kiss and lick and lap at him. "I hope that doesn't come off as degrading."

"Joke's on you, I'm into that. Which you already know." She dipped her head down and sucked one of his balls into her mouth, then the other, giving him her mouth everywhere but where he craved it.

"Touché."

A bead of pre-cum leaked from his opening. She swiped the pearly drop and licked her lips, bitter sweetness on her taste buds. "You are about ready to blow, aren't you?"

He threw his head back and thrust his hips. His knuckles whitened. "Show me your tits."

"Smooth line," she quipped, but she pulled the pliable lace of her teddy down below her breasts. After exposing what he wanted to see, she laid a row of kisses on his shaft and rubbed the underside of his crown, giving a scratchy little tickle with her nail. "I want to try an experiment." Megan popped the nails off the first two fingers of her right hand. "I've never done this before, but I've heard that it takes the male orgasm to the next level."

He stared at her face with a mix of reverence and frustration. "Please suck it."

"Can I massage your prostate while I do it?"

His eyes got huge. She thought for a second there that his tongue was about to loll out of his mouth, the greedy bastard. "Yes. I love that."

Thom was awesome. Up for anything sex-wise, just like her. She left him there for a second and grabbed a bottle of lotion off her dresser. Megan coated the fingers she was about to use and said, "Scoot up on the bed."

He got in position, hips lifted and knees up, and she worked her fingers inside his tight back hole in a corkscrew motion. Penetrating a guy admittedly gave her a thrill of role-reversal power, but mostly she was focused on making him come harder than he ever had before. The men she'd seen climaxing in pornos while receiving rear stimulation had screamed.

Megan hooked her fingers and twisted them until she pressed against a bulging node, and Thom moaned. "Is that your prostate?" she murmured, stroking up and down on the purported male G-spot, a swollen bean hidden away like the best-kept sex secret.

"You're dirty and brilliant and I'm hopelessly in lo—" Thom interrupted his own speech with a sharp cry, his prick twitching in the open air.

Time to learn if all the hype about a prostate-massage-enhanced blowjob was legit. She drew Thom's prick into the back of her throat and bobbed, never taking her stare away from his. She laved and slurped, adding pressure and backing off, her fingers doing their thing while her mouth worked him over. A few aligned strokes later, his lips parted, and he groaned a curse.

He stiffened in her mouth and sprayed her tongue with salty release, jutting his hips and howling. Thom kept coming for a good thirty seconds after he spent his load, mindlessly bouncing on the bed in jolts timed with his shouts of triumph.

Now. She winked at him. He nodded frantically, barely getting out the gesture as he was still riding aftershocks from the ministrations of her hand.

Sister Fire, build for me, secure my borders, certainly. None shall pass, friend or foe. All who breach must surely go.

A crack split Megan's ears, followed by an incredible pressure between her shoulders that forced her to drop Thom's erection from her mouth. A mammoth force pulled her up into the air, and she hurdled through a tunnel of light before reemerging to stand before the six doors with their six knobs.

ELEVEN

THE SIGIL AT THE BOTTOM OF THE STEPS BOTH BECKONED TO THOM and triggered in him an unspeakably potent sense of repulsion. He walked to a predator, instinct screaming deep within him, yet he couldn't stop his march. His bare feet connected silently with stair after stair, the pearlescent marble cool on his soles.

Where was Megan? Where were his shoes? Where was *he*?

He wore only his boxer shorts, barely dressed and wholly vulnerable as he descended into the heart of this strange, ritualistic lair. The air was still, unscented, and crisp against his neck and belly. Pale rock surrounded him in every direction. Walls arched high and tall, propelling to vaulted ceilings. At the foot of the stairs lay a sterile floor made from the same material in an identical color.

A symbol was carved on the ground. A hexagon with a simple triangle marking each juncture and stamped in the middle with a squirmy, twisted handprint. He'd seen these symbols in Megan's book. These dark insignia had assaulted his eyes previously.

"Megan." His voice echoed in a triptych of hollow taunts. "Are you here?"

"Megan, oh, Megan, you're perfect and beautiful and my dick is perpetually hard," an invisible voice called out with raw contempt in an androgynous, smooth, and bloodless timbre. "I'm gonna come again, *Meeeeegaaan.*" The speaker then switched from mockery to a serious tone and said, "She brought you here, both of you, through your little fuck and suck erotica fest that I've been forced to endure. If I were you, I'd be wholly displeased with her. Of course, I, personally, am delighted to have you. You, on the other hand, are not likely to share in my glee."

This had to be a bad dream. Yet he remembered all the moments leading up to the nightmare he now resided in. Spending time with Megan in her room, the things they'd done together, her sitting hunched over that book and brushing up on a fire spell—all the snippets were as sharp as any recent memory. Recollections that crisp didn't happen in dreams. "Where is she?"

"Megan is a fool." Evil laughter bounced off the walls. "And so are you. A useful idiot."

Fear swept over him before fury overpowered it. "What have you done with her? If you hurt her, you'll be sorry."

"Yeah, okay, sure. I'll be sorry, pal. I'm sure I will. Tell me. What do you plan to do to me, human? What's your plan to dispatch of the most powerful deity ever to exist, you stupid, useless man?"

His heart ached in Megan's absence. He should have tried to talk her out of that spell. But who was he to intrude on something personal to her? What would he have even said? He had to gather his bearings and figure out what to do. "Who are you—what are you?"

A click-clack tapped over the flooring as if an unseen predator circled him. Thom labored to regulate his breathing, and his short hairs lifted, but he refused to show fear.

"I am everything you can't explain. Synchronicities and chance encounters. I'm your inspiration and your gut feelings. I'm luck and fate. I blew the wind in the right direction the exact second that your ridiculous band broke big. I was the reason why that talent scout happened to be in a really good mood the day he saw you play. I'm the one who sucks your music out of your bones and uses it to fuel my power. I'm the tailor who will stitch your fate into the tapestry of the hologram."

Every one of those words came coated in ice and arrogance. "What do you want from me?" If he could pinpoint the motivation of his disembodied companion, he'd have a better handle on an approach to get to Megan.

A hefty sigh crashed down from nowhere. "It seems that your pesky friend Brian has gone and fucked up the prophecy. Again. I detest him. My loathing for his presumptuous, meddlesome, upstart presence knows no bounds. At first, he wouldn't die on schedule like he was supposed to, but thwarting me with his stubborn little will to live apparently wasn't enough."

At least he had this spirit talking. If he pretended to be on its side, perhaps it would continue to yammer. "Brian is quite aggravating, I agree." Thom walked to one of the high walls and, upon closer proximity, saw that it, too, was etched with a medley of carvings. He caught unrecognizable words in foreign languages that he'd never seen, numerous symbols, and snatches of text in English. Thom brought his fingers close to the grooves in the stone but thought better of touching. "He's always done exactly what he wanted with minimal regard for how his personal drives impact the wishes of others." His actual view of Brian was far more charitable, but mercy wasn't what this entity wanted to hear. That was obvious.

"Precisely. He's willful to a grievous fault. I let my guard down. I got lazy. I underestimated him, never for once anticipating that he had the fortitude or skill to close a portal." The voice trailed off before picking up. "That's where you come in."

Ah. Thom smelled leverage. "How?"

"'Deep Dark Woods.' I don't know how the four of you did it, not every detail, but you encoded me into that song. Other songs of yours host me too, but I'm most heavily resonant in that one. You've taken such ownership of those songs over the years that I can no longer control those pieces of myself without your consent. It's rather inconvenient, having these small satellite bits of my consciousness scattered about. I need them back. I need you to play it. Now."

The spirit's confession was interesting. If it had the capacity to be perplexed and stumped, then it wasn't as powerful or omniscient as it claimed. A bunch of bloody hot air was blowing his way. "Show me Megan and I'll consider putting on a private show for you."

A bitter snort was what he got for a reply. "Why do you care about this girl? Your mind fascinates me in its nonsensical attachment. You've had thousands of women. Why her?"

Because Megan was authentic and complex and liked him for exactly who he was. Because she was brilliant and funny, talented and thoughtful. She knew when to be serious but loved to have a good time. Because when she walked into a room, she was more *real* than any other person in his presence. Because of an ineffable factor that reverberated in the best nooks of his true self, he loved Megan and only Megan. "None of your business. Those are my terms. Show me that she's alive and safe."

Like a copy-paste on photo editing software, Megan popped into view, suspended in midair directly between the floor and the ceiling. She hung in an arch, belly-up, wearing the lingerie she had on earlier. Her hair fell from her head in a red rope. Her eyes were open, and her lips were closed, but she wasn't moving. Thom's heart crushed back into his chest. He ran directly underneath her and held up his hand. "Megan, love. Are you there? Can you see me? Can you hear me?"

She didn't respond, but her breastbone moved up and down. She was breathing.

"There," said the fiend. "Now play the song."

"Absolutely not. We aren't safe. Safe means back home and free of you."

"Then you'll never be safe because you'll never be free of me. Not until the prophecy commences."

"You just said that Brian fucked up the prophecy."

A low growl quaked in every open space inside his body. As if manipulated by a marionette, Megan turned upside down. Her arms and legs jerked to the sides until her limbs were wrenched into a star shape. "Challenge me again and I pulverize every bone, muscle, and tendon in her body."

The threat landed flat. Both of them were of more use to this demon alive than dead. Which didn't mean that Thom had any desire to drag out this encounter longer than necessary. He needed Megan in his arms and a clear path to escape. He presented both palms in a performance of surrender. "Set her down and then we'll talk."

Megan's entranced body cartwheeled head over heels. Her legs snapped shut, and her arms flopped limp at her sides. She floated to the ground and stood before him, gazing blankly into the distance.

He ran to her and checked her pulse. She was alive and warm. He cupped both sides of her face and fixed her in a stare. "Can you hear me, Megan? Are you there?"

"She's in fairy land with another part of me. Don't worry about her. Sing the song."

"Once I see proof of life." He hugged Megan, finding her body pliable and boneless against his, and shook her by the shoulders. "Megan, give me a sign. Blink. Say something. It's me, it's Thom. We're trapped in an alternate dimension, and we need to get out. This spirit wants a song out of me. I need your help."

"I'm more than a spirit. I'm the generator of all spirits, now and forever."

Shut the fuck up.

A faint croak crept out of Megan's throat. She twitched.

Hope propelled him into further action, firing up his mind and motivation. "You're in there. I can hear you and feel you. Keep resisting. Keep fighting. Push yourself out of wherever you're being held. I've got you."

She whispered a string of words, her utterance too quiet and fast for him to understand.

Their looming, disembodied companion snarled. The symbols on the walls lit up in a phosphorescent glow. Thom saw various lines from Fyre songs inserted into the jumble, ripped out of context and pasted in with other snippets of text to make a mishmash like that of the magnetic poetry set they'd played around with on a tour bus one summer.

He rubbed, jostled, and patted Megan, his mind souring into dark dread as the walls throbbed with creepy light, bombarding him from his peripheral vision. "I can't hear you, love. Please speak up. You're almost out. Come on. You're close."

That summer with the poetry strips, when they'd goofed off with an experimental method of songwriting, had seemed harmless, inconsequential. But it hadn't been. Those choices they'd made with words and phrases were being recorded here, wherever this was, every action and choice made by Fyre used as fodder to feed a sinister design.

The band was cursed. Their rise to prominence was never an accident, a fluke, or the result of good luck. It was all by design—heinous design. Brian was right. Fyre was an agent of cosmic downfall. Somewhere along the way, they'd picked up a key and opened a door. Plunged the world into hell and not even known it. They'd cracked a code and pushed into perpetual motion a cosmic wheel, a disc that tore through the fabric of the universe with its mysterious and destructive fires.

"None shall pass, friend or foe," Megan slurred.

The last thing that Thom wanted to hear was the words to that damn spell, but at least Megan was speaking coherently. "You've got it. Push through. You're right there, my love. On the surface. I have you. I've got you."

"Play the song," the magical being screeched.

The walls were covered now, every inch of space painted in bizarre graffiti. Messes of lettering pulsed with white-hot radiance, the wattage cranking until Thom had to squint against searing pressure. A strange and debilitating sensation overcame him, like the coils of his brain matter were unspooling before slithering off into the distance.

We flew too close to the sun. The thought struck him like an arrow despite the looseness of his cognition. *And now we melt in the glare as our wings of fame ooze in dripping wax and our broken bodies crash to the cold, hard floor of fate. We never piloted the chariot. It steered us the entire time, and the rise was never meant to be continuous. Free will is an illusion.*

Thom's grasp on reality slipped further. He wasn't sure if his last thoughts originated from his own mind or had been implanted there by some...other.

What was the nature of mind anyway? Everyone assumed their thoughts were their own, kept under lock and key like personal property in a safe, but who was to say that all thought, every thought iterated by every thinking being ever to exist, didn't orbit in an external force field where those of higher mind could mine and pull from the meager thoughts of people? What if all thought was shared by a collective of the highest order?

"Now you're getting it," purred their creepy watcher, its manner once again chilly and composed. "You're coming around. Step a little closer,

Thom James, walk to me in the surrender of yourself. Your song is in there, and I can taste it already. Simply release your grasp and let that honey of music flow into my sacred walls. Feel your grip release just like all those sexual climaxes you're obsessed with."

My God, we were never even us, in the sense of being discrete entities or creatures. Brian, Thom, Jonnie, and Jonas. Four vessels, open ports through which the songs flowed. Kissed by the gods, sweetly at first, only for lips to turn to poison death once the bill comes due. Nothing lasts forever. It's time to pay the debt now. Time to relinquish what was never yours and return those gifts to the source from which they came.

"Your mind was never yours. Those songs were never yours. You never owned them, only rented. All that is mine returns to me. Your egos claimed possession, but that was your folly. Render unto folly all that is Folly's. Now. Open, Thom, you're open. Hollow space remains in you. It's okay, you won't remember. You'll serve me here, feeding me your songs until there's nothing left of you except space for me."

He was heavy and tired. Stirrings of music swirled in loops through his marrow. The words of "Deep Dark Woods" took shape first, followed by the melodies and harmonies. The chorus clicked into place like all those strips of magnetic poetry, and he swayed in a daze as the whole of their masterpiece formed itself from his life force and lifted out of his center to seep through his pores in packets of music and lyrics.

Anger struck him, snapping the worst of his stupor. This wasn't right. He was dying, killing himself, opening a vein and draining his lifeblood into those evil walls. "No." The word came out like molasses, and his tongue was too large for his mouth, but he spat out his protest. "No more. You can't have it." He hugged Megan close before turning his attention to address her. "Please come back to me. I need you. We need to get out of here before this place steals every piece of us that's worth having."

Awful, animal yowls stabbed his eardrums, but the cries only helped to wake him up. He pressed his lips against Megan's ear. "Keep fighting."

A sickening belly cough erupted from her stomach. She dug her nails into his elbows and hacked out another round of retching before letting go of a groan that sounded much more conscious than any of her prior vocalizations. "This is bad," Megan wheezed, gulping for air like she'd been drowning. "It's too powerful. We're stuck. She has us."

"No, she doesn't. She's not nearly as powerful as she'd like us to believe. She's close to the level that she wants but not there yet. We can get out of here. Protect your boundaries. Keep your head about you and don't submit to the mind control. That's what it is, mind control magic." He looked up at the creamy apex of the cathedral and shouted, "We have free will! Your spells don't work on us!"

And to think, a few weeks ago, Thom thought magic was utter bollocks.

"You don't have shit," the severed voice hissed. "Save for the folly of your worthless ego and the traps you set for yourself. You are all my subjects."

Thom held Megan with the intent of never letting her go. She was breathing more steadily now, and the muscle tone had returned to her body. He had to keep coaxing her back from the brink until they had a method for breaking free. He'd walked through a doorway to get here, and if Megan wasn't yet fit to move her body, he was strong enough to carry her. Thom circled his grip above her wrist, turned on his heel, and said, "Run."

They moved together, dashing up the steps that he'd walked down, the temple burning bright all around him. His legs ached with effort as he ran for the exit.

Except the opening wasn't there anymore. All that remained was a slab with no knob or crack. Thom ran his hands over the smooth, cold surface, shaking his head. Perhaps there had never been an opening at all. It didn't matter. The laws of physics didn't apply in this underworld.

"Ready to face me?" The taunt snuck up from behind, curling and oily.

"I can try the firewall spell again," Megan said under her breath. "I ran through it a couple more times while I was out of commission. I think I have a better grasp on the cadence and rhythm. With these spells, I'm gathering that if even one little piece is off-kilter, the entire thing backfires badly. If we can stall her for a few more minutes, I'll feel ready. She's distracted right now and isn't reading my thoughts."

Megan's insights on the requirements of perfection didn't inspire confidence in magic going off without a hitch, but he had no cache to contest her or offer an alternative. Undermining her resolve might worsen the outcome, and Thom would offer Megan his unyielding support regardless of his reservations. The least he could do was stand in her corner. Besides, he owed it to both of them to face their tormentor with bravery. Keeping Megan in a protective handclasp, he turned around and stepped in front of his love.

The intrusion of a fearsome, fantastical intruder leveled Thom with a mighty shock.

A scream died his his throat. Awe crashed down on him. His kingdom for a weapon of any sort.

The dragon that stood poised before him was completely translucent, light passing through a ten-foot body of glassy flesh to reveal an utter absence of blood, organs, or other biology. The only color to pierce the diamond behemoth was two blood-red irises, twin pits of ruby dropped into a hulking, colorless expanse.

The creature stalked forward on muscular haunches, nostrils the size of fists opening and closing. Curved toe claws clicked against the flooring, their crystal tips as pointed as the ends of daggers.

Thom locked eyes with the monster. "I'm not afraid of you." If this thing had the ability to harm them, it would have done it already. It wanted "Deep Dark Woods" and had failed to suck the music from Thom's soul. This big show was little more than an empty spectacle.

A whoosh of air filled the room. Two demonic wings crisscrossed by delicate networks of transparent membranes expanded. "That's good." The dragon slunk forward, its red eyes burning bright and hateful. "I have no desire for your fear. Fear is useless to me and tastes bitter."

Megan's lips moved, her speech hushed and rapid.

He pressed their palms together. "You want our songs? Our creative inspiration, vomited from our hearts and funneled your way? Because you can't have that either."

"I can give you much more than you already have." The dragon's tail swished, a row of spikes cascading down the serpentine appendage to catch the light. Thom's monstrous adversary advanced until it stood two feet away from him, an unholy and primal abomination seeding inches from his face. "More money, more fame, more women. Eternal youth. Immortality even, in a sense."

Thom laughed at the cheap, tiresome appeal to the basest parts of him. "Yeah, no way am I making a literal deal with the devil."

"I. Am. Not. Your. Puny. Christian. Devil." The beast's lips pulled back to reveal two sharp rows of teeth. "I precede Lucifer Morningstar and Satan and everyone else in that pathetic menagerie of two-bit rebels. I was here before every god and goddess worshiped by your lowly kind. I created your gods and goddesses, I'll have you know. I stood upon Mt. Olympus and built the personalities of that pantheon like building blocks, structured according to my whims. I am the origin of storms and stars. *I* parted the Red Sea. From me every dream and fantasy are issued, as I turn the cosmic dial of—"

A loud and assured incantation from Megan stopped the bloviating behemoth. "Sister Fire, build for me, secure my borders, certainly. None shall pass, friend or foe. All who breach must surely go."

A wall of flame shot up to claim the tight space separating Thom and Megan from the dragon, the fires crackling an incandescent shade of orange tinged at the tips with sapphire. The flames didn't sear, or even warm, but they did divide in the center, opening to a shimmering pool of calmer blues kissed by pink.

Megan pulled him forward.

Thom looked into her eyes and followed.

The next thing he knew, his head was splitting with hammer pain. He was blind and sucking air, scrabbling for purchase against nubby material. Nausea threatened to heave his guts. His vision returned in splotches of color, and it hurt to see, but he fought to reclaim himself. "Megan. Where are you. Are you here?"

He was looking at a picture of a butterfly. Blurry, but that's definitely what it was.

"I'm here," she whimpered. "I see you on the other side of the room."

Room? He rubbed his eyes until the world stopped spinning and his stomach settled. Facedown, he hauled himself to a seat. The bed and dresser were familiar. Megan sat across from him, crumpled forward in a ragdoll pose, and lifted her head slowly until they acknowledged each other with a heavy look.

He hurled himself across the floor and swept her into his arms. They simply hugged for a long time, reconnecting with the sweet relief of normalcy. Finally, Thom got speech to leave his lips. "Are you hurt?"

"I'm fine. We're probably both physically unaffected. Do you feel anything damaged in your body?"

Now that the queasiness and general discomfort of disorientation had subsided, he was unharmed as far as he could tell. "No, I don't seem to be injured either." Grounded as he'd ever be again, Thom drew back to face Megan. "Where were we, and what the hell was that?"

TWELVE

THE AFTERMATH OF THOM'S QUESTION HUNG HEAVY IN THE AIR. Megan thought about how to answer. Even considering analyzing her book and magic spells exhausted her, but she owed him honesty. They were in this together.

With her cheek rested safely on his shoulder, she did her best to unpack the mysteries. "It's an alternate dimension ruled by magic. From what I can tell, it's called the Other Place. There's all sorts of nasty stuff there. Doppelgangers, demonic energies, phantoms that can possess people, and these weird Frankenstein monster creatures called Other Ones." She shuddered from the pictures her imagination conjured. "The Other Place, according to my book, is the domain of chaos. It's the domain of the magic giver, who may reveal valuable insights to the practitioner but doesn't always have our best interest at heart. I have a feeling that I'll know more once I read another chapter."

Thom hummed in acknowledgement and stroked Megan's hair. "This is just a thought, but what if you took a break from that book? It doesn't seem like any good comes from working with it."

He wasn't wrong, but ignoring a problem didn't make it go away. "Except now we're closer to understanding what's going on with Brian and Jonnie and how it impacts all of us. You heard the stuff the dragon was saying about the prophecy and your songs."

Thom rubbed his temple. Weariness dragged down on his handsome features, and dark circles ringed his eyes. She would have felt terrible for yanking him into this mess, but by all accounts, his involvement preceded their connection. "Yes, I heard that part. I'm not sure, though, that I want to understand."

Her pulse clicked to a higher gear. She spied the book out of the corner of her eye, those juicy secrets teasing her from her desk. "We need to understand though. I think if I try another spell, and we go back to the Other Place one more time, I'll have a solid handle on this prophecy and how I—we—can intervene." She licked her lips, jumpy from a rush of energy. "No more being in the dark."

"I never want to go back there ever again." The certainty in Thom's voice was undeniable. He was sterner than she'd ever heard him, more than enough to get her attention. "It's not healthy to get stirred deeper and deeper into that world. I'm sure you felt it. How wrong it felt? Where were you when you were in that trance? What do you remember?"

Not much. She'd been cold and alone, in the dark, not frightened but in no way content. She'd been in a waiting room with others, and at the same time fractured severely until she wasn't entirely herself. "I'm not sure. It was like, the best I can describe it is, I was being shared. My soul was being shared or taken apart. Taken *out*. I wasn't in my body."

His eyebrows lifted to his hairline. "That sounds absolutely horrifying in the most existential way possible."

The way he deadpanned startled a dry laugh out of her. He was right about the weird world of magic. It was all actually kind of horrifying when she mulled it over. "I wouldn't call it pleasant."

Tenderness returned to Thom's face. He massaged her shoulders. "Look, if this practice is important to you, I won't stand in the way. That isn't my place. I'm not going to lie though. From what I've seen, getting too involved in this is a bad idea. The book and the spells seem to have a mind of their own." He scoffed. "I cannot believe what I'm hearing myself say out loud. But we both went through that ordeal, and it was very much real, and throughout it all I had the strong impression that we weren't in total control. Or perhaps I'm speaking out of turn."

"No, you aren't." Unfortunately. Megan hungered to wield her craft like a badass. But the reality was that wasn't happening. She'd scored wins, namely the fire spell, but equally as often she couldn't shake the notion that the craft was wielding *her*. "I don't want to give up, you know? I want to be better than this magic. Stronger, and more capable. I feel like if I acknowledge that it has me where it wants me, that it's more powerful than I am, then I lose."

She'd had a fair number of setbacks recently that had only fueled her urge for a win. The particular sort of victory that came with improving at a skill she'd worked on was a high too tempting to abandon. She used to feel the dopamine payoff of successes at her old job, when she'd published papers or earned excellent teaching evaluations. That source of satisfaction was no more. *Bump in the Night* had gotten dicey when it came to delivering hits to the reward center of her brain, and even a good workout didn't cut it.

"I'm not saying give up. My suggestion is to take a short break. At least for the night. Process what we just went through. Sleep on it. Give yourself a chance to digest and make sense of what happened before you dive back in. Maybe clarify your goals, you know?"

He was being awfully sensible. The last thing Megan wanted to do was drag Thom along for a ride through spells and witchcraft if he wasn't onboard. Especially if her experimentations were making things worse. The book had her too amped. She needed to cool off. Or heat up. She ran her bare foot up the inside of Thom's thigh until her toes tickled his balls. "I can think of an alternative goal."

He brought her foot to his face and kissed her toes. "I have a scandalous proposition for you."

"You want a foot job?" She traced her big toe over Thom's bottom lip. "That's cool. I'll get you off with my feet."

"I was actually thinking we could go out. Spend time together in a way that doesn't involve magic and where we keep our clothes on." He moved her leg to rest beside his.

A tremor of anxiety traveled its course. If Thom wasn't interested in sex, was he getting bored with her? When a guy didn't want to get laid all the time anymore, that was a clear warning sign the relationship was headed for destruction. Her relationships, at least, depended on sex for their foundation. She looked at a spot on the floor. "It's cool if you need to leave. Get back to your tour or whatever."

He made a sound of confusion. "I just said that I'd like to go out."

Once again, she'd dumbly let her fears and insecurities take center stage. Thom had already reassured her that he liked her for more than sex. It was hard to believe, though, when she'd been the sex chick for a long time and for lots of people. Over the years, Megan had kind of lost sight of what else she had to offer besides her body when her body and sexuality were what got attention. "You want to what, go out for dinner and a movie?" Sarcasm offered a safe way to gauge his intentions without opening herself up to rejection. Megan wasn't quite ready to be all earnest and vulnerable with her feelings and shit. Men ran away when she showed her underbelly. They didn't like seeing their porn star fantasy shattered by the inconvenient depth of a whole-ass person.

"Yes, I would love that." He touched her face and guided her back to eye contact. "What's your favorite place around here?"

New Denmark didn't have much to offer, but there were a few nostalgia traps within driving distance. Besides, it was just dinner, not an elaborate courtship ritual where she had to prove herself worthy. "There's a decent steakhouse where I used to go in high school for special occasions. I can show you around my old haunts, if you want."

"Perfect. Take me down memory lane. I'd be honored."

Megan couldn't remember the last time she'd gone out to dinner with someone. Her recent dates had mostly flowed unimpeded down the bar-to-bedroom pipeline. "As long as you don't mind the Podunk, U.S.A. experience."

"I'm with you. That's what counts."

She might have a hard time avoiding being sentimental with her feelings when he said romantic stuff in his sexy voice and doomed her to total infatuation with those brown eyes. "Let's go. I'm starving."

They washed up, and Megan changed into skinny jeans, ankle boots, and a cute sweater. She replaced the nails that she'd pulled off and even put product in her hair. She added a little mascara and eye shadow, much lighter makeup than she usually wore. She wasn't trying to catch a lover tonight, not with such a good one by her side.

While she was touching up in the bathroom mirror, Thom came up behind her and circled his arms around her waist. "You look exquisite."

"Classier than my regular getups, huh?" She patted on red lipstick in a shade lighter than her usual blowjob ruby.

"Just different. You'd look good in a potato sack."

"Sure. With a big belt and heels, that wouldn't be any uglier than what they put on the runways these days."

He laughed and took her hand, gazing at her like she mattered.

Megan allowed a bit more of her heart to open.

VINCENT'S STEAKHOUSE MADE ITS HOME IN AN UNPRETENTIOUS building that was built like a brick warehouse and sat alongside the lazy creek that ran through the edge of town.

The outskirts of New Denmark included a time capsule pharmacy with a non-ironic fifties aesthetic and a print shop run by an eighty-year-old who'd walked his now-elderly Beagle around the block at lunchtime since Megan was in her early twenties.

To say that New Denmark was a sleepy town was a generous understatement. On life support was more accurate.

Megan pulled into the restaurant parking lot, swerving to avoid two gnarly potholes in the cracked pavement. The restaurant's sign was dimmer than she remembered, the first neon "n" in "Vincent's" blinking in sad little red sputters.

A few more of the surrounding business had gone under, leaving Vincent's flanked by the ghostly remains of a men's clothing store and a blown-out skeleton of sadness that was once a beloved flower shop.

All that remained robust was a dystopian expanse of corporate farmland, plastic-green fields lining the land in every direction with mechanically tidy rows of corn and soybeans.

Sunset spilled purple and orange over empty streets. Megan's chest ached for her steadily deteriorating hometown. New Denmark was like a Grant Wood painting but more depressing. "This place is dying a slow and painful death." Embarrassing to bring Thom around here, given that he was used to the best the world's cities had to offer.

"It's quaint. Main Street Americana."

Yeah, sure. On anyone else, the excess generosity would've seemed condescending, but Thom wasn't like that. He always tried to be kind and never acted snarky to her. "I guess having grown up here, I'm less inclined to embellish the decline with a rosy glow." She got out of the car, a warm breeze blowing smells of earth and minerals from the creek. The funky odor of nearby freshwater stirred up creative longings in her heart and set her mood straight. She'd had special times down by that creek, and Thom might appreciate a tour.

"Why did you stay, especially since you aren't close with your family?" As they crossed the lot and approached the front door, Thom laid his palm on Megan's lower back and led her to the entrance.

His protective touch sent a tingle up her spine. Though she'd been with a lot of men, she'd never quite felt claimed. Megan was everyone's temporary lover, and she was sorta okay with that usually. The subtle touch of possessiveness was refreshing though, with a startling resonance that she couldn't deny. "When I was applying for colleges, getting out never occurred to me. I didn't know anyone who had moved away. My parents and teachers were all born and raised here. By the time I was thinking about grad school, the townie persona was part of my identity. I was a regular on the local bar circuit and at the tattoo parlors, which was where I'd met most of my friends. Then I finished grad school and got offered the job at Stillwater. It was always easy to stay, and the inertia got stronger with each passing year. Life never asked much more of me than the path of least resistance, and I didn't expect it."

He held the door for her, making her feel cherished and special as she waltzed into the low-lit dining room with its dark wood and crackling fireplace. Classical music played at a quiet volume over the speakers, and the place was deserted save for a gray-haired couple and one young family.

Megan worried about the state of Vincent's. She'd hate to see the classic bastion of New Denmark fanciness go under. She'd come here for senior prom like everyone else and felt like an absolute queen in her mall dress and wilted wrist corsage. Even her hopelessly tarnished reputation hadn't managed to ruin that special teenage night.

A plain, pleasant hostess in a silk blouse led them to their booth. She did a double take at Thom but didn't say anything, which was a relief. Megan could do without the reminders that her date was important, an icon, and glaringly out of place in the flyover dead zone that she called home.

Thom sat and thanked the hostess for his menu before returning his focus to Megan. "You've certainly felt wanderlust though, right? We met in St. Louis and then again in Chicago. I take it you like to travel."

She glanced at her menu and landed on the salmon, one of Vincent's specialties. "I do. That's true. When I got into going to concerts, it felt like a happy medium in a way. Escape to somewhere exciting, party for the weekend and meet cool people, and come back on Monday to where it's safe."

"Safe, but maybe not fulfilling?" He took a drink of water, holding her in a gentle stare.

"Why do I get the sense that you're leading up to what you really want to say or ask?" She pretended to be irritated but was intensely flattered. She'd never really been pursued for more than a fling, but by the way Thom was asking repeated questions about her life and interests, she could tell he was working for her approval.

Her friends had always told her that she was too easy. Men liked a challenge, and she'd never bothered to offer one. With Thom, though, she didn't have to play those tedious hard-to-get games, hold back, or pretend that she didn't like sex as much as the guys. He wanted her for who she was, and this was practically revolutionary.

"If you stick with me, we can travel as much as you want. Live wherever you want." He bumped up one shoulder in a nonchalant shrug. "You can work or not work. Your choice. That's all I'm saying. Take it for what it's worth."

Megan honestly didn't know how to process such a novel proposition or how seriously to entertain Thom's offer. Fortunately, the waitress was now standing by the table, a convenient deflection in a men's necktie and black apron. "We'll see." Megan looked at the server, a wholesome blonde in her twenties who wore a cross around her neck. "I'll have the salmon, please."

"Good choice. For you, sir?"

"I'll go with the filet. Rare. Bottle of wine sound good?" he asked Megan.

"Definitely." A couple of drinks might take the edge off her latent anxieties about relationship status issues. She'd almost rather obsess over witchcraft. Almost.

The waitress collected the menus, narrowing her eyes at Thom. "Why do you look familiar?"

"I'm not sure." He flashed her a charming, bad boy smile that changed her expression from puzzled to melting. She sauntered off.

Megan swatted his forearm. "Don't tell me that you screwed our nice Catholic waitress."

He studied the server from across the room. "I don't believe so. She would have remembered." Thom lobbed Megan a teasing look.

She rolled her eyes. She was *not* getting jealous, and besides he was clearly kidding. "Where are you headed next? How much longer is the tour?"

"Two more cities and then it's over, thank goodness. Three months off before Brian drags us back out on the road. I'm ready for a break. Thinking of spending it in Hawaii at my beach house. I'd love for you to join me. There's this road that winds all around the island with breathtaking views of the hills and ocean. We could ride a couple of my motorcycles or get out the convertible and drive as fast as we want. How does that sound?"

Divine. Exquisite. Like a fairytale dream. Too good to be true. "Bright and sunny. I'm a natural redhead. I fry in the sun."

"That's why God invented SPF 50, my dear. Don't worry. I'll rub it all over every inch of that creamy skin of yours. And you don't have to remind me that your red hair is natural."

The waitress arrived with the wine, having caught Thom's innuendo judging by the pink on her round cheeks. She poured a small measure of wine into Thom's glass, and he nodded in approval, prompting her to fill both glasses.

"I'll have to see how the *Bump in the Night* shoot schedule looks." Megan lifted her glass to his, and they clinked. "I could do the editing and postproduction stuff anywhere, though, as long as I have my laptop and Wi-Fi."

"Cheers to that." He took a sip. "How long have you known you wanted to go into television?"

A drink of wine flooded her taste buds with rich, refined flavors of wood and dark fruit, relaxing her in the process. "It's been a relatively new development. My first goal was to be an author. I published a few short pieces in literary magazines while I was in college, but that didn't really take off. My job during those years was as a deejay at the college radio station. I got really into curating playlists and building song selections around concepts or themes. The creativity of that work inspired me to seek out more opportunities in media production."

Chasing bands around to have sex with them also started up during the college radio years. She began with the midlevel acts that played at bars or the student union, graduating to anyone who toured out of state, then moving up the ladder to groups who had real record deals before striking gold with Fyre-caliber targets. The groupies she'd hung out with back then were cool as shit too. One was now a roller derby micro-celebrity. Too bad that a couple of the girls were already dead from drugs and other ravages of hard living.

Megan left the seedy parts out. She was invested in presenting herself as a serious person.

"It was obvious from the moment I met you that you harbored this thoughtful, intense passion for music. Your appreciation shines through you in a glow."

That's a creative way to say that I took a facial in a bathroom for our first date. He was right though—good music spoke to her soul. So what if it had been a part of her sex life too? She didn't need to downplay her intelligence just because she was horny and looked hot in slutty clothes. A woman could contain multitudes. "For sure. It got to a point where I wanted to create a product of my own in a capacity that was more involved than the deejay gig. I went to grad school for English and grew to love teaching, but it wasn't more than a route to pay the bills. I've always been drawn to the paranormal since, well, you know my history. Ghost hunting became an outlet to constructively channel my curiosity. I loved all the gear and gadgets, since I'm kind of a low-key technology buff. Once we started taking footage to turn our location visits into television content, I was like, this is it. I've found my calling."

He smiled at her so genuinely that she could feel the warmth. He'd never looked more handsome. "That's wonderful. It's rare that a person can say that. I want you to know that I'm here to support you in any way I can. I don't want to put pressure on you or make you feel smothered, but please know that you have an advocate. I'm rooting for you."

For someone who'd long been resigned to hacking the world alone, that was a lot to hear. Megan's throat swelled. A stinging bolt shot up her nose. She waved a hand in front of her face in an effort to brush aside the rising swell of emotion. "Thank you. That means a lot."

The waitress returned and laid down their plates. "I know where I recognize you from," she exclaimed, pointing at Thom.

He cast the server a dose of bombastic side eye. "Do tell."

"You hosted *Rock of Love* on VH1."

"That wasn't me." Thom shook his head.

The waitress tacked her hands on her hips. "Pretty sure it was."

His smile sharpened. Utter mortification teemed behind his eyes. "I'm positive you have me confused with someone else. Someone who looks nothing like me, sounds completely distinct, and has an entirely different musical style."

"Yeah, sure, whatever you say, *Bret*." The waitress did a cheesy, theatrical wink. "Your secret's safe. I won't tell anyone you're here." The waitress walked off humming Poison's "Talk Dirty to Me."

Thom propped his elbows on the table, planted his face in his hands, and groaned. "Excuse me while I die of embarrassment in front of a woman I'm trying to impress."

Megan burst out laughing. "Hey, it's cool. Poison's a fun band and still relevant-ish."

"Stop," he moaned, still face-planted. "It's okay. My ego needed a swift kick in the bollocks."

It was all good. And funny. Thom was cute when he was humbled. "Hey." Megan pulled on his wrist until he uncovered his face to reveal a good-natured grin. The guy was able to laugh at himself. That was cool. "Chin up, that's the spirit. Now let's eat and get out of here. There's a place I want to show you."

THIRTEEN

THE DIRT PATH WOUND THROUGH THE SAME SCRUFFY WOODLAND THAT it always had, curving around the fat tree with the creepy gravestone at the base before twisting downward past the fire pit clearing where Megan and her old crew used to smoke pot. Two pudgy mallards, one male and one female, waddled out of the way. "Watch out for duck poop," Megan told Thom, who wove the trail beside her.

"I can't even remember the last time I walked through nature." He grazed his fingertips across the budding leaves of a tree. "How sad is that?"

"It's a stretch to call this area nature, but it used to be my favorite place in town."

"Why's that?" He caught her hand and interlaced their fingers.

"We're almost there. But the gist is that I'd come here in high school. It was my special spot. There was the typical getting into trouble that happened, but eventually my best friend and I kind of claimed it. We'd hide away where I'm about to show you and just talk for hours about whatever came to mind. We'd read each other our poetry and short stories. Stuff like that."

"That's really touching." Thom stepped over a rock and a crushed Pepsi can. "What was your friend's name?"

"Jessica. We'd hang out here every day. We still talk sometimes." They'd grown apart but still got along. Megan had gone to Jessica's baby shower a few months ago. They exchanged the occasional social media message.

She took them to the edge of the bank. The water was low, depleted in light of stingy rainfall, but low water was preferable in getting where they were going. Megan hiked up to the concrete drum of a storm drain and ducked inside, shrouded instantly in darkness, memories, and a sense of safety that was nearly religious in its sanctity. The inside of the tunnel was cool, dark, and a little funky with creek smells. Perfect. Songs from decades past played in her mind, and she could practically taste the cinnamon sugar lip gloss that she used to wear.

She sat on a dry part and watched the water pass by beyond the opening. More of her mind cleared with every lick that glossed the rocks and drooping branches. The stream babbled its one lone song.

Thom joined her, and his hip pressed against hers once he got situated. They sat in silence for a few moments. He traced the veins on the top of her hand with his index finger. "Do you remember any of the poetry and stories that you wrote?"

Yeah. She did. Cringe alert. "No. They all sucked."

"I'm sure they didn't."

"They did. Cheesy high school stuff about first loves and all."

"Who was your first love?"

Now there was a can of worms she didn't care to open. "Just some dorky teenager," she lied.

"Same here." Thom kissed her cheek. "Her name was Melanie. She dumped me after a week."

"Ouch, harsh. Well, you went on to do pretty well for yourself in the women department."

"I suppose." He played with a stick. "In retrospect, I wish I'd focused on quality over quantity. I missed out on a lot, living fast and burning through lovers like I have. And then you wake up one day and the people you used to run around with are all married with kids. It's lonely being leftover in that way."

She studied his profile, the angled slope of his jaw and the crow's feet around his eyes painting a portrait of a rugged life and a good heart.

Thom was a sensitive guy when he let his guard down. "Why did you go the freewheeling bachelor route?"

"I'm not sure sometimes. I suppose all that attention is addictive. There's a high that comes with landing a new partner. I never got all that into drugs or drinking. Women were my vice. Sex. I told myself that I was living my best life and having fun, but it was an empty kind of fun. I was too lazy to say no or examine why I was making the choices that I was, and at a certain point, I was just letting things happen *to* me instead of steering the course of my life onto a different track. Getting laid repeatedly is no substitute for building a lasting connection with a person." He tucked a strand of her hair behind her ear, allowing his fingertips to track lazily down the curve of her neck. "Pathetic that it's taken me until now to figure this out."

"Have you ever been in love?"

"Yes. A couple of times. I thought it was love, at least, but eventually the relationships burned out and died. Maybe that's when I gave up and assumed I wasn't meant for long-term romance. Easier to keep things casual. Of course, easy and casual doesn't implicitly mean healthy and good."

Without warning, the presence of another body ambled into Megan's field of vision. The pretty brunette wore a denim jacket and carried a few extra pounds. A second later, recognition set in. "Jessica. Hey." It wasn't all that shocking to run into Jessica at the storm drain. Megan's high school best friend had talked at the baby shower about how she still came to the spot they used to refer to as their philosopher's stone.

Jessica's eyes were bloodshot and damp. She sniffled and wiped her hand on her jeans. "Hey, Megan and Megan's friend. I'm sorry to interrupt."

Megan jumped up to hug Jessica, who returned the embrace like she needed it badly. "What's wrong?"

Jessica's chin wobbled. "There was an accident over the weekend," she eked out, her voice squeaky and shaking. "Mr. Tremble was killed in a car crash. His Honda went off a bridge and exploded. He was burned alive."

Vertigo sucked Megan's perception in and out. A mix of feelings overcame her hard and fast, shock and grief chased by a perverse sense of satisfaction that brought her great shame. "Oh my God. That's awful. You must be devastated."

Jessica nodded. "He was the best teacher I ever had. If it wasn't for that recommendation letter he wrote me, I would have never gotten into college. Not with my shit grades." Jessica whimpered. "I don't want to run you guys off. I can go to the dock." She pulled a note from her pocket and burst into a fresh round of tears. "I wrote him a letter too. To thank him for all that he did to ensure that my future was bright. I reached my potential because of him."

Megan hugged Jessica again even as a repulsive tide of bitterness flooded her. Mr. Tremble had declined to write Megan a recommendation letter for the Iowa Writers' Workshop, despite the fact that she'd made straight A's from his ninth grade English class onward and graduated Moore High with highest distinction. A letter from him would've gotten her into that prestigious program, the same one where Kurt Vonnegut had taught, and changed the course of her life forever. By senior year, he hadn't wanted to be associated with her anymore in any capacity.

"No, please," Thom interjected. "You stay, Jessica. We'll give you some privacy."

"No, no." Jessica pressed her note to her chest. "I actually want to go to the dock to read this. His funeral is tomorrow. You should come. I know that he was important to you too." Jessica hustled off, choking back sobs.

Jessica was one of the three people whom Megan had told what had happened the summer she turned thirteen. A mean girl named Bianca had overheard Megan's confession in the locker room and spread the news around school, making it her mission to smear Megan's name.

Megan had worn her scarlet letter like a badge of honor though, her first act of turning the whore tables in her favor. All had been well until Mr. Tremble decided to distance himself from the baby harlot whose irresistible, Lolita-like allure had made him the hottest piece of gossip on the rumor mill and caught the attention of the principal.

"Are you okay?" Thom stroked Megan's arm. "I'm sorry for your loss."

There were times when memories of the Tremble affair filled Megan with an unbearable rage that consumed her with hatred for all men everywhere. If she'd gotten to keep her virginity for a couple more years and lose it in a normal, healthy way, maybe she would have turned out better. By now, she was mostly healed enough to not place blame where it didn't belong, but she did have her low moments. "I'm fine." She made eye contact with Thom. None of the mess of her past was his fault. "That was shocking, but I'm okay."

He touched her face before pursing his lips. "Did something happen? It just struck me that when she was telling you the story of the teacher who died, you clammed up. It was almost as if you were conflicted."

Thom was certainly perceptive. She sat back down in the drain, having not yet having fully processed the ramifications of Elijah Tremble violently exiting the land of the living in a fiery crash. Megan patted the spot next to her. Once Thom had reassumed his place, she said, "Want to hear the story?"

"Of course. But only if you want to tell it."

"I started high school when I was twelve. Skipped two grades because I was bored, unchallenged, and acting out as a result. I was thrilled to be there, learning with teenagers. I felt mature and fancy, and like I was finally blazing my own path after growing up with a bunch of siblings and struggling to get anyone to pay attention to me. Mr. Tremble was my ninth grade English teacher. He praised me, told me that I had the most brilliant mind of any student he'd ever taught and that I'd surely go on to write the next great American novel. I basked in his glow. Hung on to his every word. At first, I started staying late after class. Then meeting in his office after school." She swallowed hard. The air felt a little colder, the rush of the creek water harsher and meaner. She hadn't remembered the sky being this dull when they'd walked down the trail. "He'd bring me these chocolates from Europe. Said it was our secret. One day he poured me a half-glass of champagne to go with them. Next, he told me about an elite summer school that he said I would be perfect for. That ended up being just me and him at his house. He kissed me on the second day and then bam, I wasn't a virgin anymore."

"Megan," Thom whispered, his fists clenched at his sides, "I am profoundly sorry for what that bastard did to you."

She flashed both palms in the air. Phantom pain snaked through the deepest recesses of her abdomen. "Don't you dare pity me. I am *not* a victim. It wasn't rape."

She'd been precocious and mature for her age. Everyone had agreed. Besides, she'd been in love with Mr. Tremble and consented to what they did, even though she hadn't been sure exactly what she was consenting to and had gotten scared when it started and tried to stop it. Still, it wasn't like he'd jumped her in an alley. She'd wanted it. He'd been gentle. Mostly. At first.

"I don't even know what to say," Thom croaked, his gaze hard and glaring over the water. "I'd love to beat him to death, except that he's already dead."

The gallows humor startled a laugh out of her. "I'm fine. I promise. I learned to take control of my sexuality as a way of reclaiming my body for myself. It was actually empowering in the end." She supposed that her attraction to older men fit into the puzzle that her past had built, but Thom didn't need to hear any musings on her daddy issues. None of Megan's experiences, nor the ensuing damage, belonged at his feet.

"As long as you accept that none of what happened to you was your fault."

"Eh." She kicked debris out of her path. "I led him on. I was seductive. You know me."

"You were a child. He was an adult who should have known better. He should have looked out for you and protected you, not taken advantage."

It was hard, after years of being put into a box that others had made for her, to view the Tremble situation from a different perspective. A perspective where he was a predator and she was his prey. Megan was never a good enough girl to be taken seriously as an innocent victim. She'd had her first drink of beer at age nine and sucked a hit off a skunky joint at ten. She'd been caught and punished both times. Everyone knew what she was all about.

Trouble kept right on following her. Eleven was around the time when she started getting a lot of male attention. Her parents imposed a strict ban on the short skirts and halter tops that she favored. Unfair because Iowa was hot as hell in the summer and her brothers were of course allowed to run around shirtless in swim trunks. When a wardrobe change didn't stop the catcalls, they ordered her to keep her eyes on the ground and quit smiling so damn much. "Sure. But it doesn't do any good to mope and feel sorry for myself over events I can't change. I knew where things were headed when he started paying special attention to me. I was smart enough to figure out what the champagne and chocolate meant. I loved feeling mature. I flirted with him."

"Even if you did, it was his responsibility to put the brakes on."

She pulled her knees into her chest. In retrospect, the memories made her sick when she thought of them in a new light. "I'd get mad. It was like the door to my childhood closed that summer. My friends were still playing with Barbies, and I was like, well, I'm a woman now, I guess I'd better play the part. I was stuck with the reputation either way."

"I wish that you would have had more and better advocates to help you process your feelings and get you justice. Where were your parents?"

"Distracted with my brothers and their own stuff. Oblivious, as usual. I think they were just happy I wasn't getting in trouble like I was in the years prior. To be fair, they didn't know what was going on." A more critical read might deduce that Mitch and Jan ought to have noticed that Megan had changed, but they instead chose to remain willfully ignorant because she wasn't causing problems anymore. Megan wasn't interested in dredging up resentment. Her parents had done their best.

"What do you need from me?"

"Just be here. Just listen."

He put his arm around her.

A radical thought flashed in Megan's mind, bold and scandalous. "Take me with you."

He brightened. "To Hawaii?"

"Yes. But before that. I want to leave this town. New Denmark drags me down, and I'm over it. It's time to get a fresh start. Can I pack up my things and leave here with you after this funeral?" Maybe the whole place was cursed and that was why her book had gone haywire. For all she knew, a change of venue would be just the ticket to shake up the mojo and clear out all the bad vibe cobwebs that had her alternately stumbling into nightmare dimensions, reliving her personal hell with Tremble, or slipping into maudlin musings on how her life path had been on autopilot for the past twenty years. As a bonus, she'd get to be with Thom and try his world on for size.

"Absolutely. I'd love that. A few more cities, then we jet to the island and start over together. Perfect." He cleared his throat. "You're positive you want to go to the funeral tomorrow?"

"I am. It'll be closure. My last act before I put this place in my rearview mirror." She'd write a letter and read it to Tremble's casket. Say all the things that she hadn't known how to express back then or was too afraid or ashamed to make sense of. Unburdened by catharsis, she'd finally be free. Megan let go of a protracted exhale that lightened her load by a million pounds. She smiled at Thom. "That's enough of my trauma. Let's talk about you."

He held her gently, but with the fullness of his strength. "Ask me anything."

"What was your family like?"

"Small. Just me, my mum, and my dad. We were a typical middle-class family. They were both professors and valued education highly, which was how I ended up at the school where I met everyone who would become Fyre. Mum and Dad's vision for my future never ended up aligning with mine, but they made peace with my choices. I'd love for you to meet them. Ever been to London?"

"No. I've never been out of the United States." Ugh. Her world was small and constrained. "They wouldn't have a problem with my tattoos?"

"You kidding? They'll be thrilled that I finally settled down."

A fuzzy feeling took hold. She forced herself not to act too giddy or eager. "Slow down there, turbo. I don't recall us discussing exclusivity."

"Well," he drawled, tilting his head, "we're discussing it now."

She kicked his boot-clad foot. "You seriously think I'd want to be with anyone else when I have you?"

"I never want to presume. I'm not as egotistical as my reputation would have you believe."

"That's clear. I feel privileged to have access to that special side that not many get to see."

He raised a single eyebrow. "I can't tell if that's a backhanded compliment or not."

She dropped a kiss to his cheek. Megan's world might be messy, but if

Thom wanted to be a part of it, she'd welcome him with open arms. "Good. That keeps you on your toes."

"I feel cheap and empty-handed. I wish that I had jewelry or some other gift to give you."

Megan's predilections for snark, deflection, and the emotional armor of sarcasm left her body. She relinquished her defenses in the harbor of his aura. "You've already given me a lot. You've given me everything." She hugged him with all her might. "Thank you for your support today."

"You'll always have it as long as you'll have me. Now and always."

"Want to head back to my apartment and watch a movie?" The night was wearing on, and the trek up the hill got a bit more arduous after sundown.

Decompression was in order. Megan had the funeral to prepare for and the *Bump in the Night* crew to touch base with before it was time to pull up the stakes and leave New Denmark in the dust. Spending a night in close proximity of her witch book wasn't ideal, but with Thom by her side, she'd be brave enough to face the supernatural drama that swirled at the center of her life.

FOURTEEN

MEGAN HAD SPENT PLENTY OF TIME ON HER KNEES—NOT ALWAYS A comfortable pose, but at least the Catholics offered padding. She might look into investing in a pew for sexytimes.

The blasphemous thought made her snicker. She rose to stand when everyone returned from taking communion.

While a young, Black priest said the concluding prayer for Elijah Tremble, she took a moment to admire the classical beauty of the wonderfully gothic St. Peter's Church.

The building where she'd spent Sundays as a child boasted an aesthetic that couldn't be beat. Vaulted ceilings arched high, drawing the eye to panels of stained glass that shone in saturated primary colors illuminated by the midday sun. Rows of candles flickered delicate flames, and smoky sweet incense perfumed the air to create a multilayered spiritual atmosphere.

The looming crucifix heading up the gilded altar didn't necessarily make her feel closer to God, but the holy place of her childhood certainly had a calming effect. Even the ever-present church soundtrack of babies fussing put her at ease. With Mr. Tremble at rest, she could be at peace. She didn't need to worry about that sick, broken man anymore, and she certainly didn't need to blame herself. He was in...wherever he was, and she was moving on with her life.

Megan took Thom's hand. The all-black dress clothes he'd bought at the last minute looked criminally cool on him, but more importantly, he'd once again demonstrated his devotion.

The priest walked off. Megan whispered, "Thank you for coming with me."

"Anything you need." He squeezed her hand. "Anytime."

Thom's support was invaluable. Megan had spotted a dozen people she knew at the service, and she bet that her semi-estranged parents were in attendance. They never missed a regular Mass when she was growing up and had worshipped Mr. Tremble to an idolatrous extent. She'd never had the heart to confess to them what he did.

Once the organ music rang out to mark the end of the service, she ducked out of her pew, genuflected, and made the sign of the cross. Megan was lapsed as hell—and, yes, a witch—but the ceremonial aspect of her former religion still lived in her as a special thing. She and Thom walked to the marble font of holy water. "I didn't even break a sweat." She winked, dipping her fingers in cool water before making the sign of the cross again on her forehead, chest, and shoulders.

He put his fist to his mouth and chuckled, clearly having gotten her joking reference to the "whore in church" expression. "Me neither. Maybe there's hope for us super-sinners yet."

The steady stream of bodies moving to the exit had provided enough cover that Megan hadn't noticed anyone in particular leaving, but when she moved to give clearance to a pregnant woman, she came face-to-face with her parents.

Years had passed since they'd last spoken. Her mom and dad had eventually surrendered their fantasy of the daughter they'd wanted and lost interest in the one they had. She'd grown tired of calling home only to be met with blah, monosyllabic answers to her questions and zero interest in her life. Yet there they stood, somber and unflinching. Her dad looked grayer and more tired than usual: a tall, stern, washed-out portrait of aging Midwestern masculinity. She swore that her once-statuesque mom had shrunk a few inches, her matronly dress swallowing her in dark polyester.

Apparently, it was up to Megan to make the first move. "Hi, Mom. Hi, Dad. It's nice to see you again. This is Thom."

"Pleasure to meet you both." Thom stuck out his hand.

"Hello," her mother said limply, offering a weak shake.

Her dad barked an indeterminate greeting and shook hands roughly with Thom.

"Are you okay, sweetie?" her mom asked in a leading, pained way.

Megan wasn't quite sure what was being discussed but sensed the vicinity. She suspected that her parents...knew, but the Tremble incident was one of those subjects that was destined to hide in darkness, never to be addressed head-on and taken with everyone into their coffins. "I'm fine. Good. Better than good."

Her dad scoffed. "You could have at least covered those up." He waved his hand in her general direction. "Shown respect for once."

She'd worn a chic, calf-length black dress with three-quarter sleeves and a scoop neck. Why bother to hide who she was anymore? Anyone who judged her would do so regardless of whether her body art was visible.

Megan sighed. Her dad was as retrograde and tiresome as ever, arrested in a bygone era that he wasn't able to relinquish. "There are other people with tattoos in this church, Dad. They're actually pretty mainstream now." She discreetly bent her head in the direction of a passerby with scripture stamped on one of his wrists.

"Those things are the purview of criminals and degenerates."

Megan excavated some of her dad's hypocrisy from the vault. "I didn't hear you complaining when you hired that tattooed college student to work on your website for bottom-dollar wages."

"I expected more of you," Mitch scoffed. "That was my first mistake."

"Mitchell," her mom hissed, "remember what Christ said in the Sermon on the Mount. Remove the plank from your own eye before pointing out the splinter in your brother's."

Megan's dad shook his head and stomped out of the church, hastily crossing himself with holy water on the way.

"I'm sorry about him." Megan's mom wrung her hands. "It's been a stressful few days, with the accident and all. We just saw Mr. Tremble four days ago, at a fundraiser luncheon."

Megan's oldest brother sidled into the mix, a husky, blond former quarterback who walked with a swagger like he owned the world. "Hey, Megan. I'm shocked you didn't burst into flames the second you stepped inside."

"You ever fess up to when you stole that stop sign in high school, Teddy? Or how about when you got suspended for drinking in the parking lot? I'm sure one of the priests will still hear your confession." Megan and Teddy had never been that close, but over the years, their barbed albeit fun banter had degenerated into acrimonious potshots.

"Theodore, quit tormenting your sister," her mom snapped. "Go check on your father. He's upset."

Teddy obeyed, forever the golden son who had trod the life path set by his parents' expectations.

"Thom." Mom's gaze drifted to the church vestibule where Teddy had joined Mitch, her attention only half-focused on the person to whom she spoke. "What do you do?"

"I'm a musician."

"Ah." Mom parted her lips and furrowed her brow. "Classical?"

"Um, no." He scratched the back of his neck. "Rock music. You ever hear of Chariotz of Fyre?"

She shook her head, cringing. "I'm not up on trends. I don't watch My Tube or Trick Talk or any of the rest. I don't follow what the young people are listening to. I do know that Justice Beaver got famous from the World Wide Web. Do you know him?"

"Yeah. We've met. He's really nice. My band has been around for decades, actually. We've outlasted trendiness, if I do say so myself. We're on the radio a lot."

"That's nice. I do enjoy my Christian radio station. You're from England?"

"Yes, ma'am."

"What are you doing in Iowa?"

"I came here to visit your daughter. We went to Vincent's last night and took a walk down by the creek. Your town is lovely. Megan made me feel right at home."

"This is serious." She didn't sound upset, but she didn't sound pleased either. Baffled was more like it, unsure how to process the presence of a man who made no sense to her and for whom she lacked any frame of reference.

Thom hadn't grown up in New Denmark and wasn't a farmer, teacher, banker, or police officer. He didn't attend St. Peter's. Therefore, he didn't compute.

"This is serious." He glanced appreciatively at Megan and reclaimed their handclasp. She smiled up at him even though the situation was super awkward.

"This is serious," Megan echoed, never happier to repeat a single statement.

"Well, I suppose congratulations are in order." Mom's lips thinned. "Excuse me. I'm going to go check on your father and brother." She shuffled off, playing with a wadded tissue that she must've pulled out of her sleeve.

"That went well." Though he spoke in a jocular tone, she caught the undercurrent of disappointment.

Megan led them through the first set of doors. "I'm sorry that was weird. We haven't spoken in a long time. I don't think she really knew what to do."

"Don't apologize. You were gracious and lovely. Are we headed to the burial now?"

Megan laid her hand on her purse, where she'd tucked her goodbye note to Tremble and packed her watch in case it miraculously sprang back to life. "Yeah. Then we're done. We can go to my apartment right after and I'll grab some things."

They marched down the stone steps in tandem, the day ripe and fragrant with lingering notes of a morning rain, and met Megan's dad on the sidewalk. Other parishioners socialized in the vicinity, chatting with each other or the two priests. Now would be a good time to mend fences with her dad, since she was going away for good. She could see how the first sight of her tattoos would be shocking, but he'd have to get used to them. Her body was her own to decorate as she pleased.

Megan's dad turned his back on the elderly man he was talking to and quick-stepped to the church parking lot. What was his problem? Did he hate her style that much?

"Dad, wait," Megan called, race-walking to catch up. Her dad had reached his Chevrolet Impala before she closed the distance. "I regret that I didn't call or stop by more. I felt like I tried, but I should have tried harder to honor you." With any luck, using the biblical language that he preferred would dent his wall. Their relationship may have been strained, but she'd hate to leave on such unfortunate terms.

Dad whipped around, his face contorted in anger. He glowered at Megan until she felt small and humiliated. "Honor me? *Honor* me? Are you out of your mind? You have some nerve turning up here, with your painted face and your disgusting tongue rings. That's right. I see all of that metal in your mouth. I know what you're all about."

Forget reconciliation. "What is that supposed to mean?"

"You know exactly what it means. A man is dead, Megan. A pillar of the community, ripped away from us by tragedy. Is this a joke to you? Did you come here to make fun of him? First you try to ruin his life with your lies, and now you set out to besmirch his memory? What won't you do for attention, Megan Marie?"

Her legs went to lead. Bile shot up her throat. A bolt of searing fire slashed through her body. She tried to speak, but no words came.

Dad's eyes were as small and dark as two lumps of coal. He curled his upper lip. "That's right, stand there and gape like the idiot you are. I should have applied a firmer hand with you and ignored those hippies who said that corporal punishment was wrong. If I'd have brought you up right, maybe then you would have developed some class and grace. You've never done one single thing to make me proud."

"Pride is a sin," she bit out.

Thom caught up. Megan's mom trotted in tow, out of breath. Teddy waited in the wings.

"Don't speak to me ever again, you foolish, wasted, worthless girl." Dad threw his hands in the air, his car keys jingling in his white-knuckle grip. "Look at you, just look at you. You're ruined. Your arms. Your *neck*. You're thirty-six, unwed, and all used up. You lost your job because, yet again, you couldn't keep your legs together. I know. Everyone knows.

You'll never have children. You think this man wants to marry you?" He laughed bitterly and pointed at Thom.

"I'd love to marry Megan, if she'll have me," Thom said, laying a protective hand on her lower back. "And you need to calm down, sir."

Jan rushed to her husband, tugging at his raised arm until he lowered it and braced his hand on the car door. "Please excuse us. This has been tough on our family."

The gaggle of people loitering outside the church had migrated closer to the parking lot, everyone either staring or pretending not to stare. The young priest who'd preached at Mass inched forward, pressing a huge book to his chest. Great. Was he going to give Megan a giant Bible and direct her to the applicable passages to study being less of a complete fuckup? Was literally everything her fault today?

Fuck it. She was already a black sheep and straight-up pariah. The priest was probably coming over to excommunicate her for good. She might as well unload her secret and enjoy a bit of catharsis before taking permanent leave from this shithole town. "Elijah Tremble raped me," Megan shouted at the top of her lungs. "That's right. When I was thirteen. He isn't just a rapist, he's a child rapist and a pedophile. He didn't deserve that beautiful funeral. I hope that he's burning in hell."

Megan's mom burst into tears. "Someone make this stop happening."

"Unbelievable," Mitch barked. "Unreal. Where did I go wrong?" He opened the passenger door, shoved Jan inside, and cranked the engine before tearing off in a squeal of tires.

Thom swept Megan into his arms. "Let's go," he whispered. "Let's leave right now."

Drained from her unburdening, she slackened against him. "I need to read that letter."

"Excuse me," the priest said in a timid voice. "Megan O'Neil?"

Good grief. She had to deal with this. She pressed her hands into Thom's chest to gently break their embrace. "It's fine. One second." She walked over a few feet to where the priest stood.

He shifted on his feet and thrust the book at her. The rosary resting against his waist swished from the movement, knocking into his white robe. His bald head gleamed in the sun. "A parishioner found this in your pew seat."

She shook her head. "I didn't bring a Bible into church."

"It's not a Bible. And it has your name in it." The priest opened the book's thick cover and pointed at the inner flap where Megan's name was written in sharp, jagged, red cursive.

She didn't feel sick until she spotted the symbol for fire. Next, she recognized the text, the signature, pulpy pages, and finally the coven daughters symbol. The witch book had followed her. There was no fleeing her curse. She accepted the wicked tome from the priest's hands. It wasn't his responsibility, it was hers. "Thank you." She forced the perfunctory pleasantry out of her mouth.

The priest's features stitched into empathy. "Do you want to come inside and talk? It doesn't have to be a formal confession, but you do seem upset. Perhaps I can help."

The well-meaning clergyman wouldn't have the faintest idea of where to begin. What was he going to do, perform an ad-hoc exorcism? "No, thank you. I'm okay."

"Are you sure?"

No. "Yes."

He tipped his chin in a curt nod that sealed off their exchange. "God bless."

"You too."

"Burn it," the voice of Folly whispered. "Until it smolders."

"Shut up," Megan gritted out through clenched teeth. She walked back to Thom, the dumb fucking book as heavy as a millstone. "I'm not burning anything. And fuck you for writing my name in this and dumping it in my lap when I'm trying to process my own issues."

"You curse your magical birthright with such cavalier glibness. Your father is right about you. No respect, no character, no reverence, no values."

"You're one to talk. What do you value? Illuminate me, oh great one."

A sinister laugh flowed from the innards of the book to Megan's ears. She stumbled over a crack in the sidewalk, woozy and lightheaded. For an instant, she couldn't see anything, and then her world went white before coming back distorted and out of focus.

She lost a firm sense of time and space. Thom stood a football field's length away from her, even though moments ago he'd only been a few paces down the sidewalk. Everyone around her was blurry and frozen. The parking lot was five times its normal size, while the church was no larger than a toolshed.

Folly said, "I value the minds of the precious coven daughters when they surrender to me as my toys. I value the role that each witch plays in bringing the hologram prophecy to fruition. I value your ability to put your magic into others, like you've been doing with your hapless musician. Soon he'll be pliable and mushy enough for me to pilot. Now before you help me crack him open and suck out the song I need, we're going to have some fun. Burn it."

Dense fog surrounded Megan in every direction. The urge to sleep pulled on her eyelids, clouded her perception, and slowed her reactions to a crawl. She stumbled through endless mist. "Burn what?"

The clouds parted in a seamless split down the middle, leaving St. Peter's presented before her. "Use your powers of intention to engulf the structure from top to bottom." Folly giggled. "Come on, it'll be a hoot. Do it. The spell you need is right in front of your face."

Megan looked at her hands, where the book had cleaved on its own. Words floated right off the page and burrowed into the spot between her eyes, probing her with intense pressure that threatened to smash her skull into pieces. She yelled out in pain, but the attempt stuck in her throat.

"Folly into skull," the malevolent spirit crooned. "Possession complete. I am your mind now. For your initiation rite as my puppet, you will burn it. Come on, live a little. Give these backward heretics a real show. You'll be a legend. A real witch. Burn it."

Megan dropped her book to the ground. Curls of white mist coiled around the pages before slinking up to shackle her ankles. She smashed her fingertips into her temples, riding throbs of suffocating agony as she battled to retain the last vestiges of self-ownership. "I know who I am," Megan cried out, her forcefulness breaking the worst of the hold inside her head. "Possession not complete. Get out of my mind. And I am not burning down a church. That is ridiculously cliché and on the nose. I'm embarrassed for you. Get out. Get out. Get out!"

The spell snapped like a rubber band, hard and sharp, and Megan found herself writhing on the ground. A circle of fretful faces gazed down at her.

"Can you talk, love? I don't think you hit your head but move slowly in case you did." Thom crouched and tried to pull her to a seat.

The instant that his grip secured around her forearms, two spears of pain stabbed through her back. Crunching, squelching, and other vicious, violent noises pummeled her eardrums.

A woman shrieked. More screams followed.

The pain wasn't stopping, but it had changed, sharp, searing punctures layered in with dull, deep cramps in her legs and tender bruising throughout her midsection. A muscle overstretched to a frightening degree of tension. Megan lurched forward and slapped her palms on the ground for stability. That's when she noticed that her fingers ended in three-inch black claws.

She staggered to her feet, sending a few gawkers scattering. "What's wrong?" She stumbled, losing her balance, which made a bearded man in Crocs howl in unbridled terror. "Why are you all freaking out?" Taking steps was a failure, each one ending in a stumble. The people around her were all short. Was everyone in New Denmark always tiny? Thom had shrunk too, looking up at her with a mix of fear and awe.

Megan was taller than everyone by a good two heads. The second she realized this, the sky sucked her upward, sending her propelling above the rooftops and grid of electrical wires before she blinked into nothing.

FIFTEEN

THOM FUMBLED IN HIS BACK POCKET UNTIL HIS FINGERS CLOSED around the hard chunk that was his phone. His mind was purple stew. Every second was an eternity. He was sunk into the moment but not present. He fumbled his phone out of his jeans, his hand shaking so badly that he dropped it on the pavement. The crack of plastic on concrete jarred loose memories of what had happened.

He stooped, snatched his mobile off the ground, and punched in 911. The world vibrated before him in meaningless color blotches. "Did anyone see where she went?" he shouted at the eight human figures still standing around near the church steps. "Which direction?"

People glanced at each other with that shell-shocked, befuddled look of the uncomfortably clueless.

He pressed the phone to his ear. The dial tone rang. He hadn't thought through a strategy. To an outside observer, his account would sound ludicrous. What was he going to say to the operator? That he'd just seen a woman morph into a demon outside of a church before being sucked up into the air? They'd either deem him a prankster and hang up or refer him to a psychiatric facility.

A heavyset white man with long hair stared at him while fidgeting with his keys. "Where who went?"

"911, what is your emergency?" the female dispatcher prompted.

"I need to report a kidnapping. Or a missing person. I'm not sure which." His thoughts stumbled round in circles. He had no cogent plan. The priest who'd led the Mass was coming toward him. He couldn't deal with all of this.

"Sir, did you see a person get kidnapped?"

"Yes...I think."

"Was the victim a child or adult? Male, female, race, identifying characteristics?"

"Adult. A woman. White, red hair, colorful tattoos all over her arms, chest, and neck. Hard to miss. She was wearing a black dress." He ached with fear and dread that the image of Megan in her stunning black dress was the last picture of her that he'd ever have. He chewed his nail.

"Can you describe the kidnapper?"

"No." Too-bright light drowned the spaces behind his eyes. The muscles in his mouth locked. He fell off a cliff. This wasn't going anywhere. Logic and everyday explanations didn't apply.

"Excuse me?"

"I didn't see anyone."

"Then how do you know she was kidnapped? Did you see a car, a license plate number? Was this woman pulled into a vehicle by an unseen assailant?"

He hung up. He was wasting time. The priest was standing in front of him, holding Megan's sinister book along with her purse. Their eyes locked in a heavy hold. They both knew that something was wrong, dead wrong, fundamentally wrong. Thom had substance to work with here. Someone who could help. The priest was near the correct wavelength.

Thom took the purse and book, the first touch of leather making his stomach lining crawl through his skin. No part of him wanted to assume possession of this cursed record. "Did you see that?" he asked the holy man, pointing at the sky. "Her metamorphosis and the force that pulled her away?"

The priest nodded somberly. "Megan's turning away from the faith is heartbreaking. I can tell she's hurting and lost. But she'll always have a home here with God. You're right to describe the lapse as a force that pulls us away. Satan's lure can be powerful when—"

"You aren't listening. I'm speaking literally. Did you see her physical body transform a few minutes ago? Did you witness her vault into the sky?"

The priest blinked. Eyes the color of oak peered at Thom with a mix of concern and fear. "I'm not sure I understand."

His phone rang, probably the emergency dispatch following up. He let it go. They called again, and he ignored the ring. The police had nothing to offer him and Megan.

Same with the parishioners, loitering and chatting like they hadn't seen a person shapeshift and otherwise defy the laws of physics. These people were clueless. Folly had gotten to them. That was her name, the spirit of the Other Place. They'd had their minds cleaned by her. Their memories wiped. They were useless. He'd have to figure out how to save Megan himself.

He clutched the book, glaring at it, his emotions punching him from every angle. "You're right. You don't understand."

"I do understand that whatever she's reading in there isn't helping her or bringing her peace. The temptations of the devil are empty and dangerous, but it's a good sign that she came to St. Peter's today. There's hope. I'll pray for Megan."

He was right, but not in the way that he thought that he was right. "Sure. Fine. Thanks."

Thoughts and prayers were nice, but someone had to take action to save Megan, and that someone was Thom.

He set the wheels in motion to get back on the tour. Brian and Helen could surely give him guidance on how to use the book to rescue Megan. On top of everything else, he had to grind through more shows and their associated obligations. Step one was to get to the airport.

Logistics tumbled over him in a blur, and he found himself in the locale of the next tour stop. Austin? Houston? Boston? Corporate arenas and hotel chains were only memorable for what they lacked.

Once inside the cavernous entertainment venue, he barged into Brian's dressing room with the book in tow, his awkward gait embarrassing him, but not enough for him to care. He was frayed and fried with no concern for decorum. The longer she was gone, the louder a dark whisper sneered that she'd never return.

Brian was lying on the floor, his eyes closed. Fyre music, *Prometheus, Avenged*, rocked the room thanks to a record turntable and Bluetooth speaker.

Brian mouthed the words while gesturing with his hands like a conductor might. In an ironic complement to his self-aggrandizing pseudo-meditation, he wore a t-shirt with a yoga symbol on the front.

Had Thom been in his right mind, he would have jumped at the opportunity to make fun of this, but he had bigger fish to fry. "Get up. It's an emergency."

Brian jerked, his eyes snapping open. He propelled to a seat. "Ever heard of knocking or boundary courtesy? You about gave me a proper cardiac arrest."

"Then lock your door. Megan is gone. She vanished. I think she was taken by this...evil that we're all apparently now battling." He thumped the book cover.

"You sure she didn't get tired of you and leave on her own accord? Typical of your ego to assume that if a woman doesn't want to see you anymore, she must've been acted upon by outside malice." Brian rose and turned down the music, a cranky look on his face. Too bad for him, but some matters were more important than his pre-show musical masturbation.

"Stop it. This is serious, and we don't have time to waste on ball-busting. She was taken. I saw it with my naked eyes. Others witnessed it as well, but their memories were erased."

The impact of Brian's full attention came in like a wrecking ball. "She was taken as in taken over by possession, or her physical body was taken by a corporeal creature?"

"Both. She grew claws and horns as if assuming a demonic form. She was too tall. Next, gravity ceased to apply. That's when this haze settled over the space. I think the mind control affected the bystanders then." Words continued to roll, falling out in a manic chain connected by invisible glue that stuck to the bones of everyone trapped in their shared matrix. "I've had visions. Fiery ones. I went to a deep, dark dimension and fought a dragon. This beast tormented me psychologically. Your name came up. Megan's rapist died in a fiery accident the same week that she vanished. Coincidence? I think not." Thom was a butterfly trapped in a spider's web. He wasn't entirely sure that he was the one thinking these thoughts, forging these ties. He was Brian in Chicago. The flaming wheel had come full circle. The pilot of the chariot had the last laugh.

"Slow down." Brian pushed a chair against the door. He turned the music up loud enough to cover their voices.

Thom couldn't bear to hear those familiar riffs and vocals. Their music was casting a spell on him. He pulled the cord of the record player out of the wall. "This isn't safe."

"I told you, I sealed the songs."

An endless loop of flame streaked round and round through Thom's lower belly. He drifted beside himself until he watched the surrounding events through glass, viewing a movie. His body was a shell, a meat suit to be worn by whomever. His nausea was unbearable, surpassing physical discomfort to become existential revulsion.

He sat on a fake leather recliner that a worker had dragged into the room. The color matched the hue of that horrible book. That had to be intentional as well, the evil monster taunting him with messages delivered in mundane symbolism.

There were a lot of wheels in the room too. The Fyre record on the turntable. An analog wall clock. Brian's golden wedding band. She'd crush them all under the flaming wheel. Brian was right. Fyre had never steered the chariot. "It's speeding up. Do you feel it? Faster and faster, burning hot. I feel it. Here." Thom laid a hand on his waistband, where a wheel had taken root and now whizzed inside of him. "Controlling us from the inside out."

Brian stalked up to Thom and yanked him to his feet. "Snap out of it. We have to keep each other solid. Do not let this control you. Do not succumb."

The spaced-out feeling collapsed in a wake of clarity. Thom shook off the dregs of that unclean film. "How do we stop this? Because whatever temporary measures you've been doing, no offense, I'm not sure that they're working."

"We won't be able to put a halt to the prophecy until we're all settled in Peru. Until then, we think in terms of stopgaps and finite fixes. We're operating from our back feet, but we don't have a choice."

"I need to transport to where Megan is and pull her out. I've been there before. I have to work from the premise that I have enough magic inside of me, magic that she transferred to me, to pull it off."

Brian looked skeptical. "We can't cast spells on our own. Helen and Eve are sure of it. We need to work in consort with a witch whom we're bonded to. If Megan is the fire witch, which sounds increasingly likely, then you need her collaboration to cast a spell."

There had to be an alternative. A solution outside the box. If not, he'd make one, because he wasn't going to give up on Megan without throwing down the fight of his life. "Let's try. I've watched Megan cast spells. I have a good enough idea of how it works."

"Absolutely not. There are so many problems with that plan, I don't even know where to begin. We might kill someone in the process. Or barter their soul accidentally. Ask me how I know about the possibility of those consequences."

They were close. Scratching at the edge of a breakthrough yet floundering out of reach. The power had reached them, but they were letting it run roughshod. It was time to take the reins. Steer the wheel. Pilot the chariot of destiny before they ended up dragged behind it.

Thom walked to the turntable, plugged it back in, and set the needle down. "What's Your Sign?" bopped along in its little rat-tat-tat of sugar-sharp, pretend hardness. "We can do better than this."

"What the hell are you talking about? You're all over the map. Now isn't the time to grandstand your airing of creative grievances."

"You said yourself that this song is magic. Lighting in a bottle. The definitive anthem of a generation with its unforgettable X factor and earworm-worthy addictiveness. Let's do it again, except intentionally make it a spell. We cast it onstage tonight and send me to Megan. She'll get the both of us back."

"You're out of your mind."

"We all are. Let's embrace it. Let's operate outside the box. The crowd will love this. If you have a better idea, speak up. If not, we need to get started."

"The show's in three hours."

"Right. We'd better be quick. Jonas and Jon will have to improvise.

Practicing is off the table, because this will need to be cast once and for all onstage. Are you ready?"

Pregnant silence became a third person in the room. Thom held his ground with his energy alone.

Brian pulled his trademark red Fender out of a closet, strapped on the instrument, and plugged in a portable amp. A whine of electronic feedback pierced the air. Thom had always gotten hot for that shrill spear to his eardrums. The promise of kickass music about to come in hard.

"Buckle up," Thom said, turning off the record player.

Brian puffed up his cheeks and blew out a gust of air. "If Dolly Parton wrote 'Jolene' and 'I Will Always Love You' in the same day, then I see no reason why we can't crank out a brand-new rock mega-hit in two hours." He put his fingers to the strings and slammed out an improvised riff that paired a metallic edge with that ephemeral, dark fantasy croon that trademarked the core of Fyre's identity. Perfect. Brian was on the level.

"That's the spirit." Thom cracked the spell book. Next, he groped in a box on the floor until he dug out five sheets of loose-leaf paper and two pens. "You compose the music. I'll write the lyrics and arrange the song."

Two hours and thirty-three minutes later, Brian and Thom were both drenched in sweat, and "She Gives Dynamite" was born.

"This is good," Brian breathed, his chest heaving.

"Fuck yeah." A pressure cooker inside Thom shook, on the brink. They needed to get this song out. Pronto. He'd filled all five pages. He folded the papers once and held them close. "We debut it for the encore. That way we can show Jonas and Jonnie the pages while we're all backstage. We don't have to offer them any more than broad strokes. All they need to know is that this song is happening for an important reason."

"Agreed. If we give too much explanation or detail, we won't look as confident and they'll have questions. We don't have time for that."

"Tell the effects people to save Pony and Tony until the encore. That way I'll be able to move through the fire and leverage the element itself to travel to the Other Place. The presence of flame will increase the odds of success." He wasn't talking outside of his arse. Spells involving inter-realm travel mostly required the use of the applicable element in some form or fashion. Megan knew her stuff.

Thom hid the spell book under the recliner, and Brian texted for a tech to come pick up the Fender and other equipment.

Brian led the way outside of the room, and they marched down the hallway in tandem. People and commotion filled the space, none of it fully real. They were on a crucial mission. Nothing else compared, not remotely.

"I suppose it's pointless to remind you how unsafe this is," Brian said.

"Since when have I ever been the practical one?" Thom slipped the folded pages in his back pocket.

His pulse cranked up higher with each step down the wide hallway. The backstage area was visible twenty feet down, an electronic city of cords and amps that lay beneath the sleeping grid of an overhead lighting matrix. The usual assortment of roadies and crew had no idea that they were about to be in the presence of a magic spell.

Brian grabbed Thom's arm and stopped them beside the short stack of steps that led to the stage. A heavy curtain cloaked the impending spectacle in a shroud of mystery. "I want to tell you, for whatever it's worth, that is was truly a pleasure working with you tonight on the new song. I haven't felt that inspired in a long time." Brian choked up at the end.

"Don't talk like you're saying goodbye. I'll pull this off. You watch me."

"I know you will. I have faith."

He was telling the truth. It was obvious in his tone, the way he held a powerful stare. Brian's faith was everything. Thom needed it, because he was so far afield with what he was about to do that he couldn't even begin to describe the level of intimidation. But this was his shot, and he'd shoot it. That was what Fyre was all about. Shooting their shot even when the odds were against them. Thom was living their credo. That had to count. "Thank you."

The standard pre-show routine moved forward like a self-contained thing. Thom's mind was elsewhere during the huddle, the warmup, the alone time where everyone got centered with his instrument. He found his place on stage and stood on the white X of tape to the left of Jonas.

The drummer sat poised at his kit, tips of the sticks touching the drums without making a sound, his locs piled on his head. Pony and Tony loomed large, silent, crazy-eyed steeds hulking weightless at the apex of the dark stage. Chatter was increasing in volume and excitement by the second, becoming loud enough to compete with the radio music that was getting everyone hyped for a big show.

Thom gulped down the rock in his throat. When he sang his designated backup vocals, the plan would set off in motion. Then, it was anyone's guess. He clenched the neck of his bass guitar. He might die tonight or send himself to an awful dimension and get stuck there. But if that was the price to pay for even a remote chance of rescuing his one and only love, he'd pay it. Again and again, he'd pay the toll with his own blood and soul if that's what it took to save Megan.

A roadie flashed the countdown cue on his fingers, and the curtain fell to reveal an ocean of screaming faces. On most nights, Thom lived for the feeding frenzy of adoration from a high-octane crowd like this one, but tonight, he was rote.

They worked through the set list, Thom playing his part, making his moves, pointing and smiling and throwing guitar picks.

Toward the end, a few of the Front Row Joes started to look keyed up and restless. A hairy pair of twins huddled in close to converse, pointing at the stage. A gaggle of sorority girls had switched from rocking out to playing on their phones. A Gen X Black man waved at the stage and pointed.

Thom got it. The set was almost over, and they wanted Pony and Tony. The fireworks usually came at this point in the show. Well, the people would have to be patient for a little while longer, and they'd get their big shebang, complete with—if all went off without a hitch—a disappearing act from the bassist. They ought to trust that Fyre would never let them down with a lackluster performance.

The set wrapped up with "Thou Shall Not Cry," a beloved power ballad that sounded like it belonged in a music video directed by Anne Rice and well-stocked with unicorns and gemstone willow trees. Thousands of pairs of eyes were pinned on those horses now. The crowd was stripped naked in its pyro lust.

Jonnie looked perplexed, tossing quizzical looks at Brian while he shredded out his famous solo, vamping it up with his throwback-to-eighties-metal hairstyle and goth-rock leather.

Once the final note of the last song struck with a bang, the curtain dropped. Cheers ensured, though plenty of unsatisfied murmurs balanced them out. The band convened backstage.

"Who changed things up?" Jonnie pushed a piece of hair out of his face. The ice-white platform boots he wore caught glimmers of dying stage light.

"We did." Thom pointed at Brian before turning his finger back on himself. "You'll see. It's important." He looked into Jonnie's eyes and handed him the pages. "Extremely important. You feel me?"

"Yeah, mate." Jonnie spoke with gravitas. He leafed through the pages.

"Does this relate to some of the things that came up when you stopped by my hotel room?" Jonas read over Jonnie's shoulder. He may not have gotten the gist to the same degree the rhythm guitarist did, but judging by the look on his face, he had an idea.

"What else?" Thom slid his thumb down the four brass strings of his instrument, each muted note he hit prepping him for the final act. The encore to end all encores. His chance. "Now let's get back out there and give those people what they want."

SIXTEEN

Cᴜᴇ ʙᴀʟʟ ᴡʜɪᴛᴇɴᴇss sᴛʀᴇᴛᴄʜᴇᴅ ɪɴ ᴇᴠᴇʀʏ ᴅɪʀᴇᴄᴛɪᴏɴ, ᴀs ғᴀʀ ᴀs Megan's vision would take her, melting into a blinding horizon of pearly uniformity. The glare pulled on her eyelids in a heavy and shimmering tide.

Her body stiff, she pushed up on her palms, the bleached void swallowing her like a drop in the ocean. She was a pinprick, an inconsequential figure in a Zen painting, mesmerized by impossibility. At least her hands were her own human ones. Memories of her physical change lingered, though they grew spottier with each passing second. She struggled to both recollect the circumstances of her transformation and make sense of where she was now. The present predicament won the lion's share of her concern.

"What is going on?" A bitter taste followed her words. The left side of her head ached. She didn't like this.

"The blank canvas represents you," Folly said, nowhere and everywhere. "The extent of your mind. A clean slate, a tabula rasa. The potential is endless. We begin our work."

Megan got to her feet, wobbly but stable. She wore her funeral clothes, a dot of ink dropped on new paper. Folly was lying, massaging the truth. The possession work had begun when Megan's body had morphed, and that work must've failed if they were starting over. "You can't have my mind." She took a few steps. Her heels landed with subtle clicks. It was impossible to gauge distance, if conventional notions of distance were even real in this place. "If you were able to control my mind, you would have taken it over already. You would have overtaken me outside of the church."

"Yes, well, the physics of that reality still eludes me. Think of that as me test driving your corporeal self. Here, I'll finish what I started. Much easier here." The confidence level of Megan's adversary wasn't bulletproof. She was able to tell by the change in tone.

There was a roadblock in Folly's plan. Megan was too formidable. She just had to figure out what her advantage was. "Good luck."

"Oh, dear fire witch. Luck is one of my best friends. Now listen carefully. Really listen to my next words and absorb them fully in your innermost core. At the center of the crystal mountain is a hole. The hole is the wellspring from which magic flows, and the hole will soon swallow the world. You must go to the hole now, Megan. Down in the dirt where the worms feed and the dead drag down the living. There is hunger in the hole. You go there now, Megan Marie. Let that hole open up wide and eat you. Feed that hole with the magic inside of you."

"No." Megan's knees wobbled. She lost her footing and collapsed to her hands and knees. Already, an odd mix of sleepiness and agitation washed over her. Resistance was futile. She couldn't see or move straight anymore, just wade in swimming blobs. "No."

Pieces of Megan dissolved into the snow of ether. Somewhere in the clean slate prison, she ended and other minds began. Other minds, other times—or was there no time? Past and present were a flat circle, a flaming hoop of intertwined consciousness spanning years, decades, generations. Individual bodies were immaterial. The concept of distinct, private thoughts was fiction. The wheel cut through them all. The wheel at the center turned forever and ever, gathering up whatever it wished in its fiery spirals.

"Megan!" her brother Caleb hollered from a submerged crevice in her brain. "Come on. They're calling us."

A high-pitched whine pierced her eardrums. She covered her ears.

There was a hole in her heart. The abyss opened up and stole everything in its vicinity. "Caleb!" she cried, dizzy. "Does she have you here, too?"

"Megan, snap out of it!" Caleb shook her by the shoulders, his voice cracking, the intonation of a teen boy on the verge of manhood. Summertime had splashed his pale face with freckles. His hair was messy and as red as the tip of a match. He had on cut-off jean shorts and a dirty, grass-stained shirt. The air smelled like warmed wildflowers. The sun was low and mellow, glazing the native plants in golden tones. "We aren't supposed to play out here in the tall grass. Mom and Dad say we'll get bit by snakes."

She was dreamy. Faraway. Why was Caleb ruining her special doze? She blinked until the fog in her eyes dissipated. He was right. They were out back behind the old barn near the Millers' property. The grass reached her knees.

She was wearing the sundress that she'd gotten from her cousin Mandy at her thirteenth birthday party. Since what happened, wearing that dress made her feel dirty and ashamed. Not wearing it made her feel worse, so she wore it anyway. "There's a hole in my heart. At the bottom of the mountain, and it's casting a spell to swallow the world. The flaming wheel spins in that hole, and I have an important key that it needs for unlocking."

"What?" Caleb let go of her arms. "You're scaring me."

"It's a misnomer that our minds are inside our heads like personal property," Megan told her brother. "In reality, we're all sharing. We're a hive mind, and Folly is the queen. I am all minds, everywhere, the final destination of every thought."

Caleb began to cry. "Your voice," he whispered, shaking. "This isn't you."

She turned around, a warm breeze animating her hair. The Millers had an old well out back, a short column of redbrick that jutted up out of the prairie and dropped downward into dank, echoing blackness. There were no snakes. The old well was the real no-no, and Mom and Dad knew why. "They're keeping secrets from us. Magic. The mysteries to everything are down there, at the bottom of the crystal mountain. Don't you want to know? Where it comes from and where it goes?"

"This is a dream," Caleb wailed, his face contorting into a rictus of horror. "Wake up, wake up, wake up."

She walked a few steps to the well, sat on the lip, and slung one leg over the edge. The cold brick scratched the bottom of her thigh. A chill from down deep crept up to cool her toes, contrasting to the sunshine warming her bare shoulders.

Caleb screamed, grabbed for her, but it was too late. A rip tore through the fabric of her dress as she slipped through his fingers. "I like it this way," she laughed. "Makes me look edgy."

Brian had uttered a similar phrase when Thom had ripped his shirt during their fight. Elijah had ripped Megan's dress, a different dress, and he'd enjoyed it. That dress hadn't been bubble-gum pink, nor had her underwear, but he'd said those words in his head. Those thoughts belonged to Megan as much as they did to anyone else.

The flaming wheel turned and turned, stitching together a tapestry of fates out of ripped seams. The wheel sliced through the fabric of many universes, sowing chaos.

Megan closed her eyes. She folded her arms over her chest and eased her bottom off the ledge. Gravity sucked her up fast, pulling her down feet first into the pit. For a time, it seemed like her fall would never end.

When she landed, there was no crash or thud, no broken bones. Her feet floated like angel feathers to connect with room-temperature dirt. The tunnel was narrow, but not claustrophobic. Orbs of floating light lit the path, an even row on each of the two walls.

A hot poke speared Megan's thoughts. She gasped. She was beside herself. Something terrible was happening. Where was she? Underground? How had she gotten here? She'd lost huge chunks of time. She turned around. Her heart sank. There was no obvious way out, no clear sense of whether to go forward to backward. Down was up. She was trapped.

There was no way that she would have crawled into a place like this had she been in her right mind. She'd been manipulated. She wracked her memories for the last thing she could recall. Pressure beat at her brain from all angles, and she was unusually spacey and forgetful. She had to fight to keep thinking, to hold on to her faculties, because every fiber of her being longed desperately to zone out. She wasn't usually like that.

Memories. Iowa. With Caleb? No, that'd been a dream. She'd taken Thom to Iowa, and they'd had dinner before going to the storm drain. She'd told him about Tremble. They'd gone to his funeral. She wore her funeral clothes and shoes, though she swore that she'd been wearing a floral dress moments ago. Beyond those broad strokes, though, she had nothing. Magic was afoot. Bad magic.

Megan set off walking. Since she had no spell book or means of combat, she'd reach out to Folly and take a stab at reverse psychology. "I have to admit, this is all interesting." The tunnel narrowed and bent into a slight downward incline. "I'm actually kind of down with this. What happens when you overtake my mind anyway? You have full access to my magic?"

"Happy you asked," Folly replied with instantaneous, jovial pep. Megan's archenemy wasn't all that smart, or at least not calculatingly clever. She was too egotistical, and her haughtiness blinded her. "Having your mind is mostly a convenience. That way I have a point of contact in your world to expedite the prophecy. Think of your little headspace like a restaurant franchise, and I'm the CEO of the entire company."

There were five other witches. Fascinating that Folly hadn't gotten to their minds. Unlikely that she hadn't tried. More likely that she'd tried and failed and was now getting desperate. Helen and whoever else was in on Operation Peru had likely wised up on best practices for psychic self-protection. Their guidance would be nice, but Megan had to wing it. "And my magic?"

The tunnel bottomed out at a rock wall. At Megan's feet lay a trapdoor with a short, rusted chain for a handle. The only ways to go were down and backward. Fitting.

"Your magic has a crucial role to play in the forward momentum of prophetic events. Fire magic, you see, is the most volatile of the elements. It touches the others and acts in consort with them. It's hardest to control and contain."

Well, that fit. Megan had never been too keen on being controlled and contained. Her fire magic lined up with her personality. Perhaps that was how it worked with all the witches. She had to see where this led. Folly seemed fairly chill and complacent for the time being, lulled into false security. Megan could work with that, and at least she wasn't being mind-monitored, as far as she could tell.

She pulled on the chain that hung from the door in the floor. The un-lubed joints gave way with metallic creaks that made her grind her teeth. A set of wooden stairs descended into a pit of darkness. Megan walked down them in small, apprehensive steps. At the bottom was a landing.

From her new vantage point, the sub-basement wasn't unlit. Faint light, a sickening industrial shade the color of pee, flickered through halogen tubes overhead. The temperature felt warmer than the typical basement, though it shared the usual cool humidity along with that trademark, dust-and-metal smell.

A concrete corridor to her right was little more than graffiti-covered walls, from what she could see. To her left were rows of run-down bathroom stalls like she'd had at summer camp. In front of her, the yellowed rock opened to a large room. Blotchy water stains bruised the walls. A bucket sat in one corner.

Debris was strewn across the floor, hunks of material the size of fists and smaller pieces. Megan squinted, her eyes and stomach adjusting to the putrid, disorienting light. She got a good look at the objects. Broken chains.

Unease seeped through Megan from soles to scalp. The air smelled foul, faintly rotten, which she hadn't noticed until now. She took two steps back. "Any updates?" she asked Folly.

The tormentor laughed lightly. "Welcome to the backrooms of your mind. I'm confident that the outcome will be favorable. Enjoy." With that, Folly left. Megan knew, because she felt a snip deep in her gut, followed by a relieving sense of loss, like a bad tooth had been plucked.

Though as she stood alone, for real, in the spooky dungeon, Megan begrudgingly missed the company of her adversary. At least Folly could be amusing in a malicious way.

"Think." She was being put to a test, tasked with solving a puzzle. A test of wits, strength, magic, or resilience? She had no way of knowing.

Maybe there was a secret passage in one of the bathroom stalls. She walked that way and kicked open the door to the first one. A sewer stench made her cough and gag. No secret passage, but plenty of filth.

The next was worse. Bad. She had to turn away, her eyes watering. Same story all the way down, and the sinks weren't pretty either.

Dead-ended, Megan set off down the graffiti hallway. The mustard light and spray-paint scribbles gave the space a weirdly dreamy, urban feel, like she was wandering through the underground of Los Angeles. She paused to read the writing. It wasn't random nonsense at all.

The future wrote her poem
On a dream that I once saw
I rode the chariot to Venus
And kissed her every flaw
Superimposed onto hope
Wish upon a star
A nightlight in the ocean
A new era close and far
Star light, star bright
I have to see her tonight
Deeper than the widest sea
Her memory calls right to me
She's a vision in the firmament
A candle in the night
She's my hope, my dream, my kindred spark
She's a breathing supernova
She gives dynamite

Of course she recognized the style of lyrics, cadence, and familiar motifs. Only one person could've written this. "Thom!" she cried out, her voice bouncing off a distant wall in the bowels of this maze. "Can you hear me? Are you trying to connect? What can I do?"

More words appeared:

Sister fire, speak to me, bestowing guidance, clarity
Let the flames before you light the wheel of the chariot and deliver my true love back to safety.

Oh no. Oh no. Oh no no no no. His heart was in the right place, but Thom should not be fucking with spells or the spell book. "Stop!" she yelled with full force. "Don't do it. It's not worth the risk." She raised her palm to the wall and wiped at the words, condensation dampening her skin, but the text kept coming. "I'm just one person. Please, don't risk this for me."

Somewhere in the distance, a low rumble cut through stifling quiet, barely in earshot. A piece of machinery firing up? A beat later, four subtle movements reverberated through the floor. They weren't close at all. They certainly weren't footsteps. They couldn't be.

Megan wasn't doing any good hanging around by the song on the wall, and Thom couldn't hear her. She took off at a brisk clip down the hall, her pulse hammering. The corridor was more of the same, except that the writings were random jumbles of words. Some pertained to her life, her past, others didn't. Or didn't immediately make sense to her.

The rumble happened again, followed by the tremble through the concrete, through her bones. Whatever it was, was closer now.

She picked up her pace, her insides ice. She ducked down tunnel after tunnel.

The vocalization happened again. It was definitely a growl.

People tended to think of fear as an acute, instant sensation, the injection of fight-or-flight adrenaline. Megan felt that, but it was compounded by a more unsettling feeling that was, in a way, scarier. To her, the fundamental inversion of her reality was more frightening than any jump scare. What she'd taken for granted no longer applied. Fear was a freefall.

The stomps and growls were getting closer and closer. Whatever was hunting her was advancing. It knew the way around these backrooms, the shortcuts, and she didn't. This thing saw, sensed, or smelled her, and she lacked corresponding leverage. But she didn't have to let her fear win. Megan was sick of running and hiding. She had to fight.

She stopped, took a deep breath, and removed her shoes. The stiletto heels were a halfway decent asset, better than being bare-handed. She also had her magic.

Another snarling growl. Perhaps thirty feet away, behind her. Megan clenched a hard grip on her shoes and turned around.

SEVENTEEN

Go ahead and disregard Megan's previous ponderings on the nature of fear.

Jump scares were scarier.

Lightning zapped her fingers and toes. Her arm and leg muscles clenched. Fight chemicals flooded her heart and veins. She clutched a shoe in each hand, embarrassed by how flimsy and feminine her weapons were when contrasted to her adversary.

The monster was eight feet tall and bald all over, its hairless skin the color of a fish's belly. The biceps were as fat as ham hocks. A pronounced hunchback drew attention to shoulders broad enough to block a doorway. The stomach looked starved, a concave dip that scooped under protruding ribs. Its head was a pin with a red wound for a mouth. Shriveled eye pits appeared incapable of taking in much visually. Smell did most of the heavy lifting, if the proportional size of the nasal pits were a reliable indicator.

The creature took two steps forward. Its legs were bent and goatlike, flimsy twigs beneath a massive frame. Judging by the skin tag that bobbed between its legs when it moved, it was, or had been, male.

The good news was that it wasn't attacking, though that growl still gurgled out from its spindly throat. Maybe the grunt was just how it communicated. She wouldn't prejudge the creature based on how it looked and sounded. She was better than that.

Though screams filled her brain, Megan stood her ground and held her calm as tight as the shoes in her hands. "Hello," she eked out, the thing at arm's length now. Its hands were large enough to hold her skull in the palm. Could easily snap her neck. Strangle her. Those forearms were thicker than her calves. "What's your name?"

It garbled out unknowable grunts and clicks. Circled her. Smelled her, the nose holes widening. The monster smelled bad. Like those bathrooms.

Its energy was negative. Tense. Aggressive body language. When it passed her on the left, skulking counterclockwise, she caught sight of an unclean backside and a stubby, crusted tail.

Megan bit her tongue and swallowed her gag reflex. Her grip on her shoes was slippery with sweat. There was no point in running, and she was physically outmatched. Her best bet was to land a single strike with her heel right between the eyes, but her target was moving. There had to be another way to solve this problem. The beast hadn't struck first.

She opted to stick with the bonding effort, which might buy time and, if she was lucky, build trust. She didn't know this monster's story. For all he knew, she was the one intruding on his world, and he had every right to be apprehensive about the stranger wandering his hallways. "My name is Megan. Do you live down here? I'm just visiting. Maybe you could show me around."

The giant completed a circle and paused, facing her. The eyes revealed nothing. The mouth was a flabby gash of raw meat devoid of frown or smile. No teeth. No fangs, at least. The thing tilted its head twenty degrees.

A measure of tension drained out of her body. Her companion had adopted a listening stance. That counted. It was what she had. She chose her next words carefully, making an offering in exchange for trust. "This might sound crazy, but I was sent here on a mission. I'm supposed to make a special donation and then leave, and I'm not sure how to do either. Could you possibly show me the way out, so that I can finish my task and get out of your business?"

A head tilt to the other side. A dim light flicked in the back of the monster's throat, the glimmer no brighter than the bulb on a firefly's tail. Whether that glow represented an effort at interaction was anyone's guess.

"The light at the back of your throat. Can you help me understand it?" She mentally backed herself up. She was putting the cart before the horse. "I should first ask...can you understand my words? If the answer is yes, would you please hold up a finger, blink, or nod your head? Whatever is easiest for you."

The light inside his mouth dimmed, then brightened.

Hope floated Megan's spirit for the first time since she'd found herself in this disquieting, uneasy place. She was making progress. "Can you control the light in your mouth? Can you blink it once for yes and twice for no?"

One blink. She breathed a little easier. The monster was able to help her, at least in theory.

"Are you happy that I'm here?"

Two blinks.

"Fair enough." A shiver slinked up her spine. She wasn't on this beast's good side, but at least they had a common goal. "I'm not all that thrilled to be here either, to be honest. No offense. I have things I need to take care of at home."

Two blinks.

Her world shrunk. "I didn't ask you a question."

He stepped forward. The glow spread to cover the surface area inside his mouth. He had no tongue. Just a gaping maw the color of spoiled hamburger. Made her wonder what the point of having a mouth even was. Perhaps he could only drink from puddles. Pools of blood. The odor from inside his hole was as expected.

"Neither of us wants me here. I'm okay with that. No hard feelings. Will you show me the way to get out?"

Two blinks.

Panic threatened to annihilate. She was tanking. She couldn't bear the stench much longer or she'd heave. The aesthetic wasn't much better. At this range, she could make out the texture of its skin, its pores. The surface was like chicken skin. Tiny bumps. A few warts and blemishes. "*Can* you show me the way out?"

One blink.

Ink filled her veins. The clock was running out. The sand ran down the hourglass. Her options dwindled. "You can, but you won't?"

One blink.

"Are you going to hurt me?"

One blink.

"Fat chance." Before her enemy had a chance to hit first, Megan flung her arm back and fired, swinging the point of her heel at a spot right between the creature's eyes. Her makeshift blade landed with a wet, disgusting crack that made her shudder.

The heel sunk in halfway, flesh and bone yielding to the object's penetration with an awful pliability that she'd never forget.

The monster stumbled backward, thrashing and howling, dark fluid oozing from the impact site. He pawed at his face, his cries blending pain and rage. Blood streaked his cheeks and mouth-type hole. She would have felt guilty at this pathetic sight, but he'd expressed his intent to harm her.

"Well, you should have helped me!" Megan shouted. "That was all I wanted." She ran in the direction of where she'd come. If she got to a quiet place, like one of those bathroom stalls, she might be able to wing a spell.

Her jog took her past Thom's song and spell. She allowed herself three seconds to stop and look. The words burned even brighter on the wall now, luminescent and golden, different letters dulling and glowing in a pattern.

The behavior of the spell song mirrored the glare in the monster's mouth. What was Thom up to? She had no way of knowing or getting involved. She retraced her steps to that terrible bathroom, using bits of familiar graffiti as signposts. No growls or footsteps pursued her. That was a positive.

She found the bathroom and chose the least repugnant stall, where the toilet wasn't overflowing and contained no shit. She sat on the toilet tank beside her solo shoe and braced her feet on the sides of the bowl.

The impulse to shield herself from the gazes of any intruders may have been senseless and irrational, but the illusion of being protected in an enclosure helped her concentrate.

Megan had studied her book tirelessly, memorizing her section and taking copious notes. She'd be able to transport herself home without reading any pages. Her mind was enough. It would have to be.

"Sister Spirit, I, a fire-born, humbly call upon your assistance." Along with water, spirit was supposedly the most effective element when seeking to travel between dimensional planes. Was Megan advanced enough in her practice to call upon elements other than her own? She was about to find out. "I am trapped in a sunken place where I'm tormented by adversaries. Please deliver me to my home, safe and unharmed, so that I may continue to practice my craft in the service of the six-fold sisterhood." Those final words sealed a pact of sorts. Megan was all in. Committed. She was the fire witch. She had to be. Who else? More importantly, in a way, she decided to be. In that moment, holed up in a nightmarish bathroom stall, she claimed the title, chose herself, appointed herself. She wasn't waiting around for any more signs. She'd received plenty.

Megan had received plenty of signs, except for the one she desperately needed. Nothing was happening. Spells were usually instant. Her perception wasn't even woozy or wobbly like it sometimes was when magic was involved. Her view of her bare, tattooed feet on dingy porcelain was sharp and lucid. She looked at the walls but wished that she hadn't when she saw the stains and crud.

Megan recast her spell, arranging her words differently and selecting alternative verbiage. Still nothing. Damn! What was she doing wrong?

The growl happened. Far away, but always too close. She clenched her fist and grabbed her remaining shoe off the top of the toilet tank. Why wouldn't this fucking creature leave her alone?

The footsteps vibrated through the air, and this time they were faster, with less time between each one. It was running. How was it running? She'd badly injured it with that strike to the forehead. Or at least she thought she had. Another growl. Much closer.

Run or lay in wait? Which would give her the best advantage?

Probably run and attack. She didn't see how the stall was helpful. The small area reduced her range of motion.

Megan had one of her feet halfway to the ground when the steps approached the bathroom. Dread dropped her down one of those toilets. Of course the monster found its way back to the bathroom quickly and easily. It was home base. He recognized and followed his own scent. Possibly hers.

A sharp *thwack*, and metal clattered against metal. A nearly identical barrage of thuds happened two seconds later. She clenched her lone shoe. He was kicking down doors. Stalking her.

Fuck it. She saw red. Megan shot out a scream to end all screams, voiding every drop of primal rage with her voice. She slammed against the door, vaulting her body out of the stall.

There he was, the same fiend, save for a gory puncture wound between his eyes. An inch-long piece of her heel protruded from his flesh. He faced her down and growled, his entire body shaking with fury.

She charged him, screaming, the point of her shoe raised high. This time, she'd try for the temple in hopes of a more direct route to the brain.

She wasn't lucky. The monster caught her wrist midair. The two of them stood there frozen for a half-second, trapped in eye contact. At least, she assumed there was eye contact, as there was no life behind this freak's eyes.

He bent her arm at the worst possible angle. Sharp pain shot through her elbow. She braced for the crack of her own bone snapping. Her fingers twitched in agony, and she dropped the shoe. It landed on the linoleum with a clunk. "It doesn't have to be this way. I can get us both out of here. Or make your life easier. I can at least try."

The resulting growl let her know that he wasn't interested in her proposition. He jerked her arm behind her back in a painful twist, but his face was tracking a different target. A distraction was good. What was he looking at?

His stare tracked her shoe. For whatever reason, the object fascinated him. "You like that, huh?"

His mouth light blinked once. The shoe enthralled him until he'd lost focus. He was slipping. Beside himself with shoe obsession.

"I feel you. I'm kind of shoe crazy myself. You want to see it?"
One blink.

"If you let go of my wrist, I'll pick it up and show it to you. I'll even give it to you." Like hell she'd arm her opponent, but she sure would like to get her weapon back in her hands.

He pulled her wrist close to his face and smelled it. His grip was strong and painful. His nostrils flared. A rolling growl tumbled out of that dead mouth.

With another, meaner growl, he shoved Megan to the floor. Her ass hit the tile with a snap that smarted her tailbone. He still had her wrist and was pushing her arm into her sternum to hold her at bay. His pale, meaty forearm flexed with corded muscle. He'd crouched but was still on his feet. This was bad. He could easily overpower her now that she was no longer standing. Think!

Twisting his upper body, he used his free hand to reach for the shoe. The effort wrenched him into an awkward angle, his arm threading through the space between their bodies. He pawed at the shoe, but it was out of his reach. Grunting and growling, he fumbled at what he wanted, bending his torso more to get better leverage.

Now! He was distracted and vulnerable. Megan didn't have perfect vantage by any means, but she had a measure. She reared back her leg, took aim, and smashed her heel into the spot between his legs. Bone and flesh cracked against bone and flesh. No squishy male bits, but he shrieked all the same, stumbling back.

The grip on Megan's wrist gave, and relief flooded the area when the pain stopped. Reaction time had to be swift. She jumped to stand, snatched her shoe, and ran.

At last look, the creature was seated, his legs bent, scrabbling to regain his footing.

She tore down the graffiti hallway, heading toward Thom's song. She had an idea. It had better work because this was her last one. She ought to have gone to the wall first and not listened to her reptile brain and its demands for shelter. No time for regrets though.

Megan arrived at her destination. She pressed her palm against Thom's words and spoke her own part. If Thom was hailing fire, then she would too. That way, she reasoned, they stood a chance at enjoying the benefit of double firepower. The idea of passing through flames as means of transport didn't thrill her, but now wasn't the time to be picky. The situation she found herself in was one of desperate times and drastic measures.

"Sister Fire, I, a fire-born, humbly call upon your assistance. You've heard the calls of my accomplice, my true love, delivered on my behalf. Join my pleas with his and deliver me from this fallen place of chaos."

Growls and footsteps were coming her way. Of course. Megan beat back tears. Frustration clamped down in a vise grip. Why couldn't she catch a break?

The words warmed against her skin. This counted. This was progress. Out of the corner of her eye, the monster advanced. He walked with a limp now, and his pace was slowed, but he hadn't given up.

He was relentless in his drive to hurt her. He was her pain personified. The second thought landed in a strike of lightning. That was it. He was symbolic. To defeat him, she'd have to address the underlying trauma that he represented.

Megan let her next words flow from the heart. "Burn away the residue from my past to purify the hole in my heart. Release me from those old hurts as they go up in smoke. Build a firewall between my old pain and my new self. Stop those wounds from touching me anymore."

Footsteps closed in. Megan chanced a glance. Where the monster ought to have been was a burning car. A sedan, tires up, its front and back seats crushed like an accordion, spewing crystalline chunks of glass on the ground. Flame blanketed the hood and poured from the ruined windows. There was a body inside. She recognized him.

"Burn it all away," Megan cried out. "But not like this, ever again. Burn it out of my spirit. Like smoke into the sky, burn it all away."

More words filled the wall now. Fire spell words that she knew from her book. Thom was still there. He was communicating with her through the spell. Through their spell, that they were building together, they'd get her out.

"Wrap my body in cooling protection from the flames and deliver me." The words appeared on the wall after Thom's. "Grant me the strength to pass through the fire. May I never return to this horrible place ever again."

Her perception loosened, blending into the words. It was working. She relaxed and gave in.

Before she could surrender, a shadow darkened her peripheral vision. Spaced out but still alert, she looked.

The monster was back. He wrapped a hand around her throat, pinching off the flow of air to her windpipe. He lifted her off the ground and pressed her into the wall. His strength was predictably mighty. For the first time since their paths crossed, he spoke. "You die now. When you die, we have you. You belong here, with us. Forever and ever, you belong to us."

The bulk of Megan's vision was lost to dancing white sparks. Her breath came in meager gulps. She heard herself wheeze. She was in and out of consciousness. She scratched at the creature's hands, tugging his fingers in a futile effort to free herself. Dried blood crusted his nose holes and thin, ragged lips. Over the shoulder of her attacker, Tremble's car roasted.

She'd be damned if these images were the last ones that she saw.

"You belong." He squeezed tighter. The crash flames burst above his shoulders like demonic wings. "With us. To us. You are us."

In her delirious state, she caught a glimpse of the vision that Thom had seen in that closet. Of what she'd been outside the church, and the odd sensation that she'd experienced in bed. Herself, merged with her demons. Her magic, when allowed to fester in unhealed hurt, made her and those she cared about vulnerable to Folly.

"No." She should have said it a long time ago, in many situations, with total conviction. But she was saying it now. She was done trembling. She was ready to be strong. "That is a hard no."

A dull, gray film spread over the creature. He ceased all movement. Even the rise and fall of his hollow chest froze. His fingers remained stiff around her neck, but no longer exerted force or pressure. He had turned to stone.

The top of his head flaked away, scattering in flecks. The same thing happened to his neck, arm, and the hand that held her until his entire body crumbled into dust. All that remained was a pile of ash no larger than what a cigarette would make.

Megan drew in a long, glorious breath. She'd never felt more unburdened. She stepped over the remains of her monster, returned her consideration to the wall, and touched the words again.

A tangerine teardrop bloomed in her mind's eye, a dancing flame perched atop a slice of white wick. Fearless, she followed the candle into a dark tunnel until flames fanned outward to consume her whole.

EIGHTEEN

PONY AND TONY ERUPTED IN TANDEM, DELIVERING THE FIREPOWER crescendo that the fans demanded. The pair of carousel crazies didn't disappoint.

Pony ejected white-glazed sapphire sparks from his eye sockets at the exact moment that Tony voided a spray of orange. The crowd shot off as one ballistic body of whoops and cheers. Their pleasure was pagan, scarily erotic, and Thom would be lying if he didn't admit that the response sent a tingle into his balls after all these years and despite everything else he was going through. Fyre lived for these moments. That there was real magic involved this time amplified the time-tested frenzy of exaltation.

Critics used to bitch that Fyre's unforgettable zenith was a gimmick, the purview of hacks who had to fall back on props to hide questionable talent. Thom didn't care about their opinions anymore. They were envious of those equine divas, because those who couldn't *do*, or teach, griped in magazines. Fyre had the modern-day equivalent of Tommy Lee's roller coaster drum set.

The pyrotechnic boom chattered Thom's teeth, shaking his bones despite his earplugs mounting their best defense. Tinnitus popped up in his left ear, bleating a shrill note. Sweat beaded on his brow. His face was his own personal boiler room. The reek of petroleum stung sharply in his nostrils.

The backstage crew leapt into action, fussing around to shut off the prop and contain potential hazards. To keep the party going for a few more minutes, they fired up the fog machine.

He squinted, battling the glare and smoke jets for a sign that something, anything, had changed. His attempt at a spell better have worked because he didn't have a backup plan.

He scanned the crowd of over thirty-thousand bodies, most of them still screaming, reveling in the loss of their collective mind. Three women near the front had gone topless. A bouquet of roses, several notes, and a bottle of bubbly ended up on stage. A musclebound bear of a man was being dragged away by security, screaming a woman's name. Welcome to the carnival.

Frustrating their desire for high-octane stage pageantry had worked from an entertainment perspective, but not to return Megan or deliver him to her. Smoke flooded the stage, compounding the confusion. Tension cramped his lower back.

Thom ran through the cloying fog that blanketed his world, cutting past Jonnie and Brian.

"What's up, man?" a fan screamed from the audience, no doubt befuddled by Thom's premature breaking of character.

Thom was by the amps at the rear of the set, losing hope, when a different audience member cried out, "Who's that new person?"

Thom whipped his head in the direction of the voice, blood roaring in his ears. A female body lay crumpled near the edge of the performance floor, in grabbing distance of the front row spectators. He recognized her instantly, curled in the fetal position, and a mix of relief and dread clobbered him with the impact of a Mack truck.

"Drop the curtain!" Thom yelled into his wireless microphone that connected him with the crew. "There's an incident we didn't anticipate. Kill the lights and audio."

"Whaddya mean an incident?" howled a fan from farther back in the seating chart.

Dark material tumbled from the top of the set, slamming down a wall to divorce the fans from the performers. People kept yelling, demanding to know who'd gotten up on stage. Little did they know the extent of what had happened. A routine concert had been transformed into a ritual before their unsuspecting eyes.

He ran to Megan and crouched beside her. "Can you talk? Are you hurt?" She was moving, twitching her legs and scratching at the ground. Red hair blocked her face. He gingerly moved a piece of the impediment to get a better look at her. No obvious cuts or blood.

"I'm fine," she said in a hoarse voice, crawling to a seat. He didn't see any injuries, thank heaven. "Relatively speaking." When she looked in his eyes, he was hit with the dread swirling behind her stare. "The song on the wall. What did you do up here?" It wasn't an accusation, but she didn't seem happy.

"What I had to." He helped Megan to her feet. She wore the same clothes that she had on for the funeral, but she had lost her shoes. "The important thing is that you're safe now."

"I wouldn't count on that." She hung onto his arm, her balance unsteady.

He led her backstage, stopping briefly to hand his instrument to a shellshocked bass tech, a hefty woman in overalls. "She wasn't there, and then she was," the tech stammered. "How did you do that? Did I just see a rock concert or a magic show?"

"Musician, magician," Thom told the gobsmacked roadie. "Same thing, in a way. Tricks of the eye, light and shadow play. You saw a knockout performance. Leave it at that."

Brian ran over, already unbuttoning the top three buttons of his uniform dress shirt. He always roasted onstage, and the impact of the spell seemed to have cranked up the humidity level. "Megan, I want to warn you that you'll end up in the public eye. It would do you good to lay low for a few days. The press will be all over this, and they won't let it go. If you don't want to be hounded, I'd keep your head down. I can run interference if need be. But I wanted to warn you that there's going to be attention following you, not all of it good."

"Always practical." Thom didn't give a fuck about reporters. If they crossed a line with Megan or upset her, he'd protect her. He comforted Megan with touch.

"No such thing as bad publicity, right?" Megan said with a crooked smile.

Thom swept her into a side hug. That she hadn't lost her wit was a good sign that the transport incident hadn't overly traumatized her.

Brian returned her quip with a jesting finger-point. "Shrewd. The finale is in a few days. I'd rest as much as possible. I have no idea what to expect."

"That makes two of us," Thom said.

"Three," added Jonnie, jogging into the fray. "And I have a feeling that we're on the radar of a presence who isn't a fan like those people in the seats."

"Four," Jonas put in as he cased the area. "Are we in agreement that we want the final show to go on?"

"Don't cancel on my account," Megan said. "We can beat this thing."

Thom had no idea how. But he admired her resilience and confidence.

"I say we discuss that topic in the morning." Brian caught a shirt that a staffer lobbed to him. His half-chest tattoo flashed as he accomplished a quick wardrobe change. "Sleep on it. Take time to think. You all know where to find me."

Everyone left separately to decompress. This was not a night for an after-party or any other type of socializing.

"Do you have my book and watch?" Dark circles had already spread under Megan's eyes, and her features were slack.

He had to get her to a safe place as fast as possible. "Yes. They're in a secure place. We'll collect your stuff and regroup."

"Thank you," she said. "Those should have been the first words out of my mouth."

"You don't have to thank me." They made haste to Brian's dressing room. "I'd do anything for you."

"Even destroy the world with an impromptu spell cast with extremely sketchy magic?"

"Proof's in the pudding, yeah?" He shuffled them into the dressing room and pushed the chair against the door. Ridiculous, the broken lock, but he had no reserves to get irritated with mundane minutiae. Corporate arenas could be surprisingly decrepit.

She crashed on the couch and pulled her knees into her chest. Her face paled. "I think I might be sick."

He knelt beside her and rubbed her back. "It's okay. Get it out if you need to. I'll have antacid and over-the-counter stomach medicine sent over. Or do you need more heavy-duty pain pills? I can find those."

She hacked a terrible, retching cough, but nothing came out. "That's okay. I think what I need is food in my stomach. I can't remember what I ate last. Can we go to your hotel and order room service?"

He gathered up his phone from where he'd stashed it under the couch and called a car. He told the man who answered, "Send over women's sneakers too. Size nine." Thom distanced the phone from his mouth and asked Megan, "Did I get your size right?"

A wisp of a warm smile crossed her lips. A sad expression, ultimately, but it was a start on the road to recovery. "Yeah. Why are you this good to me?"

Still kneeling, he bent forward and wrapped her in his arms. She smelled sleepy, and the residue of her perspiration left him sticky. He relished the sensation. She'd branded him, inside and out. "You know. Because I love you."

"I love you." She burrowed into the hold. Clutched the sides of his shirt. "But damn, I'm trouble for you."

"You are not." Sure, trouble followed them. But that wasn't her fault. The darkness had attached to Thom and his bandmates before he and Megan had met. She'd told him as much on the first morning they had woken up together. That was a fact. Unless she was wrong. He ordered his brain to stand down before his thoughts took a grim turn. "Don't internalize it. You're fighting to stop the trouble in its tracks."

"I hope you're right."

Thom concurred with that sentiment. Once the driver affirmed a five-minute arrival time, he recovered the spell book and her purse from their hiding place. If they destroyed the book and watch, would all of this go away? Wishful thinking. The instant he handed over the book to Megan, though, he was relieved of a hard, queasy affliction that he hadn't even realized had taken root in him.

The book was a sickness. Diseased. He was convinced. But how to cure the metaphysical plague? Now wasn't the time. The pressing matter was to ensure that Megan got rested and healthy.

A helper showed up with the shoes, and she put them on. He guided Megan down the wide hallway to a secret exit with a nonworking emergency alarm. This way, they had a chance at escaping discreetly.

The level of loitering outside the back exit of the arena wasn't too bad, but savvy fans always knew where to catch a glimpse or, if they were lucky, an interaction. A mixed group of around ten people had gathered in the alcove where trucks pulled in to deliver equipment.

He recognized a hot brunette in tight jeans and a barely-there top. She was a veterinarian who loved horses and had taken up ballet at age thirty-nine. Or maybe her hobby was photography or painting. He'd slept with her—four times, about a year ago—and ghosted her when he'd gotten bored.

His shame was a second person living inside of him, a selfish and adolescent troll that didn't deserve to be touching Megan.

His former bedmate zeroed in and breezed through the gaggle of people on her way to her target. "Thom James, long time no see. Were you even going to say hello?"

The goblin inside of Thom snickered. There was no escaping his past. He ought to have been more like Brian and Jonas. Helen and Laura never had to feel the ick of involuntarily witnessing their partner's late stage walk of shame. "Hi...Emily. I don't have an excuse. I hope you're doing well."

She narrowed her eyes. "It's Becky." Becky turned on her high heels, her long hair swishing behind her, and marched back to the trio of people from whom she'd diverged. "Whatever. I'm over it," she told her friends. "Let's go downtown and hit the clubs."

The Fyre Lexus pulled up on the street. Saved. He opened Megan's door for her and guided her into the leather-seated interior. He avoided looking at the book, and in Becky's general direction, which relegated his gaze to the pavement. He supposed that he deserved his moment of head-bent, downcast eyes. "I wish that you hadn't had to see that," he said, climbing in to situate himself in the seat beside Megan. The car got moving, leaving his bad decisions behind as shrinking dots in the rearview mirror.

She slipped off the sneakers and wiggled her toes. "Dude, I've bludgeoned a bloodthirsty monster in a hell dimension." She patted his knee. "A piece of one of my shoes got lodged in its forehead. I'm not traumatized by the sight of a woman you hooked up with. She seems cool. And of course her looks are flawless. I like that you have good taste."

"She's no match for you." He took her hand. "More importantly, my exes don't concern us. And I'm glad your humor is resurfacing. Lets me know you're doing okay."

"I will say that I've learned a lot from my time in that place." A disturbed expression stole in. "How long was I gone?"

"Eight hours." He'd counted the minutes of every single one. "How long did it feel like to you?"

"Forty-five minutes, give or take. Time is strange."

"What did you learn?"

She placed the book in the space between herself and the door. As soon as it was out of sight, he was able to think more clearly, and he hadn't even realized that his thinking was messed up until it felt normal again. Megan continued, "I was out of control when I got sucked up like that in Iowa. My emotions overcame me, which triggered a stress reaction in how I manage my magic. I was vulnerable to possession. Before that, I couldn't keep it inside of me. I'm better now." She glanced out the window. "I think."

It made sense how "better" was a relative term, but the way she spoke gave him a shudder. He didn't quite know why. "Speaking of thinking, do you ever feel like your mind is jumbled or soupy when the book is around? Unglued?"

"All of the time. That's her attempt at gaining possession. It's ongoing. I think that's why she sent the shadow monster after me. To get inside my head. Like a flying monkey in *The Wizard of Oz*. She has these lesser creatures do her bidding."

The driver's eyes flicked into the rearview mirror. It wasn't like he could do anything with the fantastical information he'd absorbed, but nonetheless, the presence of listening ears launched Thom into cover-your-ass mode. "Partition up, please."

Tinted plastic quickly walled them off.

"Why, you want to fool around?" Megan asked.

His dick stirred. Yes, they'd been breaking down the uglier points of magical malfeasance and mental possession, but he was insatiable. And this was Megan. "Now that you mention it. Maybe it'll clear our palates." He liked the sight of her, barefoot, her fancy black dress scuffed and smudged. Her hair was messy, her makeup streaked. She looked a little roughened, worse for wear, and he loved the thought of having her like that in the back of the limo.

"You serious?"

He slipped his hand between her thighs and stroked her velvet skin. They both needed respite. What better way than their shared favorite activity? "Absolutely."

"Can he see or hear?" She nudged her head in the direction of the partition.

The car had merged onto the interstate, the engine accelerating with a hum. City lights gleamed to Thom's left. "Probably not. Who cares?"

"I missed you." She crawled across the seat and unbuttoned his fly. He was fully hard in seconds. Her touch was irresistible. His cock was stone, the rest of him putty. She stroked him over his jeans. "What about the book? Open or closed? Visible or out of sight?"

She unzipped his pants and tugged his cock free. He was even more turned on by the sight of himself ready to go in a somewhat taboo location. He'd had plenty of action in cars and limos over the years, but since this was Megan, it felt as exhilarating as the first time all over again. Accordingly, he felt wickedly delicious. Reckless. On the edge. The peak of himself, but in a guiltless way. "You want to try another spell with it, now that you're more in control?"

She moved into his lap and gyrated against his stiff member. The fabric of her panties was silky and decadent. He unzipped her dress at the back and pulled the top part to her waist. Her bra didn't last two seconds in his hands. He couldn't get his face in her breasts fast enough. He licked and sucked her nipples one at a time. Fingered her wet pussy under the fabric of her panties. "Stroke your cock against my clit," she said.

Thom ripped her panties off her body, the tearing of fabric ruined sending another jolt into his full balls. He smelled her pussy and salivated at the sight of her red nether hair. He was a wolf. His tongue nearly lolled out of his mouth. "You didn't answer my question."

"Yeah, I have an idea." She leaned across and split the book open before returning to her position, mounted on top of him. "When you come, picture magic flowing out of the bottom of the crystal mountain and into me. This should help me get leverage."

Precum beaded at the opening of his head. All of this talk of stroking and coming had him seeing double. "Do you really want me now, or are you just using me to practice a spell?" Either way was fine, really. He'd take Megan any way he could get her, and the spell thing was kinky. Dangerous. Razor sharp.

She used her index and middle finger to part her labia. He could see both her bulging clit and slick juices. A minor scrape had scratched a pale pink line across her leg, right above the knee. In the dark glow of the moving car, right after a show, this was beautifully whorish. Thom was more than in love. He was stark raving obsessed.

"What do you think?" she asked in a sultry, gravel-and-honey voice.

"Get that pussy on me," he grunted, grabbing her hips.

She leaned back and used her hand to prop herself against the back of the seat. Her clit was perfectly aligned with the sensitive underside of his dick. She pressed her hips forward and pumped.

Megan was drenched. Her flesh slicked against his, up and down, delivering an immediate tingle of pleasure into his crown. "That's perfect. Right there." He held her at the waist. Bumped his hips up and down. Her tits bounced. He licked his lips. "You like this? Fucking in the car?"

"Oh yeah." She clamped her free hand down on his shoulder. "I'm gonna come."

"Yeah. Get it." His cock was slicked from her. Glistening. Obscene. His favorite. A vein on the side of his shaft throbbed. He loved his dick. Always had. Such a blessed thing that Megan loved it as much or even more. "Show me what you've got."

Her moans popped out closer together. He tongued her pierced nipples, sucking on the metal like she liked. "I'm close," she panted.

"I want to taste your pussy when you come." He was talking dirty more to get them both off than making a request, but Megan surprised him.

In a remarkable feat of athleticism, she flipped over until her head was between his feet, her knees balanced on his shoulders. Her magnificent cunt, all red and swollen and juicy, was aimed right at his face. "Ever thought about piercing this?" He used the pad of his thumb to rub the head of her big, erect clit.

She twisted her hips. Gasped. "That feels great. I'll do anything you want."

He continued to rub her sweet spot in a circular motion. "I'll go with you and get my first tattoo. Your name on my cock. Deal?"

"I'm there," she said, her speech muffled by the floorboard. "Taste it."

He stuck out his tongue and pressed it to her hot center, pulling away to see a string of saliva joining his mouth and her lower lips. She tasted of sweetness and the sea, a unique and complex flavor made delectable by her excitement. Thom pointed his tongue at her clit and lapped in small motions, switching to feathery flicks right on the tip when she cried out. She came for a long time, ramming her backside into his face. She made a lot of noise. The driver would be wanking like a maniac this evening. Thom drank her salty, musty juices like they were ambrosia.

One she was done, she maneuvered herself back upright. "I felt it." She pressed her palms into his cheeks. Her eyes were wild and had changed color from green to a golden-rimmed hazel. "The magic."

He was horny as fuck. She was dead sexy, satiated but still hot for more. He bet she could climax again. "Take care of my dick before I die, sweetheart. I want to feel the magic too."

She laughed. Her hair was a mess, and her laugh was stunning. He was still fully erect when she glued her warm, wet goodness back on his member. "How's that?" She pumped up and down.

"That's the good stuff." The tension built quickly. Underneath his navel, the rubber band was taut. His brain drained into his balls. He loved to fuck. And come. And see his cum. Cum was coming. "Faster."

She obeyed, her acquiescence as luscious as the speed with which she rubbed on him. On every upward stroke, her perfect piece hit the base of his crown. The orgasm was sudden, painful almost, a valve deep inside of him blowing. He moaned on each squirt, totally shameless, watching in awe as the white cum spurted up to land on a dolphin tattoo near her pubic bone.

The aftermath of relief was almost as unbearable as the explosion of pleasure. Thom hugged Megan tight. He loved her. That much he knew. The rest of the stuff in his skull was scrambled eggs and jelly. His command of language was zilch. He made a dumb noise. He was an empty vessel. After a few stunned seconds spent learning to become human again, he got out a question, with proper syntax and everything. "Do you figure that the magic effort worked?"

She whispered in his ear, "Look to the space beside me and see for yourself."

NINETEEN

MEGAN PICKED THE BOOK UP OFF THOM'S HOTEL BED AND SHOWED him the relevant part again. They had made progress. Their effort was working. With his help, she was harnessing control of the magic.

He glanced at her, furrowed his brow as he scanned the written words, and cast her another long look. Clearly, he had trouble believing his eyes, but it was all right there.

She ran her finger down the lines of undeniable text. "Your new song. 'She Gives Dynamite.' When you cast the spell song, you wrote the words in the dimension of magic. When we used sex with a spell in the limo, we put them in the book."

He had changed into sweatpants and a Linda Ronstadt tee that'd lost its integrity to many washings. "I still don't understand what this means." Standing near the edge of the bed, he twisted his freshly showered hair into a bun. "Have we permanently encoded the song into a repertoire of spells or what?"

"That's the thing." She traced several of the words, the script encoded in cursive on the rough material of the paper. Awe held her in rapture. "I don't think that any of the content in this book is permanent, strictly speaking. It's a living document. The ultimate definition of a work in progress. Collaborating with us, the users, to continually redefine its environment. Sentient but not entirely independent."

Her mind was buzzing. Overly active. She was heightened. She felt an extra presence inside of her, like her brain had gained the ability to splinter into two and work double time. It was exhilarating. She had leveled up.

"And you're sure that's positive?"

"It's all trial and error. But that's how I learn."

"I wish there was another way to learn." He checked his phone. "Food's here."

"I'll get it." She had to move around. A run would be good, but some extra steps in a hotel room was second best.

Megan breezed through the bedroom and into the corporate-chic living room suite. She opened the door to an empty hallway that looked like every other four-star hotel hallway. Nice carpet, generically pleasing wall art, a potted tree or two. No delivery person with the Chinese food, however. "Hello? Delivery for Room 237?"

Footsteps puttered nearby, footfalls absorbed by the carpeting. They must've been looking for the room. Megan patted the pocket of the lounge pants that she'd borrowed from Thom and set off down the hallway.

The rhythm of the steps was persistent. Ever-present. Methodical. In front of her, beside her. Behind her. Getting louder. The hairs on the back of her neck took notice. Her fear chemicals kicked in, tingly and pressurized. She walked faster, unsure now where she was headed. Her vision tunneled to the elevator. Her lizard brain had located the main escape route. She clung to the illusion of normalcy. "Is there someone here looking for the room that ordered Chinese food?"

The steps were right behind her. Running. Chasing. Her throat and stomach collapsed into a single wad of stress. A rush of anger came in next. Who was fucking with her? A bored teen looking for kicks on his delivery job? "This isn't funny."

She turned around.

There was no one there, just a hypnotic stretch of hexagon-patterned carpet, magenta geometric shapes stitched against a luscious backdrop of cream. Yet she couldn't move. The hexagons on the rug sucked her in.

The presence inside of her rose up to eclipse the thinking part of her mind. She was far away yet stuck in place.

The shapes on the carpet were three-dimensional now, a matrix of hexagons interlocking to make a cage, which was also hexagon-shaped.

"It's a little funny," Folly said inside of Megan's head. "How easy you are, in every sense of the word. Keep moving forward."

She didn't want to, but she also did. More importantly, she couldn't stop. Megan wandered toward the floating container in the middle of the hallway. She had enough reserves left to interact. She had to figure out what was happening in order to stop it or bring it to heel under her own power. "It's the book, isn't it? I have to write my own fate into the book with spells. That has to be the key. You control me, but not completely."

"You had good luck with my friend down in the backrooms," Folly said. "But your luck is about to run out."

Megan's feet continued to move forward. The rubber of her sneakers squeaked. If she walked into that cage, it was all over. She couldn't stop walking. She was too dazed. The prison was about three feet away. Each side of the hexagon exerted a magnetic pull that was pleasurable to feel. Like a tide in the ocean, but shot through with electricity at the same time.

She passed a decorative, oversized mirror in a gilded frame that leaned against the wall. Instead of her reflection, the monster from the magic dimension stood in the glass. Unlike then, she wasn't afraid. He put his hand to the glass, making the barrier between them wiggle in silver rings. More lines than she ever could have imagined crossed his pale palm, a city's worth of white lattice intersections. A palm reader's playground rendered in wrinkles.

Except there was a strange feature inherent in his palm lines. They weren't simple markings on the skin. They were made of words, tiny words, crisscrossing the surface of that sallow skin in an intricate, nonlinear network of poetry. The poetry strips that Thom and the others used to write songs on the bus that one summer were all right there, in the flesh.

Vertigo sucked Megan's perception in and out. Her boundaries blurred. Those words took her for a ride. They moved in a circular procession across the monster's palm, knitting a wheel through time.

She remembered every detail of that summer on the bus. The smells, the laughter, the memories forged in friendship and fleeting, passionate affairs. That summer was sculpted from appetites and longings, drenched in booze and that careening, almost-sad sensation of a party on the verge of ending. A manic drive to keep the lights on as long as possible before the circus folded up its tent.

That summer, Thom had worn a lot of black and spent many nights awake writing songs. A couple had become hits, others forgotten. An elegant, manic disaster of a muse, some socialite, had been at his side. Megan yearned for that version of him, to have known him his whole life. The bus broke down outside of Boise that summer, and Brian had fixed the engine. She never would have guessed that the business-minded front man was so handy.

"Join with him," Folly whispered from deep inside Megan's inner ear. "Pull him into the hologram with you and feel the depths of that unity. You can have what you want. Memories of having known your lover back then. Of being in love with him. You can take the place of that other woman in his memories and yours. Retroactively become his one and only, his forever."

She hung onto herself by a thread, but she hung on. She was close. About to crack the code. This magic was befuddling. She wanted with an unhinged hunger to give up and scream. But she didn't. She recited the words to "She Gives Dynamite" over and over until they wore their own dedicated groove into her brain.

"It's a living thing," she said out loud. Clouds fell from her eyes. "The ultimate unsealed song. Volatile, dangerous, but with much potential. It's timeless. Eternal. 'She Gives Dynamite' has always existed, even before it was formally created. It's the richest mineral at the bottom of the crystal mountain. The lifeblood that fuels all of this. It's elixir."

"What, you think you're a muse?" Folly sneered. "You are nothing but a tool. A hole. A simple, temporary prop. A consolation prize."

Megan ignored the taunts. The lies were cheap. This was too big. Her thoughts were flying out of her head before she could pin them down. The words to the song filled the lines of the hexagon now, every word glowing in a shade of hot pink so saturated that it put neon to shame.

"That song is mine. Ours. All of ours. It's our lock and our key. Our communal magic."

She had a hunch. Brian was only partially right about sealing songs. That method was a bandage, a precaution, a means to play it safe when one didn't fully understand the might of what he or she was working with. But sealing songs wouldn't get them anywhere. It wouldn't lead to breakthroughs.

She had to test an experiment. She sang the first few verses of "She Gives Dynamite."

The walls shook as if constructed in jelly. The monster blinked out. The hologram followed. Megan stared into her own eyes, reflected in the mirror. Her head was clear. She was right. As long as she held the reins of the chariot and steered "She Gives Dynamite," she had her magic where she wanted it. The song wasn't meant to be hemmed in or contained. It demanded to be shouted from the rooftops. Flung far and wide.

Tears pricked her eyeballs. Emotions bubbled up from the core of the crystal mountain and laved her heart with floodwaters of magic. She had to collaborate with Thom and figure out how to optimize "She Gives Dynamite" and give it the life it deserved and cried out for.

"That was a cool tune." A man's voice startled Megan.

She jerked, then laughed when she saw a shaggy guy in combat boots and a stocking cap holding a bag of Chinese food. "Thanks. It's going to save the world."

"Rock and roll." He handed over the food and flashed her metal horns with his free hand.

"Rock and roll will save the world." She accepted her dinner from the delivery guy. "I love it."

"Rad."

Buoyed by new revelation, Megan quick-stepped back into the hotel room.

Thom sat on the couch, texting. "That was quick. They left it right at the door, yeah?"

Right, time moved oddly when magic was involved. She didn't bother to bring up her interlude, not seeing a point. She opened the plastic bag and placed a small army of white cartons on the glass coffee table in the middle of the hotel living room. "I have a theory that 'She Gives

Dynamite' is more powerful than any of us can imagine. It's your songs of songs."

Thom glanced at his phone before plunging his chopsticks into a container of beef lo mein. "Brian certainly seems to agree."

"What do you mean?" She speared a saucy bite of orange chicken, the intrigue bringing out the tangy and sweet flavors.

"We're getting noticed in a big way for that show. All the usual sites plus the conspiracy webpages. The typical nutcases are saying that we performed a satanic ritual onstage and junk like that. Which, who knows, maybe we did." His laugh was unsettled. He ate a nest of noodles. "I shouldn't have a negative outlook about that type of attention, I suppose. We've leveraged the conspiracy circuit before to our benefit."

"I know that you're concerned about where this is going. Believe me, I sympathize with the worries about the runaway train factor. But we can harness this. I get new information constantly."

"Okay." Thom said to his food, pushing the chopsticks around.

In posture and tone, he had closed off more than she liked. "You don't believe me? Don't trust me?"

"It's not a matter of that. It's just that I feel now that I'm in the presence of an outsized adversary, we all are, and it's dwarfing." His brown eyes met hers with a piercing intensity. "Do you ever feel that it's arrogant or presumptuous or hubristic to lay claim of ownership to such a powerful supernatural force? Like we shouldn't be monkeying with these forces at all? You've said something to that effect before. You still believe it?"

Her stomach closed up around the breaded chicken and rice. She stabbed her chopsticks into random bits of the meal. She could do without Thom being a foil. She was in control of her magic, piloting the wheel. Mostly. "Don't let those conspiracy websites get in your head. It's perfectly fine to utilize magic. In fact, it's our calling. We have to. We're duty-bound."

"How is this my calling and duty as well as yours? I'm not trying to be contrarian, but I feel we've made a leap in logic here."

She explained her theory behind "She Gives Dynamite."

For a few seconds, Thom looked dumbstruck. The chuckle that came next matched his bemused expression. "Brian agrees."

Brian had come up twice in the span of a few minutes. He clearly had a lot of input that had resonated with Thom. "That's who you were texting with?"

Thom murmured an agreement, nodding as he worked through more of his food. "He's working both the business angle, per usual, and now this supernatural angle. Wearing both hats. Just now he wanted to brainstorm on strategies on how to blast this song out as widely as possible. I believed that he's scrapped the sealed songs approach entirely. I told him I was too tired to deal with this tonight."

Brian was on the level. Great, great news. Thom's bandmate would make a stellar ally when it came to getting things done. Megan chewed on the end of her wooden utensil. How to get a song in front of many people quickly in hopes that it would spread at a rapid pace?

A light bulb went off. Spread, that was it! Like a virus. They needed "She Gives Dynamite" to go viral. With her background in YouTube productions, Megan had ideas how to get them there. First and foremost, they needed the stimulating allure of visuals. "Let's make a music video."

He didn't look immediately enthusiastic. "At the risk of mansplaining, there's a lot of process involved in that. Legal garbage. Hiring a team. Sets, location, director, more."

"Have Brian handle the legal. I'll take care of the rest." Her pulse went ape. She had a project. A good one. She had to get her stuff out of the Iowa studio and access her technology and computer programs.

"That's a lot to take on. I won't put a damper on your vision, but are you sure this is the approach you want to take?"

"Yeah. It's win-win. Not only will we make gains in getting this magic where we want it, but you'll have a nice piece of promo dominating the airwaves."

"I admire your boldness." He played with his food. "What if it backfires?"

"It won't. I'll make sure of it."

"Get a good contract for your contributions. Don't be afraid to play hardball with Brian. He probably won't try to undersell you but head it off at the pass by knowing your worth. Remind him that you're savvy about visual productions."

"Can I see your phone?"

He handed it over. Megan looked up *Bump in the Night*. The latest episode, the haunted brothel one, had been uploaded. It was popping off. The big, fat numbers made her eyes bulge and her heart swell with pride. Nearing six figures in views and fifty-thousand likes. Their best episode yet. She angled the screen to Thom. "Proof's in the pudding."

He kissed her cheek. "Congratulations. I'll defer to your idea on this. As long as you promise me that you'll put your well-being first. And that you'll talk to me if this starts to go bad. Let me help if I'm able."

"Deal." She wasn't exactly sure what he was asking, or if she was able to fully agree, but she'd try. "I need to square up a few things."

Thom had retrieved her phone, cards, and demon-trapping watch when she'd gotten sucked up in Iowa. Her clutch was on the kitchen counter. She got out her phone and ducked into the bedroom to call Gary.

He answered after one ring. "The amazing disappearing Megan resurfaces." Predictably, bone-dry sarcasm crusted his tone. He didn't sound surprised, either, that she'd pulled another ghost out. That part embarrassed her. She hated that she was earning a flaky reputation with her crew, but they'd soon see the significance of her efforts.

"The haunted brothel episode is crushing it."

"Would've been nice to have your help with the final stages of the editing process, but we did our best. The only reason I'm not furious at you is because you gave us gold-tier content to work with."

"You're welcome."

Gary sighed. "Are you back with Thom?"

"What's it to you?"

"Their latest concert is making waves for being super weird. Reporters can't tell if it was a gimmick or if some really off-the-wall hijinks went down. I figured that you'd be in on that action."

Even though he was being snarky, Gary was correct. He knew her well. "I need to ask a huge favor."

"I'd say no on principle, but we just locked down three big advertising contracts thanks to the brothel episode."

"Awesome. I need you to mail me my computers. I'll contribute a good deal of editing. And some clothes and essentials from my apartment. Please."

"You can't be serious. I'm not your gofer."

"Of course I'm serious. I'm working on a project for Fyre. A video. My involvement and name will drive traffic to *Bump in the Night*, and you know it."

"Does this mean you're leaving us to go work with Fyre?"

Such a move would violate her sense of loyalty. She'd find a way to manage both her show and the video. "Depends. What's going on with Logan?"

"Fuck if I know. He's been MIA since the brothel episode aired. Won't return any of my calls. I think he's mad that we edited out his parts."

Logan was a douche, but he had grounds for being pissed in this case. If she dedicated her labor to a production only to be cut, she wouldn't want anything to do with those involved anymore. "Sounds like he's off the team permanently."

"Yeah, I think he's done. He's been posting on TikTok, but from what I can tell, he's moved on to other sponsors and collaborations. He won't return my messages there. Or on Insta."

Gary could be cringe when it came to pandering to Logan. At least that phase seemed to be nearing its sunset. "Let him go. It's not worth it."

"Yeah, you're right. We don't need his money anymore."

"That's the spirit. You'll mail my stuff?"

"Will you contribute five to ten hours per week to editing for us?"

"Yes." She wasn't about to turn her back on the show.

"And you'll stop ignoring my calls and messages?"

She winced. She had to stop flaking on Gary. It was unprofessional. "Yes. Promise."

"We want to get back out on a shoot in the next two weeks. You think you can make that a priority?"

"Yes. Any more demands?"

"That should do it."

Megan laughed. Gary could be a pain, but he cared about *Bump in the*

Night deeply and was committed to its success. She admired his conviction. "Deal. Thank you."

"Can I ask you a kind of hardcore question?"

"Shoot."

"What happened at that concert? I have a feeling you have an inside track. Is it true what they're saying, that there was black magic involved? Entities more...troublesome than ghosts?"

Megan pursed her lips. She didn't quite know how to answer Gary's question. "The paranormal is real. We both know that."

"You didn't answer."

She gave Gary the details of the courier service that Fyre used and hung up. He'd be just fine in the dark. The only aspect of her extracurricular activities that concerned him was the video, which he'd see soon enough. When her creation saved the world.

TWENTY

W ITH T HOM BY HER SIDE, M EGAN SAT ACROSS FROM B RIAN IN THE singer's hotel room. She'd made a point to go shopping for the meeting, an opportunity to tour Boston with Thom and pick out a new dress and shoes. Fyre's mail crew had received her computers and editing equipment and delivered them to Thom's room. Once she had a chance, she'd buckle down and edit a ton of *Bump in the Night* content. She'd tie it into the video in any way she could.

For now, she was ready to pitch her latest business venture. Beside her on a loveseat, Thom held her hand.

Brian had arranged his couch into a makeshift workspace, folders and a tablet lined up neatly on the middle cushion. He'd already laid a stack of paper on the coffee table, even though she'd only provided him with the barest details of her video vision. Brian had helped write "She Gives Dynamite" and been present for its stunning debut. He knew what the song was capable of. He had to have an idea of her agenda. He'd dressed up too, in slacks and a collared shirt. She took these as good signs that he was taking her seriously.

He wasted no time on niceties. "Why are you the right person to take the lead on a music video for us?" His blue eyes were piercing. His posh accent was disarming.

She was unbothered, armed with passion and purpose.

"First of all, the magic. You need me. My input, my power. You've seen what I'm capable of and the forces that swirl around me, within me. I can harness them effectively. As we know, our collective well-being demands it. Not only will my direction be more effective than sealing songs, you get the added benefit of publicity. It's a win up and down."

He held on with his stare.

"You look ridiculous when you try to mad dog someone, mate," Thom put in with a laugh.

Brian sliced Thom a narrow-eyed look. "Thanks for the feedback." He turned to Megan. "Do you have any experience in creative writing and/or directing?"

"Yeah. I've written fiction, especially when I was at my old job."

"What happened there?"

"Fired."

He raised a single eyebrow. "Oh?"

"Personal issue with management." Sounded better than "humped and dumped."

"I don't want to know."

"You really don't. More importantly, my show, *Bump in the Night*, is a breakaway success. Go online and see for yourself."

Brian picked up his tablet and poked at the screen. His eyes widened. "Impressive."

She was certain that Brian had watched the show prior to the meeting. That man for sure kept his pulse on all up-and-coming content. Of course he'd pre-screened her work. She let him play it off cool and pretend he was just now learning about the show. "Thank you. I'm not being entirely noble or selfless here. I'm thinking of cross-promo. A boost for my original content. If we act fast and ride the energy from your last concert, it'll work out for all our benefit. I see a lot of crossover in our audience bases."

Brian leaned against the back of the sofa, still sizing her up. "What's your vision for this video?"

She launched into the setup that she'd pictured. The main character, played by her, is tapped by wise mages for an elite mission to travel to the hole at the bottom of the crystal mountain in order to fulfil an ancient prophecy.

The inside of the crystal mountain would be a dimension in itself, a thriving world hidden in a hollow, crystalline core. The protagonist must secure a sacred key and return it to its rightful place before reentering the everyday world armed with a new set of sacred powers that she'll need for her final mission.

While traversing the bowels of the crystal mountain, she fights many adversaries and experiences a number of crushing setbacks before finally prevailing against a formidable opponent with the power to control minds. "It'll have action, mythology, magic, creatures, and lore. Every piece of this video will enhance your brand, not dilute it. Guaranteed. Beyond that, this will be the production that 'She Gives Dynamite' deserves. Through this, we'll gain control of the chariot once and for all. No more sealing songs. We'll be steering the prophecy exactly how we want it. No more exhausting yourself with weird shit rituals down in Peru when you really ought to be working on your career. You guys can't do everything yourself, nor should you be expected to. Let me lend my expertise to take on some of the load."

A few beats went on. An unpleasant clench commandeered Megan's innermost muscles. She'd made a misstep. She was losing Brian.

"Have you talked to Helen and Eve?" Brian asked.

There was the rub. He was worried she wouldn't be able to handle this on her own. He didn't realize how fast they had to act. How involving additional opinions would slow them down and diminish the control they needed.

"I'm not looking for outside feedback. I'm trying to save everyone the trouble of wasted time and labor."

"I don't think it's prudent to keep them clueless. They'll want to be involved in this effort and won't appreciate that you've gone behind their backs."

"Your reservations can't be that strong, because you've agreed to meet with me. Let me guess. You're worried that they'll have concerns and try to put the brakes on this lucrative opportunity, and you want to head that off at the pass before we get in too deep. We can't afford to dawdle, or we lose our perfect timing and waste time debating and debriefing when we really ought to be getting to work."

He pursed his lips. Glanced at Thom. Scratched his temple. "I don't want an air of secrecy to cause any trouble in my marriage. Sprinkle in secrecy in any relationship and you're playing with dynamite."

Thom put in, "Why did you want to hear the idea in the first place? Why agree to this meeting instead of voicing your issues right away? Because it's starting to feel like you're toying with us. Dangling a carrot."

"Come on, you know me better than that." Brian met Thom's eyes. Nothing about the man was dishonest or shifty. Megan wanted to hear his perspective, but at the same time Thom was right. They couldn't afford to hem and haw. Brian turned to address Megan again. "I'm enthusiastic about your idea. I knew it'd be good. And connecting you to the video, a recognizable face with an existing media presence, after you appeared onstage? Genius. There's even a hint of reimagined, MTV-era nostalgia tied in with an up-and-comer getting her big break—think Courtney Cox pulled onstage at the Springsteen concert. Speculation and press attention is all but guaranteed. The iron is red hot right now. It's for sure time to strike with this initiative. We have at least a seventy-eight percent chance of going viral, if recent metrics on viral patterns are any indication."

"We see eye to eye. What's the problem?" Megan pressed.

"It's almost like a liability thing. We can't be continually reckless when working with magic. We were at the stage show, yes, but the stakes were in the stratosphere. We had no choice. It's time to approach this more carefully from now on."

"Tell Helen to come see me if she wants, but that this is happening. She'll thank me when it's done. I'm fine to meet her on the set, or give her the gist, but I want this project to be my own. Not a co-created effort where I end up bouncing ideas off anyone."

"I'm afraid I can't support that plan," Brian said.

"You aren't being particularly helpful," Thom said. "And you realize that we don't need your permission to make the video."

Brian looked taken aback. "If you wish to use our music, elements of our story world, and brand name, you most certainly do. Allow me to remind you that you didn't write that song by yourself. Let alone perform it solo. 'She Gives Dynamite' is all our intellectual property."

"Talk about getting lost in the weeds," Thom scoffed. "Megan and I are over here trying our hardest to halt a prophecy and save the world, and here you are pretending to be the contracts lawyer you've always dreamed of becoming."

"Maybe one of these days you'll learn to make a cogent point without insulting me," Brian said. "At the risk of being smug, I think it's fair to say that I've more than proven myself capable of handling our business and legal matters. You never had a problem with ceding that sort of control before, as long as someone else was willing to shoulder the adult responsibilities of what we do. But now that you're emotionally attached to a pet project, you're perfectly comfortable belittling me for pointing out what are very real, practical concerns."

"Spare me the sanctimonious lecture." Thom folded his arms across his chest. "Why don't you save us all the time and admit that you're not willing to do anything without asking your wife's permission."

Brian's mouth hung open.

Megan inserted herself into the verbal melee before Brian had a chance to fire a shot. "Enough arguing." Thom and Brian could unpack their disputes another time. This meeting was about productive collaboration. Squabbles had no place. "Thom, we'll get the video made. We just have to be patient and work through these hurdles. Brian, I see where you're coming from. Get Helen in here. I'll deal with her right now."

"You always this forward?" Brian sliced her a dry look as he picked up his phone.

"What do you think?" She lobbed a wink.

She'd turned Brian's head a time or two back when she was running around on the scene. He was a serial monogamist who'd always been too faithful and scrupulous to respond to her in a sexual way, which was just as well. Their emerging relationship as business associates would function better since there was no sordid history to contend with.

"Don't let this opportunity slip through your fingers." Thom spoke to Brian in a tone of warning. "We can get this video out in a week, while we're still in the news cycle."

Brian finished his text. "I can do without the used car salesman pitch, thanks. Helen's on her way. And since you're keen to talk business all of a sudden, Thom, how about we stick around here while the ladies talk over their part? I could use your help buttoning up the last of the details for Rockstock 2024. Pepsi needs a Zoom meeting. A couple of the endorsement deals are in shambles, and I have no idea who we're going to subcontract to secure Pony and Tony on that pathetic excuse for a stage. Oh, and one of our regional marketing directors just quit. Family crisis. Perhaps you can fill in for him until my search team secures a replacement." Brian smiled sweetly.

"I walked right into that," Thom groaned.

"Into what, your obligations?" Brian reached into a designer briefcase on the floor, pulled out a fat manila envelope, and plopped it in Thom's lap.

"What the hell is Gabrielle doing? What's the point of having a manager if we end up doing all the management work?"

Brian handed Thom a leather-bound folder. "She's doing a million other things, and she's doing a great job. Why don't you review that dossier and give your opinion on whether it's within our budget to expand our management team?"

Megan did *not* want to get in the middle. Everything that Brian had mentioned sounded like a total drag to deal with, but no doubt it had to get done. Thom would be fine. He and Brian bonded over bickering, though Thom would never admit as much. Who was she to interfere with their special time?

Brian's phone dinged. He pointed a finger in the air. His signal that Helen had texted to announce her arrival was welcome.

When a knock landed on the hotel room door, Megan stood. Thom rose with her, and she gave him a kiss on the cheek. "Hope you don't get bored to tears."

"It's fine." He gave her a hug. "I suppose it's what I deserve for taking a hands-off approach all of those years."

"Mmm, I'd say you were more hands-on." The kiss she pressed to his lips was more sensual than the first.

His breathing quickened. His fingertips traced the curve of her waist and hips. "If only we had ten minutes to ourselves before parting ways. Alas, I'm now at the whims of our self-appointed CEO."

"CEO," Brian said over the rustle of papers shuffling. "I quite like the sound of that."

"It's going to be a long afternoon," Thom said.

Megan kissed him once more before gathering her purse and walking to the door. She had a case of stomach butterflies. The energy of the first meeting was charged. She slipped out the door to greet Helen in the hallway. Her fellow witch wore jeans and a sweatshirt. She'd tied her brown hair in a messy topknot and applied light makeup. She looked like a typical pretty woman of their generation. Little did the world know.

"I don't know what to say that won't sound stilted or dumb," Megan admitted. "It's good that we're connecting. We ought to have done this sooner."

"I'll say." Helen pulled a phone out of a cross-body bag that rested against her front. "Want to get lunch and try to find somewhere to begin?"

Megan laughed. The tension within her eased. Fortunately, Helen was friendly and receptive.

They ended up at a hole-in-the-wall sushi restaurant that Helen endorsed based on glowing recommendations from the crew. Chimes dinged when the door opened.

A massive fish tank full of colorful, lazy specimens kept goggle-eyed watch over the entryway. Dim lighting made the entire place feel like an aquarium, murky and mysterious. Wood-paneled walls complemented the aesthetic with an outdated charm. There were no other diners. Helen had picked a good place to convene discreetly. Which Megan should be thinking about given her public spectacle onstage.

An elderly Asian woman in jean shorts grabbed two menus and led them through the dining room. Helen asked for a booth in the back corner, and the hostess obliged. She set down two plastic cups of water and vanished into a back room.

"Part of me wants to be mad." Helen pushed her glass back and forth on the table. "You didn't come to me right away and instead kept this a secret. I realize that's not fair. I'm sure you had your reasons for keeping this to yourself."

Megan fidgeted with a paper placemat with a crossword puzzle on the front. "I heard you and Eve talking about Peru. At that point, I didn't want to know. I think I wanted this magic situation to resolve on its own, even though deep down I knew it wouldn't."

"I don't blame you." Her light brown eyes were heavy with knowledge. "But it's too late for that now, isn't it?"

The air in the restaurant took on a certain chill. "I take it you saw what happened onstage? Heard the story behind it?"

"Yeah. I wasn't thrilled that Thom took it upon himself to put magic into a song. Or Brian for that matter. But it is what it is. It made no sense that they'd be able to do that themselves without outside influence from someone like, well, us. From there, I concluded that Thom had to be connected to one of the witches. I'd seen you around. When I saw the footage of you appearing onstage, I connected the dots."

A spiky-haired waiter sidled up to the table, and they each ordered a couple of sushi rolls. Once he left, Megan said, "I should not have been secretive about my experiences. I didn't know how to handle it. I think that the prospect of one more thing on my plate was overwhelming."

"Why don't you tell me about yourself?" Helen served up a warm smile. "We'll call this a fresh start."

Megan painted a picture with the relevant strokes. How when she was a child, her grandma had told her that she was gifted with a special sight that allowed her to contact supernatural worlds. How Gran had given her the watch to trap dark energies when Megan's travails with the shadow person became too much to bear. She explained that the watch had been helpful in the past, working reliably, but recently it had stopped. Literally ground to a halt, the gears frozen in stasis.

She told the story of pulling her book out of the floor at the haunted orphanage where she'd done a paranormal investigation a couple of years ago. Since then, she'd been hearing things. Seeing things. She'd encountered a bizarre woman. Felt inexplicable sensations in her body. Possibly put magic into Thom. Gotten sucked into other worlds that felt hostile. At times, she confessed, she felt as if she shared her body with some presence who had no love for her.

"Yeah," Helen said gravely. "That's the architect of the prophecy at work. She's always trying to possess people, and once she's in, she's hard to get rid of. It doesn't sound like Thom's been compromised. That's good."

"Why do you think he was able to resist?"

"It might be a crapshoot for all I know. This magic is a mindfuck."

"I wish there was more I could do to help. The spells I've attempted have raised more questions than they answered. Which has been the case every time I opened my book to try to learn." Merely mentioning the book sent a spike of anxiety into her nerves. She hated to leave it unattended given its recent behavior, but hauling it around didn't make practical sense. The book was fine in the hotel room. It would have to be. Besides, why would it want to leave her?

"Yep, that checks out with what we're dealing with. Inverted realities, ever-changing facts, up is down. My mentor got trapped in one of the books for a while. But that's a whole separate story." The food arrived. Helen picked at a grain of rice. "That's a bad sign that your watch stopped working."

Megan hazarded a grim guess. "Because that means that it's no longer able to trap dark energies, since they're too strong?"

"That's my read." Helen ate a small roll. "A lot of damage was done before we figured out that the Fyre songs were connected and that we had to seal them."

"Is that what you do in Peru?"

"Yep. Continually and repeatedly. The seals wear off. We're always playing defense. Scrambling to plug a leaky dam before it bursts. I think we're too far behind to sustain this method for much longer. It's exhausting. We have to pivot, and soon."

Megan explained her theory behind "She Gives Dynamite."

Helen paled. She put her chopsticks down. Lips pressed, she shook her head.

"Say something," Megan prompted.

"I don't like it."

"Give this a chance. Give me a chance. Like you said, we need to try something different."

"This is the opposite of everything that I've learned or been taught."

"None of which is effective anymore. You admitted this." Megan seized the opportunity to eat. The fish was fresh, and the rice was perfectly moist. At least she had a good meal in front of her to help keep her brain in top form.

"The only thing that makes me even remotely hopeful that this might stand a chance is that you're the sixth witch. With you, we're complete."

"Should I feel flattered or horrified?"

That startled a laugh out of Helen and got her eating again. "You feel however you like. None of us know what we're doing. It's like trial-and-error city over here."

"We'll surely be more successful with all six of us. An unbroken circle. We'll establish a seamless chain reaction where we draw from the others while they draw from us."

"I do like that you've studied," Helen said.

"Let's give my method a try. If we get this video out into the world immediately, it'll make an unforgettable impact. The energy will be a bulwark. This dark spirit that wants to possess us and overtake the world won't stand a chance."

"You sure about that?"

"No. Guessing. But that what we're all about, right?"

"I suppose." Helen smirked but wasn't able to hide a deeper look of admiration. Megan was winning her over. "You know what? Fuck it. Let's try this. We'll fly to Peru tomorrow and shoot the video. I'll spend the rest of the day securing props and crew. If we can get the video out close to the last show, we'll put together a spell to reinforce its energy. It might fail spectacularly, but we'll be giving this our best shot."

"I knew you'd come around. You won't be sorry."

"Oh, we might all be sorry. However, you're correct in your intuition. This is novel. Creative. Innovative. And, if done right it just might work."

Megan had gone to lunch with Helen to plead her case, but suddenly, winning felt like a pyrrhic victory. Because now she had to overcome odds and uncertainty to succeed. The weight of the world rested upon her shoulders, and she wasn't going to shrug. At least she had connected with an ally who understood the intricacies of their magic as much as anyone did. Helen was a resource. "Will you meet me in my hotel room after this and bring your book? I'd like to compare notes."

TWENTY-ONE

MEGAN'S HANDS SHOOK AS SHE PUNCHED IN THE CODE TO THE HOTEL safe. Having the book go missing with Helen as a witness sure would be a bad look. She held her breath and pulled the metal handle. Her brain summoned a horror montage of what she'd see in there. A pile of squirming maggots. The head of a family member. Abominations mating.

Just the book. Worse, in a way, than the reel contrived by her imagination. Thick, dense, and watching them. Megan sighed, her exhale ragged, relief mingling with dread. Every time she cast her eyes on the grimoire, she felt more acutely that the book was staring right back at her with intentionality. Its sentience was growing. Or she was going crazy, caught in a death spiral. Or both.

"You thought it would be gone?" Helen said.

"I don't know. Maybe. Or morphed into something horrible." Megan looked away. The book was glowering at her. It was pissed. She felt sick in her belly.

"Was part of you secretly hoping that would be the case? To give you an out from facing the truth?"

Her pulse was erratic, an unregulated thread of jumps. "I don't know what to say." She didn't want to admit her true feelings and anger the book even more. Unless Folly could read her mind anyway and use her thoughts to gain leverage, rendering the entire subject moot. She slammed the safe door. It banged shut with a tinny clack. "I never should have touched this fucking thing, let alone opened and read it. I'm going nuts." She stalked out of the closet and sat on the edge of the bed. At least she wasn't face-to-face with her enemy anymore. "You might be right about the video. I think I bit off more than I can chew. I'm not strong enough, or advanced enough. Not competent enough." She held her head in her hands. The world was spinning. Ugly eyes peered through the closet door. Folly had eyes on her no matter where she ran to and hid. Tears prickled the inside of her nose.

Helen sat beside her. She'd brought her own book, which looked similar to Megan's but somehow less awful. She set her copy next to her hip. "Don't beat yourself up. These feelings inside of you are by design. That's her aim. To keep you off-balance, unsure, and in a state of dysregulation. You're easier to control that way."

"It's working. What should I do?"

"Try to find your center. Whatever that looks like for you. Positive self-talk, meditation. A walk. Journaling. Anything to help you stay grounded."

"Do you feel manipulated by your book?"

"Not anymore. But it was a struggle initially. My magic completely took control of me at first. It's a stretch to say it was even mine. I was a vehicle. A puppet. In the beginning, my mentor gave me a clear crystal to use. She may have been duped, because it turns out that crystal had dark energy attached to it that escaped and caused a lot of havoc. I eventually trapped the dark energy back inside of that crystal, but not before a lot of scary things happened. I won't subject you to the whole saga now, but there was an evil clone of me in the picture for a bit, running around and causing problems. Thom doesn't trust me at all due to the clone's mischief. That's all a ton of fun."

Hearing that Helen had gone through a rough ride and lived to tell was comforting. "That makes me feel better."

"We'll get through this, but we have to keep our heads on straight. Can I see your watch?"

Megan got her clutch out of the nightstand and took out her precious, dormant heirloom. The gears were as immobile as ever, frozen, a thin wisp of black smoke curling over the tiny brass teeth. She gave it to Helen.

Helen cradled the sleeping watch as if she was holding a baby bird. "Do you mind if I check with my mentor about this?"

"Go right ahead." She'd take any guidance she could get. The fact that a mentor was in the mix was a positive development.

Helen balanced the watch on her thigh and sent a text. She watched her phone in tense silence, twitching when it chimed seconds later. "That's what I thought," she said, her voice flat.

"More bad news?" Megan was numb to it. She expected as much.

"Sounds like the watch was acting as a buffer between dark forces and you. Based on my description of the gears and the black smoke, Nerissa said it's spellbound. As in, halted from protecting you. You said these dark energies have been following you your whole life?"

"More or less."

Helen turned the watch over and pulled the underside close to her face. "This little guy has been working tirelessly since then. Even before you connected with your book, you were identified as a conduit. Your subconscious knew that you had a tie to this magic before your surface mind did. You know who did also." She gestured to the safe in the closet.

"At the risk of whining, why me? I can't help but feel targeted."

"To some extent, that's our destiny. It's pointless to spend energy searching for rational explanations. It just is." Helen reached over and ran her fingers through the sigil on the front of her book, her short, red nails tracing a path through a maze of swirls. "There's significance to you being the fire witch too. You're distinct from the rest of us. We had conversations about you before any of us even met you. Your element is the most fickle. Versatile. Untethered, if that makes sense. Consider how mobile and adaptable fire is. Always meshed with other elements."

The gears in Megan's watch may have been frozen, but the machinery in her brain kicked into motion. Having someone more experienced to talk with about magical matters took the edge off. She wasn't alone. That counted. "You can make a fire anywhere, or a fire can start anywhere, given the right tools and conditions."

"Exactly. The other elements are either place-bound, in the case of earth, or ubiquitous, like spirit and air. Water is also more flexible, but not to the extent of fire. You can't conjure it out of its absence."

"If only I knew how to direct that power to help me. Or all of us."

"I feel like you do know. From what you've said, you're the most keyed in to the mythology of our magic than any of us. You've demonstrated an ability to pass to other worlds seamlessly. You're tied into the songs. That's valuable. You're susceptible, hence the possession efforts, but you're hard to pin down. That's why the spirit in your book is mad. She wants desperately to get to you, and she's close, but she can't. You're too ephemeral. Intangible. Like your element."

"Can you help me unclog my watch?"

"I can try."

Megan rubbed the back of her neck. Did she have a low-grade headache, or was the dull, murky sensation behind her eyes the result of supernatural infiltration? Either way, she wanted it gone. "I need to be unpolluted to give this video my full attention. I don't want to blunder this. Not at all."

Helen hauled her book onto her lap. "There's a spirit spell called Banish Intruders that I think will be a fit with what you need. My thought is to cast it in partner work with your element and build a firewall."

"A one-two punch. Kick out the unwanted guest and put in a security system to stop their return."

"Bingo. And you were correct a minute ago. We need to ensure that we're in prime shape for the video. This does mean that you'll have to get out your book and work with it."

The entire closet seemed to exude a stifling gravitational pull. The hotel room's thick curtains were open, the room suffused with both natural and artificial light, yet an unwholesome darkness vibrated in that black cube of a metal safe. Megan's archenemy was inanimate, portable, yet no less frightening. She was full of surprises, and she was learning. "I don't want to touch it anymore," Megan confessed.

"I know." Sympathy rounded Helen's speech, but there was a "but" coming. "But you have to. The video is our chance to defeat this once and for all. We have to put our best foot forward. Go in strong. Unblemished. As the best version of ourselves."

"Meaning I need to get my shit together fast." Unbearable pressure, and even more uncertainty. Present circumstances made Megan bitterly nostalgic for a time when her biggest concerns were sleep paralysis and a hulking shadow at the foot of her bed.

"To put it bluntly, yes. Don't be too hard on yourself. We're seeing to a few loose ends before we make our final push. That's all."

Helen was good at reframing negativity in more palatable terms. That was a gift. "Okay, let's get it over with."

"I can put a simple protection spell on you while you handle the book. Think of it like an invisible hazmat suit."

"I'll take all the assistance I can get." Megan rose to her feet. Her knees were looser than she would have liked. If Helen's spell would steady her, she'd accept the support.

Helen rattled off a quick incantation. Her book was open on her legs, but from the natural, smooth way that she spoke the words, it sounded like the protection spell was committed to memory.

The assurance of expertise soothed Megan. She wasn't alone. A few more steps, a few more efforts, and she'd be free. They all would. She'd be free to work on her show and enjoy being with Thom. Part of her wanted to throw that damn book in the trunk of her car, speed to the abandoned orphanage in Iowa, and stick the cursed volume right back in the hole where she'd found it. The pit she'd been *lured* to. Which probably wouldn't solve anything, now that the demon had clawed its way out of the paper bag.

She quick-stepped to the safe, flung open the door, and snatched the book before she could hesitate. Pain seared her palms. Her brain short-circuited from the flash of hot-coal agony. "Damn!" She dropped the scalding weight on the ground, rubbing her palms. "It's red hot." Her skin throbbed. "It doesn't want to be touched."

Helen crouched by the book. She pressed her hand into the cover and didn't flinch. "I think it's sucking up your magic to use as both a weapon and a shield. Taking it out of you. That's why the book is burning."

"How do you know that?"

"Experience, anecdotes, and research. She takes our magic from us and turns it against us. It's part of the possession process. We have to act fast." A shimmery, phosphorescent cloud trickled from Helen's fingertips. She moved the light in a circle over the cover as if she was applying polish to the leather. "A different simple protection spell. Try to handle it now."

Megan bit her tongue. She thrust her arm at the book, expecting another uncomfortable jolt, but the leather connected with her skin without incident. Her stomach in knots, she trucked back to the bed, telling herself that all would be well. Helen had a plan. Together, they'd pull off their strategy.

"Ready?" Helen asked.

"No. But I'll do it."

Helen let out a wry laugh. "That's the spirit."

"Fitting, because you're the spirit witch."

"An unintended yet clever play on words. Okay, follow my lead. I'm going to open to my section and read off Banish Intruders." She cleaved her book. A sweet, musty smell teased Megan's nostrils. She always enjoyed the old book aroma, even if the book in question was suspect. "While I'm doing that, you repeat the words to the Firewall spell in your mind. That way we aren't talking over each other, but we're still building the energetic chain that allows for our magic to co-create."

Megan got her book open and flipped to the Firewall spell. The appropriate page was crowded with words written in cursive. Notes in different handwriting and ink colors filled the margins. Much of the penmanship was illegible, and big chunks had been blurred by what looked like water damage. Rust-colored stains pockmarked the pages in pinprick droplets. This section had seen usage.

She recited the phrases in her mind. Endless repetition made her spacey and distant. Her thoughts came unglued. There were spaces between her mental words and images—big ones. That had to be where the fire went. Her guardian. "Is it working?" she heard herself ask.

The dead center of her skull rumbled. Sharp pain made her scream, unless she was only thinking about screaming. The effect was the same. Burning. Screaming. A primal, unspeakable hurt pinned her in the crux of teeth.

Her body lurched forward with roller-coaster violence. She flailed a body part—arms? legs?—cartwheeling for purchase against a void.

Eyesight left the picture. Her universe was a controlled inferno. She kept on reciting the words of the spell even as syllables ran together into a mush of gibberish.

Somewhere in the wasteland of eternal nothing, Helen's voice called out. She wasn't more than a whisper, but she was there, and a lifeline.

A savage glare barreled down on Megan's eyeballs, white-hot. She squinted. Squeezing her eyelids shut didn't help. The brightness was severe. After a battle against rapid-fire blinks, her vision adjusted.

Three faces peered down at her. Not faces, technically. Three smooth, reflective slabs. One gold, one bronze, and one silver. They wore black robes.

"Where am I?" Megan asked. Her voice was hoarse enough to sound alien. She felt like she'd slept for a year.

"At the bottom of the crystal mountain." She couldn't tell which one of them spoke, nor ascertain the gender.

"Helen?" Megan lurched to a seat. She was in an enclosure with bumpy, ridged cave walls like frosted glass. Helen was somewhere in there, whispering, but her vocalizations were faint. Megan couldn't make out even a piece of a word.

"At the bottom of the crystal mountain," one of the trio repeated. It was impossible to tell if the same one spoke or one of his companions.

This was the video. This had to be the video, and she'd lost time and memories of events leading up to the shoot. Yet there was no production crew anywhere. Just pale walls and the three white-robed figures with faceless faces.

"Come," the bronze one said, beckoning with a crook of four gloved fingers. "Your ceremony begins."

Déjà vu sucked her forward and back through a circular hoop of infinite time. Non-time, because time was an illusion. She rapped her knuckles on the material that she lay in. A hollow echo returned her call. She could finally see well enough to comprehend. She was in a pod. Time might be a false construct, but matter was real.

She swung her legs over the side. Her bare feet connected with room-temperature ground. With as much grace as she could muster in her dazed state, she hauled herself out of the chamber. After a couple of dizzy, queasy seconds, she was secure enough in her bearings. "Where's

Helen?" The other witch ought to have been more accessible. On the set. She was supposed to be present on the shoot, but where was she? "Helen!" Megan called out. "Are you there?" Anxiety began its python squeeze. This wasn't right.

"Your friend had her very own piece of the crystal mountain in her pocket," Silver said. At least Megan was with it enough to be able to match voices to those who spoke them. Not that it mattered, because their voices were identical and uniformly devoid of emotion. Creepy didn't begin to describe the depths of that uncanny valley.

"Bequeathed to her at her initiation by her mentor Nerissa," Gold said. Megan's spinal cord was a lightning rod for unnatural tingles.

"A conduit for our very own dear mistress and her ilk. Little did your friend know how much use she'd be to us." Bronze giggled, and the others followed, their tinkling chortles blending into a blood-curdling chorus.

"Oh how we captured Nerissa's judgment," Gold prattled, "and presented her with one clear crystal from the crystal mountain. All witches return to the crystal mountain."

"Crystal mountain." Silver linked arms with Gold and Bronze.

"Crystal mountain," the trio chanted in perfect synch. Connected by a chain of black fabric, they stepped closer. Closed in on her, their words and bodies swallowing her will.

"No!" Megan took off running. She didn't know where she was going, but she had to go. She caught Gold by surprise and smashed through the arm link he'd made with Bronze.

Then she was off, running, sprinting, her lungs and calves electric with blood and burn as she ran, ran, ran to nowhere. Her mad dash took her through turns and straight stretches, each as monochromatic as the last. She halted herself, panting and high on adrenaline, and felt a wall.

She pawed for a door, latch, window, anything. Nothing gave. There was nowhere to stick her fingers, and the rock of the mountain walls didn't yield to a push. She repeated the words to the Firewall spell out loud, knowing in her heart that the effort was futile. The spell had failed. Or hadn't worked in the way they intended. Either way, she was operating from behind, as usual. "Helen!" she yelled.

Helen responded, but she could have been in a distant galaxy.

Megan got moving again, a knock of her big toe against a hard object halting her momentum. Three objects lay before her on the diamond ice ground. A beaten broadsword. A 9mm pistol, ebony on ivory. Her demon-trapping watch.

"We'd never undertake a battle of wits against the unarmed," crooned a member of the masked trifecta. They'd gone invisible, apparently. Or communicated via telepathy. "You will have but one chance to accomplish your goal and close the door between your world and ours. Choose wisely."

It was a trick. A trap. It always was. The triptych of choices stared up at her, mocking in their muteness. The gun seemed to be the most straightforward, but she'd never handled one. She couldn't point to the safety or bullet chamber, let alone operate those crucial pieces of the machine. The broadsword was the most conducive to Fyre's vision, which made sense if she was operating from the premise of the music video. Too bad that the laws of physics were optional around here, casting doubt on the efficacy of direct combat.

Finally, the watch. Sentimental, mysterious, and time-tested in its paranormal efficacy. Broken, however, and lacking a clear pathway to repair. Unfixable perhaps.

Just like her.

No contest. Megan scooped up her demon-trapping watch and said, "Let's do this."

TWENTY-TWO

B RIAN WAS BANGING ON ABOUT R OCKSTOCK 2024 AND HAD BEEN FOR
ages. He'd covered the pros and cons of having food trucks, expert
reviews on various types of suspension cables, and liability clauses for
bungee jumping when an insight more powerful than any epiphany or
intuitive spark struck Thom.

The truth struck Thom from up above, loud, in a voice that wasn't
his. The truth travelled a pipeline from his mind to his lips. The truth
would not stay silent. "That music video can't happen."

Stop the video. Stop the video. Stop the video. Stop the video. His gut
instinct wouldn't stop screaming.

"You weren't listening, were you?" Brian glanced up from a bunch of
files to give Thom a withering look.

"Not really, but that's beside the point. This video can't happen. We
have to stop it." The voice gave the order. The voice was right. The voice
had always been right, since time immemorial, and who was he to
challenge omniscience? He was lucky that the voice had chosen him. The
least he could do was heed her demand.

"What's with the abrupt reversal? Barely an hour ago, you and Megan
thought that this video was the solution to all our problems."

"I misjudged a key element."

Chiefly, how that video will break my cord to you. That damn video will leach my magic from you and give it to our enemies. I have to have you. Your mind. Your music. "She Gives Dynamite." All belong in the crystal mountain, with me, to fuel the hologram.

"Yes, ma'am," Thom muttered.

"What?" Brian set down a messy stack of mixed paper and placed a highlighter atop the jumble to serve as a paperweight.

Brian was getting suspicious. Thom had to hold his cards close. He couldn't let Brian know that he'd formed an alliance with Folly. He wouldn't understand that their partnership was invaluable. The hologram prophecy had to happen. It had been decreed. There was no other option. Megan's will was not a factor in the equation. "I didn't say anything."

"Well, you're sweating, and your eyes are pinned out. Don't tell me you've picked up a drug habit. I thought we put that behind us."

"Shut up." Thom sprang off the couch. He was full of bugs. Filled to the brim with minuscule, fiberglass peepers, watching him. All eyes on him. He darted to the kitchen, pulled a bottled water out of the fridge, and drank half in one chug. Brian was right about one thing. He had to cool off. Sharing a body with Folly had him too worked up. He had to play it cool. This claustrophobia would take getting used to. He wasn't all that great at sharing what was his, least of all his soul. But he'd have to learn because this was how it would be from now on. "That's quite rude, to accuse me of being an addict on the basis that I changed my mind. Why do you even care? You subjected Megan to a cross-examination fit for a criminal, having her defend that video."

"Okay, you're right. That wasn't called for." Brian showed up by the stove. He knew. He could tell. Thom could see suspicion in his eyes. Brian was on to him.

"He may have to be handled," Folly whispered from within. Her voice sounded odd, deeper. Male, like his. "Permanently. My apologies in advance."

I won't hurt him, Thom told her with his mind. *He's my best friend.*

"He means nothing," she snapped. Were they merging? "Conversely, the prophecy means everything."

I know. He felt helpless. If she took over completely, he might be unable to protect Brian from his due punishment. A consequence that would be inevitable if he stood in the way of the prophecy. Brian had already interfered once. They couldn't let that happen again. *I won't let it come to that.*

"Then you'd better stop that fucking video from getting made."

"Are you talking to yourself, mate?" Brian's discernment was as sharp as Japanese steel. He saw right through Thom. He inched closer, his hand outstretched.

Thom was about to be cornered between the fridge and the wall. He needed out. "You know what it's like," he gritted out. He refused to lie or gaslight, but telling the truth could seal Brian's doom. Folly was dangerous. He had to abide and appease her without leading his best mate into a lethal trap. He ought not to be cavalier with his thoughts either. She was in there. Listening. He covered his ears. "You've been where I am. I need space. Please leave me be."

He got himself out of the room before Brian could stop him with actions or words.

He didn't remember making the short trip to his hotel room, opening the lock with his key card, or walking to the bedroom. Yet there he stood, facing down the pristine, made bed.

In an instant, he thought that he was dreaming, or had woken up from a blackout even though he never drank enough to go blotto. The bed was wrong. Red decorative throw pillow instead of gold. A vortex sucked him under. The room was entirely different. Foreign décor, unfamiliar furniture placement. He'd been mind-wiped. They'd switched locations on him. But why?

Panic crashed down in a thunderbolt. "Megan?" he cried. No answer. He stumbled to the safe where they'd stashed her book. The combination didn't work. "Fuck!" An interloper had scrubbed him clean. Transplanted him. At least he had his phone. He called Brian. After two rings and an answer, he demanded to know, "Where am I?"

"Excuse me?"

"Where the fuck am I, Brian? Cut the shite. Who switched out my room? What happened after we parted ways? Did you and Helen decide that I was too much of a wild card and clear out my memories? Fucking lobotomize me with your spooky black magic?" He collapsed on the strange bed. He didn't feel like himself but was unable to identify what the problem was. The last time he'd seen Brian, they'd gotten into an argument about Fyre business, meaning business as usual. Rockstock 2024. Petty crap. He'd left Brian's room in a huff. There was a sense of urgency without a referent. An event had to happen immediately or be stopped.

"Look, I don't know what's going on with you, but you need to get a grip. Helen and I haven't done anything, but something might have. Retrace your steps. What's the last thing you remember?"

Something? What was this "something" that might have meddled with his fundamental sense of reality? "Where's Megan?"

"I haven't seen her since Boston. I figured she was with you, or with Helen working on the video. When did you see her last?"

Boston. That was their last tour stop, where they'd unveiled the "She Gives Dynamite" spell performance. "She Gives Dynamite" was a problem. Ditto for the video, but he wasn't sure what was wrong with one or the other. This "since Boston" thing, though, was a problem that made sense. "You're telling me that we aren't in Boston anymore?" The pause of a lifetime. Dull, static-filled dead space wormed into Thom's ear. "Talk."

"You're taking the piss," Brian said.

"Where the fuck are we?" Thom shouted.

"Memphis, Thom, we're in Memphis. You can't be serious. We played our finale show an hour ago, and it went spectacularly. You seemed completely present."

His world inverted. He had no memory of playing an entire show, or of changing cites for that matter, and he was sober as a nun. "Nothing out of the ordinary happened at this show?"

"No. It was perfect. Can you please back up and give me more details? How do you feel specifically? Try to recall your last clear memory. What you saw, smelled, heard. If you read any text or had text read to you."

You have no memories or recollections. All you have is the eternal now, guided by my command. I'm in you, with you, and always around you. Forever and ever. I feel my powers shifting and merging. Each moment, my strength increases. You are a most habitable and gracious host. Thank you.

"Did we play 'She Gives Dynamite'?" It was all he could think to ask, as the question seemed significant.

"The crowd wouldn't let us go without it. Now try to concentrate. You have me worried about Megan. And my wife. Helen told me that she'd be ducking off the tour after Boston to get started on the video and wouldn't be checking in as frequently, but now I'm concerned that the entire endeavor went sideways."

Dominoes careened into each other. This video project had to be snuffed out. Nothing was more important. This video, if allowed to exist, would be worse than nuclear war. "When did you speak to Helen last?"

"When we landed here in Memphis. You were with me when she texted. Her message was very brief."

Brief—and for all intents and purposes, deleted. "You have to connect with her immediately. If she's involved in the video, tell her to stop at once. If Megan is with her, tell her to call me."

"You haven't even attempted to clue me in on your obsession with this video or this whiplash insistence on grinding it to a halt after it meant more to you than anything we were planning."

"Doesn't matter. Just do it." Thom hung up. Observing from a nook behind his frontal lobe, Folly was satiated. For now.

ARMED WITH WATCH AND WITS, MEGAN MARCHED DOWN A STAIRCASE of ice. The only place to go in the crystal mountain was deeper, lower. That's where she went.

There was no way she was in the video. The setting was otherworldly and wholly immersive, the way that spells were. The magic subsumed one's entire body in its system, saturating physically, mentally, and spiritually. She had no idea how even the most advanced witch was capable of mastering such a mighty force. The thought of such a feat struck her as impossible. It probably was.

Once Megan reached the bottom of the steps, wonder washed over her. A thriving city in miniature existed at her feet, every component rendered from the same transparent rock that comprised the rest of the mountain. There were tiny, glittering homes no bigger than shoeboxes, complete with dollhouse shingles carved delicately into diamond rows.

She crouched, a giantess in this little place. See-through rose bushes sprouted from glassy grass, each petal chiseled from cubic zirconia. Cars were ice cube sculptures. A hailstorm of rounded treetops sprayed yards and lined streets.

A white dot scampered past her toes. She jerked backward, her instincts telling her to give berth to the spider. Except it wasn't a spider, it was an elfish, not-quite-human creature with pointy features, angel wings, and a tail. The humanoid was small enough to fit in her palm. He (she? they?) carried a pickaxe. There wasn't only one, either. The first one she spotted was an outlier from the herd. Thousands of these small wonders scurried through their manicured town, hurrying toward the mountain walls. Marching to a beat not heard by her, meticulously on task, they ascended the wall to her left in a swarm.

Megan followed the elven army. They used clawed spikes attached to belts to hang from the wall. With their pickaxes, they hammered chunks out of the mountain, the chorus of their project creating a tinkling wind-chime melody. A smaller group of the workers stood at her feet sweeping the shards into bags. "What are you doing?" Megan asked. Her watch wasn't reacting. Either their activity was either benign or her device was still broken.

"Clockwork," one said cheerfully in a sexless voice. "We tune the machine of the mountain."

A co-worker added, "And hence, the workings of the universe."

Enraptured, she followed the group that had picked up the crystal scraps. The legion of little ones hauled their spoils to a hole in the wall at the far end of the city. The chute was about the circumference of a basketball. The elves dumped their yield inside, heading back to the labor site once their bags were emptied. "What are you doing?" she asked.

"Seeding your world," one said. "That way, your kind can find us, and nobody disbelieves ever again."

Megan lowered to her belly and peered in the hole. A honeycomb of flickering imagery, like dozens of movie screens each playing a different show, floated in blank space. In one square, a crystal chunk appeared in a bowl of mixed rocks in what looked like a new age shop.

In another, three of the chunks sat at the base of a tree trunk. Every window played a distinct situation involving a crystal. Helen had talked about a magic crystal being an integral part of her initiation into witchcraft. Now, it apparently had dark energies trapped inside. This had to be meaningful. Megan needed more information. She ran back to where the elves worked. "Do the crystals always end up in the right hands? As in, do they always go where they're intended, or destined, to go?"

A little one laughed, striking its axe into the rock. "Not at all. We try our best, but we aren't perfect."

"What happens if a crystal ends up in the wrong hands?"

"It must be purified. We do that here."

That was it. Megan had to get Helen's clear crystal and return it to the mountain. That was why everything was still catawampus. Her clear crystal had gotten into her hands on accident, and the course had to be corrected. Megan would have to magic herself out of this place, connect with Helen, and secure the crystal. Then, she would come back and return the rock to the chute. Once that was taken care of, she could get on with the video, let that do its work, and finally be done with magical interference in her life.

She was beyond ready to launch the operation. If she used a spirit spell to transport home, with any luck she'd have a better chance of success through connecting with Helen's magic. "Sister Spirit, I, a fireborn, humbly call upon—"

Megan mouthed the next words, but they stayed lodged inside before she could put them to speech. She couldn't talk. She'd gone mute. She grabbed her throat. Tried again. Useless.

Fear got up on her heels. If she couldn't cast a spell, how was she going to get home?

Megan didn't have much chance to ponder the topic when the next shock came calling. Before her eyes, the tiny city disintegrated. A glitter cloud of pixie dust blew through the air, and she was back to being in a nondescript crystal mountain chamber. Megan ran to the only place in the room that was unique from the rest—the chute. Maybe she could teleport to one of those real-world places and figure out from there how to reconnect with her people.

She stuck her head inside, where the scenes kept playing. She had her sights on the rock shop, which she figured would be a sympathetic audience to hear her wild story of witchcraft and prophetic songs, when a tentacle of corpselike complexion shot up and clamped around her neck.

Megan thrashed against the stranglehold. She couldn't swallow. Or breathe. Her eyes bugged. The appendage was as thick as a man's forearm, scales dry and rough against her throat. Mighty muscles flexed, choking her out. She scratched and clawed, tried to jam her fingertips between the murderous flesh and the skin above her windpipe. Not a millimeter of leeway.

As a last-ditch effort, Megan leaned forward in an attempt to gain even a fraction of slack. The tentacle yanked, and she tumbled down the slide. Dizziness was her next sensation. She smelled grass and dirt. She was rolling down a hill.

"Return the crystal to the mountain," Folly taunted from nowhere and everywhere. "As if you have the capability. It's time for you to surrender to me, fire witch. I have your paramour, Thom, secured in my clasp. If you ever wish to see him again, you would be wise to acquiesce without protest. I have been known to be charitable when approached with obedience. Perhaps if you relinquish your will to me, I'll let you have a bit of yourself now and again when I'm using your body."

"Fuck you." Megan got herself to a crouch. It was daytime, and hot. Muggy. She faced a swampy ditch, a shallow creek littered with trash and scruffy foliage. A few mopey trees bent toward the water, their sagging branches bereft of leaves. She looked behind her. A road. "Help!" she howled, scrabbling up the hill on all fours. "Help!"

Before she could move herself to the street, a punch of invisible energy knocked her backward onto her ass. She'd been blocked by an energetic field. Foolish to think she was somewhere that was bound by natural law. The sudden movement ended with her wrist in her face, where her demon-trapping watch was going berserk. Megan grinned. The spell to fix her device hadn't failed.

"Little girl, little girl, let me in." The deranged singsong came from the roadside wetland.

Megan stood tall and faced her adversary. Out of the brackish water jutted what looked like a cross between an octopus and a many-headed serpent. The fat base of a body lolled out of the water, larger than a pickup truck, its dark green flesh slimy and blending in with the mud. A spray of serpentine tentacles, each wider than her body, shot from the trunk and wiggled against the dirt. Several were pale as death, while others camouflaged with the environment. They were headless but moved with purpose. The actual head of the hydra was a column resembling the others, except it stood tall and erect. Instead of a head or face, it had a skull-sized opening that teemed with a dark, glimmering energy. "Your soul goes here," Folly said. "Now walk forward. You are unable to resist. Come along and follow me. You feel me in your head, don't you? Taking hold, taking over. Come along to where you belong. Into the deep."

"You've got it reversed." Megan pointed the face of her watch at the gaping maw. "You're coming with me."

TWENTY-THREE

It didn't take long to get to the bottom of the ins and outs of the video production plan. A few phone calls, some quality time with Google Maps, and a handful of logistical arrangements, and off Thom went to track down Megan in Peru.

He'd stop the insanity in its tracks. None of this video. Not one frame. Folly knew what was best. *He* knew what was best. They were essentially the same now, humming along in smooth alignment. He'd always love Megan for putting her magic into him and enabling this union. The ideal outcome had transpired. Everything happened for a reason.

Thom's knees came up to his chin, the compact motorboat he rode in affording sparse extra space. The driver, a sunbaked man named Carlos, steered the banged-up, sea-green vessel down a wide, gray river that wove twisted curves through dense green blankets. At the river's edge, snags of old roots plunged into the silt-clouded depths.

The boat bumped along with the current, the motor's lone song an incessantly humming soundtrack. Carlos's dark ponytail bobbed under his baseball cap. They were close. He could smell magic in the air. Its base note, as crispy as a burnt match, undercut the funky, fishy river odor. Thom dug his fingertips into the backpack he'd brought.

Almost there, he assured Folly with their telepathy.

Almost there. His own thought simply mirrored back to him in no distinct tone. The past day, he'd lost track of the discernment to pinpoint where he ended and Folly began. That was okay. It was supposed to be like that. Boundaries were a nuisance.

The speedboat grumbled to a halt on a slice of riverbank indistinguishable from all the rest of the rainforest and river. Carlos got out and hitched the boat to a post. "The production crew's a few miles that way." He pointed to a lightly trod trail bifurcating two trees beset by spools of weeping vines. "Watch your step."

Thom tipped the man and set off. His feet moved faster than his brain, the new hiking boots he'd bought allowing him to step with confidence through leaves, sticks, branches, and whatever else lurked.

Stop the video, stop the video, stop the video.

Yes, he would. By any means necessary.

Minutes passed, the vicinity of a half-hour, as he blazed his way through underbrush that tried its best to snag his socks and the cuffs of his jeans. The overhead canopy blocked out the sun, creating a shadowed, insular dome to bubble his mission. He was forest greenery and purpose personified. A missile wound up and pointed. *Stop the videostopthevideostopthevideo.*

The trail opened to a clearing. A dozen people walked around carrying things. Several wore headsets, two held clipboards. The crew had pitched a yellow tent, and next to it was a pop-up awning supported by stakes. Underneath, equipment on card tables. Editing equipment. Laptops. Good, good sign.

An acne-scarred college guy in a summer camp hoodie ran over to him. "Thom, hey, we didn't know you'd be linking up with the shoot. Good to see you here. Did you get a chance to watch that short film I had sent over to you?"

"Where's Megan?"

The young man made a face of shock. "It's just that I heard you were genuinely enthusiastic about watching it. I was hoping for a couple of notes, even a line or two."

A strange sensation rippled through Thom, almost like he was being torn in two. He recalled taking the boat to Peru to find Megan, but the rest of the brushstrokes of his intent were too broad, lacking form or dimension.

He'd hurt this young man's feelings and felt terrible, though his memory failed him as to how or why. Piecemeal recollections of broken events jingle-jangled through him in a hacked-up montage. He'd fought with Brian. Ended up in the wrong hotel room. He had to find Megan. Stop her. Fight the video. Fight off Folly.

NO.

A part of him got sucked out through a straw. Whatever he'd been thinking a moment ago slipped through his fingers like grains of sand. He was plummeting, the bottom gone out from under him. He stared into the fallen face of this person he'd apparently disappointed and for whom he had no answer. What did the guy want Thom to do? Watch him take notes? "I'm sorry." He meant it. He was wracked with remorse for whatever was happening. He needed help but couldn't begin to assess what kind or from whom. "I'm not myself at the moment. Try me again some other time, okay?"

The guy quirked his mouth in a half-smile of pain and resignation. "It's cool. She's over that way." He pointed at a cluster of large trees with another trailhead marking the entrance to a path.

Stop the video, stop the video, stop the video. Don't fight me. It'll only make things worse for you. Just listen.

"Who is over that way?" The only individual in existence was Folly. The mere idea of separate beings, of individuality or differences in consciousness, was absurd. "That doesn't make sense. She's everywhere. In all of us, those who came before us and those who will follow us. There is only us. She is us."

The crew member rolled his eyes. "Whatever, man."

Thom had no idea what had gotten into the guy. Apparently, he had a problem with universal truths and incontestable facts. That was okay. Lots of people did. They'd have to face them anyway, when the hologram prophecy came to devour their life force. Mr. Production Elf wouldn't be rolling his eyes then. He'd be content and brain dead in his feeder pod, supplying Folly and the Other Ones with nutrients to sustain their reign.

Thom went where he was directed. A short, wide trail, beaten from regular foot traffic, deposited him where the action was. Two screens were set up against the trees, one green and one bright white. A different crew, two more tents, and other types of equipment and props rounded out the activity hub.

And there she was. Even though his faculties were half-gone, the remaining half commandeered by his possessor, the sight of her left him breathless.

A raft of memories returned. All that they'd done together. Shared. His love for her, for them, an unstoppable bass beat that hammered through his jaded heart. Their future, in jeopardy.

She wore leather pants the color of the darkest blood and a black bustier top that showcased her curves. Her hair was teased to the sky, and the heavy makeup on her face rounded out the look. Silver-spiked cuffs cinched her wrists and neck, a key dangling from the choker. Her heels were spears. Megan stood over one of the tables, surveying a spread of medieval-type weapons. She picked up a mace and set it back down. "Megan," he called out, with no game plan of what he'd say next.

Her face lit up, her smile sending an arrow right to his heart. She waved and walked in his direction.

He had to fix whatever was wrong with him and get back to being normal. He couldn't hurt Megan or let her down like he had that crew guy. She was precious. But he didn't know why he was all chopped up and disintegrated. Every time he grabbed enough of a handful to make sense of what he was living through, he lost the important stuff just as fast.

Stop the video. Stop the video. Stop the video.

Right. He had to stop the video. But why?

You think too much.

"Hey, you." Megan took both of his hands in her smaller ones. "What a perfect surprise. Isn't this look wild?" She twirled. He was sick. Why did he have to stop the video? She was clearly happy about the video. "I wrangled a ton of creative control over the styling. I told them to dress me like a woman on the cover of *Heavy Metal* magazine. That was always my dream, to look like that."

"Megan, we need to talk."

"I know what you're thinking." Her eyes were content underneath her ferocious makeup. Triumphant almost. Stick-on jewels that matched her spikes caught winks of the morning sunlight. "You're worried this is foolish, that working with 'She Gives Dynamite' to unleash it versus seal it will cause problems. I assure you, though, that won't be the case. This video will succeed in its goal. Hands down."

That's precisely what he and Folly were worried about. "Hear me out. You're right. The video isn't safe to make. You've been misinformed." He ran with that line of thinking. "Brian and Helen got it wrong. They said that we need to go back to sealing songs. That's the only way to get this prophecy under control. Pushing on with 'She Gives Dynamite' will speed up the hologram."

She narrowed her eyes. "That doesn't make any sense."

"It doesn't have to make sense. Just listen."

"I can't accept that. I just saw Brian and Helen earlier today. They're still onboard. In fact, they're more sure than ever that our approach is solid. Helen and I worked through a Psyche Splitting spell back in Boston. After we did Banish Intruders and Firewall. We put a part of me down in the magic realm to learn my mission, what I must do. I got my watch working again. I need to shoot the video and return Helen's clear crystal to the mountain. Then this is all over."

Oh no. They were further along than he thought. If Megan made it through the video, then returned to the magic realm and deposited Helen's crystal, Folly's connection to Fyre would be forever broken. Without the firepower of those songs, she'd have to start over at square one to push on with the prophecy. Losing Fyre represented an enormous setback, a devastating loss of a crucial toehold. They couldn't bear such an unacceptable failure. He had to use a different tack to halt her momentum. "Don't shoot any more of this video. I won't allow it."

Warm breezes ruffled the leaves, the same wind amusing a slice of her glam rock hair. "What is wrong with you?"

His real voice screamed for help, but it was buried too far inside to make even a squeak. Folly pushed her way to the surface and stole his tongue. "I should be asking you the same thing. First off, I hate the look of this video. It's trashy, pornified, and completely out of touch with our band's aesthetic. You look ridiculous, and you're diluting our brand. I won't allow this sideshow spectacle to continue in Fyre's name."

Good job. That should suffice.

Her jaw dropped. A red tint colored the whites of her eyes. "Why are you speaking to me that way? You were there when I told Brian about the concept for the video, and you didn't voice a single objection. It's not like you at all to have such a stuffy, judgmental take on the costume or aesthetic. More to the point, you are being mean right now. You know what? No. I'm pushing ahead with the video. Whatever your problem is, work it out on your own. You don't have nearly as much say as you think you do."

Fuck, she was still all in. However, the approach to undermine her claim to the product seemed to have gotten under her skin. Folly thrived on confusion, chaos, and the destabilizing demolition of predicted expectations. He leaned harder into what had shown results. "You have no say, actually. You never have. From the beginning, you've been a hanger-on. A parasite, following us around to suck up whatever secondary fame fumes you could get. If I say the video stops, it stops. The others will back me up. You're done. You're gone. Find a new piece of celebrity tail to chase. This video is over, and you're done."

"Wow," she whispered. "Tell me how you really feel. I thought we had a special connection."

You sure did. And I shit all over it. Tee-he-he-he-he.

"Goodbye. Go home." His heart broke in two and bled out onto his boots.

Why was he saying these awful things that weren't true and that hurt Megan?

His conscious self swelled up like a rising tide only to recede when he needed answers more than ever. Folly was the moon that pulled him back the instant he began to crawl out.

Her jaw hardened. "Fuck you. You never meant shit to me either. I only got with you because you were an easy lay. Brian was the one I wanted. Or Jonnie. Nobody's first choice is the bassist. Yuck."

He doubled over and clenched the sides of his head, screaming. If only he could force Folly out, dislodge her hooks from those parts of him that she'd turned into her lair.

"Oh, now that I've bruised your ego, now I get a reaction? That's how this works? You get to be as nasty to me as you want, but once I give back what I get, it's time for your narcissistic meltdown? If only I cared about your little manbaby feelings."

A crew girl with a pony mane of blonde hair crept over. "Hey there, Thom. Hope everything's okay with you. Megan, are we ready to film the first take?"

"You know what?" Megan's angry green eyes glared right into his soul. Past Folly. Past everything. It was torture because he could see her but not go to her. The blockage between them was immovable, despite how badly he wanted to detonate it. "Yes. We're shooting the video. Thom, you can sue me if you have a problem with it. I have it in writing that I'm in the clear. A signed contract. Your tantrum doesn't matter. Kiss my ass." She gave him the cold shoulder and followed the cringing crew member to the white and green screens.

You've lost, you moron. Folly was furious. *Now Brian must die.*

That accomplishes nothing except punishing me, he told her with his mind.

Of course it accomplishes something, it amuses me and ruins your life. However, with him subtracted from the equation, Helen becomes an easier mark. If we kill Brian right now, she and Megan will lose their chance to deposit the crystal in the Other Place. They're going to cast their final spell during the video itself. News of her husband's murder should throw in a wrench and give us the time we need to reclaim the crystal. But we have to dispatch him before the video shoot is through. Now.

"No," Thom slurred. Nobody heard him over the commotion and the recorded track of "She Gives Dynamite" being played on one of the computers under the canopy. He stumbled behind a tree. "I won't harm anyone. I refuse. It isn't happening."

Oh yes, it is. He's staying at a cabin on the edge of the base camp. Now. Here's what you are to do. Grab that oversized axe off the prop table and take it to Brian's cabin. Chop him up until he's good and dead, then cry for help saying he's hurt. That'll send Helen running and stop their little crystal spell cold. Then we handle her as we see fit, seize the crystal, and throw it into this skunky river. Nobody will ever find it. We're safe here after that. You and I, friends forever. I'll be Fyre's number one fan.

If only he had Megan's book. He could look up Banish Intruders and boot this parasite from his head. The book had to be in the jungle. In her tent or cabin.

Don't even think about it. One foot in front of the other. Get your ass to that table and wrap your fingers around the axe.

On command, one of his feet went in front of the other. He was walking as if remote-controlled. Lurching like a zombie but unable to stop his forward momentum. That was the worst part. Awareness but no control. Folly had him pause near a shaggy bush to wait for an opportune moment to strike. He hated himself, his life, every choice he'd made leading up to this moment.

Once the crew and Megan either had their backs turned or had wandered off set, Folly gave the marching order. Thom lunged forward in his ungainly stagger. The big axe was the second weapon from the left, evenly placed between a barbed whip and a sword polished to shine.

He resisted with every fiber of his being until he got too tired and gave in. Then, he grabbed the axe. With Folly as his pilot, his body jerked down a trail wide enough to accommodate a horse or a dirt bike.

The cabin at the edge of the base camp stuck out as on its own, a more private domicile than the rest. The structure was small—three rooms max and one story, a single square of wooden logs. A light was on behind the lone window on the side of the building. People were in there. "Run," Thom spat out through his mouth full of molasses.

Nice try. Keep it moving.

Thom dragged his aching, thousand-pound body to the front door. On Folly's whim, he reared back and kicked.

The first thing he saw was Helen's bare back, her loose brown hair spilling down her shoulders. She sat on Brian's lap, both on the living room couch. Bouncing on him, her hand on his shoulder. All of that was happening until the door crashed down.

The action froze.

Helen's hair flew, and their eyes locked.

Brian craned to see around his wife, to see what had happened.

Nobody screamed.

"Forgive me," Thom shouted in his weird voice. "This isn't me."

Sudden movements caught him off-guard. Helen jumped off. Brian charged him, grabbed the handle of the axe, and bent his elbow at a painful angle until he dropped the weapon.

Folly was bellowing with rage, everyone was screaming, and rips and tears shredded the fabric that held him together. He pushed, physically resisting Brian's pull. At the same time, he shoved against the force inside, pressing every ounce of his will into Folly, determined to vacate her. Pressure stretched his eyes. Sparks bloomed in his vision. She was almost out. Hanging on by a thread. A snap, and his world went white.

TWENTY-FOUR

MEGAN HAD RACKED UP A DECENT NUMBER OF MISTAKES IN HER LIFE, but trusting Thom James now topped the list of bad decisions based in poor judgment. Bad decisions, poor judgment. Those words belonged in a tattoo across her heart.

Megan distracted herself from her emotional pain by practicing her mace moves, swinging the spiked ball with aim and care. There was a fair amount of skill required by her to make the role look seamless. Yet Thom kept invading her mind, the sweetness of their memories lingering even as their goodbye tasted bitter.

She should have known. Men like him didn't stay interested for long. She'd threatened him by advancing on his turf with the video. His ego hadn't been able to bear the competition. He'd tried to shut her down. He'd seemed off when he'd said those unkind words, but she wasn't about to second-guess herself. His point had been clear. He was done with her. She'd lost her luster. She should have known that the infatuation would fade. Oh well. At least she still had her creative project, which she wasn't about to let him take from her. The video for "She Gives Dynamite" was the one good thing she'd gotten from their star-crossed attempt at a relationship.

"You ready?" This from a crew member, tweaking the set dressing.

The green screen supported the most fantastical of the effects, but physical props added texture and dimension.

The crew had built a cave out of plaster and cardboard, and one of the goblins was an old-school special effect made from rubber and other prosthetics. He even spewed neon-green gore from his neck stump when slain.

She'd show Thom. She'd make such a great video that he'd regret cutting her loose. He'd regret that he'd gone cold on her. Not that she'd take him back, even if he begged.

Megan didn't have a chance to answer the set person in the affirmative when Helen and Brian raced onto the set. Both were wild-eyed, hastily dressed, and looked like they'd faced down the apocalypse. Helen had her spell book with her. Brian carried the axe from the prop table.

"Change of plans," Helen said through labored breath. "We need to return the crystal right now."

A bald staffer wearing white earbuds tried to engage Brian. Brian waved the man off, the full focus of his attention tunneled on Helen.

Things were not normal. A creeping doom rolled over the set.

Megan needed answers. "What, why? That'll mess up the whole video and derail the spell. I'm supposed to endure the ordeal in the cave before the spell is cast. Otherwise, the order is all wrong."

"Desperate times call for drastic measures." Helen jammed her hand in her sweatpants, pulled out the clear crystal, and plopped it on one of the prop tables. "We move, now. As fast as we can without compromising the integrity of the incantation. We'll try another Banish Intruders before we take the stone to the magic realm and cancel the Psyche Splitting. Then we should be able to transport up here and complete the video to finish it off."

"You're talking too fast." Megan put her hands up. "Banish Intruders? We got the possession out of me."

"We got the possession out of *you*, yes." Helen's complexion was sallow. With her words, a bomb came down to level the world. "But it's far from done with us."

She thought back over the last thirty minutes. Two and two made four before anyone had a chance to respond. "Shit. This is what I think it is, isn't it?"

"Thom was overtaken," Brian said. "It was bad, and we can't risk another incident of that severity. He's safe for now. Locked in the basement of the guest cabin. But he's in trouble. If the consensus is that returning the crystal is the answer, I vote to do it. Fast."

Remorse and concern for Thom made a meal of her. Had she seen through the conflict debacle at the time, she'd have tried to help him. But she'd retreated to her old insecurities about not being enough to hold onto him, assumed the worst, and let him push her away.

Now that she had a clear and complete picture of the situation, she'd do her part to repair the damage. Folly had gotten the best of Thom. And Megan. She was that good. But not good enough. "Fast. Agreed. Right now."

"Is your book on set?" Helen slammed her own version of the grimoire on the table by the crystal. She wasted no time skipping through chunks of pages until she landed on the section she sought.

Megan ran to the hiding place that she'd used and dragged her copy out from under a hill of boxes. She set it beside Helen's. At least they had as much ammo as they ever would.

"I'm not sure I understand," said the set director, a woman with a shock of black hair who was tall enough to dunk a basketball. "This isn't in the script. Brian, are you reclaiming creative license?"

"Megan is," Brian said. "And you need to listen."

That was all it took to get the set director off their backs. Megan and Helen got to work.

If the crew was disturbed by the chanting and recitation of arcane material, they kept their thoughts to themselves.

Following an ordeal of queasiness, freefall, and an episode where Megan felt like her head was being torn off by a wild animal, she found herself back at the bottom of the crystal mountain. The elf city was gone. Helen stood beside her, the crystal in her hand.

Megan said, "At least we're getting better at the travel aspect." They needed all the positive, calming energy that they could get.

Helen cast a panoramic glance around the new territory. "Where do I return it?"

Megan pointed to the portal hole. "There. That's the drop-off chute."

Helen padded to the depository. She looked at Megan, then the hole, then Megan again. "Just throw it in?"

"Go for it." Not like this place came with an instruction manual. The books hardly counted, given their fickleness and caprice.

Helen pitched the crystal into the gap. It tumbled down, getting smaller and smaller until the flickering grid of scene screens absorbed the chunk of mineral that'd caused trouble.

They waited in silence for a short time. "That's it?" Helen asked.

"Looks that way." For once, a plan went off without a hitch. Not that her knotted stomach had registered closure. "Let's get back up to the regular world and do the rest."

A hard object hit the floor with a clunk. The crystal sat at Megan's feet. Positive vibes evaporated. The portal had spit the crystal right back out.

Reflexively, she picked it up to pitch it back down the chute, but the gap closed before she could release the rock from her hand.

"I need those songs," Folly said in her disembodied voice. "And I'm not letting go of your paramour up there. Now sing them to me. 'She Gives Dynamite.' 'Deep Dark Woods.' I know that you know the words to both. Now sing them."

"Absolutely not," Megan said.

"Sing. Them. To. Me."

"No." The weight of Megan's watch was her only solace, her lone weapon. The gears went ballistic.

"I'll give Banish Intruders another go," Helen said. "I have it committed to memory."

"Fuck your memory," Folly said. Sooty smoke filled the room, leaching out of the walls.

Instinctively, Megan covered her nose and mouth, though the fog was odorless.

Helen mimicked the gesture. But her effort didn't stop what happened next. Her feet lifted off the floor as her body went rigid. She hung like that, in midair, her mouth open in an awful, slack expression.

Megan ran to her comrade in witchcraft and pulled on her feet. She didn't budge. "Can you hear me? See me? Blink once if yes."

Helen's chest rose and fell, but that was it. The lights were on, but nobody was home. "What did you do to her?" Megan's screams echoed off the prison of alabaster.

"Sing to me. Now. Release whatever blockages are holding you back and release those words. You can do it, Megan. I believe in you. You're a good girl. The best girl." Folly's voice changed for the final sentence. She was every parent, teacher, lover, and friend who ought to have said those words but did not.

The seduction was too much. Too warm, too safe. Megan would die to escape to that nice, false world, to go back and have what never was all over again. To have it all be different, where her parents *saw* her, and her teachers heard her cries for help and attention. In that soft-soaped version of her past, Tremble wanted her to flourish in her talent.

"You can do anything," Folly continued, all those voices from the past merging and blending. "Fade into me and let me hold you."

Megan's lips parted. Scaffolding fell. This was a trust fall. Not like the one where Teddy dropped her and laughed. Utterly opposite. The two songs swirled and churned below the surface. Twin lakes of fire that would arise to raze. Finally, she had a special, precious, and unique essence inside of her.

"First verse of 'Deep Dark Woods,'" Folly said. "You were meant for this. Your fate and destiny expect nothing else. Your purpose demands your submission."

The opening lines curled in a blazing current from synapses to tongue, weaving their path of flame. The gears turned, turned, and turned, like they had for eternity. Megan was a tiny cog. Her purpose in the machine was determined and fated.

The gears.

The gears.

The gears!

That silent scream pulled back to the forefront a slice of her that'd slipped. Though clouds had beset her eyes and she saw double, she could make out more than the white walls. The guts of her watch spun in perpetual clockwork.

Folly was wrong about her purpose. Her purpose was the video. *Bump in the Night*. Stopping the prophecy, not facilitating it.

Megan ripped her perception out of the fog of hypnosis and shot her stare to where Helen floated. She could reach in with Psyche Splitting and cast Banish Intruders. This time, Folly had a container and wouldn't be free-floating to bother anyone else. She had a final destination.

Megan linked herself to Helen, tapped into the spirit magic, and launched both spells.

The rush of force leaving her body was vicious, the pressure excruciating, but when it was over, she was lighter. Folly had been amputated. The thread of dark smoke still inhabited her watch, but this time it didn't gum up the gears. Megan had put Folly there intentionally, and all of her this time.

Helen tumbled to the floor and landed at an awkward angle, limbs akimbo.

Megan rushed to her and crouched. "Are you okay? Hurt?"

"I'm fine." Helen got to her feet with relative ease. "You get her?"

"Got her." Megan showed Helen the watch.

"Nice work." Helen gave her a hug. The embrace was a thousand times better than the false promises from Folly. Real friendship was within Megan's grasp.

The portal was back, unsealed in the wake of Megan's banish and contain activity. Helen tossed her crystal into the hole. The stone made contact with a screen where doctors in lab coats tinkered with machines in a hospital room. A patient, a long-haired young woman, lay on the cot. "I really hope that's the end of this," Helen said.

There wasn't much point in analyzing the final destination of the crystal or what it meant. They'd done their best, Folly was contained, and they had to leave. She needed to get to Thom.

With Helen, Megan spirited herself back to the physical world. Brian waited by the books, where he and his wife embraced. The crew was dumbfounded, but they were able to finish the video, which Megan did for good measure.

Her costume still on, she raced to the guest cabin. The front door was locked. She hurled a rock through a window and plucked away sheets of glass until she cleared a passageway that was safe enough. She made a stepstool out of a pile of nearby firewood and crawled in.

The living room was messy, blankets and pillows from the couch fallen to the floor. One of the cushions had come loose and sat cockeyed. The wall to the left of her had a fist-sized hole in it. A nerve-pricking smell of fear sweat permeated the space.

Brian had said that Thom was in the basement. Megan ran to the only door that could lead to such a place and opened it. "Are you there, babe?" she called down the stairs. A light was on below. A washer and dryer sat at the base. The floor was finished with gray tile.

"It wasn't me," Thom cried out, pure agony in his voice. "I didn't mean any of those awful things I said, and it wasn't me that tried to hurt Brian. It swear that it wasn't me."

"I know." Megan's heart broke. She ran to him. He sat on the floor. His hands were tied behind his back, wrists bound to a pipe. A lump on the side of his head had flushed to an angry shade of red and purple. "She tried to possess all of us, and she got to you. I should have noticed, but I was too blinded by emotion." She undid his wrists, casting aside coils of white nylon rope.

The instant he was free, Thom threw his arms around her. "I should have been stronger or fought harder."

"Not your fault," she murmured into his warmth, his scent. His strength held her even as she held him. Solace and tenderness flowed between them as a give and take. Just like how she'd always wanted it to be with another person. Not like this, exactly, but the universe was strange about granting wishes. "How did you get down here?"

"I don't remember exactly. My mind was almost completely gone by then. I imagine that Brian or Helen knocked me out and carried me down here. Please don't be angry with them. I more than deserved it."

Their ordeal over, Megan broke the hug and collapsed beside him, the tension inside of her melting when she rested her head on his shoulder. He stroked her arm. They breathed in consort for a long time.

"Let's go to Hawaii," Megan said.

"Now?"

"Yes. I need to get out of here. I'm sure that you do also. If we get called back to Peru, we'll pivot. But I think a break is in order."

He looked at her for a long time. Saw her like she'd always wanted to be seen. Behind his brown eyes, he was there and no one else. The circumstances couldn't have been crazier, but this was her person. They vibrated on the same wavelength. She gave an equal energy right back to him, attuning emotionally though they spoke no words. Their present was beyond speech. They were soul mates, their bond forged in the bleakest depths of outlandish insanity.

Nobody said that true love was warm and fuzzy all the time. Yet the madness made their connection deeper. Denser. More real.

"I love you," Thom finally said in the most reverent of whispers. "More than I have ever loved anyone or anything. I didn't have the faintest idea of what the concept of love even was before you came along, and now it pulses through my heart with every beat."

"I love you too. You know what? I don't regret one single thing that happened to bring us to this moment. Because each one of those things brought us closer."

"How does ten days on the beach sound?"

"Make it two weeks."

"Deal."

He pressed a kiss to her lips, a kiss of darkness coming into light. A kiss of communion. A kiss where the whole was greater than the sum of the parts, where the two of them co-created a new reality forged in the inferno of their love.

THREE DAYS LATER, TANGLED IN WHITE SHEETS, THE FRENCH DOORS to the second-story deck flung open to let in sea breezes, Megan had all but forgotten the ordeal in the jungle.

On the nightstand, her demon-trapping watch was back in business, metabolizing the sister of chaos that it'd dutifully trapped during their stint in the crystal mountain.

"Write a song for me," Megan murmured against Thom's lips.

When was the last time they'd gotten out of bed? They should probably consider that. A walk on the beach to stretch legs. Too bad they were having far too much fun while horizontal.

He rolled to his side and picked his phone up off the end table. "Of course. But I want to congratulate you first for your accomplishments."

"What do you mean?" She watched with curiosity as he poked the screen, the light reflecting in his eyes.

Thom showed her YouTube. Her jaw dropped. The video for "She Gives Dynamite" had gone mega-viral. Millions upon millions of views. Beneath the small box showing the thumbnail of the opening image, a medium close-up of Megan with her mace at the base of the mountain, were additional screens picturing related content. And there was a lot of related content.

"Your video made the news for its success. It's all over TikTok, Twitter, and all the rest. Absolutely blowing up. Bigger than anything Sam Smith has put out, Miley Cyrus, everyone. This is being hailed as our comeback song. The dawn of a new era." Thom handed Megan his phone.

In total shock and awe, she surfed. He was right. The sensation of "She Gives Dynamite" had spilled over to *Bump in the Night* to give a massive boost of views and subscriptions to their YouTube channel.

She fumbled on the stand for her own phone and switched off silent mode. Voicemails galore. Triple-digit texts. Lots of all-caps and celebration emojis from Gary and the others. Sweet stuff from Logan, wheedling to get back in her good graces. No thanks on that one.

She checked her email. A solid wall of offers for endorsement deals, television contracts, agent representation, advertising, and more financial opportunity. Money for the video was already pouring in, thanks to the writing and production credits she'd negotiated in addition to the acting component. Megan checked her bank account. Tears of joy pricked her eyes. She could finally sustain herself on her passion. "I don't even know what to say."

"I'll start. Congratulations. Your vision was perfect. Absolutely synergistic with our existing brand while suffusing it with fresh energy. This wasn't luck either. It was your genius. If you want to write more with us, I'm sure that the door will always be open. If not, that's okay too."

"I'll need time to think it over." She set her phone aside. These were big decisions, and she was on vacation with the love of her life. She'd mull over her career path down the line. She had options and good problems for the first time in recent memory. Problems that could wait for solutions. "Now, where were we?"

They picked up where they left off, in decadence and the delicious flow of breath and touch. With her sacred heirloom back on track and the next phase with Thom about to begin, Megan was ready to let go. Of her past, compartmentalized where it belonged like the demon in the watch gears. All that mattered now was the present, the joy of passion and kisses.

Megan's heart was full, and on fire. She was free.

***

Thank you for reading! Did you enjoy? Please add your review because nothing helps an author more and encourages readers to take a chance on a book than a review.

And don't miss more in the *Coven Daughters* series coming soon! Until then read EMBERS, the first novella in the *Coven Daughters Origins*, available now. Turn the page for a sneak peek!

Also be sure to sign up for the City Owl Press newsletter to receive notice of all book releases!

SNEAK PEEK OF EMBERS

Thom James couldn't pinpoint, with absolute certainty, when awareness of a void in his heart switched from minor nuisance to undeniable ache. On the latest routine morning in a long string, though, the abyss had stolen more than usual.

He pulled in a drag of cigarette smoke, the woodsy flavor more rote than satisfying as a rush of chemicals cancelled out the minty flavor of toothpaste. An exhale left his lungs in a choppy whoosh, his breath ejecting filmy gray residue. Here he was again, going through the motions.

He touched the cold glass of his hotel suite window and stared down at Nashville. Or Raleigh. Or perhaps his band had played Atlanta last night. Maybe they'd delivered their music to an arena of thirty-thousand cheering faces in Orlando or Dallas.

Didn't matter. This midsize city at morning was the same as any other: paper doll cutouts of buildings, drab redbrick and concrete tones, crumbling infrastructure. The theater of the mundane unfolded twenty stories below while he watched in a fruitless search for affect or even inspiration. A smattering of affordable cars lurched to jobs. A man wearing a backpack scurried down a sidewalk, prompting a cluster of pigeons to lift off in frantic flight.

Nearing the end of his forties and having played cities like this since his teen years, Thom had seen it all.

He'd felt the previous night, yes he had, high on the usual maelstrom of lust and fame.

At night, cities were sexy, glitter-sprinkled light shows teeming with promises, spectacles tailored to cater to the appetites. Come morning, though, they were little more than blight on the landscape. Interchangeable, half-real, used.

He spied a silver arch not far off in the distance, an artistic piece of architecture curving toward the clouds amid downtown buildings that weren't quite skyscrapers. Right, they'd played St. Louis the night before. That's where he was, not that it mattered.

A cynical bark of a laugh jumped out of his lips. Hollow mornings were the price he paid for his indulgent nights. The rock star's debt always came due.

From behind him came a soft, feminine moan. The bed squeaked, and the latest woman occupying whatever he called his bed sighed. The tomb in his chest gaped wider, a mocking reminder that a well-adjusted man would feel tender emotions right about now. His stomach tightened as his head spun. He stubbed out his smoke on the windowsill, snuffing his ennui.

Water rushed from the bathroom sink. Bodily noises of teeth getting scrubbed, gargling, and spitting followed. Thom smiled sadly. If their time together had been intended to be more than one night, the sounds of her freshening up might inspire intimate anticipation.

"Hey." Her voice, thick with sleep, belied a lilt of hope that toppled dominoes of guilt and regret inside him.

He turned to where she stood. A thin, white sheet swaddled her supple form, shielding the soft breasts that he'd enjoyed to the fullest. Her full-chest tattoo peeked out from the top of the material in coy glimpses of flowers crawling through emerald networks of jungle foliage.

His gaze travelled through the artwork on her chest and up to her lips, across freckled cheeks and northward to eyes as green as fresh-cut summertime grass. An inferno of chaotic red waves blazed past her shoulders.

She was quite pretty. Beautiful even, in an unconventional way with her strong features and robust bone structure. Ultimately, though, just another groupie. Another American woman in a city he couldn't place.

He didn't even know her name.

God, she deserved so much better than an empty fuck from the lowlife likes of him.

"Hi." He slid a piece of her hair through his fingers, appreciating the silkiness as he reminded himself not to be a dick. Quality aftercare in these situations kept his reputation sterling. "Sleep well?"

"Yeah. You knocked my ass out. I think it was that second orgasm that did me in. Or maybe the third. I'm pretty sure I'll have sweet dreams of the sexy British rocker for the rest of my life." With a siren's smirk, she snagged his pack of smokes off the nightstand and lit up.

Blowing rails through her nostrils, she jutted her chin in parry. Or defiance, daring him to condescend to her. Bloody hell. This bird was a live wire like none other, crackling with white heat.

Thom tilted his head to one side. Her brazenness, a shameless quality to her, piqued his intrigue. He slipped a finger into the swell of her cleavage and loosened the fabric concealing her breasts. "What's your name?"

She blew smoke in his face, the blast making him cough and blink as his eyes burned, though she didn't resist when her sheet fell to the floor. "You're an absolute pig." A touch of levity to her true statement betrayed affection. "Luckily for you, the accent *almost* makes up for it."

"You're still here. And naked again, I might add." Beneath his unbuttoned jeans, his prick swelled. He plucked the cigarette from her mouth, laid it in the ashtray, and guided her back to bed with two firm hands pushing against the velvety slopes of her shoulders.

"Touché." She walked backward in accordance with his motions, running slender fingers through the mat of hair covering his bare chest. The redhead flopped on the bed and spread her legs, her crooked smile both vulnerable and caustic. "I have a lot of problems."

His hands were busy attacking his zipper when fresh waves of shame and disgust pummeled him. Christ, what was wrong with him, screwing women as if they were mere objects? What a scoundrel he was.

"I'm so sorry." He slashed a hand through his hair, the strands as unkempt as the rest of his life, and pulled his thick mess into a ponytail in some pitifully symbolic effort to order his chaos. "Are you hungry? I can have some room service sent up if you'd prefer discretion, but if you'd like to go out, that's fine too. Or I can call you a car if you're ready to get out of here."

Her smile spread while she appraised him with a knowing, green-eyed gaze. "You don't need to pay me with food. I'm a slut, not a whore.

Nothing against whores, but judge me correctly." Though she spoke in a jesting tone, her words cut like a scalpel.

She hadn't closed her legs—gorgeous pink pussy, trimmed strip of red hair—but now Thom wasn't sure if he felt aroused, embarrassed, ashamed, or some unwholesome mix of all three. He stood there blinking like an idiot, his face hot and a nest of brown pubes sprouting through his open fly while a spotlight shone on his mortified conscience.

"You aren't either one of those." He stammered, his mouth dry. Though he meant what he said—his promiscuous arse had no right to pass judgment—the words came off forced and ridiculous. "You're a beautiful person. I wished I would have gotten to know you a little better before we ended up naked."

He meant that too. Yet some unseen force stopped him, time and again, from seeking out a deeper level of intimacy with women. It was easier to approach them as empty conquests.

Easier to forget them. Easier to keep his emotional wall high and solid.

She smacked her forehead. "A beautiful person? That's the cringiest platitude I've ever heard. Can we please fuck? I don't need to witness you thumping every branch on the way down to rock bottom."

Tension and self-consciousness flew out of him in an inexplicable gust. For all his cavorting and playing the part of boorish lout, Thom never quite felt at ease or at peace. He envied the woman on the bed, how she lay there open and free, unshaken.

"Nice metaphor." He swiped the half-burned cigarette out of the ashtray, drew down a hit, and handed the smoke to his temporary partner. "Were you an English major?" She had to be in her mid-thirties and was articulate enough to be a college grad.

Her ample chest swelled as she partook, falling when she blew out three wobbly smoke rings. He studied the multicolor splash of ink capping her breasts and marveled at the way those inquisitive eyes of hers tracked the vapory hoops as they floated before dissipating. "I'm an English professor."

He sat next to her on the bed, and she scooted over to accommodate. Considering her cue, he trailed three kisses from her shoulder to her collarbone, seeking her scent. Floral and spicy notes mixed with her tang from below. Her exotic scent suited her perfectly, even in the stark light of day. "That's sexy. Will you read to me?"

"Why, can't you read?"

For the first time, he noticed precise details of her voice. Beneath the smokiness and snark lay a melody. She spoke like a song, her rhythm rising and falling. Thom buried his face in her neck, sampling her flesh with teasing flicks of his tongue. She whined a little pleasure noise, and with that he was stiff as a bat again. "Tell me your name. Please."

"No. It's more fun this way. Anonymous."

He urged his cock from his pants and rubbed the swollen head against the soft expanse of her outer thigh, seeking relief from the pressure building in his lower belly.

"Well, you're anonymous to me, sweetheart. I'm a famous bassist, and you know exactly who I am."

The feel of his own hot breath against her skin, the arrogant truth of his cocky words, made boiling cum swirl in his balls. Sure, he got off on his own fame, notoriety, and status. No fool would dare nominate him for sainthood.

"Your ego is out of control." She punched her hips up, and he took the cue and danced teasing fingertips down her smooth stomach. "And I actually don't know you. Right now I have the idea of you, the fantasy. Which is precisely what I want."

"Fair enough." His pulse accelerated. Blood fled his brain and filled his engorged cock. As his eyes feasted upon his partner's inviting form, he took a moment to admire the length and girth of his impressive member, the healthy purple coloring of the swollen tip. He could not wait to feed this luscious, vexing piece of feminine excellence to his hungry beast.

But for now, her pleasure was his priority. Thom might be a cad, but at least he left his bedmates with fond memories of his skills. "What do you want me to do, love? Finger you? Eat you? Rub my dick over your clit?"

"Damn, I'm all about your dirty talk." Her thighs quivered, the musky smell of her arousal intensifying.

He played with the soft curls on her mound, kneeling between her legs to admire her swollen folds and the visible bulge of her sensitive nub. He sunk two fingers inside her, licking his lips at the first touch of pussy, a tease of what his prick wanted so bad. In smooth motions, he moved those two fingers in and out, every ounce of his being committed to holding off on the raging urge to plunge inside of her and take, take, take.

"Yeah," she said, eyes glazed and lips parted.

"You want me to use my fingers?" His rod flexed, a bead of pre-cum leaking out.

Driving women crazy with his talents made him feel like a god. The potent rush of ego beat a quick one-off any day.

"Please." She sat up, her eyelids and pale lashes hooding her eyes when her gaze fell to the piston work of his hand.

"Jesus, I can see your clit. I can see how big and full it is, ripe." He withdrew from her opening and used the two slick fingers to spread her folds, making a V through which the glistening button popped like a red candy apple.

She moaned a reply and began to pinch and rub her own stiff nipples.

"I'm going to stroke your clit now, slowly with my thumb. I don't want you to come too fast, but you're so round and red I don't know if I'll be able to prolong your climax. Forgive me."

Another unintelligible grunt from Ms. Articulate English Professor. Christ, this was fun.

He'd circle back to this very moment every time he felt a flare of remorse about how freely he fucked around.

He brought the pad of his thumb to her target, admiring the smooth, slick feel of the bump as he stroked in a big circle. A few passes around, and her clit went into spasms. She lost control, bucking and moaning as she came apart.

Using his opposite hand, Thom slid a finger back into her, hooking his digit on her equally flush G-spot, and rubbed methodically. Her inner muscles clenched and released all around his plunges, her body's responses proof of orgasm.

With a sharp cry, she froze. Her eyes stretched wide, and her jaw dropped. "Oh fuck, I'm coming."

"You sure are." Once she was done, he grabbed his dick and stroked up and down, slowly, offering a little show. "You ready for more?"

"Hell yes."

"Ah, give me that fiery red pussy, baby." With an unbridled growl, he fell on her and plunged inside her pocket of warm, liquid heaven. She'd sworn last night that she was on the pill, and he trusted that she was telling the truth.

Firm walls molded around his cock, sucking like hungry mouths as he mindlessly thrust in and out. "Goddamn, that's some bloody good snatch." He cupped one of her large breasts, pumping hard and fast in selfish pursuit of release.

"Thanks." She wrapped her legs around his hips and dragged her trimmed nails down his back. "I take good care of it. Only the best."

A laugh, this one earnest and bereft of the poison of cynicism, sprang from his lips. A weird, bubbly sensation cavorted in Thom, unnerving but not unwelcome. He slowed his strokes and gazed deeply into his partner's pretty eyes. "Does this feel good?"

"Yes," she whispered, squeezing his shoulders. His lover smiled at him, and the bubbles in his chest and abdomen swelled larger.

He kissed the tip of her nose before resuming his work, taking care this time to angle his pelvis so the root of his shaft connected with her clit when he withdrew on the down stroke.

When she began to moan again and her walls tightened and released in time, Thom closed his eyes and savored her. Her smell, her sounds, the comforts of her softness and sex. A lump lodged in his throat, and the inside of his nose stung. He'd never made love, but perhaps his current experience of the sex act amounted to a poor man's version.

"Thom, you're so good." She fell limp.

Before he could think too much about those false words she spoke and what it would mean for them to become true, he sped his plunges to the frantic, needy pace required to bring him home.

Her eyes darkened into a dirty, sinful stare. "You're about to come. Your balls are high and tight now, huh? Full of a big load you can't wait to blow."

"You're so fucking hot I can't stand it." He clutched her tit, his skin tingling as he rushed to the end. Base, unspeakable need overcame him, the tension below his waist ratcheting to a fiendish craving.

"Come all over me."

Heat unspooled near the base of his shaft. He gaped at the spot where their bodies joined, marveling at the wonder of his prick slipping in and out, his rigid flesh coated with the glisten of her juices. The second relief tore in, he pulled out and gave three final tugs right below the ridge of the head.

Thom cried out while he splintered into shocks of ecstasy. Blank and blissed with awestruck emptiness, he gawked as thick white ropes splashed her breasts, hair, and cheek.

"Fuck." Aftershocks reverberated through his body. He rubbed his stomach and squeezed his still-stiff member until the final drops of fluid eked out and dripped onto her chest.

"Now lick it off me and feed it back into my mouth."

"Pardon?" He struggled to regulate his breathing, clobbered by the double whammy of a life-erasing orgasm and her request. No woman had ever asked *that* of him.

"You heard me."

Lost in the haze of her thrall, he obeyed, scooping up his own bittersweet semen with eager lips and tongue. When he took her mouth, he forgot all about the nasty, kinky deed and melted into their first kiss.

And what a first kiss it was.

Her effort was predictably assertive, skilled from practice, though more sensual than he would have guessed. But as their tongues stroked, played, gave, and took in a series of caresses and lazy searching, a frighteningly glorious thought sunk hooks into Thom's mind and heart.

I could get used to this.

"Oh, shit." She broke the kiss with a start and lunged for a bedside table, grimacing when she palmed her wristwatch.

"What's wrong? Are you alright?" He reached for her, overcome by an irrational worry that he'd bolloxed something up and caused her to hate him. Absurd that he cared, because if she hated him, she'd leave without a fuss.

She shook her head while bending over, her pale and naked bottom a curvaceous temptation dangling just outside his reach. Last night's clothes flew onto the bed—the red bustier, black leather miniskirt, and matching jacket she'd worn to the Chariotz of Fyre after-party where they'd met. "I missed my flight."

Her body in that outfit had turned his head hard and made his tongue wag with an unspeakable urge to have her. But by now, he ought to have been feeling profound relief when faced with her impending departure.

As his nameless lover shimmied and wiggled into her clothing, the reality of her slipping away lanced him. He glanced at his hands, then the floor. *I do not want to lose her,* Thom thought with an odd and startling clarity.

Normally, he lost interest in a woman after the two of them had had their fill of sex and laughs. Yet here he was moping like a schoolboy in puppy love when he damn well ought to be thanking the good lord above that the groupie of the day was about to bolt without tears, begging, or his insistence. "Can I help?"

"No." She took a cell phone from her purse and rang someone while sliding her pretty feet into danger heels.

"What's up, Megan?" A faint male voice spoke through the line.

Thom clenched his teeth and glowered at a random spot on the wall. Megan. The stupid bloke on the phone got to know her name, but he didn't. What had this wanker done that Thom hadn't to earn the privilege?

"I'm so sorry, Gary, but I'm gonna be late for the setup tonight. I travelled to St. Louis for a work thing, and I missed my flight out. I'm going to rent a car and jet up there right now, so if the drive goes okay, I'll be onsite in time to help with equipment."

What sort of equipment did an English professor need? If he'd conversed with her in more depth than his usual flirtatious small talk allowed for, the context would have meant something. Since he hadn't tried, though, he got to sit on the bed as a clueless outsider, cursing his thoughtlessness and stupidity.

Worse, he was nothing to her. Less than nothing. He was a lie, a "work thing." Served him right, he supposed. She was using him just like he'd assumed that he was using her. Karma was having a right-and-proper point and laugh moment.

Megan popped open a tin of mints and tossed three in her mouth before chucking the box in her bag. "Thanks for everything, stud."

She dropped a chaste kiss to his cheek, a literal kiss-off. He actually felt himself shrink.

He caught her fingers and thought fast. "It's already noon, and the sun goes down so early this month. Please, let me arrange a flight for you." That way he'd learn of her destination, her home state.

"It's only a five-hour drive to Iowa from here. I'll be fine." Glancing at the door, she slung her purse high on her shoulder.

Iowa. Noted. Megan the English professor from Iowa. Might be able to piece a puzzle together from those scraps. College departments had directories with pictures, and with any luck, there was a syllabus floating around out there somewhere with her cell number on it. "Why the rush? Aren't most universities still closed for the holiday?"

Though he'd graduated college over two decades ago, he hadn't forgotten about the existence of a winter break.

"Oh, I'm not going home for my professor job. I have a side gig." She slipped free of his hold and made haste for the exit.

"What's that?" He laid his empty hand to rest on the mattress, clinging to the phantom sensation of her final touch.

"I'm a paranormal investigator. And just so you're aware, when we were at the party I detected a negative entity or presence near your band. I don't say this to scare you, but you may want to think about getting in contact with someone who deals in exorcisms. Thanks again for last night and this morning. Bye."

Before he could ask the first of about a hundred questions invading his confused, vaguely horrified thoughts, Megan dipped out and shut the door behind her.

Don't stop now. Keep reading with your copy of EMBERS available now.

Don't miss more of the *Coven Daughters* series coming soon, and find more from Kat Turner at katturnerauthor.com

Until then, discover the *Coven Daughters Origins* with EMBERS

✳

Thom James is tired of his wild but empty rock star life, so when he meets a fan who is as uninhibited and unapologetic as he is, he falls hard. Problem is, she's busy chasing ghosts and has no interest in a serious relationship. Before she says goodbye, the enigmatic groupie leaves Thom with a dire warning about dark forces that are attached to his band.

Freshly fired from her professor job, Megan O'Neil is strictly focused on pouring herself into her side gig: ghost hunting. She can't get her latest hookup out of her mind, though, and her connection to notorious rocker Thom James inconveniently persists when she forgets her demon-trapping watch in his hotel room. When he tracks her down to return the lost object, she confronts her growing feelings for the famous bassist along with a realization that she must tackle a nasty curse that's way above her pay grade. Too bad the curse, which has followed her since childhood, is *not* about to be neutralized without a fight.

Now, Thom and Megan must battle not only a malevolent spirit, but a fierce attraction that feels doomed by the demands of their incompatible lives. When Megan excavates a strange book of witchcraft and taps into a world of magic with ties to a terrifying prophecy, she and Thom face down not only the challenges of making a relationship work, but of somehow halting the machinery of magical fate before everyone pays the price.

✳

Please sign up for the City Owl Press newsletter for chances to win special subscriber-only contests and giveaways as well as receiving information on upcoming releases and special excerpts.

All reviews are **welcome** and **appreciated**. Please consider leaving one on your favorite social media and book buying sites.

For books in the world of romance and speculative fiction that embody Innovation, Creativity, and Affordability, check out City Owl Press at www.cityowlpress.com.

ACKNOWLEDGMENTS

Thank you to everyone who has bought, read, reviewed, boosted, hyped, and otherwise supported my stories. Your encouragement is my fuel to keep writing, and I appreciate each one of you more than you will ever know. May you love Thom and Megan as much as I do. This couple holds a special place in my heart, and it is truly my pleasure to share them with you.

ABOUT THE AUTHOR

KAT TURNER is an award-winning author of paranormal romance and urban fantasy as well as the occasional thriller. Her favorite stories to write are those that combine action and adventure with magic, dry humor, and steamy romance if the situation allows. She lives is Kentucky with her family, where she can mostly be found practicing yoga, taking nature walks, or getting lost in the corridors of her own imagination. Kat loves to connect with readers, so don't be shy about getting in touch!

linktr.ee/katturnerauthor

ABOUT THE PUBLISHER

City Owl Press is a cutting edge indie publishing company, bringing the world of romance and speculative fiction to discerning readers.

Escape Your World. Get Lost in Ours!

www.cityowlpress.com

facebook.com/YourCityOwlPress
twitter.com/cityowlpress
instagram.com/cityowlbooks
pinterest.com/cityowlpress

Made in the USA
Columbia, SC
20 October 2023

24284028R00164